The
Alder Saga

Curse of Heirs

LUCIAN CROMWELL

authorHOUSE®

AuthorHouse™
1663 Liberty Drive
Bloomington, IN 47403
www.authorhouse.com
Phone: 1 (800) 839-8640

Published by AuthorHouse 09/13/2018

ISBN: 978-1-5462-4484-4 (sc)
ISBN: 978-1-5462-4485-1 (hc)
ISBN: 978-1-5462-4483-7 (e)

Library of Congress Control Number: 2018910985

Print information available on the last page.

This book is printed on acid-free paper.

PROLOGUE

Thesia, a minor island continent brimming with myth and legends, occupied by war torn clans bent on conquest, laid the first bricks towards an ever quickening expanse of history. With mankind developing martial weapons, mighty forges, agriculture techniques for larger production, and diversified regional architecture, a new world emerged as clans collided for control. During these events, many men and women found new abilities to control many of the natural elements around them and quickly rose to prominence through incredible feats.

As smaller clans slowly consumed one another until a singular clan remained, a young upstart began his honor-bound war path with his followers as they steadily defeated any who opposed them in the southeastern corner of Thesia and established their kingdom. Named after their king, the first settlers of Kay struck out into the farther reaches of the land to claim more territory. Kay pressed north-west as he drove into the heart of Thesia, but upon reaching its dense forests, filled with wildlife and game, he was beset by a group of exiled northern fighters lead by a young man similar to himself, but wielding the power of metal. Kay and Arthlyn, an exiled northern chieftain, crossed blades, hours seemed to pass for mere moments as both men attempted to subdue the other. As the smoke finally cleared after a day's worth of combat between the two men, Kay stood victorious with Arthlyn kneeling at his feet. By the customs of the old laws, Kay was to take Arthlyn's head and absorb his followers; however the fight between both men moved Kay to choose a different path. For the first time in Thesia's history, a blood pact was struck between the two men in peace as Arthlyn was proclaimed an ally to Kay and would be assisted in building a kingdom of his own in the north. As the combined forces marched north, Arthlyn studied Kay's methods, adopting many into his own ideals as he defeated foe and granted them the right to rule under him as nobles. Once a small band of followers soon arose as a strong warrior nation of refined soldiers and skilled engineers, and became Thesia's second Kingdom, named Alder, after Arthlyn's father.

Thesia found itself ruled by eight separate kingdoms by the time of the next yearly harvest. With Kay and Alder, Kingdoms of Evest to the forested northeast, Ulferth within the northern mountains, Barner along the western coastline, Vaine to the sprawling plains of the east, Parthus to the southwest, and Epharth in the south. Now poised for peace, Thesia prospered under the reign of the first and second generations of kings and queens. A large central portion of central Thesia was declared to be a place that any person, common or noble, could travel free of banners to a large citadel known as King's Hold. Although the lands held no ruler, each kingdom held the responsibility to maintain and oversee the prosperity within their kingdom's districts within King's Hold, as well as the roads to and from. Each harvest after the completion of the citadel, Royal Families, Noble Houses, and commoners alike would journey to King's Hold for feasts, tournaments, and hold court for any disputes between kingdoms.

With each passing harvest, Thesia's lands prospered and flourished as larger cities across individual kingdoms arose alongside noble family keeps. With watchful eyes and understanding, two centuries passed with kings and commoners alike growing accustom to know only the ways of peace, except for the historians that became known as Sages, men and women with gifts of transcribing detailed events with minimal effort as they began to grow the grand archives within King's Hold. Although not without treachery, Thesia combated the raiders and bandits with individuals of seemingly poor origins, granting them the title of "Hero" for such tenacious deeds of selfless bravery. Any person, regardless of age, gender, or kingdom of origin, would be awarded the title equal to that of a noble, and after adoption into that kingdom's noble house, would receive lands to instill such courage into others.

As Thesia celebrated her two hundred and fifty-seventh year of peaceful harvests, the fifth generation of kings entered King's Hold to celebrate. Drawing closer to the end of the Harvest Festival, kings and queens turned their sight to the future aspirations within the central confines of King's rest, a sealed area of which only royal blood could enter. With the final sunrise of the festival rising, King's Hold found itself sieged by usurpers and their coconspirators that vastly outnumbered the guards within the walls. Many guardsmen of the city were slaughtered or simply abandoned their posts in terror as the traitors roared through the separate districts of the eight kingdoms until they encircled King's Rest and the royal families.

Each king and their personal guards entered the fray, and against such numerous forces, began to fall one by one to unending forces that opposed them. Last to fall was King Ralford of Alder; minor remnants of the remaining forces seemed to hastily return into King's Rest after their leader's demise, and for two weeks the citadel was sieged as new kings were legitimized. Slowly reduced forces within the walls, the new regime assumed that whatever remnants survived would not be capable of striking back with a force worthy of note.

As King's Rest outermost walls were breached, invaders quickly found themselves standing across from healthy heirs of each kingdom and royal guardians tasked with protecting them. Less than twenty-five heirs and their soldiers stood against the combined forces of nearly ten thousand, yet despite all odds, less than a hundred of the attackers escaped King's Hold before the heirs sealed the city and the walls fell silent.

Word reached the newly appointed kings and queens of each kingdom of their staggering defeat, many sent thousands of soldiers and mercenaries to kill what remains of the royal families and secure their place, for even though the king lay dead, no ruler could call themselves royalty without the complete eradication of the previous bloodline. Each force that attempted to capture the remnants of the prior kings, less sightings took place until the royal families had all but vanished into smoke. Enraged leaders set thousands of pounds of silver and gold forward to any man, woman, or child that could capture an heir, dead or alive. With each passing harvest that failed to yield results, many kingdoms closed their borders to one another out of suspicion and rumors surrounding their possible attempt to house another kingdom's heirs.

With the twenty-first harvest festival after "The Great Uprising" set only a few weeks away, many of the kings once again proposed bounties for the hunted heirs, in addition to insisting that any hero or noble wishing to present gifts for the king's favor retrieve an item from King's Hold, a now cursed place filled with only bones and horrors.

"Y ou won't get away with this!" A plump noble shrilled, his constraint tightening around the old wooden chair as he struggled to free himself. "No low born treasure hunter will ever be able to accept a quest from the king without a noble to sponsor them. Even if you use my seal it won't allow you to pass through the gate. You will pay dearly when I get out of here, you masked bastard!" His velvet garments soiled in blood, one eye swollen shut and his nose broken, Lord Larus Carthill sat facing his captor in an old abandon house. Though Carthill was only missing for a few days, his captor delivered numerous beatings within an abandoned house located inside a recently diseased and cordoned portion of the common district. Lord Carthill's prison was in a state of disrepair, the floors creaked from the slightest movement, windows were boarded closed from the outside, and any holes in the wall were hidden by dark cloth to keep any light from entering. Only a burning fireplace behind Larus provided a source of distorted illumination.

Grabbing the only other chair in the room, a masked man brought it forward to face the noble lord, smoke from the fire stinging Larus's wounds as he tried desperately to identify the brigand as he sat down and leaned in. The cold blue-green eyes of the masked figure pierced Lord Carthill's soul as he began to speak, "No one's coming to save you. No matter how you scream or cry for them, you are alone; with me. I'm not here to rob you or kill you, but you are going to deliver a message to me to King Sepius Vasilli himself, do you understand?"

Carthill exhaled in relief and nodded his head in acknowledgement, a burning pain erupting in his shoulders from the blue and purple bruises delivered during one of his beatings.

Grabbing Larus' face and twisting it to the side, the masked man forced a wretched squeak from Larus as his eyes tried to keep the man in view. A hard cold sensation brushed against his ear as the mask moved just out of view, "The noble houses of Alder will fall to the rightful king's hand and a new day will dawn with your crimson blood upon the streets. The low born will rise and drive the knife through your frail king's heart. A Crow's wings will spread and the six winged death will take his throne."

With his message delivered, the masked man stood up and kicked Larus in the chest, sending him backwards onto the old floor before heading for the door laughing maniacally. Lord Carthill winced from the pain and muttered under his breath, "Low born scum. I'll find your true face and skin it off of you, personally."

❀   ❀   ❀

Rylan sat as his usual table within the Ogre's Nest, one of the larger mercenary pub's where nobles would come and hire low born mercenaries selling their skills to a highborn in quests past down by the Noble's Guild. Both guilds and quests were located throughout Alder offering coin and prestige to any who would take a mission, however true renown and coin came from a noble sponsored quest from a noble house. Sipping on his preferred pale ale, Rylan scanned the room for his competition; the "Silver Dragoons" were gathered around the bar, a group of hand to hand combat specialists, and cream of the crop for protection duties. Two members of the infamous "Serpent's Fang", a nefarious group responsible for many of the untimely ends of individuals at the wrong end of a wealthier party, sat at a table near the back corner playing a game of cards with a few unsuspecting mercenaries, cheating their way to the mound of coins piled in the middle of the table. A handful of lesser known groups made up the remainder of patrons, discussing their sought after riches, and a handful of barmaids running between bustling tables with their hands full of tankards or plates of food.

Horseman's Square outside was filled with more mercenaries and merchants selling both services and wares that were not permitted into one of the taverns for one reason or another. A large bell tower erected in the middle of the square stood surrounded by statues of past heroes, each different from the others is both style and form. Atop the tower, the large bronze bell began to ring as the gates of the kingdom's noble district opened as many hooded figures sitting atop horses flooded through the gates about their own personal business. Many of the commoners quickly rushed outside of the dusty pub, either cursing their luck or shouting offers in hopes of acquiring quick work. Rylan cracked a grin between sips and muttered rather loudly, "Greens, they'll never learn." Several of the Dragoons turned in Rylan's direction, raising their glasses in agreement.

Time passed quickly as nobles rode directly for renowned groups in their usual locations. Rylan remained stationary in his seat; the low murmur of the Ogre's Nest was preferable to the calamity happening just outside the tavern walls. Knowing harvest season would soon be upon the kingdoms and festivals would have desperate nobles hoping to impress the king to gain favor, they were likely to search for a man like Rylan and his small company of brothers. No other gifts provided more favor then old kingdom relics, none more so than one's located within King's Hold, filled with old kingdom relics and tournament grounds. Rylan finished off his drink and motioned for another towards a young woman named Amelia. Amongst most of the staff, she was a friend and veteran, and provided with the right metallic incentive, would easily move profitable nobles to a "desirable" group. Amelia nodded, grabbed the pitcher of ale, and proceeded to make her way over to Rylan. As she began to pour Rylan placed his hand against her arm and murmured, "What's your asking price today? If you're looking for a dress, I have a stunning one that would make the noble women look like they adorn rags."

Amelia giggled, "The Silver Dragoons have offered three dresses and a whole basket of honey scones for first priority with a protection task. I shouldn't be even saying anything about it, but since you are likely to have several requests, I suppose you could put something better forward than a dress that I probably wore once or twice back when we were together."

Rylan smirked and retorted. "Damn you always were able to see through my ploys. Besides Bansel's Dragoons always throwing their weight around, what's the average going for a dress nowadays?"

Amelia took his flagon and began to pour; her gaze focused between pouring and monitoring the doorway as nobles marched over the threshold, "around forty silver pieces last time I checked."

Rylan scoffed and adjusted himself in his chair. "You must be looking at the jewel studded dresses, my last glance the exceptional dresses were barely eighteen."

She shot him a scowl, "Are you saying I'm only deserving of exceptional?"

Rylan subtly removed his hand away and leaned in to whisper in Amelia's ear. "Far from it, your beauty rivals that of late Queen Maree."

Her gaze quickly turned back to the flagon as she finished pouring; her tone now hesitant and scared, "Don't curse me like that. You never say someone was more beautiful than a queen unless you want them to die a painful death."

Rylan leaned back and placed his hand over his chin, trying to throw off onlookers and quickly reassessing his words. "I certainly don't want that to happen, you look much lovelier alive. You are as beautiful as the moon in a black ocean of stars, and I will give you five gold pieces so you can buy as many dresses as your heart desires. I'll even hand make your scones for you if you so desire."

Amelia giggled and touched Rylan's hand, the symbol for accepting an offer so other groups knew that a bid had been raised. "I still remember the last time you tried to cook; we were both sick for a week and stuck in your bed. I'll take the gold and I imagine you'll want your normal recovery requests?"

Rylan cracked a pure smile and nodded in agreement. With the deal made and his cup refilled, Amelia was off toward another table.

Nobles and their guards began to fill the tavern, most heading directly to the Dragoons, however a handful of masked individuals made their way to the table where the Fang were sitting and took seats next to them as they began to pass scrolls and whispers to one another. A large thud from the doorway echoed through the tavern as four well-dressed noblemen entered. An elderly gentleman, Lord Darden of Draedin Keep and his three sons, Renword, Lucas, and Arbain, proceeded directly over to the Silver Dragoon's Leader, Bansel, and was received with open arms. Bansel had served under Lord Darden for many years before taking up the mercenary life and founded his band of well trained protectors. Other nobles sighed in dismay, and like scavengers to a dead beast, the smaller bands began to move in and attempt to work deals. The barmaids corralled the more desired nobles towards requested groups however Amelia did not send any nobles Rylan's way.

"Odd," He thought as he sipped his ale, "the nobles are never in clear standing with the king and always seeking to gain favor. Fact they're all focusing on either protection or the seedier side of work must mean there is going to be a rather sizeable change to the position of noble houses and names."

As the flow of nobles began to slow and quest boards began to fill, Rylan looked for Amelia and found her busy dealing with a very dashing young noble. Although not in their normal activities, flirting with nobles was an easy way to earn money if the end result is a child that the noble would pay to disappear. Amelia was very beautiful as well, however both individual's business never allowed Rylan to start anything with her, except for a fool's dream that only lasted a few weeks. Finishing the remaining ale in his flask, Rylan began to stand up to check the board when two hooded individuals approached him and sat down at the table. The first to sit was a large armored man with the crest of a two headed wolf, the sigil of the Bernak family, visible on his chest plate. House Bernak was a long line of strong warriors and high ranking amongst the King's High Guard. Although mostly hidden, Rylan could see the charcoal black hair of the main bloodline and the features of a man relatively close to the same age. The other was far more concealed and much thinner, a woman without doubt as she descended into her seat with her arms crossed, careful not to touch the table and signify the start of a discussion with Rylan. There was no crest visible that signified a family house, but he caught the slightest movement of vibrant red hair; it was the legendary female of the era and surely soon to be made a Hero of Alder for her efforts against the roaming bandits that plagued much of the kingdom for nearly a decade. She was Lady Isabelle of Violet Embers, a powerful fire wielder that could scorch a large wheat field to ashes within a moment. She was known for her aggression getting the better of her during fights and often causing more damage to her surroundings than the bandits, however the results left no doubt. Over three hundred rebels charred to a crisp against one young girl of only fourteen made her quite the reckoning force; and also a target. The months after her "eradication" of the bandits, her fame spread, she was arranged to be married by her low born father to a middle class merchant and well known abuser. The day before the wedding he found his way to her bedchamber and attacked her; the city guard only found ashes of the merchant and she was promptly disowned by her father and banished by the village. She was adopted by the Bernak family and given a noble adoption. It was rumored however; King Sepius had requested this happen as to keep her within Alder and outside the influence of other kingdom's whispers.

Rylan sat back down is his chair and leaned back, "Sir of Bernak and Lady-". He stopped as the hooded man raised his hand and shushed him. Agitated Rylan smirked; he had never been the typed to be treated so rudely and did not take kindly to it. "What can I help you with my lords?"

"You know who we are and we know of you." The man spoke as he pulled back his hood and revealed his face. "You are Rylan, leader of the mercenary troop known as The Six Crows. The only incursion group that has completed every artifact extraction from the King's Hold with success, correct?"

Rylan nodded, "Yes that is my brothers and I, Lord Tiberius Bernak. I must ask what artifact you are attempting to recover. You are, after all, the favorite of your house to acquire the title of 'hero' after the countless tournaments you've won, on top of being known as the 'Wall of a Thousand Winds'."

Lady Isabelle met Rylan's eyes as she produced a sealed letter. "I ask that you keep this matter private. Although Lord Tiberius is accompanying me, his reputation is not in question. I am asking this be done so that I may bring honor befitting my new family. I trust that you and your brothers are the men for the job. I am not wrong in this assumption, am I?"

Rylan bowed his head and took the letter carefully, ensuring not to touch Lady Isabelle's hand, "No my lady you are not mistaken, my brothers and I will see the delivery of the artifact desired. I will meet with them tonight and we shall set out at sunrise tomorrow morning from the west gate. Roads to King's Hold will soon be filled with companies and bandits alike with the Harvest Festivals beginning soon."

Tiberius laugh echoed across the inn, but quickly regained is composer. "You must know what she's done to bandits to achieve her current position, I'm sure between both of us we could beat a small army without breaking a sweat. Never the less, we should discuss your payment."

Rylan stood abruptly and bowed to Isabelle and Tiberius, "Upon reclamation of the item you seek and return to the capital, we may discuss payment. The Six Crows have not garnered such a reputation from bargaining before a job is complete."

The two stood up and bowed in acceptance. Tiberius held out his hand and Rylan did the same, the handshake signifying the Six Crows were now bound by contract. As they walked out of the inn, Rylan proceeded to the barkeep and set two gold coins upon the bar before following suit out of the Ogre's Nest and into the busy square.

❊   ❊   ❊

Rylan began to make his way from the Horseman's Square down the main street towards the Scholar's Academy. Guilds and academies shared the district between nobles and the lower classes. Although the capital's smallest district, the Merchant's Quarter catered to thousands of people selling their wares or honing their talents in hopes of being selected to join a company of mercenaries or one of the noble guilds that selected heroes and recorded the history of the kingdoms. Dalkas' Scholar Academy was a location for everyday historical studies, as well as a place for magic wielders studying to one day become powerful magic wielders. Sages were garnered as treasures due to their supreme power without specializing in any specific form of magic. Several sages were gifted with the ability of foresight, while others were empowered with the ability of longevity, living to see several crowns change heads from father to son, continuing for thousands of years. It was also common place of mishaps to occur around the academy, from sounds of explosions to flames erupting from open windows every few hours. Rylan peered at the academy and reached into his cloak, producing a flat, clear crystal with a blue hew. An Arcane Receiver was used for two way communication between people, as well being purposed by royal families to activate other items. It required only a small amount of focused ability to activate, and only the users would hear the conversation. Rylan stepped away from the main road and leaned against one of the merchant stands, carefully concealing his face and the gem from any observing eyes. "Aldis" He muttered under his breath, careful not to speak the name too loudly. A dull glow began to emanate from the crystal as it changed form from a blue hue gem to a flat, clear mirror like crystal. As the illumination dimmed, a young man with messy black hair and a stack of tomes around him appeared.

Aldis turned towards his receiver and grinned, "Hello brother! How are you? I didn't expect to see you until the selection ceremony tomorrow."

"I'm doing very well little brother," Rylan smiled back and chuckled, "I need you to do something for a retrieval we've been contracted to perform. Any information you can gather on the artifact in question, as well as the safest possible route for arriving at King's Hold. I'll have the requirements within the letter I was given."

Aldis nodded in agreement, "Does that mean you won't be at my selection ceremony tomorrow? I've been selected to go to the royal academy to further my studies with House Vasili."

"That is very impressive, is that your wish to join the Academy of Sages? I was under the impression that we would skip the ceremony tomorrow and you would become the Six Crow's sage. If you'd prefer to join the academy though, I certainly understand your wish. A Royal Sage is quite the prestigious honor." Rylan said as he brushed his loose hair back behind his ear.

Aldis's eyes enlarged and nearly jumped out from his coffin of books around him as several fell against the tile, "Are you speaking truth, I can join the Six Crows? I would never let you down if you allowed me to join my brothers. I'd rather that then ever be part of a dusty bunch of old, boring historians."

"You will always have a place amongst your family; otherwise we would only be the Five Crows. Now come down here, grab this parchment, and find out everything you can on the desired artifact of our noble requester. I wish to make it back to the house before I'm forced to do anything else today. We have preparations ahead of us." Rylan waved his hand in front of the crystal and as it reverted back to its dormant state, scanning the crowd guardedly as he returned the crystal to his pocket. Although the streets were bustling with merchants and traders, it was all too common for thieves from lesser guilds to steal a contract and replace the group on the mission.

❖ ❖ ❖

Aldis bound over his pile of tomes as he tossed his crystal into his coat and hurried down the hall. His fine, grey robes with ornate black and gold patterns glistened in the firelight, and the symbol of Arcane Magi, a specific order of gifted individuals that dedicated themselves to the pursuit of knowledge of pure magic over specialized forms that involved the elements of life centered on its back. For twelve long years of sleepless nights and endless reviews of ancient texts, Aldis acquired all he could absorb of the old kingdoms, ancient wars, and all relics imbued with the royal power. Seemingly endless halls of the academy were lined with tapestries of old heroes of Alder and their deeds that earn them the title. Although made of simple fabric, the tapestries moved in glorious fashion as the woven fighters clashed and fires burned in the background. Torches were not simple wood and flame, but short staffs with gems positioning to give a maximized light from an arcane glow. Downward spiraling staircases appearing perfectly seemingly spotless with a solid marble pillar in the middle stood near Aldis as he nearly flew down the steps, hurried around several other students as he rushed to the front door, and with a quick waive of his hand opened the ancient doorway into the street. Aldis' young appearance scurried down through the crowds as he brushed his way through the bustling street over to Rylan with ease. Jokingly Aldis bowed, "what brings you to the academy this day my good sir?"

Rylan gave Aldis a stern glare and crossed his arms, "Focus Aldis, this is a very serious matter and I hope you will endeavor to take this with more restraint than your normal studies. In the letter you'll find the noble's name and their object that they desire. I will need everything you can to find it. Where it was last sighted, our fastest route, and any possible dangers we may face along the way. Also make sure you and Sayren draw up a contract this evening. If you need further assistance, find me and I'll do what I can. Although this is your first expedition as an official member of the Six Crows, I still expect the same excellence from you that you've given during your time at the academy. Do you understand?"

Aldis silently nodded and retracted his excited smile, "Yes, of course. I will see that everything is taken care of before I rest tonight."

Rylan returned the nod as the two split, Aldis to the Academy's study, and Rylan to home.

❊ ❊ ❊

As the midday sun rose to its peak, most people moved inside to escape the autumn sun and consume their lunch, Rylan quietly made his way to the gate dividing the Merchant Quarter and into the Militia District. Merchant District streets drew closer to the wall, they narrowed closer and closer until the space available would barely fit a cart. Shouts from the more seedy taverns echoed through the desolate alleys with sour songs of a mission gone poorly or a missed opportunity while others cheered of recent success and promises of great future endeavors. Rylan ensured he passed quietly by without drawing any attention to himself, the lesser groups that performed the same relic acquisition often whispered insults and foul words just within the audible range of Rylan as a way to irk him into any response and hoping for his detainment. Between the dangers of other guilds, thieves, and rabid, diseased rats lurking in the shadows, Rylan feared the guardsmen above all. Between Commoner's Militia and Royal Inquisitors, the threat of going from a sustained existence to an impoverished lifestyle was becoming more prevalent with each passing harvest. During a successful mission, many guilds accrue other rivals of higher status and can lead to a very low chance of survival within the militia district. With the Festival of the Harvest drawing near and steady increases in raids from small bandit and rebel forces suspected to be commanded by fallen heirs, Alder's capital of Dalkas had begun increasing its militia presence within everyday life through checkpoints and random searches.

"Clear the road! King's Militia is coming through!" A voice echoed from down the road as a fast moving carriage followed by horsemen sped towards Rylan. With only moments to react, Rylan leaped into an alley and onto a stack of old, empty chicken crates that shattered on impact, "By Johan's Mace those rebels are gonna make it impossible for the guilds to find work. That must be the fifth noble in only a few weeks that have been held hostage. I feel sorry for whoever was on the receiving end this time around." Rylan propped himself upright and began to clear off the shards of wood when two men passed by discussing between themselves, without noticing Rylan, "soon the king will start giving us bounties against the rebels. There's no way he would risk sending his own men against people he knows nothing about. That's when we'll start working for both sides and make our fortune."

"It'll be dangerous," the other man replied as they passed the alley where Rylan was standing, "but the payments would be worth the risk and more. Let's hope he does it before the festival begins so we'll be outside of the city while everything gets fortified to the point where guards will start checking our bread rolls for hidden messages."

Rylan peered around the corner as their voices faded into sounds of the capital to see if any further riders were approaching, but with the street still mostly empty, he re-emerged and once again tossed the hood over his head. The Militia District was not far off as Rylan started to see more and more armed patrols moving in formation. The gate gradually came into view as the towers began to peek over the rooftops. Many of the people stood waiting in lines to be randomly inspected for contraband by guards; however Rylan seamlessly passed through unnoticed and continued into the militia grounds. With a seemingly endless number of militiamen moving to and from, Rylan proceeded with the utmost delicacy. One wrong move into a guard provided a never ending amount of problems, questions, and delays. Most of the people passing through the area carried wrapped goods or letters sealed with noble crests; however many of the traveling merchants passing through the district were bringing foreign relics and diplomatic communications from other kingdoms. Rylan passed between moving patrols, cautiously avoiding eye contact as he made his way around a sizable training courtyard brimming with guardsmen recruits. With the training yard surrounded by separate barracks and administrative buildings, Rylan spotted a golden robe amongst the militia's tarnished grey and red tunics. The robe belonged to a member of the King's Inquisitors, a group of highly skilled nobles who sifted through the shadows to find any traitors to the royal family or properties. Inquisitors themselves still represented their families by wearing a black crest on the robe; Rylan could not distinguish the noble family this particular inquisitor belonged to as several soldiers moved around the figure. Rylan returned his eyes to the ground and continued to move quietly away. Turning to head down the steps with two guard captains, the inquisitor's long faded grey hair and blue eyes belonged to a son of Lord Gaius LeBlanc, a noble born hero who killed Ralford, the late King of Alder. Out of the corner of LeBlanc's eye, he caught sight of Rylan's cloak with six crows and called out, "You there with the cloak! The man of Six Crows, come over here!"

Rylan stopped mid step and hesitated for a moment as a handful of militia turned in his direction. He took a deep breath, exhaled, and began to move towards where the inquisitor and captains were standing. Rylan stopped at the bottom of the steps and removed his hood. He gave a low bow, "Good afternoon Lord Inquisitor, is anything that I may assist you with?"

"What is your name?" The inquisitor scoffed as he leaned against the railing.

"I am Rylan of the Six Crows, Lord Inquisitor."

"Are you the leader of the company?"

"I am, sire."

"Very good, you've saved us the trouble of hunting you down across Dalkas."

"Have I done something to offend you Lord Inquisitor? I do not believe we have ever met." Rylan cautiously spoke as he tried to determine the inquisitor's identity.

"Oh no my good man, you have done nothing to displease the crown. Your work carries quite the expectation of success behind it, so I'm told by my sources. I do, however, have a minor problem with one of your brothers, Toren to be exact. He had a rather destructive dispute with some militia while they were breaking up a tavern brawl. Your brother seemingly single-handedly incapacitated several of the guards, broke a jailer's wagon and injured a horse's leg to the point of having to end the poor thing's agony. Many of the men have had to be placed in beds for serious conditions stemming from his actions."

"I must apologize to you Inquisitor; my younger brother has been troubled for the past few years since our father's passing." Rylan paused as he ran a hand through his hair. "Our father passed not but a few harvests ago, and Toren's mind has become clouded in his decisions. I've mostly had him running simple errands and tasks to steal his mind from the troubles; I feel he still struggles at times though. If I may provide any corrections to amend for his misguided actions, please say them and consider them done."

"Your fathers passed away you say? I have seen the toll it can take on men. Although I am the youngest of the LeBlanc line, many of the families have faltered when a loved one is killed. I see that you mean well to cover your brother's affairs; however they are still quite severe. The capacity of his destruction warrants death by hanging for such actions against King Sepius' name. How would you amend a situation such as that?"

Rylan paused; his mind raced to find the inquisitor's identity, Lord Gaius had five children; four sons and one daughter. The oldest son, Liarn, was killed in a tournament at one of the last festival games held within Dalkas's walls. Halen, the only daughter, was married with Prince Faust only days after her fourteenth birthday and birthed her first child only two years later before passing away in child birth. What three sons remained in the shadows and were rarely spoken of. One became a world traveler; the second became governor of Althra, a border city on the southern portion of the kingdom's border. Finally the youngest had become somewhat of a nightmare due to an unfortunate accident with a mysterious dark magic that was said to have twisted his mind. "Lord Mauro, it is an honor to make your acquaintance. I would be unable to amend such a situation should death be warranted. Loss of a man such as my brother would still be a much greater loss for Alder. If he was able to defeat a patrol of common militia, I would hope he has proved himself valuable to the defense of Alder and her people."

"Ah," Mauro clapped his hands with a devilish grin across his face, "men of the militia do not give you enough credit Rylan, you certainly have a mind for command. Many of the men that know of my father have never heard my name, let alone have such an eloquent set of words to stand defense against such charges. Tell me what type of man is your brother?"

"A man of Alder, sire. Toren is a man of honor, even though he is prone to be misguided by his loss. He has served by my side for over ten years without fail. My brother is a man for the king."

"A man for the king you say?" Mauro started down the stairs, his finely crafted leather boots pressing against the old creaking boards with each step. "That is quite the bold statement to be made about a man who would attack the king's men. I do see the benefit of having such a man amongst the ranks of the common militia. I believe a year with him working patrols without pay when you are not on a mission would provide such an opportunity to exemplify such qualities as a 'man of the king'. Toren was found with thirty some odd silver in his possession when he was detained, if you can afford to pay five gold coins, I can see no reason not to harm your brother and release him to your charge. What say you, Master Crow?"

Rylan bowed once again and reached for his coin purse, "That would seem like a most honorable and fitting chance for Toren to prove himself. I have just recently received a contract to escort a group of nobles to King's Hold in order to retrieve an artifact. If you'll permit, I will bring my brother along and he will start his time immediately upon our return. I will provide the requested amount immediately as well, to whom should I deliver the funds to?"

"Perfect," Mauro said as he placed his hand on Rylan's shoulder, "That is expected from a man of your profound character. Captain Rolan will accept your payment and Captain Neir will fetch your brother. If you don't mind me asking, how did your father pass?"

Rylan pulled his coin purse from his side and pulled out five golden coins with a griffin printed on one side and the face of King Sepius on the other. "He fought in the uprising at King's Hold against the Tyrant Ralford. He was struck by a swarm of arrows that cost him his ability to walk. He told me that while he laid against the hard stones of the roads leading to the Royal Citadel, he said a flock of six white crows soaring over him. They made several passes over the area before landing around him, and stayed by his side until he was brought back with the other wounded. He believed they were his guardians and wanted his sons to maintain that same honor when my brothers and I began to pursue mercenary work." Captain Rolan took the coins from Rylan's palm, nodded to Mauro and preceded into the barracks with Captain Neir close in tow.

"I must say that seems rather exuberant. I don't think anyone who stood again Ralford would be protected by the very symbol of the old kingdom. However who am I to question the stories of heroes that sacrificed their lives for pursuit of freedom of tyranny. My father, Lord Gaius LeBlanc, has his fill of battle stories and loves to talk endlessly of Ralford and his prowess in their conflict. The man may have been a tyrant, but he held his honor until the end. It truly takes a honorable man of Alder to face certain death while his family escapes into the shadows. I can only hope that your brother will be as true of a man as Ralford... Ah! Here he is now."

Toren was never in the best conditions after he found trouble, for the sneakiest of four brothers; he never truly learned how to defend himself in a fight. This particular event was different; most times he would pick fights with fellow thieves or random bar patrons. The guards were a different matter entirely, he appeared bruised and bloodied from the retaliation for injuries sustained by fellow guardsmen. His cloak was stained with mud and crimson blotches, pants ripped at the knees from where the guards dragged him away. Captain Neir gripped Toren's cloak tightly as he pulled him along, Toren starring angrily at Neir's face with every step. In his other hand was a tied belt with Toren's daggers, an empty coin pouch, and a dusty old book that was unfamiliar to Rylan.

Captain Neir stopped a few paces away from Rylan, slammed the personal belongings into Toren's chest and gave him a strong shove forward. "One future militia guard, as promised, delivered unharmed."

"Well I see you didn't get yourself beaten cripple. Hopefully you will learn from this that the guards are here to keep the peace, and there are far more of them then there are you." Rylan patted his brother's shoulder as he quickly moved him away from the barracks. Toren winced from the pain, but remained silent as Rylan continued, "We've a mission in the morning and you will be repaying me for saving your ass, again. I couldn't save you entirely though; upon our return, you'll be joining the guards to make amends for injuring their ranks."

The Inquisitor turned to start back up the stairs and motioned to Captain Neir to follow. "Well said Rylan of Alder, I hope that upon you're return we'll be able to discuss your adventures. You have quite the list of nobles that swear to your band's actions, yet every time I ask the same people, they seem to know very little about you."

"Of course Lord Inquisitor, I look forward to our next meeting, but I fear I don't have a fable past worthy of much note. I am simply a man for Alder and family." Rylan returned as he bowed.

Mauro waved his hand in the air, "It will at least be something new to the same dreadful stories of the noble quarter. Also, my name is Mauro LeBlanc, I absolutely despise Lord Inquisitor, it makes me feel as if I possess no soul."

"Very well, Lord Mauro, I will be sure to bring only my best to tell." Rylan turned and exited the drill square behind Toren. His younger brother's appearance instantly drew the gaze of all who passed by, and seeing Toren's grimacing face, he quickly removed his cloak and placed it on Toren's shoulders. The whispers of the surrounding people instantly fell silent as they looked at Rylan, his leather armor decorated with intricate patterns of a crow emblazoned on his chest piece above the heart, and a single dragon flame-forged armor over his right arm. Although the armor was a simple design with mobility taking priority over protection, the Orden Forge produced the best quality work available to the common man. Several people bowed as

Rylan crossed in front of them; a wide path opened with both passing merchant and pauper made way.

❈ ❈ ❈

Passing from the Militia to Common District, it was clearly apparent that Rylan had achieved a level of respect from all who knew him name and that of the Six Crows. Several people fell to the ground pleading for Rylan to give them a chance to serve under his command, while merchants held out free pieces of weaponry, armor, and food for him to take in an effort to attach their business to his reputation. Closer to their residence, the pleading crowds began to diminish and disappear. Although people respected Six Crows enough to maintain a gracious distance, the last unfortunate soul to attempt to step foot within their home was meet with two of the Six Crows, Rylan's step brothers, Wilhelm and Ebon. Their message was made clear to stay away from the residence unless you were there for an official purpose.

As they made their last turn through the winding streets, a house emerged into view with a small patch of grass out in front near the street. A young girl lay in the grass watching the clouds as they rolled by, her dirty blonde hair messily lying against the green blades of grass. As Rylan drew closer to the house, a woman around Toren's age emerged from behind a line of bed sheets and waved, "Welcome back Rylan, Toren, how was your day?" Her voice flowed through the air as if a cooling gentle breeze had moved in during the height of a burning hot summer's day.

"My day was very successful. In fact we will be setting out again tomorrow for another collection with the newest member of the Bernak family, Lady Isabelle. Where are Sayren and your brothers?" Rylan motioned for Toren to proceed inside. Abagail looked at Toren's face and placed a hand over her mouth as she gasped at his bruises. The little girl turned her attention to Rylan and quickly ran to him, wrapping her arms around his leg.

"Ophelia, why are you attacking my leg?" Rylan patted her atop the head.

"Because you're home Uncle Rylan!" she shrieked with excitement, tightening her grip.

17

"Did you practice the motions I showed you?"

"Yes, I can do them with one hand now!"

Rylan looked to Abigail, "Is that true?"

"Oh yes," Abigail said as she pulled the first sheet off and carefully folded it into a large empty basket, "She insisted on practicing until she could do it better than her teacher." A low sigh voiced her displeasure.

"I am pleased to hear that. Why don't you head inside and we'll go over some new movements to help you improve even more?" Rylan pulled a loose blade of grass from Ophelia's hair as she giggled and raced inside. "Does my training displease you?"

"No," Ophelia disappeared behind the next sheet, "I don't know how to feel about my daughter being able to use metal magic at a pace that rivals that of your own when you were her age."

"I can see how this would be troubling to you, and her level of skill has already exceeded my own when I was eight. The only reason I am teaching her isn't for power, but one day she will be met with an obstacle she cannot defeat on her own, and her knowledge on how to control her abilities should be her greatest defense." Rylan pulled back the sheet to clearly see Abigail and make his point, "I don't want her to live in fear as many people now do without a way to protect what matters."

Once again Abigail sighed, "I understand, I just wish she spent more time being the girl then your apprentice. I would feel better if Sayren would take her hunting then have her learn such dangerous abilities."

Rylan nodded and released the sheet, "are they out hunting again?"

"Yes, I worry more with the whispers of rebels becoming increasingly frequent. One day the guards are going to mistake them for traitors and take them into custody because of something foolish one of them blurts before their mind can catch their tongue. With rumors and latest kidnapping of a new noble, I'm getting worried that we will not be safe for much longer, even within Dalkas' walls."

The sounds of laughter and banter came into earshot as Rylan turned to see three men turning down the alley "Well not to worry, it will be a while longer before we need to take any precautions. Even if rebels attack the city, this house connects to the old escape tunnels. When the time arrives we will all be ready to do whatever needs to be done."

"Brother!" Wilhelm and Ebon yelled in unison as they drew closer, although similar, both men had fair hair that touched their shoulders, however Wilhelm had his pulled up into a single ponytail most times. Both had dawned their light leather brigantines and leather gloves to hunt with. Both men's fronts were caked with heavy mud from where they had no doubt crawled through the mud to stalk their prey. Though they carried a sack each filled with their kills, both men had no arrows remaining, However Sayren was the complete opposite. His braided, ash blonde hair moved with the slightest breeze as he walked towards the house with his dark oak bow in one hand and a satchel filled with coins in the other. His quiver was still filled with his sixteen arrows; pristine due to his sentiment that each arrow was worth a prized target, or not worth having in the first place. Not a single spot of dirt tarnished his clothing, his leather vest untarnished, and his shoes covered in minimal amounts of mud built up along the sides.

"Hello everyone, I see that you've all had a successful day of hunting." Rylan chuckled as he embraced Wilhelm and Ebon. A unified laughter began as the three stepped away to see Rylan now covered in mud as well.

"I swear," Abagail said as she shook her fingers at them, "If you two don't learn how to hunt without crawling through mud, you're going to end up hunting for another woman to do your clothes."

Wilhelm and Ebon locked eyes and gave off a devilish grin, "Oh but Abby, you know how much we love you. Come and give your brothers a hug." Rylan grinned as they approached her, Abigail attempting to push them away until all three tripped and fell onto the clean sheets.

"You idiots," She scolded as she tossed them off and stormed off, "those are your sheets. You can clean them! Since you wanted to get my clothes messed up as well, you can also cook dinner tonight."

"Now that's unfair to everyone dearest." Sayren's voice was soft and harmonic, but the group laughed more as they glanced at one another. "I'll cook dinner tonight, Rylan would you mind helping me?"

Rylan nodded and began to brush of the mud, "Certainly, we have work starting tomorrow that we'll need to discuss. Aldis will officially be joining us starting in the morning as well. I've asked him

19

to research all the information required, however from the growing fears of the rebels, we'll have to travel off any main roads. I suspect our employers will not want to stay away from any inspection convoys."

"I can certainly assist him. Will all six of us go?" Sayren inquired as he crossed his arms.

"Not for this one no; I want Wilhelm and Ebon to remain here if rebels decide to make their move. We'll meet at the other end of the tunnels if that happens. We'll be leaving at first light tomorrow." Rylan grinned as he patted Sayren's shoulder, careful not to place any mud on his clothes as well.

Sayren grinned and moved for the door, "Then there is little time to stand about dawdling. Wil, Ebon and I will get started on finishing things around the house. I will come get you once we are ready."

Rylan bowed and began walking away from the house towards the stables to tend to his horse.

❈   ❈   ❈

Lord Carthill painfully awoke to find himself inside a room with several tables filled with instruments of torture. Sounds of a burning fire crackled behind him, and a dull red glow from a partially concealed evening sun that peaked through the only window as it slowly sank beneath the horizon.

"Lord Carthill? I see that you are awake. I almost began to worry they had brought me a dead man," The unfamiliar voice came from behind him, but as he attempted to turn, new metallic restraints halted his movement.

"I swear, if you are friends with that masked bastard, I'll find you all and personally gut you all from roots to apple!" Larus shouted as he clenched his fists with rage.

"My, my, I never thought a noble lord on the council would use such a foul tongue to speak to an Inquisitor." Mauro stepped into view and ran his fingers over his instruments of torture.

"Inquisitor, you must understand that after being taken from my home during the night and assaulted for three days; any man would be angry and uncouth. I would ask you forgive my hasty judgement before forming any conclusion about me."

Mauro moved to a table with a vase filled with dark ruby wine and poured it into a plain goblet next to it. "I completely understand my lord. I must ask why you were taken. It would seem odd to me that you of all people would be taken from your house in the noble district and moved to a condemned structure within the slums on the other end of Dalkas. I would be more inclined to believe that you were out chasing skirts, drank far beyond your limits, and found yourself in a crowd of the wrong fellows."

"You must be daft! I was awoken from my chamber with a masked fellow standing over me who clubbed me over the head with my own walking cane. Next thing I knew I was sitting in a chair like this and tortured until the man saw fit to leave me with a message for King Sepius' ear. If you would kindly allow me a water bowl and some proper garments, I would like to deliver the message to his majesty before that masked cutthroat distances himself any further."

"I am an inquisitor, Lord Carthill, the enforcer of King Sepius and son of the Hero of Alder, Lord Gaius LeBlanc. I would think that you would convey more respect to someone who stands in my position. I believe that you should tell me this message, and I may deem it necessary for it to reach the king's ear by your lips or my own." Mauro grinned and sipped the wine before smacking his lips loudly to unsettle Larus.

Lord Carthill squirmed in his bindings, "I will only tell the king the message. I do not answer to you, or your father."

Mauro sat the glass of wine down and walked to Larus' side. Mauro gripped the noble's collar and began to pull him towards his face, the binds pressing into Larus' skin. "You will tell me this message or I will be forced to draw it from you by whatever means I deem necessary. Now what did your captor say?"

Carthill grunted as the constraints pressed against his chest uncomfortably. "He said a low born would rise up to kill all the nobles and take his place on Alder's throne! Ignorant fool said he was leader of the rebels and heir from an old kingdom! Now let me go dammit!"

Mauro released his grip and let Carthill fall back into his chair, "He claimed to be a leader and a mere pauper would steal our king's throne? No affiliation to any group of rebels or mercenaries in particular? I could believe that a fool would claim he was the leader of the rebels, but I doubt an heir would ever be present within the walls of the kingdoms that hunt them. There must be something more to what he said. Do try and recall it for me, my friend."

Carthill swallow the lump forming in his throat, "He said the low born was part of crows, that's the only other thing I can recall him saying, honestly, he did not take torture lightly."

"Crows you say? Are you sure that he specifically stated crows?" Mauro began to ponder silently.

Carthill nodded.

"That's quite odd, why would he say crows in particular unless he had specified which crows?"

"I don't know! The fool wore a mask and plain clothes. I couldn't have told you anything except the mask looked like nothing I'd ever seen before. Made from some pristine substance that did not stain or clump dirt upon its frame, it was a truly a masterpiece item that I've never seen within Alder's borders."

"I met a man who leads the Six Crows mercenary band; I think you know of him as well. He seemed like an honorable man and respected by all around him with some powerful supporters. If this is the man you're speaking of, I find it highly improbable that a man with such an open presence would seek to destroy his support. If you cannot provide any further information I will have to start my interrogation to collect further facts from you." Mauro's face was cold. The interrogation from an Inquisitor was not something taken lightly or often survived without serious trauma.

Carthill jolted in fear and nearly tipped the chair onto its side. "I have told you all that he said! If you harm me I will see you hanged by your ankles and beaten bloody! Now release me at once."

Mauro exhaled and moved for the door, "I'm sorry you feel that you believe that defiance is an avenue available to you." He cracked open the door and motioned to a guard standing just outside the door, "Fetch my gloves, the lord has decided he will not give me the answers that I have asked for."

With a silent nod, the guardsman moved away from the door, and Carthill gathered his remaining strength, attempting to break his bonds. The leather straps moved slightly but remained secured. He began to sweat from his brow as the inquisitor moved back to the tools and began to pick up a lancet, its small fanged edge glistening with reddish-brown glow. Mauro moved over to the other table lined with more devices and picked a small bundle of thin nails. A knock on the door forced Carthill's eyes to dance from the door to the inquisitor. Mauro placed his tools down onto an empty table and proceeded to the door as it cracked open slightly, taking the gloves, and smiling as he watched Larus dart his eyes to both guard and inquisitor, visibly shaking in fear.

"Well then Lord Carthill," Mauro slid the leather gloves on to his hands, "your actions have been found questionable. Possibility that you have incited unnecessary panic within Alder's borders and claimed rebels have infiltrated the capital city of Dalkas warrants a full interrogation to discover whether you are telling the truth or covering up your own failures in your noble position. Your bonds will remain in place until I release them and King Sepius has a worthwhile answer. Be aware that you have the right to confess the truth at any time to cease my interrogation, however if I do not find it to be sufficient I will be forced to continue until the necessary information is found."

Lord Carthill pushed back in the chair, forcing the legs to rise and topple over. Larus' head slammed against the cold cobblestone floor, his vision blurring from the impact. As he gingerly blinked to bring the room back into focus he saw Mauro standing over him, the gloves etched with a bright orange pattern, as the inquisitor reached for him. As the gloves drew closer to his face, a searing pain from inside his head flooded his mind as if he was being suffocated by darkness within his own head. He screamed out, a flow of inaudible words flying from his lips, his body began to shake terribly and tears began to fall from his eyes.

❈   ❈   ❈

Inside the house, Rylan and his brothers sat laughing merrily at the story of how Ebon had attempted to catch a white stag with his bare hands, but in leaping for his prey, the deer moved out of his way and Ebon went head-first into a muddy ravine, coating him from head to toe in mud, but he found a small coin purse with a gold bracelet within, free of rust and wear. The family sat at the table, with the exception of one; Toren, who sat atop one of the barrels beneath the staircase holding his plate in one hand and nursing his bruised face with the other. As their laughter died down, Rylan raised his glass to speak.

"Tomorrow we will set out on another job to escort nobles to King's Hold. Although this will be nothing out of the normal, it will be the first official mission with Aldis as our sixth crow. I am proud of each of you that have improved your abilities to the point that we may be so selective in our tasks. As the newest member of our troop, Aldis will inform us of our task and route we will be taking. You may begin when you are ready."

Aldis nervously shot upright and almost instantly fell back down as he planted his foot on the back of his robe and nearly choked himself as the clasp pressed against his neck.

"Easy now little brother," Sayren chuckled as he assisted Aldis and patted his arm in reassurance, "Tell them what you've decided."

Aldis nodded politely to Sayren and glanced at his brothers. "Thank you for such kind words brother; it is an honor to stand with you as a crow, and not simply the youngest nuisance. We have been contracted by Lord Tiberius and Lady Isabelle of House Bernak. Tiberius is known as 'The Wall of a Thousand Winds'. He garnered that title after victory in almost fifteen tournaments and never being struck once. Although his proficiency with wind magic is renowned to say the least, he is also the man that killed King Sepius's nephew in the grand tournament four years ago after the match was called and Sir Panfir of House LeBlanc attacked Lord Tiberius's back. His attack never connected, the gust of wind that Lord Tiberius used to counter collapsed Panfir's breastplate and he passed on shortly after. Lady Isabelle's story is widely known, so I will move on to the artifact desired and the information about the route we will take."

Aldis moved away from the table, grabbed his satchel with two large scrolls from his bed, and returned with a noble sealed letter in hand. "The artifact Lady Isabelle is requesting to be found is the Ring of King Ralford, also known as the Ring of Alder. It is said to produce the ability for the wearer to use the strength of Alder in defense of her lands. During the Uprising, King Ralford was killed by Lord Gaius LeBlanc; however the story becomes something of myth after that due to accounts of soldiers that spoke of a metal winged heir of House Bassadora taking up arms against the soldiers using a total of six complete wings. If this account is true, that heir would have been the most developed metal wielder in the history of not only Alder, but all of Thesia. Named 'Six Winged Death', the heir was said to have been killed during the fighting, however no body was ever recovered. Same is true for King Ralford, and the ring has been lost to time. King's Rest is the center of King's Hold, location of the last stand for all kings of the eight kingdoms, and our target location for search. Departing from the western gate at sunrise, we will travel alongside the King's road until we reach Havenhome, at which point Sayren has suggested taking a Sen Portal to House Bassadora's estate within Alder's district. Journey to the Sen will take only a handful of days travelling at a normal pace. With the Harvest Festival less than three weeks away, any chance of finding the artifact will have to be found within three days of arrival before any groups that may have left a week or so prior reach King's Hold via normal routes."

Rylan gave a serious look to Sayren as he leaned forward at the mention of the ring, "We will have to be very cautious when we find our objective. Such a ring was made to empower King Ralford and is recognized by all kingdoms as right to rule. What are the reports from the travelers in regards to problems along your path?"

"I was able to found out about several attacks from an unknown creature, several have been killed and many provision caravans were destroyed." Aldis began to flip through his book at several notes, "I've also found there is a minor bandit encampment near the town. There have been several raids of military equipment forcing the militia to offer a reward for recovered equipment. Those are our only current threat without normal sittings of wolves and threats of rebels outside Alder's borders."

Rylan nodded and raised his cup, "A fine first introduction for Sage of the Six Crows, Aldis. We are being asked directly by Lady Isabelle for assistance. Because all Heroes are judged for position during Harvest Festivals, she seeks the most powerful item. It is bold and we will oblige, however with the increase in patrols, we must do our utmost to conceal not only our accompanying nobles, but the artifact as well. Wil, Ebon, I ask that you protect Abagail and Ophelia in our absence. If anything should arise, take the hidden tunnels outside the walls and hide at our hunting cabin. Everyone should get some rest, our journey starts early tomorrow." Rylan thrust his cup forward, "To the crows!"

"To the crows!" the brothers shouted in unison as tankards collided with one another above the table.

With dinner finished, Toren buried his face within the tome he had brought home, Aldis began to pack his things away, Sayren cautiously stood, his third cup of ale forcing him to move at a snail's pace and nearly tripped over the seat as he made his way with Abigail to their bedchamber. Rylan turned to Ebon, "Would you see that the horses are ready for travel in the morning? I would prefer as few surprises as possible on this journey."

"Of course, I'll bring Wil along to make things go quicker." Ebon patted Wilhelm on the shoulder.

"Yes of course you'd volunteer me." Wilhelm moaned as he clanked his fork against his plate.

With the day's work done, Rylan took a deep breath and closed his eyes, his mind wandering about King's Hold and the nightmares he'd had before ever trip. He pushed the thoughts aside as he walked to his straw bed. He knelt down by his personal chest, popped the lock with a quick turn of his key stuck in place and pried the lid open. Aside from his fine leather armor and travelling cloak lay a finely crafted sheathed longsword and a metal battle-axe made entirely of fine metal. Rylan rubbed his tired eyes and closed the chests lid, ensuring the lock was closed completely before laying down onto his bed. Pulling the sheet over him, Rylan quickly fell asleep an ominous violet flicker of energy sprang from Toren's tome as he sat staring at the starlit pages.

CHAPTER 2

King's Hold stood desolate in the middle of all kingdoms, a stalwart memory of a peace that once reigned across Thesia's lands. Its stones now weathered and forgotten, sections of the outer wall collapsed down to overgrown sections of grass and dirt. The Uprising of the Eight Kingdoms left inner cobblestones stained red with skeletons donned in armor littered the outer limits. Banners of old houses still stood, Alder's white crow soared on its post still shuddering against the cold northern winds of Ulferth, kingdom directly north of King's Hold. A citadel resting center of innermost grounds, known as King's Rest, still remained in pristine condition, it's finely crafted marble pillars from the south-eastern kingdom of Kay stood unscathed by the uprising, and the large doors crafted from the Laumawood sculptors of Evest in the Northeast stood unharmed by weather and decay. Even the fine metal hinges from Alder remained without a spot of rust.

Within the walls of King's Rest, Royal families would feast, discuss political matters, and relax socially without the constraints of leadership during the festival. Only Royal Guardians, members of a noble family that displayed strong martial prowess and chosen to serve within the citadel with a necklace containing a drop of royal blood, would be allowed to enter. Atop the citadel's roof stood a covered platform with paths leading up to the circular table from the cardinal directions. Trees braced the ceiling from the intermediate directions as posts for the open air chamber where kings would engage in discussions of disputes, trade, heroes, and problematic wildlife.

As the western tower door's metal hinges creaked open, the

masked man emerged with his cloak off and a chain adorned with a circular blue gem around his neck. His hair was an odd, faded blue color, yet dark blonde roots revealed themselves as the wind tossed about his hair. As he made way for the chamber, he proceeded around to the southern doorway, inhaled and pulled back on the handles.

As the doors opened and revealed the inner chamber, the masked man's ashen hair moved with the escaping breeze as he stepping inside the chamber. Ornate arrangements of colorful flowers planted along the edges of the room and a sturdy marble table with the divisions of the eight kingdoms cut into the stone's surface, although each king's chair was made differently, no one chair stood out over the others as a reminder that peace had been met due to each king's respect for one another. Residing in the center of the table floated eight separately colored gems all surrounding a keyhole without a key.

Three others sat inside with the masked man, a stalwart man with a strong physique and supporting a strong amber beard, somewhere within his thirties. Secondly, a woman in her mid-twenties with pale skin, eyes as blue as the sky, and her hair's color matching the masked man. The third was a young bald headed man, slightly younger than the woman, but covered in roots and flowers.

"Take off that stupid mask Alkith," the young man said as he opened his eyes, "you may be able to hide from prying eyes; however my plants will never mistake your scent."

"I honestly didn't even remember that I still had it on, Gianni. That would explain the odd looks I got from the guards." Alkith pulled the mask away from his face and moved for an empty chair.

"I certainly don't think that is a quality of an heir, especially one of Kay. I trust you have completed what you set out to do?" Gianni began to move as the vines around him retracted and return to the dirt.

"The cards are in play for Alder's heir to finally join our fold. Once we have all heirs inside, I will be able to send word to our allies across the great sea and bring the reinforcements needed to retake our homes. Where are the others?"

"Most of them are out recruiting within their kingdoms. Ellice is out on another patrol along the northern border." The bearded man said as he leaned on the table, his arms crossed in regret that he was not the one to go.

Gianni walked to his chair and sat down, "Don't worry about Halvor, he's been mopping about since he hasn't been outside of the walls for over a week. I've been wondering when you would discuss your 'allies' further. I don't trust outsiders for aid, let alone supply us with an army large enough to conquer Thesia."

"I believe that will be something we must discuss once we have all players sitting around this table. Why don't we discuss more of Alder's current plan?" Alkith said as he sat down in Kay's chair, the woman walking up and resting her arms atop the seat's back.

"I'm glad you made it back so quickly this time, brother."

"I see you have maintained things quite well in my stead Naria. Maybe next time I'll stay away longer." Alkith laughed at his own notion as he lifted his gaze to meet hers.

"You know how I feel about giving orders and ruling. Once we get Ralford's son on our side, this will be much easier. How do you figure things will work for acquiring our last piece?"

Alkith leaned back into his chair and laced his hands together. "The noble I captured has already been taken for interrogation. I can only imagine it will take a few days for King Sepius to hear my message and force the truth from the shadows. I wasn't able to stay long enough to locate the heir's residence, but I was able to make contact with a few fellows that knew a man by the same description. If the plan goes awry, they have pledged to help us and fall under his banner once he is safely brought to the hold."

"Good," Halvor sat back and ran his hand through his hair, pulling it away from his eyes, "Once we have Alder's aid, our men will be in position to retake our homes. Ulferth will fall before winter ends."

Gianni sighed, "You cannot be serious. If we move separately, none of the heirs will reclaim a throne, let alone return Thesia to her prestige. If we are to win we must attack a centralized location and give Alkith's allies a place to make port. Evest has no docks large enough to allow an army so numerous to land and help us retake Thesia. Kay will be heavily fortified to the point that most of the ships will never touch the harbor without sustaining severe causalities. Our only hope is to move into Barner with a small force that can capture the harbor and hold it while his allies unload their forces and support in the offensive to capture the capitol. If we can accomplish that, any ships that need to dock will be able to with minimal losses and we can establish a foothold as we retake the eastern kingdoms."

"That will be something far down the path from where we currently stand. If we are to ever make it that far, we must prepare to fight off the kingdoms that will know the location of all Thesia's heirs. We should first complete our table before we can strike anywhere. Now, onto more pressing matters, how are the repairs to the outer walls going?" Alkith's voice changed from its regular calm tone to a focused and direct one.

"The wall along the south west portion of Parthus' District have been repaired by Alissia's troops, however many of the broken segments within Alder's have yet to be restored." Gianni pulled a scroll from his satchel draped across his chair; the tree of Evest sealed in wax across the letter. "The current reports from my agents are showing a large growth in unity amongst all kingdoms with the exception of Epharth. I feel as though Elwarth will not aid either side in this conflict."

"I must agree," Alkith nodded, "If we are to reunite the kingdoms like our forefathers, we must have Epharth join us. For now we will leave him to their dark ways until we must intervene. I believe that it is approaching noon and I am famished from my journey. Shall we reconvene this evening after sunset?"

"Aye, lunch sounds good to me."

Arising from their seats, each heir gave a slight bow and exited the chamber. Bustling sounds of marching, commands, and tireless automatons moving about filled the air as Naria leaped onto Alkith's back as he proceed towards the door, "I can't wait to see him again." She whispered with a deep grin forming across her face.

❊   ❊   ❊

Western Gate of Dalkas, known as Arthlyn's Aegis, designed as Alder's only gateway that led directly to King's Hold, and her last line of defense. Walls surrounding the gate itself were lined with turreted towers for both archers and trebuchets. No army had ever reached

Dalkas before, however during such times; King Sepius grew weary of the other kingdoms and their ambitions. Wooded gates had been reinforced with strong metal braces as well as a recently constructed wooden wall along the outside to give the defenders a funneled position to contain any invading foes. Dalkas' gates remained opened at all times, however posted guard checkpoints were in place for control of any contraband that was attempted to be smuggled into the kingdom. Rylan and his brothers sat atop their horses, cautiously waiting, and watching for their nobles. Toren slumped in his saddle from a blatant lack of sleep and his snoring forced Sayren to tap the back of his brother's head with the end of his bow. Bustling sounds of caravans moving about filled the air as Rylan gazed up at the wall, each time he returned to Dalkas, the daunting approached sent a shiver down his spine. Rylan looked to Aldis who sat fiddling with his notes; once again trying to memorize all the reports of bandits and wild beasts on their route should either noble inquire.

"Calm down little brother. If you constantly read the pages of the area, you'll never see its beauty when we ride through it." Rylan gestured and smiled to ease his brother's anxious demeanor.

Aldis rolled the scrolls tightly and placed them in his satchel, "I know brother, this is my first time as your sage, and I am terribly nervous. I don't want to make you, or our family, look bad."

"Don't worry about that. You're the smartest out of all of us, and still young. Simply enjoy the journey and make mistakes. We are all here for one another, should any of us fall, the others will be there to raise him back up and continue forward." Rylan patted Aldis's shoulder and gazed at a commotion coming down the road. A caravan lead by the Silver Dragoons moved through the streets, the bright silver armor, specially crafted to appear like silver dragon scales shifting with each step of their horses. Bansel rode ahead and stopped in front of Rylan, "Not here to take our job, I hope."

"Oh no," Rylan smirked and chuckled, "I'll leave the protection business to you, Sir Bansel the Slayer. My brothers and I have work of our own this morning."

"You know how I detest being called such titles, but I digress. Once we've returned from our escorts I want to speak with you about your journeys. I think we may find common ground in some work after the harvest."

"Very well, I have to see an inquisitor upon my return, but immediately after we will meet at the Ogre and discuss our tales." Rylan extended his hand and Bansel shook it before spurring his horse and returning to the formation as they began to pass through the gate.

"Bansel seems like quite the respectable fellow Rylan, perhaps you can introduce us when we return." Tiberius called out as he approached with Lady Isabelle and a large entourage of servants.

"Lord Bernak, it is a pleasure to see you and Lady Isabelle as well. I trust you've rested well?" Rylan replied as he began to look over the accompaniment of bannermen behind them.

"I've never had a better nights rest." Tiberius laughed as he grabbed the longsword on his hip and held it in place. "I must ask your cost though before we begin our trip."

Rylan leaned back, his eyes catching on a priestess of late Queen Maree, "If we are to travel with the entirety of your group it will cost six hundred gold and we will not be able to return before the harvest I fear. My brother has developed a route that will only take two weeks in total; however it will require a smaller group and lightly encumbered to meet the goal. If you choose four others and the priestess to accompany you, we can meet that goal and I will only charge you three hundred and fifty gold."

Lady Isabelle waved off the group accompanying her, "Only Brilla will accompany me on this journey. Lord Tiberius, I leave it to you to take the others."

Tiberius pulled on the reins and turned to face his men. He cleared his throat, "anyone without a horse will remain. Lorn, Orsen, Falder, and Afnir will accompany as protection. The rest of you will return home and say nothing of this to my father. You are dismissed!"

The four men rode forward, each armed with a spear, as well as a sword attached to their side, and shield resting on their horses. Tiberius turned back to Rylan and nodded. With a bow and snap of his reins, Rylan called, "Crows! Fall in, Sayren and Toren to the rear, Aldis you are to stay in the middle to keep watch!"

Tiberius and Rylan took point followed by Orsen and Afnir.

Isabelle, Brilla and Aldis fell in behind them with Lorn and Falder to the rear with Sayren and Toren. A mass of merchants surrounding the gate area made way as Rylan and his party moved forward. They approached Arthlyn's Gate, as movement slowed and guards randomly searched anyone not accompanying a noble or holding the documentation of a mission requested by one. Rylan approached as Captain Neir called out to him, "Halt! State your reason!"

"Captain Neir, I am Rylan of the Six Crows accompanying nobles on a recovery escort. I ask that you let us pass." Rylan spoke calmly as he produced the letter with the Bernak seal in clear view.

"I don't see any nobility with you. We will have to stop you for a search in the king's name. Move to the side for inspection."

"I don't think you have the best eyes for this captain." Tiberius spoke without looking in Neir's direction.

"Oi! Which one of you said that? Was it that little bitch brother of yours again? I don't think any of you are going anywhere!" Neir's voice snapped as he raised his clenched fist at Rylan.

"Captain Neir, I believe you know the man beside me as the Wall of a Thousand Winds. Do you not know of Lord Tiberius of House Bernak?"

Neir cautiously looked over Tiberius closely before letting out a short squeak at the revelation of the obvious Bernak crest emblazoned on his chest plate, "Apologies my lord, I beg your forgiveness for my rude words. I meant no offense to you or your house."

Tiberius spurred his horse and began forward without saying a word, his group followed suit. Toren and Neir's eyes meeting as he passed, a silent nod from Toren gave Neir a crazed look as a vein appeared atop his forehead. "Next!" He yelled as he motioned the next person forward.

❀　❀　❀

As the sun continued its rise Rylan pulled the hood over his hair and motioned for Sayren to move to the front, "Scout ahead and if you see any problems before we clear the farms and make our way into the forest. I don't want to be seen entering if possible."

"I will return shortly." Sayren nodded and raced off with his horse in a full gallop.

"What is your brother doing? He's mad to navigate the king's road that fast. He'll kill himself or someone else being so reckless." Tiberius remarked as he watched Sayren pull further away at a quickened gallop.

"Fear not Lord Tiberius, Sayren is one of the best riders I've ever seen. He's an archer by trade and even on horseback he's yet to miss his mark. If I may ask, why would you choose to accompany Lady Isabelle instead of being next you your father as his heir during the harvests?"

"Normally I would spurn that type of questioning from people beneath me, but your reputation for confidentiality precedes you. I detest being my father's heir. I was born the middle child and runt of all my brothers. My oldest brother Lein has a far greater claim than I, however, my father doesn't believe that age makes a man, but the deeds he does will show him to be worthy. I was enlisted in the tournaments with my brothers and each time I defeated all who stood against me, even Lein. I hated the affairs of court afterwards though; I have no time for the masked games of nobles."

"Sounds of a true Alder warrior," Rylan said as he adjusted the knife on his leg, "I didn't paint you as the type to turn away from your father's decision though. How is it that you defeated all your brothers and won all the tournaments you ever entered if you were born sickly, my lord?'

"I would be a fool to disobey my father; I don't have a choice on leading the family. I was trained by Aethelwulf, Hero of Alder, who fought with King Ralford during an uprising within Alder's district in King's Hold. He trained me for three years of my youth before he was hung for treason against King Sepius. I never knew a stronger fighter. He wasn't even noble born, but he held himself to that of a noble and made him respected by all. After he passed I was so furious I went to Northern Alder and stayed at Othgerd for a few months fighting raiders from Ulferth. The winds there gave me a new perspective on how to use my ability without relying on it. I never lost a match after that. How does a commoner like you come to dealing exclusively with nobles? I find it hard to believe that one man could build such a reputation without having either an abnormal ability or a man on the inside of the hold itself."

Rylan chuckled as the group past a returning company and a

very weary looking noble. "I am just a normal man. I work hard at maintaining a good reputation and ensure that my brothers do the same. When I was being trained to fight, I crossed with several other companies and found a niche for finding old relics. It bought me both friend and favor within the whispering ears of Alder's Nobility. We've even been requested by the Kingdom of Vaine at one point. As for inside the hold, after being there so many times you get accustomed to searching the bones of dead souls. Most times when we've gone, we find additional relics and secure them to ensure they are not taken by others."

"Does that mean you've found Lady Isabelle's artifact in question?"

"Unfortunately no, King Ralford's body was never found after the Uprising. I've never been close enough to the innermost walls to search if I'm to be honest."

"Damn, I was hoping this would be a short trip. My father's leaving today for the harvest out at our farmlands, near Sonnaer. I'm sure to catch an earful from my brothers about how I have duties to my house, but I was selected by my father to oversee Lady Isabelle's indoctrination as a Hero of Alder."

"I see. We'll try to make this trip as quick as possible. If you don't mind another question though, why are you being accompanied by a priestess of late Queen Maree?"

Tiberius gazed down at the cobblestone road and sighed, "King Sepius requested that Lady Brilla accompany Lady Isabelle until her acceptance."

"Lady Brilla? Is she a noble?" Rylan peered back at the two women who were discussing something back and forth.

Tiberius shook his head, "I honestly don't know. Before Sepius took power, only commoners were priest and priestess of past heroes."

Rylan gave Tiberius a puzzled look, "Queen Maree wasn't a hero thought."

"You're right. However, she was a hero to the people. For all the good deeds she did for the poor-" Tiberius stopped suddenly as the sounds of shouting and hooves clattering against the stones.

Toren shouted, "Riders approaching! No banner!"

Tiberius reared his horse and turned to the approaching riders, "Go without me! I will catch up after this is finished!"

Rylan broke off and pointed to Aldis, "escort them to Sayren and wait for our return!" Rylan spurred his horse as Aldis nodded and raced towards the oncoming riders with Tiberius just ahead.

Tiberius looked back to Rylan, "I told you to get them away, not follow me! This is something I must do alone!"

"I'm not one to run away from a fight, and if it is your brothers as I suspect, you'll need a second! Like it or not I'm with you until our contract is complete!"

Tiberius pulled the reins back and slowed his horse to a halt before dismounting with Rylan close in tow, leading their horses off to the side of the road along a fence to tie the horses. As riders drew ever closer, Tiberius pulled his shield from its restraints and placed a readied hand over his sword. The eight riders reared their horses and four dismounted, each with armor similar to Tiberius.

"Why are you here brothers? You should be escorting father to Sonnaer!" Tiberius barked as he tightened his grip on the pommel of his sword.

"You should be there too brother," Lein pulled his mace from his holster, "I would ask you to come with us, but something tells me you've decided against that."

"That's very astute of you. I was tasked with seeing Lady Isabelle to her status as a hero. Father will understand my decision to stay by her side for now. Your actions will not be given such kindness if you don't return, now."

Lein pulled his shield off of his steed and motioned for his brothers to follow, "I don't take orders from the family runt. I take it your mercenary will be taking your second?"

Rylan bowed deeply and stepped to Tiberius's side, "I am Rylan of the Six Crows, I will be Lord Bernak's second if this is to be a duel with single combat."

The four brothers laughed heartily before Lein raised his hand to hush the group, "This fight is brother against brothers. Tiberius will not require you to do anything if he is as remarkable as father has painted him. What do you say brother? Will you fight us honorably, or will you hide behind the commoner?"

Rylan discreetly nudged Tiberius's shoulder, "If you want me to dispatch them, I'll do it without charge."

Tiberius grinned and replied, "I wouldn't want my brothers to suffer such embarrassment to fall at your hands, but it would be dishonorable for them to fight me four against one as well." He paused for a moment before drawing his blade and pointed it at Lein, "I will fight you alone brother, the others will have to fight my second. If they can beat him then they may join our fight, however if they fail, they will never set foot against me again. Do you find my terms agreeable?"

Lein motioned for the others to surround the group as Rylan drew his blade and started backwards slowly, "Very well brother. I hope you've paid your hired help enough coin to pay for his recovery after they're done with him. As for you though, I will see to it personally to put you into your place."

The travelers on the road halted as the men began to spread out. Tiberius and Rylan instantly cut off from one another as the three moved around Rylan. A silent pause fell over the road as the fighters readied themselves and onlookers waited with bated breath for the battle to commence. One of the horses released a loud neigh as it adjusted the reigns on its face and Lein raced towards Tiberius. Roars for the growing crowd filled the air as Tiberius swung his longsword downwards forming a streak of air rushing towards Lein who continued forward with his shield in front. The wind connected to Lein, nearly stopping him in his tracks, but Lein continued forward, dissipating the wind. Sounds of clashing metal and grunts from behind Tiberius made him nervous, but he reset his blade and began walking to meet Lein. As the two drew close to one another, Lein leaped into the air, swinging his mace down atop Tiberius's shield, a tornado like spiral of wind swirling around his weapon. As Lein connected with the shield the wind forced Tiberius's shield back and began to scratch against the Bernak emblem. Tiberius stepped forward, pushing the mace away, countering with a strike of his own. Lein blocked with his own shield, but his footing began to give way under the immense power of Tiberius's magic.

Both men continued to trade strike after strike, gusts of winds forcing loose dirt up from between the rocks and obstructing many of the onlooker's views. A large crowd had formed around the fighters enough to garner attention from guards along the wall and signal down to dispatch a detail. Lein launched a strike forward with his mace and Tiberius countered by side stepping and sending his shield into his brother's unprotected arm. Lein's mace fell to the ground with a lifeless thud as he grabbed his arm and tried to reconstitute himself before Tiberius moved into attack. Lein moved his shield clumsily in front of him as Tiberius swung his longsword, colliding directly with the shield and sending Lein toppling backwards across the stones and onto the trodden dirt, unconscious. A boisterous cheer erupted around the fighters as Tiberius sheathed his blade and walked over to Lein, gently placing his hand on the breastplate to feel his brother's chest breathing. Tiberius let out a sigh of relief before turning to see how Rylan was faring against the others. Much to his astonishment, Rylan was holding his own by parrying and nimble dodging the last of the three brothers. The other two lay against the ground, both clutching their limbs and streaming tears from their eyes.

"Hold!" Tiberius shouted as Rylan and the brothers stepped back from one another, "This fight is over. Licinius take our brothers home to be seen and prepare to ride with father. I will not tolerate any more embarrassment from you. To let a common man beat you is beneath our house and disgraceful. Leave my sight before I finish you myself!"

Rylan listened intently to Tiberius spoke as if he was commanding his own soldiers, the bark just as tremendous as his bite. He patiently waited for Licinius to make his decision before saying anything. A silent lull fell over the gathered on lookers as Licinius paused, his eyes darting between Tiberius and Rylan.

"Very-y well brother, I apologize for my misconduct; I believed Lein was just in his actions. I mean no disrespect; I will see them home immediately." Licinius bowed and sheathed his blade before walking over to the closest brother and motioning for the other riders to approach.

Tiberius walked over to Rylan and placed a hand on his shoulder, "I'm glad you made it through without problem," his tone back to its original state, "however I wish you had taken a little more discretion when you defeated two of my house."

Rylan smiled as they proceeded back to their horses, "Here I thought you didn't care for the business of nobles."

"I don't. I care for the business of my family. Thank you for assisting me, if this had dragged on I would not have been able to fulfill my duty to Lady Isabelle."

Rylan swung his leg over his horse as he situated himself back into his saddle, "You don't have to thank me Lord Tiberius; I am to assist you until we recover the artifact and return you and the lady safely back home. I am honored that you allowed me to second you. Perhaps if we have the opportunity we could cross swords, I'm intrigued how well we would stand against one another."

"If we have time I would also like to see how you defeated two sons of Bernak and nearly a third. I believe I hear the guards coming though, we should take our leave before we get detained for fighting along the King's road."

Rylan nodded and both men rode off down the road as Captain Neir and a handful of guards drew closer to the dispersing crowd shouting, "Disperse or be confined for blocking the road! Who fought here?"

❈ ❈ ❈

As Rylan and Tiberius reunited with the group at the edge of the forest, Sayren rode out to meet them, "Is everything alright?"

Rylan nodded, "We're completely fine. Some men attempted to deter our path, however Lord Tiberius is every bit the skilled fighter as they speak of."

"I've scouted ahead," Sayren said as he turned and moved alongside Rylan back to the others, "Our trail is clear for the most part, a few animal tracks scattered about, however nothing larger than a fox from here until we reach our first destination."

Tiberius leaned forward, "Our first destination you say? Where will that be?"

"A small hidden lake within the forest that few know about or seen with their own eyes. It's an open area that old sages would travel to for seclusion. Mostly animals live around the area now so we shouldn't see any other riders while we rest." Rylan conveyed as he pulled his hood back over his head, "There are still a few pests out though; I would suggest donning a hood if you have one."

"Very well," Tiberius motion to Orsen, "hand out the cloaks. Ensure none of your armor is seen."

Orsen nodded and began to untie a bundle from behind him, tossing the cloaks to the others as he pulled them apart. Donning their cloaks, the party continued off the road on a obstructed path through the woods. Rylan and Tiberius returned to their position at the front before settling in to the sounds of nature around them. Alive with birds' signing and a slight breeze moving through trees, the forest leaves began to show colors of red and yellow hues from the changing seasons. Rays of sunlight shot through fluttering leaves, cascading into an ever changing show of lights around them as them moved further and further into the thickening trees.

After traveling through the woods for the better part of the afternoon without any direction other than carvings of various hunter's markings into trees, the forest instantly split open, and a wide dirt path carved into the ground emerged. Rylan motioned Aldis forward.

"Aldis, which way do we head from our current location?" Rylan called out as he pulled back on his horse's reins.

Aldis peered at his parchment before pointing to the path on the left, "this way will lead us to the lake. Soon the road will fork left and we'll be at our destination in just a few minutes."

"Very good, thank you," Rylan gestured to Aldis in praise and motioned the group forward.

Weary from the long journey the horses began to trot slower over the trodden path as the group moved within a large clearing around the lake. Its majestic crystal waters shined with the fading sunset as they drew closer. Rylan dismounted near the shore with the others following suit leading their steeds to water.

Rylan passed out his orders as he pulled his pack off of his horse and tossed it to the ground. "Sayren will you go gather firewood, Toren, clear a place for the fire and Aldis will you check the surrounding area for any dangers?"

Tiberius retrieved his shield from his horse and motioned to his men, "Assist the brothers as best you can, Lorn and I will set up the tents for the ladies. Orsen see to our horses."

Isabelle and Brilla moved off to the side of the horses and waived to Tiberius, "We're going to head into the woods for a moment, we will return promptly."

"Very well milady, should you find yourself in danger, shout and we will be there to assist." Tiberius bowed before returning to his task. Sayren and Falder walked along the lake's edge for a distance before disappearing into the woods, while Toren and Afnir began to clear separate areas for fires. Aldis moved over to an old tree stump and sat his satchel to the side before resting his back against the old wood. He closed his eyes and fell silent as he remained motionless, focusing on his ability.

"What is your brother doing Rylan?" Tiberius inquired as he dropped his third pack of supplies to the ground.

Rylan looked back to Aldis and smiled, "Aldis is a selected sage for the noble academy. From my understanding of what he's able to do other than combat abilities, is something similar to that bird flying above us." Tiberius looked to the sky as a White Esper Hawk flew over the lake. "The sage can see his surroundings without the limitations of his own body. I don't believe it works for long distances; however the immediate area will be under his watch until we're ready to settle for the night."

Tiberius returned his gaze to the task at hand and began to unbundle his bag. 'That's quite the power for such a young sage. I'm sure that comes in quite handy at times."

"I wouldn't know. I do my best to maintain my capabilities and that of my brothers separate from one another. It is far easier to accomplish more varied challenges with multiple skill sets."

"I don't believe I've ever heard anyone talk about your power. What is it that you do?" Tiberius inquired.

"Hopefully nothing you will ever have to witness for our journey. It can be troublesome at times, however my father made me practice it tirelessly until I surpassed any of the other wielders around me, including himself." Rylan answered.

"If it is some form of forbidden magic, I would hope you would let me know now what it is. I won't risk Lady Isabelle or my men's life if you are set to endanger them."

"You have my word it is nothing of the sort. I detest the use of forbidden magic unlike the men and women of Epharth whom thrive off of that sort of perversion of might. It is simply a magic that is not well liked due to its past wielders." Rylan placed his hand over his chest to show his sincerity.

"I see, my stance still remains though. If you do something that puts my people in danger I will not hesitate to crush you under my wind." Tiberius' tone was resolute as he met Rylan's gaze.

"You have nothing to fear. My brothers will never let you or the lady come to any harm. You have my word." Rylan nodded in understanding as he did not shy away from the Bernak noble.

Tiberius nodded and moved to Lady Isabelle's horse as he began to remove her supplies, his eyes glancing upwards to see the hawk soaring away from them, flying further into the woods.

Aldis found himself surveying the surrounding woodlands, searching for wolves or any signs of bandits within proximity to their camp. A pair of deer grazed just out of sight, however the sounds echoed through the trees as if Aldis was sitting next to them. Dozens of small birds sat amongst the trees chirping and singing in a harmonic flow that calmed Aldis as he continued his search.

"I see now why this was such a wonderful spot for study. I can't imagine the advancements that have been made in this place." His voice whispered within his mind as he swayed between trees.

As the sun rested just above tree tops, Aldis began to make his way back to the campsite. From the corner of his view he noticed Brilla helping Isabelle adjust her shoulder pauldron, he hesitated and quickly hid himself behind the closest tree. Although he had studied with many young female classmates none had ever caught his eye like Brilla. Without her headdress, her long flowing black hair fell against her back. Aldis attempted to look away, but her beauty infatuated him. Sounds of a snapping branch forced him to jump from his gawking stance and locate the origin. A large Willow Bear appeared walking east away from the campsite in the direction of King's Hold. Aldis remained motionless as it past directly in front of him, stopped, and began to sniff the air. The bear turned towards the direction of Brilla and Isabelle and began to silently move towards them. Aldis quickly turned to see where the two were standing, but only a handful of cloths were set hanging on a tree branch. Aldis moved behind the bear quietly, watching for its movements, but as it drew close to the hanging pieces of cloth, the bear sniffed the air again and began to move back in its original direction. Aldis sighed and returned to his body. He opened his eyes to three separate campfires and his brothers finishing up their final tasks.

Aldis approached his brothers and sat next to Rylan, "The surrounding area is safe, but there is a bear moving away from us towards our next destination. We should be weary as we travel tomorrow."

Rylan nodded, "Agreed. Sayren, take the first watch, stay alert should any beast attempt to move at us during the night."

Sayren nodded, grabbing his bow and quiver as he stood up to head for the outskirt of the camp. Toren laid down to rest, muttering something under his breath as he adjusted his cloak beneath his head.

Rylan looked at Aldis, "Get some rest now, I need to do a few more things before lying down, but you'll need all the strength you can for tomorrow. We'll need to be on our guard tomorrow after what happened today with Lord Tiberius and his brothers. We may have drawn some unwanted attention."

Aldis set his satchel to the side as the wood cracked and popped from within the fire, his eye grew heavy as his mind began to wander off to his dreams and that of Brilla.

CHAPTER 3

Wth morning rays of sunlight peeking through the tree branches, Rylan arose to calming sounds of water gently washing up onto the banks. As he scanned his companions, he could see Isabelle in the distance practicing with her sword while the others all slept. He deftly moved towards her, drawing his sword silently with each silent step. As he drew closer, he could hear Isabelle breathing heavily with each exasperated swing of her longsword.

"I don't mean to interrupt you Lady Isabelle, but I couldn't notice you seem rather wearied." Rylan calmly spoke as he approached.

Isabelle recoiled at his unsuspecting presence and swung wildly at him. Rylan quickly parried and disarmed her before she could speak. "You should know not to sneak up on a lady! It's very rude." Her voice half yelled and half whispered, "What by Thesia are you doing awake?"

"I could ask you the same question milady. As I awoke, I couldn't help but notice you practicing without opposition. Would you like me to assist?"

"I don't need you to question my actions; I'm not the simple farm girl," Isabelle paused for a moment before continuing, "I wouldn't mind the assistance though. Tiberius has had me practicing against him every day for months; he says 'you must learn to fight with a sword before you fight with your flames.' I find it ridiculous to say that I would get close enough to anyone to fight hand-to-hand."

"I see," Rylan replied as he picked up Isabelle's sword and tossed it to her, "Then I will have to ensure you don't have an opportunity to use your fire against me I suppose. Ready yourself milady."

Isabelle scoffed as she raised her hand, but before she could call forth her flames, Rylan lunged forward and forced her to parry. Rylan swept his leg underneath Isabelle as she stumbled backwards surprised as he connected with her feet. Isabelle fell backwards, releasing her weapon as she attempted to catch herself. As she tried to stand Rylan stepped beside her with the tip of his blade over her chest, "I don't mean any insult Lady Isabelle, but I do hope that Lord Tiberius has only just begun your training."

"On the contrary, she's been training with me for the past few months." Tiberius said as he walked up behind Rylan.

"I see. I wouldn't imagine many heroes pick up the sword as quickly as you though Lord Tiberius." Rylan replied as he removed his sword and held out his hand to Isabelle.

"I would be out of an occupation if she picked up combat as fast as I. I'm curious to see how well you'll do Rylan, considering you've crafted your skills from dealing with bandits and odd beast." A grin slightly formed against Tiberius cheek as he motioned Lady Isabelle away from both men.

"I would be willing to show you milord, however I believe it is about time we set out. I don't wish to cause any delays our journey. Perhaps when we get back from our travels I will try my hand at beating your winds."

"I see no reason we cannot try now." Tiberius spoke as he drew his sword.

Rylan readied his blade, bringing his right hand forward as both men locked eyes. "Very well, we may begin when you are ready."

Tiberius readied his shield in front of him and lunged forward at Rylan. Stepping horizontally as he stepped to the side, Rylan knocked Tiberius off balance and forced him to a knee. Although Rylan had only just nicked the side of his shield, Tiberius couldn't withstand the power of Rylan's swordsmanship. Rylan quickly followed with a flurry of strikes, forcing Tiberius to remain knelt in the ground, unable to regain his footing. Tiberius seized his opportunity between strikes to lung forward with his shield, sending a forceful gust of wind upwards, taking Rylan's breath away as he recoiled several feet backwards. Tiberius swung his longsword vertically at Rylan and formed a razor-like blast of wind that cut into the earth as it drew closer and closer to its mark. Rylan quickly rolled to the side and threw his open hand back in the direction of his horse. A second attack from Tiberius quickly followed his first as a metallic substance flew from one of the bags atop the horse and moved in front of Rylan, flattening itself into a shield as the gust of air collided against it. Tiberius paused for a moment as Rylan regained his footing and recalled the metal to his side in the form of a shield.

"I see now what you meant. Not many are bold enough to risk their lives using the abilities of the late king." Tiberius sighed as sheathed his sword.

Rylan nodded and jammed his sword into the loose sand. "It was my intention of being someone of note before the fall of King Ralford, however after his demise I was forced to conceal my magic for obvious reasons. I hope that I may believe in you to keep this within your confidence, Lord Tiberius. Such information would needlessly endanger those around me."

Tiberius nodded, "Of course. Hiring someone with your abilities, even if I was unaware of them, is dangerous to all of our health. I believe we will have to hold on the rest of our exercise, we've drawn a crowd of hungry eyes it seems."

Rylan turned to see the others who were asleep now standing watching the fight as it unfolded. "Good to see you're all up! Let us pack up and continue our travel. Aldis, clear the fires. Toren, Sayren, pack up and scout ahead! We should arrive at Havenhome this evening!"

The group nodded and went about their work to prepare for the day's travels. Packing their belongings and saddling their steads, Rylan's brothers watched while Tiberius's guards all knelt by the lake, cupping water in their hands and splashing it against their faces. Brilla and Isabelle both disappeared into the woods again as Sayren and Toren leaped into their saddles and began their reconnaissance. Aldis stared into the woods until Rylan brushed up against him, "Is everything okay, little brother?"

Aldis scratched the top of his head, "Yes...well, no... I don't understand why they keep leaving. It doesn't make any sense to me."

Rylan cracked a grin and wrapped his arm around Aldis, "When you've been in the academy, do you have classes with a lot of women?"

"No, classes are divided by genders, but what does that have to do with anything." Aldis inquired.

"As we grow up we change and develop. You grow taller; your hair grows longer, even your abilities change. There are things that happen to women that we do not have to deal with. It is a discussion for another time, but for now, put your mind to the task at hand." Rylan pat Aldis's back and walked to another fire pit, kicking out the small bits of embers and burying them amongst the dirt.

❀ ❀ ❀

As Sayren and Toren continued through the woods, creatures began to stir and move about. Several pairings of Black Thorn Deer meandered around the two as they grazed their morning meal. Three Root Barrow Foxes scurried through the shrubs chasing mice and small lizards. Toren even pointed out a lone Harbinger Wolf that stood on a large stone surveying the forest, watching both brothers with an unflinching gaze. Much of the forest had grown past its original limits on the outskirts of Alder, surrounding many towns, as nature began to reclaim its unmanaged lands. Sayren pulled back on the reins of his horse, quickly stringing his bow and dismounted from his horse, his hand held out to halt Toren as well.

"Stay here. There's something going on ahead. I'm going to check it out." Sayren whispered as he began to subtly advance. Toren quickly grabbed the loose reins and moved to a young oak tree to secure their horses to. As Sayren continued forward, stepping carefully to minimize noise, stopping behind a dense shrub just off the road, sounds of a large number of people shouting filled the air as Sayren peered over the shrub. A fully loaded wagon with a small family was being raided by a large number of bandits. Sayren attempted to gauge the number of troops, which seemed endless as they disappeared into the forest on the opposite side and reappearing with two innocent travelers. A man was being beaten while his apparent wife was being interrogated. Sayren quickly drew back his bow when he saw two children laying on the ground with bags over their heads, a single guard standing over them. Toren slowly approached and placed his hand on Sayren's arm, "Not now. We should follow them until we find their hideout. This isn't our job."

"Forget the job, they have innocent children." Sayren replied, his voice a low bark as they exited his lips. One of the bandits appeared to have heard Sayren started towards the tree line. Sayren and Toren both began to step back as the bowman made his way through the shrubs and began to look deeper into the woods. With a nod from Sayren, Toren drew his dagger and leaped at the man's legs, driving his blade deep into the bandit's unprotected leg, twisting his dagger to sever what muscle remained intact. A howling cry erupted from their target as he fell, forcing Sayren to quickly grab the bandit's neck with his free arm, and twist. A loud snap erupted from Sayren's grip and the brigand fell limp against the soft grass. Other bandits heard the cry and began to instantly rush over. Toren quickly reacted by giving a low guttural growl, stopping the bandits dead in their tracks.

"Damn it! We need to get out of here if it's those sodding wolves again! Grab what we can. Leave the people, but take the kids! They'll go for a good price!" A bandit called out to the others as many of them began to scurry around the cart grabbing whatever they could carry and disappearing into the woods. Sounds of horse's hooves and wagon wheels breaking fallen branches could be heard as they disappeared deeper into the woods.

Sayren looked at Toren, "Get the horses now. We're going after them whether Rylan objects to it or not. I'm going to check on the people."

Toren nodded and rushed off back into the forest. Sayren grabbed the quiver of arrows from the dead archer and emerged from the woods with his bow drawn to full tension. Clutching one of the carts wheels, a woman desperately attempted to maintain her composer as Sayren emerged. Sayren scanned the tree line for any movement and returned his arrow to the quiver as the forest fell silent.

"My lady I need you to scream," Sayren spoke softly as he held out his hand, "If those bandits fear you've been attacked by wolves, they won't return and you'll be safe."

Without a moment's hesitation, the woman instantly screamed and Sayren suddenly muffled her mouth, nodding that she had done well.

Toren emerged from the forest with both horses in tow and his sword drawn. Sayren made his way over to the man who lay motionless against the dirt road, cautiously checking his chest to see if the man still lived. Faint heartbeats pulsed through the man's chest and into Sayren's hand, "He's unconscious, but he'll live for now."

Crawling from the cart to her husband, the woman pleaded to Sayren, "Please sire, help my children, they're innocent in all this. I will give you anything, I beg of you to save them, milord."

Sayren gently picked up the man and carried him to the back of the cart. "I will save your children, but you must save your husband. Take these coins and ride away from here. This should help get him the medicine he'll need, what brought you out here during these dangerous times though?"

Silent at first, woman followed Sayren as he carried her husband and fell to her knees as he finished his question, "We had no choice. A masked man approached us and said we were to deliver these supplies to King's Hold. We've barely enough money to feed ourselves and if we didn't do as he said he promised to take our children."

"Would you not have been able to leave them at your home?" Sayren's mind began to ponder as he thought of Abigail and Ophelia.

"No milord. We cannot afford a place of our own so we've been forced to live on the streets. The slums wouldn't even accept us because we are from Parthus. Please save my children! I cannot live without them!"

"I will rescue them, you may rest assured." Sayren turned to Toren, "See that her care is in order and help her on her way, but be sure to return the others and inform our brother of what is going on. He'll want to know what has transpired here."

Toren nodded and handed Sayren his horse. "Just try not to get yourself caught; I don't want to have to save you too."

Sayren didn't reply, his mind focused as he mounted his horse and snap the reins. Sayren and his steed tore off down the road for a moment before darting in the bandits' direction, disappearing into the woods. As he raced to catch up to the bandits, Sayren restrung his bow and watched his surroundings for any movement or markers that would give the groups position. The smell of burning meat pierced the air as Sayren raced forward. Sayren slowed his horse to a trot as he tried to pinpoint the origin. Several small tree stumps began to appear to his right as he drew closer. Sayren halted his horse and dismounted, careful not to make too much noise in case of any patrols around. Faint sounds of grunts and cheers in the distance meant that Sayren found his mark. As he approached a clearing, trees began to thin and multiple shacks stood in a clearing where the bandits sat around a large table clamoring with one another on their haul while other grunts moved boxes from the carts to a large warehouse. Sayren scanned the encampment; however, the children were out of sight. Four men sat about a table playing a game of cards while three others stood off to the edge of the encampment conversing in secret.

"There's almost thirty in total. I don't have enough arrows to fight them all, but maybe I can distract them." Sayren thought to himself as he turned his bow parallel with the ground. Sayren took another arrow from his quiver and strung both against his bow, aiming at the three on the outskirts. Sayren released both arrows, quickly restrung, and fired a third at lightning speed. Soaring through the air, the first two arrows found their marks, hitting both men in the back and sent them down to the ground, dead. As the third arrow flew through the camp and pieced the final targets leg. Collapsing to the ground, screaming in pain, the man clutched his wound. Many of the men rushed to the sound of the injured comrade while Sayren quietly moved around the tree line to the opposite side of camp. Two bandits darted towards the woods as Sayren moved, each armed with a spear. Sayren quickly released two more arrows and silenced both men as they reached the tree line. With the camp now on alert, many bandits began to move into the woods where their first companions had fallen. Carefully watching for any more men that didn't follow the others, Sayren made his way to the first shack. Making his way further in, Sayren found two men guarding a shack with broken doors and sounds of young children's wails perforating the gaps. Sayren fired another arrow as he rounded the corner, striking the closest guard's throat as he rushed the other bandit, drawing his sword as he approached. Both men were taken completely by surprise as the first fell gasping for air, and the second found himself falling to the ground as Sayren tackled him. Tossing Sayren to the side, the remaining guard grabbed his dagger from his boot and attempted to run Sayren through. Sayren quickly countered the strike and cut the man along his side. Sayren quickly drove his sword into the man's chest and twisted. For a moment the bandit writhed in agony before falling listless as he exhaled.

Sayren sighed as he retracted his blade and cleaned the blood off of the side of the fallen bandit before holstering it back into his sheath. Looking at the door, Sayren noticed the rusted state of the latch, and with a single well placed kick, snapped the lock and latch off of the door. As the doorway slowly revealed two children, both with the bags over their faces and their hands clasped together, Sayren pulled out his hunting knife and cut the bindings, "Hush now, I'm going to get you out of here. Be ready to run, okay?"

A young boy's voice sniffled, "Okay."

Sayren pulled off both hoods at once, revealing a young boy and slightly older girl who had an angered expression toward Sayren. Stringing his bow once again and moving to the edge of the door, Sayren scanned for any additional foes that may have been alerted by his actions. Sounds of enraged commands barked from the woods as they slowly disappeared behind the wind. Sayren hurried the children off towards a post where the bandits had tied their horses and lifted them into the saddle before handing the young girl the reins, her brother tightly holding his hands around her middle.

"Ride towards the road and then turn to Dalkas. Your parents will be waiting for you there."

With an anger look, the girl muttered, "They're not our parents." under her breath and snapped the reins.

Sayren stood in awe for a moment from the ruse he had just been fooled by. If the couple were not the guardians of the children, then they were part of a trafficking ring that took exceptional children in the night and sold them to other slavers. Sudden sounds of footsteps pulled Sayren back as he turned around and notched another arrow in his bow. Several men dressed in unfamiliar blue tunics with an unsheathed sword behind an open palm emboldened on their tunics stood around Sayren with weapons drawn. Sayren scoffed and dropped his bow. Although he dropped his weapon, the soldiers did not move until a man moved from behind the shack, his mask hiding his face.

"Ah," Alkith's masked appearance moved to one of his soldier's sides and cleaned his bloodied sword against the man's tunic, "what brings a man like you out here? I didn't expect we'd find a son of Alder in the confines of a bandit camp."

Sayren clenched his fist, "Who are you? What do you want?"

Alkith moved past the line of soldiers and motioned for them to leave, "I am simply here to acquire what is mine. I should ask you the same question. You may pick up your bow though, there's no reason to leave such a fine piece of wood lying in the dirt."

Sayren bent down and cautiously retrieved his bow before responding, "I was here to find something that was lost. I have done so, if you and I have no quarrel, I will take my leave."

Alkith smiled under his mask and raised his sword. Sayren quickly drew his bow back in response. "I have no quarrel with an heir; however, I do believe I would like to see just how strong you've become since the fall."

Sayren gave Alkith a startled look for a moment, "I am no heir you masked fool, I'm just a hunter. If your wish to fight me won't be swayed, then let us not waste words."

Alkith chuckled menacingly, "Very well Sayren. Let us see if you are worthy of Ralford's throne."

Alkith rushed Sayren in a full sprint, sword pointed outward whimsically. Sayren drew back his bow and released an arrow directly at Alkith. Flying through the air, the arrow appeared to find its mark, however, sounds of metal striking wood mystified Sayren; however Alkith was no longer standing in the same location he was in a moment before. Sounds of a sword cutting through the air forced Sayren to leap forward, nimbly dodging Alkith's attack from behind. Sayren quickly notched another arrow and fired at Alkith from his roll. Once again, Alkith disappeared from sight without a sound, but Sayren caught a faint flash of light as he vanished. Sayren regained his footing and quickly ran into the trees, many of his arrows jostling in his quivers. A sudden flash of white light burst through the tree line and forced Sayren to fall to the ground, scattering his remaining arrows amongst the small bushes.

"Run if you're going to flee, son of Alder! I'm impressed that the rumors you had the gift of foresight to be true. It is truly impressive! We'll see if it can save you from my abilities!" Alkith's voice echoed throughout the forest.

Reaching to his leg, Sayren pulled a metal rod from its sheath and strung his bow, its shape changing into a metal arrow. "You will not have a chance to use your abilities should you continue to pursue me. I am Sayren, Archer of the Six Crows. Do not trifle with me lest you are prepared to receive my arrows! What say you, you masked freak?"

"I'm hurt," Alkith said as he stepped from behind a tree, his sword hanging loosely in his hand, "I thought you'd give me more credit. If I actually wished you dead, I wouldn't give you a moment to react. I want to see just how strong the brothers have become; many of the other heirs are waiting for your return to begin retaking their homes."

Sayren released his arrow without a word and moved behind a tree to draw another arrow. Alkith blocked the metal arrow as it clanged against his sword and flew into the distance. Alkith outstretched his hand towards his opponent and opened his palm; a shimmering light formed as another beam shot forward into the wood, burning through the wood. A whistling sound of another arrow forced Alkith to check his surroundings as the first metal arrow returned and connected with his mask, shattering a small piece just below the right eye. Alkith recoiled from the unsuspecting attack and disappeared yelling, "Very well done! I await our next confrontation, Archer of the Six Crows!"

The forest fell silent as Sayren stepped out from beneath the hole in the tree and returned the metal arrows to their place as they reverted back to metal rods. Sighing in relief, Sayren began to look around for any loose arrows he could salvage before returning to his horse.

❖　❖　❖

With the campsite removed and saddles replaced on their horses, Rylan slid his foot into the stirrup and swung his opposing leg over. Tiberius and his men were packed and ready, each starring at their tranquil surroundings as Isabelle and Brilla were gathering their belongings. Aldis sat atop his horse, his eyes closed and his mind focused on the area around them. He felt no signs of the willow bear near them, however a feint multitude of hooves stampeding in the direction Sayren and Toren had taken gave him a sense of unease. A sudden nudge pulled Aldis from his trance and as he open his eyes found Brilla attempting to balance off of him as she struggled to find her poise with the saddle.

"Are you okay?" Aldis as ask he offered a hand in assistance.

Brilla chuckled and gently placed her hand is his as she steadied herself, "Yes, thank you. It is my first time outside of the walls. I had always been told it was a very dangerous place, however, with a place so tranquil, I cannot imagine this would be filled with treachery."

"I thought that way too when I first joined my brothers," Aldis replied as he retracted his hand and grinned, "Although this is a very peaceful place, many are not so quiet, but filled with dangerous monsters and dangerous men. While you travel with the Crows though, you will never have to worry about your safety."

Brilla blushed and silently nodded before moving over to Isabelle as the group began to move again. Brilla whispered something into Isabelle's ear and both chuckled. Aldis blushed and quickly pulled his hood over his head and went back into his meditation. All while Rylan and Tiberius glanced back at the two.

"What made you want to bring a priestess of the late queen outside the walls? It's highly irregular to even see one now days after the queen was killed in the square." Rylan inquired as he pulled his hood up slightly to cover his neck form the sun.

Tiberius shrugged, "It wasn't my choice to be honest. She appeared at the estate with a letter sealed by the king stating she was to accompany us; I didn't have time to ask why. I would rather talk about your skills though. What makes a man delve into the ability of royals instead of something more useful?"

Rylan smirked, "I was taught at a young age that to be powerful you may either succeed where few have accomplished similar deeds, or you may blend in with the multitudes simply looking to get by. Using metal is every difficult, but the fact remained that few people possess the ability to wield it properly. Using it in King's Hold helps make things easier as well."

"I still don't understand what made you choose it though. Using the ability to control and shape metal is forbidden since King Sepius said that only royals may possess the skill. You would have been alive for King Ralford's time though. Did you wish to join his guard?"

"I did for a time," Rylan despondently replied as he looked up into the sky, "I dreamed of the day when I could serve with honor amongst the best fighters of Alder. After the harvest festival I was to apply for selection, but the revolt left my father broken and I was forced to choose between family and a wanton goal. I elected to protect my family and provide for them. I would not be the man I am if I had left them for my own selfish gains."

Tiberius nodded and pulled a pendant from a pouch on his side. "I cannot fault you for your actions; I too wanted to be a part of the Royal Guard when I first met Queen Maree. I was only a small boy, but when I was introduced to the court, she walked right up to me and held me in her arms. Many of the other nobles were shocked that she would do such a thing, but the moment she embraced me I knew that I would work to protect her. After she was caught in the Horseman's Square and quartered, I could not bear to have my name amongst the chosen few that belonged to the royal guard."

"I see," Rylan looked at the cylindrical pendant with the image of the late queen's face upon it, "I suppose your brothers would feel differently if they were given the chance to join."

"Aye, they would jump for a chance to step beyond my fame. I only hope that my brothers do not do anything reckless outside of what they have already done."

"If they do, we will be ready. Any nefarious move against you or Lady Isabelle would be treachery against a noble and grounds for royal punishment."

Tiberius sighed and returned the pendant to his pouch, "I agree, but my brothers can be brash at times, not thinking of consequences their actions may yield."

"Rylan" Toren shouted as he busted through the trees, "we encountered a caravan beset by bandits! Sayren pursued them after they took the children and sent me back to retrieve you! We need to go, now!"

"Damn him!" Rylan shouted as he snapped the reins. "Aldis, find Sayren! We ride now!"

Aldis snapped from his trance, "We need to go, there is a group pursuing us from Dalkas but I cannot see them."

Rylan jerked his head to face Aldis, "How many?"

"I'm not sure. They must have another sage with them to block my ability to locate them. I can only hear the hooves against dirt. We should quicken our pace to stay ahead of them."

Tiberius motioned the group forward, "We ride for Sayren, and then to face our pursuers! Toren lead the way and we shall follow!"

Galloping through the tree line, the group raced behind Toren as dark clouds drew closer from the west. Sounds of pursuers drew closer in Aldis's mind as he attempted to find Sayren's location with no avail.

❀   ❀   ❀

Sounds of Lord Carthill screaming in agony echoed throughout the hallways surrounding his torture chamber as Mauro continued to work. Although specialized militia, both guardsmen attempted to appear steadfast, yet with each shrill and cry, obvious shuddering motions or gagging sounds from both men could be observed without investigation. When the screaming stopped, footsteps could be heard drawing closer to the door. A loud, sudden creak from the door as Mauro pried it open enough to stick his head through forced the guards to snap to attention.

"Which one of you would do me the pleasure of fetching a clear crystal from my storage room and return swiftly? I wish to be done with this before the sun sets again so I may actually rest my hands." Mauro's face was dotted with droplets of coagulated blood as he grinned at the men before slowly pressing the door close. Both guards turned to one another before a quick nod and the sound of clanging armor trailed down the hall.

Mauro returned to Carthill, his grin still affixed to his face as he looked at a bloodied noble. Several of Carthill's fingernails were missing on his right hand, while tarnished metal rods stuck though the tips of his fingers with rusted metal wings on the ends in his left. His face had become far worse, his bloodshot eyes were forced open and several teeth lay on the table in front of him.

Mauro rested in his chair and folded his arms, "You should know, this is not how I wished to proceed with you, Lord Carthill. You've given me little choice but to follow the king's instruction. Will you not simply tell me the truth so that I may make this all stop and you may be attended by a healer and return to your home to rest?"

Lord Carthill whimpered as he attempted to formulate words; however a low inaudible mumble and a steady flow of drool fell from his bloodied lips. Mauro slammed his fist atop the table and shouted, "How rude! I would expect someone like you to not insult me with your lowly whispers! Now speak to me like the man of prestige you claim to be!"

"You... Monster... I am a noble of the King's Court." Carthill voice cracked and sputtered as he gingerly raised his head, "I will see you hang for this."

A sudden, manic laugh erupted from Mauro as he cocked his head back and wiped a tear from his eye. He exhaled to recover from his laughter, leaned forward, and rested his arms on the table, "You're quite the fool to insult a Royal Inquisitor; to call me a monster is simply childish. I am simply a product of my father's discipline. When I was young, I possessed little aptitude for martial skills; however, I was fond of a talent I learned from a dream. You see my father had a marvelous war hound. Doaclus was his name, powerful and very much my father's prized pet. Doaclus always guarded the family; however he had a nasty disposition towards me. He even bit me once when I feed him." Mauro paused as he pulled his collar to the side and revealed a continuous scare that traced itself around his shoulder. "Thankfully the family healer was quite wondrous, but I hated that dog, and roughly a year after, I had a dream that showed me how to alter thoughts and emotions in others. So when I awoke in the middle of the night I snuck up to that sleeping mutt and changed him. Nothing noticeable mind you, however when the dog attempted to attack me again in the morning it suddenly went into a crazed frantic state of hysteria and wouldn't stop. You see I had changed his mind to fear me if he ever sought me harm. That fear would go away the moment I patted his head, but I was never able to do so before the smug bastard's heart gave out. My father was very displeased that he had lost his pride and joy, but after he discovered why, he saw the benefits of having my ability. For two years I found his enemies and removed them by my father's order. King Sepius eventually caught wind of my father's actions and gave him a choice to give up his son to his Royal Inquisitors, or lose my talents all together. I suppose I should thank him for not letting the king behead me, but he still despised me for killing his damn dog. It's quite the conundrum would you say?"

Carthill's facial expression instantly changed to terror as he attempted to free himself from his bonds. As he attempted to grip the chair's arms, however, he writhed in excruciating pain from injuries done to his hand. A pained whimper exiting his mouth as he stopped his attempted and slumped over in his chair, yielding to his cruel fate.

Mauro crossed his hand underneath his chin as he rested his head and continued, his cheerful voice eerily filling the room, "Oh come now, I haven't even gotten to the good part. I can't believe you'd be so rude to try and leave before I've finished my story. As time progress, this occupation became less and less bothersome. At first I could barely stand the sight of blood, however, after I was given the ability to torture rebellious traitors on my own, I grew to like this bloody calling. It gives me a sense of completion that I cannot find in my day to day living. These actions, over years, allowed me to develop a way to seal personal memories into Sen Crystals, even ones that people hide in the deepest, darkest corners of their mind. It's quite excruciating for the person as the memories are ripped from your mind, and unfortunately not very many survive this process. I am able to provide King Sepius with a very clear image of what has transpired, and what actions will need to be taken afterwards. That is our best course of action at this current point I feel, but should you survive and be proven innocent, then we shall rectify the situation as the King sees fit. If you are lying to me and have secrets though, I will tear them from you, and leave you a broken, forgotten wretch in an alley." Mauro's voice changed from a lighthearted tone to one of cold and precise. "You will give whatever I choose to take Lard Carthill; that is absolute."

Thoughts of torture at Mauro's hands forced a cringe out of Larus' bloodied face, his body shaking uncontrollably in pure fright. A sudden knock on the door forced a shrill out in panic as Mauro cackled in response. Mauro slowly arose, Carthill's garbled pleas became louder and louder, until the door opened slightly and Mauro's bloodied hand reached out of sight and returned with a crystal in hand.

"No! No! You can't do this to me! Someone! Anyone! Help me and I will pay your weight in gold! Do not let him touch me, please!" Carthill's clear voice shrieked as he lurched back in his chair causing it to rise onto two legs. As the wooden chair began to tip over the edge Mauro darted over and cupped Larus' head, preventing it from smacking the soiled ground, "I see you're ready to begin." Mauro smugly replied as he eased his hand out from under Carthill's head and placed his open palm over top Lord Carthill's face. A dark blue aura began to form underneath Mauro's hand, and in an instant, the aura pierced Lord Carthill's consciousness and blanketed his eyes black. Searing pain forced a garbled scream out of Carthill as he arched his back and writhed in agony.

Mauro's vision blurred for a moment before he could feel himself drifting through Larus' memories. A swift motion of his hand placed him inside the abandoned house, standing beside Lord Carthill as he sat restrained, receiving a remorseless beating at the hands of the masked man. Mauro slightly twisted his hand as time propelled forward until he arrived at the same moment the message was delivered.

"The Noble Houses of Alder will fall to the rightful king's hand and a new day will dawn with your crimson blood upon the streets. Low born will rise and drive the knife through your frail king's heart. Crow's wings will spread and The Six Winged Death will take his throne."

As the words echoed from the masked man's concealed lips, Mauro twisted time back and forth listening carefully to the message over and over again. While the message was delivered, Mauro carefully moved around Larus' captor in an attempt to solve his identity. Dark robes seemingly covered the man from head to foot; however, the faintest motion revealed the same blue as the Kingdom of Kay underneath the black. "Ah," Mauro said as he grinned, "I see the other heirs are attempting to stage a revolt here, important news indeed. Mauro opened his palm and began to tear the memory away for Lord Carthill and into the Sen Crystal, turning its clear form dark crimson. Mauro pulled back more memories, delving deeper into Carthill's past, several meetings will cloaked individuals staring at indiscernible scribbled reports lay scattered on a table, the briefest of moments as he gave his daughter's hand to an finely dressed young lad as his sons stood off to the side next to two others, and final a crystal clear view of Queen Maree drenched in a dirty, blood spattered dress with two young boys and a small babe pressed tightly against her womb.

"Help us Larus, please." Queen Maree's body began to shiver and fail from exhaustion. Mauro stopped the memories progression and moved about the Queen as she fell; noting anything of remote value, the two boys that stood beside her seemed almost unrecognizable from their filthy appearances.

"Come now Lord Larus, you can't keep them hidden from me now. We've come so far already. I want to see everything you have to offer the king. Give me their faces!" Mauro tightened his grip as Carthill arched against the cold cobblestone, his mind in absolute agony as his muscles seemingly burst as he could feel the inquisitor pulling the young heirs faces into focus against his will.

Against Larus's cheek, a single tear fell as he muttered, "I'm sorry Ralford... I have failed you. Please forgive me..."

Mauro saw the faint blonde hair and wondrous brown eyes from one heir, while the other hand deep chocolate brown with a dark blue eyes like the queen herself. The baby remained hidden from view as Mauro tried to force the images forward and back to catch even the faintest chance of glimpse of the youngest heir. The memory around Mauro began to blur and crumble as Lord Larus past the point of no return, "Not yet you old bastard!" Mauro yelled as he forced his hand open and managed to hold back the collapse, "There's got to be more somewhere!" Mauro quickly moved to the doorway and peered outside to see a young man glistening with six metal-like shard wings. The boy's face and demeanor plagued him with a familiar look that he could not place. He strained to leave the estate's doorway, but with each passing step Mauro felt a tremendous pressure begin to surround him. Lord Carthill was dead, but with just a single detail of the fabled Six Winged Death, he could reveal the identity of a fourth heir. The pressure felt as if his chest was being enveloped by boulders crushing his every breath. Mauro pulled the memories into the Sen as reached out for the boy, however, a sudden flash of lightning flashed across the motionless sky and the boy reached out with his hand, "You will bow before your king."

Mauro felt the pressure around his surmount to more than he could bare and fell to his knees as he attempted to recoil from the memory and back to the present. Vision of the fourth child began to blur as Mauro began to return, but a metal vine ensnared his throat and pulled him back to his knees before the Six Wings.

Mauro grasped at the tightening metal around his throat, "How is this possible? You're only a memory!"

The boy's face was obscured by shadows, but Mauro could hear him clearly, "This is a dark realm that you carelessly wander through Inquisitor Mauro, dreams and memories are safeguarded by those who seek to protect the sovereignty of this world. Should you mettle further against Thesia, you will not see the real world again."

"Who are you...if not Ralford's...Heir?" Mauro choked as his hands began to bleed from pulling against his restraints.

The boy released his metal grip around Mauro and muttered, "I am amongst the chosen" before dissipating entirely and forcing Mauro back to his own body.

For a moment Mauro felt as though he could not breath before he inhaled a long gasping lungful of air and picked himself off the floor. Mauro's Sen Crystal, now saturated ruby red, reflected the light from the candle, the edges leaving minor lacerations along his palm. Mauro moved towards the door before slamming his hand against the wood, "Open the door...I am done with the traitor." A thud from the retracting latch resonated as it slowly creaked open and the guards returned to their positions of attention. Mauro braced himself against the doorway as he moved over the threshold and down the hall, his voice coarse from the mystery boy within the memories. "Throw good Lord Carthill to the dogs, may his soul find no rest for his treason against the one, true King of Alder." Stopping for a moment Mauro laughed mockingly, "King Sepius will finally have his absolution!" Mauro turned to the guards, "Come to think of it, dispatch a message to Lord Gaius that I will have to speak with his majesty tomorrow morning at his earliest convenience. It seems I may have some more work to complete after all."

"At once Inquisitor Mauro!" and the guards disappeared into the chamber to collect Larus' corpse.

Although he had multiple memories within the crystal, the one of Lord Carthill's daughter being wed struck Mauro as odd. Larus had three children, but they gave up their titles for some unknown reason before disappearing entirely into the realm of commoners and paupers. "The image of the heirs and the other men within the wedding could have been one in the same which means they will lead me directly to my targets." Mauro started again, this time with his stride faster and his mind fixated on his new tasks.

CHAPTER 4

A lkith sat atop a fallen tree as he gazed at the bandit's burning encampment in the distance. His men busily scurrying about gathering fallen comrades and any usable materials left behind. Four full carts sat along a western trail that twisted into the forest away from the ambush. Although he was focused on the task at hand, Alkith sat recalling movements Sayren had made as he held his broken mask; his minded concentrating around how quickly Sayren had returned the arrow without any noticeable change is expression. "With such ability," Alkith thought to himself as he moved the mask to the side of the log and ran his fingers through his hair, "he has to be the heir. Why deny it though? I could've sworn I've seen him all those years ago. I will have to delve deeper; I know I'm correct."

From alongside the carts, a single man made his way over to Alkith and bowed, "Milord. I have the report."

Alkith grabbed the mask and slid it into a satchel, "What is your report, and why is Romnu not giving it?"

"I'm sorry milord," The soldier fell to a knee and lowered his head; "Romnu and three others are dead. We've secured the supplies you requested, unfortunately, the children that were supposed to be delivered are missing still. I will send out riders on your orders."

Alkith leaned back on the log, "Damn." He sighed as he entwined his fingers behind his head. "Romnu was one of my best men. That puts our numbers down beneath forty for this excursion. Forget the children, we'll return to the Hold without delay. What is your name kid?"

"Gauld, Sire. I am Gauld of Bannefir, just north of the capital of Kay." The young soldier responded as he lifted his head, his dark blonde hair shifting with the forest's gentle breeze.

Alkith grinned and gave a slight chuckle, "I recall Bannefir quite well. I spent almost five years there when I began my campaign to regain my title. I always adored its beauty and serenity of the lands around it, so peaceful and majestic. One day we'll return there and retake our homes, what say you Gauld?"

"It will always be an honor to stand by your side, milord."

"That is a very good answer. You'll be my new second Gauld from this day until our last. Will you ready the men to travel?" Alkith turned to look at Gauld.

"At once, milord, it will be done immediately!" Gauld leaped to his feet, bowed to Alkith and raced through the brush to the caravan shouting orders to ready the wagons.

Alkith looked up to the tree tops as the rays of sunlight shifted through the ever changing openings between the trees and danced across the branches. A low guttural growl forced Alkith to glance around. Suddenly leaping forward from its surroundings, the Willow Bear forced Alkith to roll off the log and press himself against the ground, dodging the mighty claw as it tore through a large portion of the wood. Alkith quickly returned to his feet and readied his hands, both giving off a slight glow as the bear's hulking form maneuvered over the fallen log. Alkith launched a single hand forward, sending a beam shooting through the air just to the side of the bear; however the beast leaped at Alkith once again, his form bounding over Alkith's attack.

"Tch, looks like you're not the type to be scared off so easily." Alkith grumbled at the bear drew close as he teleported away moments before its claws tore through his leather brigandine. Alkith turned to see the bear collide with a tree and shook its head in an attempt to regain its composure.

Alkith shot another hand forward, this time aiming for the bear's hind foot and found its mark. Howling, the bear turned to face Alkith; enraged the beast rushed forward ignoring its newly acquired injury and crashed head first with Alkith's chest before he could move away. Alkith rolled along the ground until he collided against a tree and gasped for the air that had been knocked from his lungs. As Alkith clutched his chest, he could see the blurred image of the Willow Bear as it began to close upon him. Reaching back with its large paw, the bear attempted to rip into Alkith in a singular attack. Gauld roared "From Death!" as he leaped into the fray and threw three knotted daggers into the Willow Bear's reared arm. All three knives sank into the bears arm and prevented the attack while Gauld bravely held the rope. Alkith staggered upright, resting against an oak tree for support as the bear roared and turned to face Gauld. Charging towards the wild beast, Gauld reached behind his back to grab a short sword. As the bear swung his massive claws, he leaped into the air and moved in front of Alkith, tugging the rope and forcing the blades to tear from the bear's arm and return to his free hand. A distressed whimper from the Willow Bear sent it scurried back into the woods and disappearing as it hobbled away, nursing its wounds.

Gauld propped Alkith against his arm as they began to walk back towards the caravan, "Are you okay to stand milord?"

"In a moment," Alkith's voice wearily spoke as he placed his hand over his bruised ribs, the shear act of breathing causing him to grimace in agony, "Once we get to the carts, I'll move to my horse and ride."

Gauld gave Alkith a concerned looked but nodded in agreement, "I understand. Morale of your men must not waiver, not until you regain your throne milord. I'll see to it the men think nothing of any injuries."

Alkith stopped and stood on his own, "you're quite the astute learner Gauld, who taught you to be so understanding of tactics?"

"My grandfather, he was the Duke of Bannefir lord."

"What is the grandson of a duke doing serving in my forces? You could be ruling in prominence, living a life of ease."

"My father died in service to your father, King Arbuk, and our title was stripped. My mother fled with me to King's Hold where I willing serve the true King of Kay as my father did for as long as you'll have me, milord."

Alkith gave a pained grin and patted Gauld on the shoulder, "As long as I am alive, you will have a place at my table. When we return home you will regain your title of Duke of Bannefir."

Both nodded to one another as they broke through the woods and onto the path, Alkith to his horse, and Gauld to the lead cart barking orders to prepare to move. Faint dark clouds of an approaching storm peaked just above the tree line as Alkith looked back one last time at the woods before snapping the reins and beginning their ride back.

❀   ❀   ❀

"How much further Toren?" Rylan shouted as he tightened his grip on the reins, his eyes darting from side to side looking for any signs of Sayren or his horse as they raced down the road to the billowing trails of smoke.

"I'm not sure, he must be close though! I doubt he's gone far from where that smoke is coming from!" Toren replied, unsheathing his sword in case any of the bandits remained.

"Hold!" Sayren shouted from the group's left as he dropped out from a heavily forested tree, "Don't move towards the smoke!"

Rylan and the others quickly halted their horses and moved to Sayren, sounds of crackling fires echoing just off in the distance as Rylan dismounted and embraced his brother. After a moment Sayren stepped back, "We need to continue with our journey, the bandit encampment that was near this area have been taken out by rebel forces. I fear those same men may still be nearby. Brother, they're recruiting gifted children and using them as warriors. There was also a masked fellow that made mad accusations."

Rylan crossed his arms, "I agree with your motion of continuing onward, we're being pursued by a large group that Aldis has been tracking. We may have lost them for the time being, but we'll need to move again soon. As for the masked man, he may be just another fanatic who is trying to recruit whomever he thinks he can find and convince them of any falsehoods possible. Pay him no mind; however your actions have put us in a troublesome spot. Should any of those bandits have seen you and survived, when we make our way to the village, we very well may have to contend with an additional adversary, an enemy we are not being paid or commissioned to dispatch. Remember what we are here to accomplish. Are we at an understanding?"

Sayren looked to the ground with a long sigh, for all the love he had for his brother, Sayren disagreed with Rylan's ways when the lives of innocent people were put into harm's way. He begrudgingly retrieved his horse and returned to the group. Tiberius looked over to Sayren, "Did you deal with all of those bandits yourself?"

Sayren cracked a grin, "Nothing a little fire won't do when your enemy has no idea where it's coming from."

"Don't tell the lady that." Tiberius chuckled as he motioned to Isabelle.

Rylan interrupted as he turned his horse to face the group, "We'll need to gain as much ground as we can before our pursuers reach us. If it is the Serpent's Fang, as I believe it to be, the storm will need to be upon us when we face them."

As the sounds of the rolling thunder clouds echoed closer to them, Rylan and the others once again raced near to Havenhome. Sounds of the other group drew within ear shot as Aldis continued to track their movements from his trance. His attempts to reveal the group were unable to ascertain any detail. He was able to distinguish their numbers as he carefully singled out each horse's hooves as they crashed against the cobbled dirt. "There are sixteen riders! We should stop now and prepare for them if you want to fight during the storm!"

Rylan pulled back on the reins and turned to face the others. "We've run far enough. Now it is time they learn not to mess with Crows!"

Following Rylan's orders, Toren and Sayren moved off the road on the left to prevent an ambush, while Aldis, Isabelle, and Brilla moved to the right side to balance their strengths. Rylan and Tiberius stood forward of Tiberius's readied guard. With axe and sword in his grasp, Rylan looked to both sides of the roads, then Tiberius, "Once they arrive, they will dismount. These assassins are not fools; they'll seek to draw us out without thinking. Depending on the leader and their sage, we may have to use your winds to full effect."

"That will be difficult," Tiberius replied as he rested his shield upon the ground, "If this storm is being carried by strong currents, my winds will be ineffective."

Rylan tapped the edge of his sword against the ground, "I don't suppose your men possess abilities as formidable as yours?"

"No, unfortunately my men are trained in hand to hand combat. All their abilities are used to strengthen their defenses against ability wielders like ourselves. What about you? Are you going to use your hidden talents?"

"I will if it cannot be prevented. I will refrain from it until it is unavoidable, the less that see my ability the better for our overall health." Rylan tightened his grasp as the riders stormed into view before pulling back on their reins and coming to a halt.

Concealed behind masks or helms, the riders were indistinguishable, with the exception of black cloaks with crossed snakes. As the Fang riders dismounted, Rylan walked forward until the others drew weapons and formed a line behind a single man with dual swords. Their leader moved closer to Rylan as he pointed to Tiberius, "I want nothing from you mercenary; I am here for Lord Tiberius and Lady Isabelle of House Bernak. Give them to us and you may go on your way."

Rylan smirked, "You must have me confused for someone that you can push around with your daggers," as he tugged against his cloak as it fell to the ground and revealed his armor and crest, "I am Rylan of the Six Crows, the nobles you seek are under my guard. You should turn back now if you wish to see the next sunrise."

Throwing back his hood, the leader tore off his mask and revealed his face. A slender pale skinned man with scars carved across his face and a grizzled look of fury seething from his demeanor. He locked cold, glaring eyes with Rylan for a moment, "You have nerve ever showing your face in front of me again. It has been five years since you delivered a unprovoked attack against my family, and I have longed for the day that I could repay you in turn."

A streak of lightning shot through the sky followed by a booming roll of thunder. Drops of rain began to plummet downward onto the road as Rylan looked closer at the man, "I am sorry but I don't recall your face, did your family attempt to hurt mine? I can think of no other reason to attack a commoner without reason. If I had delivered such unbearable pain to your bloodline; why would you attempt to strike back at me knowing that you could not harm me?"

Gripping the white stone pommels of his weapons, the man scoffed, "You don't recall me? I knew you had no honor Crow, but to deny any involvement with men who wished to serve under you is heartless. My brother and I wished to join and assist your family. When you denied us, my brother was outraged and attempted to reason with you. You took his sword arm and left us for dead in a back alley street! No one wanted to hire a crippled man, nor the brother that would have to take care of him. I was forced to turn to the Fang and spend two years completing my trials to gain the position I hold. These twin blades were given to me after I was forced to take my brother's life so that I may use them to take from you what you stole from me! I am Kraste; I will kill you for what you did to my brother!"

Rylan pointed his sword at Kraste, "Then I propose we be honor bound to duel until one of us lies dead in the mud and should you fall, your men will leave and not attempt anything further against those under my charge. Will you agree to the terms?"

Kraste drew his swords, two light-weight blades with large hilts carved with images of crossed serpents spiraling towards a black gem in the center. "Very well, I accept your terms. Men! Spread out! If this dishonorable fool attempts to pull some underhanded tactic, kill them all!"

Rylan stepped forward again, "Say I'm without honor one more time night-taker and I will be sure to place your head atop your horse when I send it back to your masters!"

"Rylan, what are you planning?" Tiberius called out as he stepped forward.

"Do not interfere, Lord Tiberius. Even if you are noble, this is honor bound and any interference from either side will be dealt with swiftly. I will dispatch with this man and we will be on our way to the others."

"Enough talk Crow!" Kraste roared as he raced forward through the downpour of rain, his swords ready to strike.

Rylan winked at Tiberius before turning to his opponent and moving forward. As the two clashed, Rylan parried the first attack and countered with his axe, however, Kraste was nimble and swiftly rolled away before launching his next attack. Rylan saw the wild attack and stepped away from the blades as they swept by before thrusting his sword at Kraste's back, cutting his left side slightly before having to leap back from a surprise counter. Kraste's blade connected against Rylan's armor, cutting into his leather armor. Both men paused checking the damage before resetting their stances and leaping into the fray again. For each of Kraste's attacks, Rylan parried or countered. However any time Rylan pressed an opening, his opponent closed the distance between them and forced him back into a defensive posture. With each clang of sword striking one another Tiberius could see both men tiring, as well as the other members of the Fang disappearing into the woods with the exception of three men all wielding hatchets. A deluge of blanketing rain began to fall, covering the surroundings in a fog like appearance. Thunder bellowed across the sky continuously drowning out the sounds of the two fighters.

With both men's equipment saturated and burdensome, Kraste attempted to rush forward at Rylan with both swords ready to strike. Rylan heaved his axe into the air and sent it careening downwards while Kraste swung low at Rylan's legs. Both men connected, Kraste's blade sliced Rylan's unprotected side of his leg, cutting deep into his flesh, while Rylan's axe crashed into Kraste's thigh. Rylan hobbled away while Kraste rolled along the ground wailing, "Honor-less trash! He's attacked my leg and shown his tasteless virtues! Kill them all!"

Rylan felt his surroundings slow as a venomous poison began to numb the wound on his leg. Tiberius ordered his men forward to Rylan's aide as the other Fang members still on the road raced forward towards him. Shouts from the woods echoed as both sides clashed from within the trees. Rylan stumbled forward towards Kraste as he smirked and crawled away in agony, both his blades dirtied from the mud and crimson blood slowly washing away by the rain.

Tiberius rushed forward in front of Rylan as the first man arrived with his hatchets raised high above his head, cascading downward at his target. Shield met hatchet as Tiberius shoved the man back and swung in a wide arch at the assassin. Tiberius's guard quickly rushed in after their lord and engaged the other troops as Rylan and Kraste backed away from the battle. Tiberius quickly pulled Rylan's arm over his shoulder and moved him out of combat some distance before seeing more members of the Fang emerge from the right side of the road on their flank. Two arrows flew through the air and struck their targets in the back, sending them sprawling into the mud. Toren emerged behind another assassin, running him through from behind before disappearing back into the woods. The remaining exposed men quickly turned their attention toward Sayren and Toren's general direction before befalling victim to Tiberius as he slammed his shield again one man forcing him against a tree and slicing the other from behind as he turned to strike. Tiberius quickly turned to the other man as the spear man thrust his weapon forward, only to have it clang off Tiberius's heavy plate armor. Tiberius plunged his sword in the man's chest, twisted and wrenched it out as the Fang gasped for breath as he fell back against the tree slumped over and motionless. A sudden piercing scream forced Tiberius around to see Lorn lying face down and Afnir with both hatchets dug into his collarbones as the female assassin moved forward, gripping both handles firmly while placing a foot against Afnir's chest and forcibly prying both blades out. Enraged Tiberius rushed forward as Afnir fell back, shuddering as he lay under the falling rain before he slowed to a twitch and stopped all together. Both Falder and Orsen quickly moved to either side of Tiberius and took up a defensive posture, readying their shields together to form a barrier between the opposition. With three remaining assassins on the road, they glanced at the soldiers and off towards Rylan as he struggled to stay upright.

A unified silent nod between the assassins occurred as two rushed towards Rylan and the third slowly followed, cautiously facing Tiberius as he continued backwards.

"Rylan, look out!" Tiberius shouted over his shield as the two men drew closer to Rylan, a sudden flash of lightning and the assassin's leaped at Rylan. Rylan quickly rolled away, dropping his axe in the process. The two quickly stepped between Rylan and his weapon, their masks menacingly glaring at Rylan as he slowly pushed himself upright, his armor covered in a thick layer off mud. Rylan readied for another attack, pointing his sword low towards the ground and placing his injured leg in front. One of the men quickly launched himself forward with a hatchet held high above his head and the other across his body for protection. As the man approached Rylan, he flashed his blade against the radiant lightning and sliced upward as he stepped to the side, away from the hatchet's path. A howling scream erupted from the man as his severed arm fell to the ground still clutching his untarnished weapon. Rylan quickly spun his sword around to point at the Fang and pushed forward as the man turned in fury to strike at his target. Before the other assassin could react, Toren appeared form the bushes, tackled the man to the ground, and began to stab repeatedly into the cloaked figure's back. Both members of the Fang choked and gurgled underneath their masks before becoming motionless in the deluge.

"Stop Kraste, I will not let him take victory away with his cowardice and spite!" Rylan sputtered as he collapsed to the ground and began to breathe heavily.

Sayren emerged from the tree line and released an arrow at Kraste, missing wildly due to the winds, "Damn. Toren knock Rylan out now. We need as much time as we can have. Lord Tiberius! Leave that last one to me and head into the woods. Aldis will not be able to withhold the remaining forces on his own!"

Tiberius and his men moved into the trees as the remaining assassin turned to face Sayren and chuckled. Placing the bow on his back, Sayren removed his four iron arrows from their holster and waited. A bolt of lightning struck a tree in the woods with a loud crack and Sayren turned his gaze to ensure he was in no further danger. The Fang moved in quickly, sprinting through the puddles of water formed by the footprints, and leaped at Sayren. He returned his gaze to see the woman mid leap and grinned as he threw all four metal arrows forward and struck the defenseless woman, sending her body flying through the air before crashing into a large oak tree. Sayren rushed over as the woman wailed in agony as the metal sank into the tree and pinned her limbs in place, "Tell me where the antidote is and I will end your suffering quickly! Refuse and I will take my time to prolong your suffering!"

She stopped screaming as the female shook her head and forced the mask to fall to the ground. As she lifted her head Sayren saw her face and recoiled in disgust. Skin had been flayed from parts of her face and burned or lacerated to create horrific scars. "I won't tell you anything! Your brother will die and rot before the next sun sets. He will soon delve into madness before breathing his last breath!"

Sayren scowled as he clenched his fist and forced the metal to begin working its way into her limbs, wrenching muscle from bone as they began to swell and crack. "Tell me where, now."

"I won't break, not to you, you worthless bird!" The woman cried out.

Sayren unsheathed his hunting dagger and drove it into the woman's stomach, pulling it upward as he began to open her stomach. "My brother will not die. Not to the likes of you or your kind."

A gasp for air and a grimaced expression filled the assassin's face as she reacted to the immense pain. "Okay, okay... I'll tell you, but you have to keep your word to end it!"

"Speak!" He shouted as he lightly pressed against the knife.

"The Sage...argh... the Sage has the sodding antidote!"

Sayren retracted his blade, felt against the woman's ribs and drove the blade back in, piercing her heart and twisting. A short breath and she immediately fell limp. Sayren motioned for the arrows to retract, quickly flying into the air and returned to Sayren's hand as he drew back his bow and moved into the woods, leaving Toren to watch over Rylan as he lay unconscious propped up against a tree.

❀ ❀ ❀

Sounds of raging battle roared in the distance as Aldis sat with his staff placed across his lap, watching the battle in his trance. A sudden cracking of a fallen tree branch threw him back to reality as a spearman found him, Lady Isabelle, and Brilla. Aldis quickly rolled to avoid the point of the man's spear and countered by slamming the end of his wooden staff into the man's face and forcing him stumbling backwards.

"Get behind me Lady Isabelle!" Aldis shouted as he made a circular motion with his hand and sent a blast of pure energy forward, striking the man and propelling him further off balance until his head collided against a tree and he fell motionless against the dirt. Several shouts erupted in front of them as the other assassins moved into view. Three sword and shields, two hatchets, and two additional spearmen emerged with their Sage stepping into view but concealing himself behind the heavy rainfall. Lady Isabelle moved around Aldis and lifted her hands in front of her, "Come meet death if you dare to face me!"

A resounding roar from two assassins wielding spears and hatchets pierced the sounds of the ongoing storm above as they quickly rushed forward around trees and over bushes. Isabelle clapped her hands together and as she began to reopen them, a bright illuminated mass of flames began to grow until she forced the mass into two separate flames and thrust her right hand forward. Without pause the flames erupted in a wide arc and flooded over the soggy terrain as the two Fangs drew closer until it washed over them, instantly searing their armor and unprotected skin. A lone swordsman burst from behind a tree on Aldis's left and forced him to force his hands into a prism like shape forming a crystal-like wall between him and the swordsman. Aldis shouted, "Brilla, in here quick!" as he separated his hands and formed a dome around them. Isabelle stopped her flames and looked to Aldis, "You can beat these men, right? Your brother said you all had bested them before."

Aldis recoiled as the swordsman began to lay into the crystal-like shield with tremendous force. "I have only gone with my brothers a few times before, mostly to another town and back. I've never even seen the Fang outside of the capital's walls before."

Shocked, Isabelle drew her sword as their enemies began to encircle the dome, "Will you be able to hold out against these men until the others arrive at least?"

"Possibly," Aldis said as he focused on channeling his power to withstand the blows, "If I cannot I will ensure both you and Lady Brilla's survival. I will give my life before I let either of you see harm. Sayren taught me that women and children, although both are powerful in their own right, will never be harmed as long as we draw breath."

Brilla grabbed Aldis's wooden staff from the dirt and readied herself, "I thank you for the noble sentiment; however these men will not live to fear our power. Lord Tiberius and the others will aide us before this shield falls."

All three nodded and waited as strike after strike crashed against the shield rained down, the lightning flashed across the ominous sea of clouds above. Cracks began to form as the endless attacks continued for what seemed like an eternity, but as one of the hatchets pierced the glass, the thunderous sound of a unified charged echoed through the trees forced the assassins to turn towards its origins. Tiberius, Orsen, and Falder stormed through the forest as they clashed with the assailants, cutting the first unsuspecting Fangs down without resistance. Their remaining four assassins quickly reformed together as

Orsen removed his plunged sword from a deceased foe. Tiberius shifted his sword into his shield hand and retrieved a spear from the ground, "Aldis, find the Sage and finish this! We can't-" A sudden orb of energy flew through the trees and shattered just in front of Falder, sending shards piercing his armor and propelling sending him backwards, dead before every touching the rain covered underbrush. Aldis quickly dropped his shield and shot a blast forward in the direction of a group of trees. A quick shuffle of feet and robes revealed the sage running away from the falling branches. Aldis quickly raced after the cloaked sage as Tiberius and Orsen engaged the remaining foot soldiers.

As Aldis sprinted after the sage, his mind focused on his surroundings in the event his opponent had laid any traps. Several loud crashes of thunder roared around him drawing him out of focus and tripping over a large root protruding from the ground. Dazed, Aldis shook his head and quickly stood upright to spot the sage standing before him in a small clearing, his hands filled with two more spheres, much like the one that killed Falder.

"I never imagined the Crows would employ a sage amongst their ranks. They seem far too inadequate to support a proper sage's employment. Just what did they promise you to gain such a power?"

Aldis brushed off the dirt from his leggings, "They aren't paying me," his voice cold and concentrated, "I joined them because they are my blood."

A loud laughter erupted from the sage as he threw both spheres forward, "I am paid to kill those that others wish dead boy! Your ideas of what a sage should be is probably what they taught you in the academy, but on the field of battle the sage is the strongest weapon of all! No one can match our strength! Not even royals!"

Aldis threw his hand forward and recast his shield in front of him as the spheres collided and exploded. "A sage is not a weapon. We were chosen to be recorders for history. Gifted with pure abilities allows us to better embrace the world around us and record it so others will see the history! If you believe yourself to be a weapon, you are truly not worthy of the title!"

Sphere after sphere crashed into Aldis's shield as the sage continued his bombardment shouting, "I will show you worthy! All will fear my power!"

Aldis reached into his satchel as he continued to block wave after wave, and produced a small cylindrical bone rod engraved with ancient markings. Drawing from his own power, Aldis pulled his energy down into the rod as its runes began to glow until a spear of energy formed from it and forced the sage to halt his attack.

"What is that thing?"

Aldis removed his shield and stood upright, "This is a tool granted to sages that pass through the Eight Trials of Wilforn. Special artifacts made from the bones of ancient beasts and imbued with offensive abilities are gifted to sages that pass the trials and are selected to the Noble Academy. Your abilities are not strong enough to defend against this. Surrender now and I will let you leave with your life."

"Only a handful of Grand Sages have passed those test, how were you able to accomplish such a task?" The sage replied as he began to slowly back away.

Aldis readied the spear as if to throw it, "Do not move another step. I succeeded the trials two months after I was granted acceptance into the academy. If you wish to live you will surrender now."

With his body frozen in horror, the sage gazed at Aldis before removing his bag and placing it on the ground. "Very well boy," the man's voice cracked as he remained motionless in the rain, "I must know how you accomplished those trials though if you aren't even allowed to take the trials until you are accepted into the Noble Academy! You lie and surely do not know how to use that weapon!"

"Don't force me to use it! I do not wish to kill you!" Aldis returned as he began to lose his calm demeanor.

Several streaks began to crackle near the sage as he drew his power around him as pooled it into a large orb in front of him, "Die boy!" He screamed as he propelled it forward.

Aldis threw the spear forward and quickly raised his hands to create a wall between him and the sages attack. He closed his eyes as the two entities collided and sent out a brilliant light followed by an enormous surge of pressure, completely destroying his shield and propelling him backwards into the brush.

As the dust settled the Fang's Sage slowly crawled in the dirt away from the small crater in the ground, his clothes shredded and his wounds too numerous to count. He clawed his fingers into the dirt as he moved painfully forward until a pair of boots stepped into view.

"Tell me Fang, where is your antidote?" Sayren's cold voice commanded as he drew back an arrow from behind a heavily destroyed oak.

"That kid...is...he's a monster. The Fang will return...to extract revenge...revenge against you. This... this isn't over." The sage gasped as he slowly lay in the dirt.

Sayren quickly moved around the sage's body and began to search the devastated surroundings in hopes of locating the bag. Several trees appeared as if pieces of wood had simply been scorched away by a searing blade. Several large divots carved out the dirt forming dozens of miniature pools of water. From the corner of his eye, the leather satchel of the Fang hung from a partially torn branch with several different colored streams of liquid flowing from its seams. Sayren carefully reached for the bag and opened it in hopes of the antidote lying unharmed, but as he gazed inside, only shards of glass and broken corks remained with a small leather bound book with a serpent imprinted on the front. Sayren carefully removed the book and tossed the satchel aside. He opened the pages to find them undamaged by the water and began to search for a recipe for the antidote.

Sounds of ruffling leaves pulled Sayren away from the book to see Aldis emerging from the bushes, his cloak covered in mud and leaves as he propped himself against a tree stump and recalled the bone to his hand from somewhere within the dirt crater. Sayren turned to Aldis and tossed him the book, "I need you to find the antidote recipe for a poison called Serpent's Kiss. Rylan has been poisoned by one of their men's blades."

Aldis grabbed the book out of the air and rubbed the back of his head in pain, "Is that sage still alive?"

"No, whatever you did ripped him to pieces. Now I need you to focus on finding that page while I check on the nobles. Understood?"

Aldis nodded, paused for a moment, and then emptied his stomach at the thought of killing his opponent. His body wretched for a few moments before he wiped his sleeve over his mouth and began to scan the book to find what Sayren had asked.

Restringing his bow, Sayren moved past Aldis and silently raced towards the noble's location. Feint sounds of swords clanging off of shields gave him his destination, but as he arrived, Sayren found Tiberius and Orsen resting against a tree with Brilla attending to them as Isabelle endlessly slammed Aldis's staff against the remaining swordsman's shield. A look of shear horror was present on the woman's face as she could only attempt to defend. Isabelle slammed the wooden staff against the shield as she screamed out, only to strike the woman's unprotected knee and causing the limb to contort and snap loudly as the swordsman screamed in agony.

"Enough!" Sayren called out as he revealed himself and pulled Aldis's staff out of Isabelle's grasp.

Tiberius quickly arose and moved between Sayren and Isabelle, "Did you just say something?"

Sayren did not budge, "I said that is enough. Our enemies are either dead or defeated. We are not butchers. If you and Lady Isabelle are safe, we will bury our fallen and move on."

Isabelle roared as flames burst from her hands, but Tiberius knocked her hands away, "Enough! He is right; we are not in the right state of mind. I will bury my men and we will continue on our journey. Thank you for finding us Sayren, we will be with you and your brothers shortly, Orsen was struck on his side before we had beaten the Fang."

Sayren moved away from the nobles and over to Orsen as he clutched his bandaged side that Brilla had just finished applying. He pulled the bandage down to reveal the wound, the black poison already showing its first effects as the skin around the wound began to slightly darken as if it were a bruise. Sayren began to suck the poison from the wound to the surprise of all, "He's been poisoned. It's only a small wound so it will be easy to remove but we'll need to get to the town soon to make the antidote. We'll need to split up."

As Sayren spat the dark gray poison from his lips before opening his canteen and cleansing his face, Tiberius looked on in amazement. "Is that the same as what has happened to your brother?"

Sayren nodded in agreement, "Yes, however, we've built up a small immunity to it since our first encounter with them. He'll survive the night, but if we cannot get him an antidote before sunrise I fear the poison will take hold of his heart and he will die in agony. If you'll permit it, I will send Aldis ahead with Orsen and Rylan to see them given proper treatment and we will rejoin them after we have buried your men and found out what we can about the person who put a price on your head."

"Agreed," Tiberius nodded as he moved to help Orsen stand. The crippled assassin silently began to shuffle her way away from sight and disappear into the forest. "We will reconvene at the town as soon as we are able. Orsen, I must ask you to ride ahead with the brothers, as well as Lady Isabelle and Brilla. Once I have found who has sought to end our lives, I would see you bring the message to my father. I will come for you the moment we reach town."

Orsen nodded silently and slowly returned upright as he braced against a tree and Brilla. Together the group returned to the road with Aldis moments behind, his finger firmly securing his place between the book's pages shouting, "I've found it!" as he waived it over his head. Toren retrieved the horses as Sayren looked over Rylan, the infection was showing signs of progressing, his pulse weakened and several streaks of poison moving through his veins. With Rylan being asleep though, he could tell the progression was much slower than had he still been awake. With Tiberius's help both men pulled Rylan from the road and positioned him on his horse. With the rain showing no signs of letting up Sayren quickly pulled a shovel from his horse's saddle and began to dig alongside the tree line as Brilla stood over the bodies and gave them each a leafless branch within their hands. She clasped her hands around her pendant and silently spoke of their deeds. Tiberius took a few steps from where Sayren dug and began to dig with his own shield. Aldis and Orsen ensured Rylan was in place before spurring their steeds forward towards Havenhome with Isabelle and Brilla close in tow behind them.

Toren looked on in dismay as the storm clouds above them seemed unyielding as they released their relentless torment of lightning and rain, his mind stood in disarray as he looked across the line of fallen men and women that lay motionless in the rain. Although it was neither his first time to fight against the Fang, nor his first time in deadly combat, it was the first time he had seen his own allies lying dead. A single tear streaked from his face as he envisioned Rylan lying amongst them before wiping it away and moving to search the enemies for any clues he could find.

CHAPTER 5

Naria stood daydreaming inside the Great Hall of Kings. She gazed upon the statue of the first king of Kay as memories of her father, King Arbuk, paraded her around atop his shoulders as glimmering rays of colorful light danced through dust filled air from finely constructed mosaics behind statues. Each king carved from fine stone and stood seemingly untouched by time. Naria slowly returned to King Kay as her mind brought her to the same question her father would ask every time they entered the hall.

"Who is this, my jewel?" Arbuk would always ask in a soft tone, reserved for his daughter.

Naira's young finger always pointed directly to the King of Kay's mighty beard, "That's Kay the Honorable Blade! He was the very first king of all eight kingdoms!"

"That's correct," Arbuk hearty laugh filled the quiet air as he pried her from his knee and set her down in one of the many rows of wooden pews for members of the royal families, "Now tell me; do you remember how the early tribes became the great kingdoms they are today?"

Naria smiled as she remembered her father's gentle face, "Of course," she whispered to herself as she echoed her younger reply from years prior, "the times before the eight kingdoms were filled with bad people who killed one another for land and power. Once a tribe lost its leader, it was killed or splintered to the wilds. Eventually, King Kay fought young King Arthlyn, but instead of taking his life, he spared Alder's king and made him an ally. Not like a servant, but an equal, something that was a big no-no for that time."

Arbuk patted Naira's blonde hair before turning towards the doorway, "What happened next?"

"Well," Naria mimicked her father as she ran both hands through her hair, "After Alder and Kay brought the kingdoms of Barner and Evest into their circle, King Kay was killed by Ulferth of the northern mountains, but Arthlyn beat Ulferth and forced him to yield and join the other kings. King Yanis Vaine joined out of respect of Kay's passing and left only Uruuk, the evil sage in the south. Parthus, the seventh kingdom, was liberated after the First Accord between the kings to unite and liberate the south from dark magic. Once Uruuk was vanquished by King Arthlyn and King Alm-Kay, a man named Epharth was appointed as high regent. He lived really long and soon after the eight kingdoms built King's Hold, Epharth fell into darkness and became a land of forbidden abilities once again."

Arbuk moved further down the aisle away from Naria, "That is wonderful you remember all of that my princess, you'll make a fine queen one day. One more question and then you can run to the kitchen and get a slice of pie as big as you can see, but you have to promise to go straight there from the hidden passage I told you about and not go outside."

Naria nearly bounced out of her seat in enjoyment, "Of course father, ask anything!"

"Very well, tell me why the kings named the kingdoms after themselves and built this place together rather than each building a keep of their own."

"That's easy!" Little Naria jumped for joy as she stared at the simple wooden throne sitting at the end of the hall, "Each king built their kingdoms off of a code of honor they used to unite Thesia, and wanted all to remember who had done so. King's Hold was different though; it was built together to show that no matter how strong any one king is, a unified Thesia is strong enough to build an impenetrable castle for all the people to live in and celebrate the honor and sacrifices of the kings and their people."

Arbuk smiled back at his daughter as she turned to meet his gaze before the large entrance doors burst open with flame and sent them both flying backwards. Sounds of other impacts from trebuchets and catapults echoed through the hall as men raced in front of the doors, clashing with the uprisings forces. Naria looked at her father as he lay on the ground motionless for a moment before racing over to him and seeing a large splinter of wood protruding from his right side.

"Father!" She screamed as she placed her small hands against his regal chest, his robes stained with blood and ash.

Arbuk stirred for a moment before wincing and clutching his wounded side, "Naria, run to your brother. I will protect our family."

Naria nodded, "Yes father of course. You're hurt though, shouldn't I fetch a healer?"

"No. Get to your brother and find your mother together. As a leader you must realize that no matter what you do," Arbuk gasped for breath as he propped himself up against a fallen pew before pushing himself upright, "you must never let your men see you run from the field of battle, even if you are in the rear. You must always stand for them as a sign that you will not abandon those in your charge until the battle is won and they are attended too. Remember that above everything else I have taught you, because you will be regent for the people when I am gone. Do you understand?"

Naria began to sob as her father waited a moment for an answer before stumbling through the threshold of the great hall and onto the citadel's grounds, barking out commands. As she sat on the floor, she could see her younger self crying with her hand outstretched, begging her father to return before an image of Alkith in his youth burst into the room and grabbed Naria by her collar and began to drag her away to safety.

A sudden, loud boom jostled Naria out of her memory as a man dressed with common garb and a crude sword fell to the ground with two guards close behind. One of the captains of the guard scurried behind them, panting as he placed his hands upon his knees to catch his breath he failed to notice Naria sitting just beyond the man.

"Captain, what's the meaning of this?" Naria demanded as she arose to her feet, straightened her sword belts, and cautiously stepping away from any sunbeams to conceal her tears.

Shocked, every guard snapped to attention and bowed, "My Queen, I apologize. This man was found to be stealing supplies and information. When we tried to apprehend him he ran until he stopped here. We are truly sorry for the inconvenience, would you like my men to enter and apprehend the thief?"

Dropping his sword to the ground, the lowly man placed his head against the dirty stone floor, "Please my queen! I have done nothing wrong! These men stopped me from speaking the truth of their fellow guardsmen and the cruelties they are committing. I beg of you please spare me and I will tell you everything I have seen!"

"First," Naria drew one of her swords, the thin blade reflecting streaks of color from the remaining shards of stained glass still in place, "tell me your name, then I shall decide your fate."

With a shocked expression the man fumbled his words for a moment before sitting up on his knees and blurting out, "Lora."

Naria paused for a moment and looked over the man, several scares raced down his body concealed by his worn tunic. A pair of boots that were all but destroyed clung to his feet by tightly strung string, but a large coin purse sat along the man's belt, full to the brim and nearly overflowing. "Tell me Lora, how is it that you wear such clothing, run from my guards, yet you carry a large purse of amassed wealth at your side. I find it hard to believe your story; however, I will afford you a choice for being a spy against your rightful rulers. You may either say nothing and die by my hand, or tell me everything you have told our enemies and I will allow you to live out your remaining days in the dungeon."

Lora quickly grabbed his sword and leaped backwards away from Naria, "You little bitch!" He cursed as he looked back at the guards before turning his attention back to her. "I have been poor for all of my life; your father saw to it that any man who stood with him would never have a chance of a life outside his service. I fought for him during the uprising! I lost my family, and nearly my own life in defense of a sniveling bunch of brats who have done nothing but hurt this world with your prolonged existence. I sought you and your brother out to take me back in and help me rebuild my life, but you refused my service simply because I had disappeared to bury my family after the battle was over and grieve. When I was given the opportunity to repay you for what you had taken from me, I accepted without hesitation!

You will never know what I passed on to your enemies, but you must know that not all of your foes reside outside your walls! I can only imagine what they will give me for bringing them your bloodied head! I will be rewarded with riches that I could not begin to dream of and finally bring peace to my family's souls!"

Naria sighed and drew her other blade before readying herself for combat, "You seem to be forgetting that to claim such a bounty still includes defeating a royal heir. I feel you may have over stepped. Captain! Have you and your men remain outside, whether or not this man has already condemned himself, any who enter here without invitation will be executed."

All three guardsmen quickly nodded and took up a secured position around the entryway to prevent Lora from escaping. As Naria began to close distance between herself and Lora, the man kicked the wooden pews forward and forced Naria to halt her advance, "Don't think I'll give you any chance to use your abilities against me! Royal blood or not I will still kill you!"

Lora leaped into the air and swung his sword downward at Naria's head. She crossed her blades, catching the attack well above her head and side stepped away from Lora as he landed and crashed into a fallen beam. Naria pressed her advantage as she began a flurry of attacks, each forcing Lora to fall further and further off balance until he fell backwards completely and rolled away to separate himself while he caught his breath. Although she was confident in her skills, Naria's mind blurred as she saw the image of her father walking away from her once again, allowing Lora to knock both swords from Naria's grasp before he swiftly kicked her in her crest, sending her sprawling to the ground.

"Now I've got you, you frail brat! Die!" Lora screamed as he plunged his sword down into Naria's chest, however as his blade plummeted towards it target, the sound of sword clanging off of metal forced him to assess why. As Lora peered down, his blade had plunged into the ground underneath him with Naria nowhere to be seen. He instantly turned to locate Naria's swords and found her standing atop a broken pew with a sight that sent him cowering to a knee. Naria stood perfectly balanced as her body's vein's glowed bright silver and her eyes pupils were a blur. "No! How can you have awakened your magic in the middle of combat? Not even King Arbuk could perform such a feat during battle!" Lora screamed as he rushed forward and swung his blade at her legs. Naria leaped weightlessly though the air as she landed behind Lora and struck both blades against his back, sending crimson blood arcing through the great hall. Lora, although deeply wounded from deep gashes in his back swung wildly, and appeared to connect against Naria's side; however the blade passed through cleanly as her figure disappeared and reappear further back. Without a moment to react, Lora attempted to dodge, however Naria seemed to move faster than light and drove both blades into each of Lora's shoulders, forcing him to release his weapon and cry out in pain. From outside the hall, the captain and his men looked on in horror as Naria twisted her blades and severed both of Lora's arms from his shoulders before he fell to the ground with his neck pressed between the edges of her swords. Lora looked up to plead for mercy, but Naira's face was emotionless. He fell silent as he looked into her soulless eyes before she swept her swords and sent his head rolling backwards. Naria's skin dimmed and her eyes returned to normal as she looked to the captain and his men standing inside the hall with their weapons drawn and slowly approaching her, "Damn." She said faintly as trails of blood formed from her nose and mouth. Naria attempted to keep focused as she felt her body become heavy and vision blur before falling against the floor, unconscious.

"Alvas, you think she's dead?" one guard said to his captain as they all drew closer.

Alvas knelt over Lora's body as he retrieved the sack of coins, "I doubt it. I don't think we should leave it to chance though either. Move her onto that throne and take her head. Dead or not, that will finish her and send a message to those other royals."

"Henvi," Alvas motioned for their final cohort, "help me move her. It's hard enough trying to run in this armor, let alone carry someone."

"Yay-yay, quit your fussing. I'll be there in a sec." Henvi scanned outside for any onlookers before moving away from the threshold, "I'll help you move her if I get to make the kill. They'll call me 'The Queen Slayer' back home when they hear what we've manage to accomplish."

"They'll call you what?" An unfamiliar voice called out as Henvi and his companion began to lift Naria. Turning in unison, all three men moved to see Gauld standing just outside the threshold of the hall.

"Damn. Henvi take care of that one. Ulk and I will finish with the girl." Alvas tapped his cohorts shoulder and began to move for the throne. Henvi retrieved his spear from the ground and rushed forward at Gauld. As he drew close, Gauld grabbed the spear and tossed Henvi over his shoulder, snapping the spear and sending the assassin crashing against the ground. Before Henvi could react, Gauld pulled one of his daggers from its sheath and hurled it directly into his unprotected forehead.

"You two will remove yourselves from the hall and face me. If you do not, your lives are forfeit." Gauld readied the broken spear to throw.

Alvas and Ulk both looked at one another and began to laugh as they propped Naria unto the throne, "You're not that smart boy! Why would we give you a chance to save your queen, you can condemn yourself to die if you want to attempt and save her!"

Gauld sighed and lowered the spear before he stepped over the threshold and launched the spear at Ulk, striking him through his ribs. Alvas quickly aimed his sword and thrust forward to silence Naria, but before he could meet his mark, Gauld's daggers dug into Alvas' shoulder, forcing him to drop his sword and attempt to pry the serrated blades from his flesh. Alvas tugged against the dagger in his shoulder with no avail as his wound worsened with every attempt until Gauld pulled back on the ropes and forced him away from Naria. Fearing for his life, Alvas grabbed Lora's sword and aimed it at the ropes tied to Gauld's daggers. Alvas swung with all his might as Gauld jerked the rope once again, extending Alvas's arm out as the blade delved deep through flesh. Alvas wretched in anguish as the dull blade fell to the ground and left him clinging to his wound. Gauld walked forward, determined to protect Naria regardless of his own fate, and drew his sword from its sheath, pressing it under the captain's chin, "Who sent you?"

Alvas refused to look Gauld in his eyes as he continued to apply pressure to his hemorrhaging wound, "I will tell you nothing. We follow those that rule Thesia, not petty brats like you serve. Do what you must."

Gauld retracted his daggers, forcing Alvas's arm to extend and reopen with a puddle of dark crimson settling into the stones on the floor of the hall. Alvas cringed, crying out as both daggers fell from their place in Alvas' shoulder. "You will answer me. Your paltry life should matter more to you than those you serve! Now bark, dog!"

Alvas looked upwards at Gauld, but only smirked before leaning into the blade and impaling him through the neck. Gauld retracted his sword immediately and spat on the ground as Alvas choked against dark blood freely flowing down his throat as he fell to the ground shuddering for a few moments before his convulsions ceased and he lay still on the cold, hard stone floor.

Gauld observed both of Naria's swords lay together at the base of the steps beneath the throne where she now rested unconscious, with a bright red stream of blood trickling down from her nose. Gauld quickly made his way over to her, carefully watching his surroundings for any further enemies, but after reaching Naria the hall was still and quiet. Quickly placing her over his shoulder, Gauld started to make his way for the threshold. A subtle sound of movement forced Gauld to lunge forward as large thorn covered vines lashed out at him from under the pews. With Naria on his back he could only evade so much, and as the vines continuously attempted to strike him as the lashed out like vipers, Gauld reached the doorway. Gianni stepped into view from the outside of the great hall with swarms of roots protruding from the ground around him, his face scowled and arms crossed.

"My Lord, Lady Naria is injured and requires a healer quickly!" Gauld's voice cracked as his nervous feelings began to surface, he was in no position to command an heir, but with Naria unconscious he had no other choice but to force the issue.

Gianni silently raised his hands from his sides, forcing the roots upward and forming a cage like area around the three, "Who are you to tell me what I should do? No dead man would ever insult his executioner when he stands at judgement's door. You should drop the heir now, traitor. If you think you'll harm her or escape my wrath, you're mistaken. I will grant you a merciful and quick death if you do as I say immediately."

Gauld failed his attempt to sway Gianni, and he could not bring himself to fight an heir of one of the kingdoms only to damage his honor. "My lord, please understand that I would not stand against any rightful king or queen, however, I must see that she is cared for, after that my life is forfeit. I am sorry Lord Gianni, but I will stand against you if I must choose whether save my queen."

A strong breeze brushed between both motionless men. Gianni clenched his fist, his tone and appearance fueled by anger, "you will not escape your fate! Now die traitor, there only has to be one heir to continue our plans! You will not succeed in any endeavor to stave off your end!" roots swarmed around Gianni as he outstretched his hand and sent them forward towards Gauld and Naria. Gauld quickly pulled Naria underneath him and shielded her from the attack, yet after a moment he felt no pain and open his eyes. Puzzled, Gauld slowly turned to see a large portion of roots cleared away, and Alkith standing near his side with his hands extended.

Alkith lowered his hands and turned to Gianni, "What is going on here? Why would you dare attack a member of a royal family? Have you lost your damned mind? Tell me why I shouldn't destroy you where you stand, now!"

Gianni looked at Alkith, and then to Gauld before finding his voice, "What does it look like? This man was caught within the Hall of the First Kings! There are four other bodies that lay inside dead, he clearly is a spy and attempted to kill Naria! I did not attack her; she is simply at the same place as that man!"

"Is that so?" Alkith questioned as he looked to Gauld as his second carefully lay Naria's head against the ground, the signs of blood becoming apparent as her head rolled to the side. "Tell me what happened to her Gauld, immediately!"

Gauld turned and bowed his head, "Lord, I went to find your sister as you instructed and found three men dressed as guards attempting to kill her after she had fallen. I killed all three men who said they were working for someone other than you and the other heirs, but I could not get any more information out of them. I was forced to enter the hall to save her life and accept your decision if you feel I must die for entering the hall without invitation."

Alkith as he returned his glare at a dumbfounded Gianni, "You sought to kill my second without asking him what was going on. I suppose you are going to give me some excuse as to why you attempted to threaten my sister's life after her savior rescued her from the grip of the actual traitors! Go ahead, Gianni, speak, before I lose what patience I still have!"

Gianni inhaled and turned away from Alkith, twisting his wrist and recalling the remaining roots, his calm demeanor returning. "I will leave you to deal with your man's failure to obey our laws. Saving a royal or not the line is clear; I will have my men sweep King's Rest in search of anymore traitors. You should see Naria to a healer; she doesn't appear to be in advantageous condition."

Alkith nearly drew his blade before Gianni could walk out of sight before his second called out, "My lord! Your sister is still breathing, but you'll be able to get her to a healer much faster than I. If you wish to kill me I would ask your do it quickly not for myself, but for Lady Naria's sake. I have never seen her in such a state before." Gauld lowered his head as he knelt down beside Alkith and waited.

"Why did you enter the hall?" Alkith inquired with his voice calm and steady.

"I entered to save Lady Naria, lord." Gauld maintained his posture as he answered, awaiting his position.

"Did you enter out of honor, or duty?" Alkith's voice continued without any discernable conviction.

Gauld looked up to see Alkith with his hand outstretched to aide him, "I did it for the respect I hold for both you and your sister. I would give my life a thousand times over to see your family stand in your rightful places as the rulers of Kay. I did not do it for coin or reward, I acted as a soldier my family taught me to be."

Alkith smiled and patted him on the shoulder as he proceeded to Naria and lifted her into his arms, "That is why you'll have your life Gauld, not because you saved my sister, but because you acted as a soldier and protected your queen without regard of personal goals. I grant you full pardon for your action and will see to it you are given a letter of invitation to enter King's Rest as needed. Thank you for what you have done for me."

Gauld bowed, "Of course my lord. Thank you."

Alkith nodded and disappeared into the distance leaving Gauld to exhale deeply. Charred remains of Gianni's roots crumbled underneath his feet as he looked into the hall to see coins scattered around Alvas's corpse. He paused for a moment before walking to the doors and pulling them closed, leaving both coin and corpse in the darkened hall.

❈   ❈   ❈

With relentless droplets continuously pelting Aldis's cloak and darkening skies looming overhead, Aldis tightly gripped the reins of both his and Rylan's horse as they came into view of Havenhome's eastern gate. Although no sunlight pierced the darkened skies, a solemn candle lantern illuminated the gatehouse as with a low red hue.

"Halt!" A voice called out from behind the wall, a small latch pulled open, revealing a weathered guardsman standing with the lantern pressed against his wrinkled skin and saturated beard, "Who goes there?"

Aldis looked to Isabelle as both dismounted and trudged through the mud soaked terrain, pulling back their hoods as they reached the guardsman's latch, "I am Lady Isabelle of House Bernak, this is my sage, Aldis. My guards are injured and require the attention of your healer."

Unconvinced as his eyes combed Aldis and the others, the grizzled guard looked back to Isabelle, "Who injured 'em? Doesn't sound like very good guards if you ask me."

Aldis looked back at Rylan's leg, the darkening red in his dressing growing with each precious passing moment, "Please understand, we were attacked by a large willow bear. It claimed two of the men before we could even arm ourselves. We need to get to a healer quickly, every second they both draw closer to death's embrace."

A disgruntled scoff from the guard before he slammed the looking door closed and pulled open the latch. Isabelle and Aldis raced back to their horses before the gateway opened with an additional guard standing looking out towards the tree line with his crossbow trained behind the group as they moved in. "Go past the inn, you'll find the apothecary hut just off a ways behind it. Best of luck to your guards milady, but I must warn you that after it grows darker there will be a curfew in effect. There've been quite a few reports of bandits roaming these areas looking for unlucky souls to rob."

Aldis nodded in response, "Thank you for the kind warning, we'll heed them as best we are able."

Turning to one another, both guards subtlety motioned towards Isabelle before one began making his way towards the guard barracks a few paces away. Isabelle carefully watched the man disappeared from view near as he passed through the entrance. Brilla tugged against Isabelle's arm to return her gaze to the front with Aldis as they continued through the town.

Although the storm's intensity made it difficult to see beyond a few feet, the group silently made their way forward with watchful eyes observing their moves from atop the smaller palisade wall of the governor's manor near the middle of the village. As the group passed further along the road, an old sign swayed on its tarnished chains flashing, "The Murder's Brooke" with each swing.

Isabelle looked to Aldis, "That seems like quite the terrible name for an inn. Surely you haven't planned for us to rest there tonight, right?"

"I am afraid so," Aldis said as he peered insight the illuminated front area, empty of any customers, "this place was where Rylan directed me to plan for. It's supposed to be run by a trustworthy business acquaintance of my brother, but I have personally never met the man who runs it."

Isabelle sighed as she stared inside and spotted a young man watching them from a window on the second floor, before the thunder flashed once again only to reveal the window closed and the young man nowhere to be seen. Turning her attention back towards the front, Isabelle saw Aldis and Orsen pulling Rylan from his horse as he began to convulse wildly and begin to carry him up the steps to a small cabin with a single lamp on the porch and an elderly woman beckoning them inside. Isabelle and Brilla dismounted their steeds and quickly tied the reins to the post before rushing up the steps and throwing back their hoods as they past underneath the overhanging thatch.

"Ma'am, my brother is hurt; I need to lay him down somewhere so I may purchase an antidote from you." Aldis's voice cracked as he grew more nervous with each passing convulsion.

As the elder woman moved for the backroom, she nodded silently and motioned for them to follow her. Orsen clamped down on Rylan's shoulders as he struggled with his own wound; all three passed through cluttered shelves before finding the old woman standing next to an open door and a small bed setting back against the weathered planks of wood, a handful of buckets collecting the rainwater as it slowly dripped from the ceiling.

"What's his affliction young man?" The apothecary asked as she began to untie his cloak and examine his wounds. A sudden gasp made Aldis jump as the woman realized Rylan's face as she pulled back his hood, "Tell me, did your brother get into a fight with the Fang once again?"

Aldis looked perplexed as he tried to identify the woman and her knowledge of his brother, "Um...yes. We were attacked by the Serpent's Fang as we drew closer to the town and he was struck in the leg. Sayren believed the poison is the Serpent's Kiss and I was able to find a recipe for an antidote within the pages of a book taken off of their sage, but I don't have any of the ingredients."

"My name is Yvette," she said making her way to the door, "Elyscia, help this young man retrieve whatever he requires for an antidote while I attend to this other fellow!"

Orsen gingerly eased himself into a chair on the opposite corner of the room and began to doff his armor. With Brilla and Isabelle looking on from the doorway Yvette turned to them, "if you're going to be here, help me get those soaked clothes off of Rylan, if the poison doesn't kill him, his soaked clothes will."

Isabelle quickly turned to Brilla to see her blush, "you attend to him priestess, and I will assist Aldis with the ingredients for his concoction." Brilla swallowed the large lump in her throat before proceeding over to Rylan.

Outside the backroom, Aldis quickly thumbed pages of the small booklet the enemy sage had in his possession before finding the antidote ingredients and scouring the disorderly shelves. A gentle tap on his shoulder forced Aldis to turn, revealing a beautiful woman with dark golden blonde hair that illuminated itself in a reddish hue from the candlelight. Emerald green eyes stopped Aldis breath for a moment as he was smitten before she asked, "What is it you're looking for?"

Aldis sharply inhaled as he refocused on the task at hand and turned to his list ingredients, "Paisley and Bone Lily petals, as well as Idris and Arcanis roots, and finally venom from a Southern Blood Viper. I'll also require a mortar, pestle, a cooking pot and some water."

Elyscia moved along the shelves as she pulled jars down, "How much of the roots will you need?"

"A handful of Idris and only a partial handful of Arcanis should be sufficient."

Elyscia pointed towards the lower shelves opposite of her, "You'll find the flowers on the lower shelves down there. Who is it you're trying to save?"

Aldis quickly set his book down beside him as he began to search, "My brother Rylan; he was injured trying to protect all of us from a group of assassins."

"Rylan", Elyscia stopped searching and lowered her hands to her sides, "the one that leads the Six Crows?"

Aldis nodded as he continued searching through the numerous cases. Elyscia brushed past Aldis with an enraged expression as she stormed off and slammed the roots down upon the counter before entering the backroom, angrily shouting, "You bastard! You've been gone for years and you think you can simply show up now because you were hurt and expect me to help you –" Her voice stopped as she saw Rylan positioned upright with his shirt pulled above his head revealing a multitude of scars across his back. Rylan's years of combat had changed the boy she remembered playing with in the river when she was barely twelve. Her sister, Raine, would play with Rylan since they were roughly the same age and being the younger sister, Elyscia would be dragged along to the dismay of her sibling. Although Rylan was not free of his collection of wounds, Elyscia could not count the numerous fresh scars acquired since the last time they saw one another.

"Did you finish with the antidote yet?" Yvette asked as she continued to dress Orsen's wound, "Thankfully, this one got lucky that the rain removed most of the poison before he was injured, however,

Rylan will still need the serum before much longer, I can already feel his soul weakening."

Elyscia looked to her mother and back to Rylan as she began to scan his body for poison. Several black streaks of poisoned veins appeared to be growing as the poison drew closer to his chest. She quickly retraced her steps and grabbed for a small cooking pot already filled with water. Aldis sat at a small table muddling the ingredients together with the exception of a small vial of dark brown liquid sealed with a small parchment attached with the letters "S, B, and V" scribbled down the side.

Aldis looked to Isabelle as she stood leaning against the wall watching Aldis and Elyscia work quickly, "What do you think made her do that milady?"

Isabelle smiled at Aldis's innocent question, "Women can be quite complex, sometimes when we see someone from our past we embrace them, however, there are those that when we see them, their very name emits a deep anger. Something must have happened between those two sometime ago for her to act like that. Tell me, what will you do with the venom and the ingredients once they're combined?"

Aldis continued to muddle as he tapped the small vial, "The book doesn't give a clear way to combine the ingredients, however with the boiling water, I'll add in the vial and then the ingredients. If I allow the poison to dilute, it should provide the changes I need when the other ingredients combine with the venom to create the antidote."

Elyscia carefully retrieved the boiling pot from the rack and set it down next to Aldis on a large stone. Aldis quickly opened the vial and emptied its contents within the pot before dumping the muddled roots and petals into the mixture. Elyscia handed Aldis a wooden spoon as he began to stir, steadily mixing the contents as the metal pot began to cool. "Will you fetch me a small cup?" Aldis motion to Elyscia as he watched the concoction change into a dark amber color. "I'll need to have a second one as well for Orsen too, if it is possible."

Elyscia reached above the fireplace and pulled down a metal goblet, "You'll only need the one for Rylan; my mother said your other companion will be fine. Whatever poison was applied to the weapon that wounded him was washed away before it made contact with his skin. I'll bring additional vials should you require any for future use."

Aldis nodded in gratitude as he reached for the cup and began to pull the antidote out with the spoon, cautiously pouring to ensure not to waste a single drop. "Will you deliver this to him? You'll need to apply a few drops to the wound itself and then have him drink the remainder." Aldis handed Elyscia the first antidote as he carefully grabbed a case of empty vials and began to pour the remainder. "I'll be sure to pay for the supplies whenever your mother is ready."

Elyscia silently nodded and proceeded back into the room. Orsen lay back in the chair gingerly holding his wound, but with a well applied herbal remedy secured tightly in place, he would recover fine with rest. Rylan lay under the sheets with his leg exposed and cleaned, however, a dark discoloration around his wound and several streaks of darkened veins reveal his severe condition. Yvette extended her hand to Elyscia for the antidote as Brilla sat beside Rylan chanting a prayer. Elyscia watched as Yvette carefully poured a few drops onto the wound before slowly pressing her hand over the wound as a slight glow began to illuminate. Rylan let out a pained groan as he began to sweat and toss about, "Hold him steady while I give him the rest." Yvette motioned to Brilla as she moved around to the other side and attempted to steady her worn hands. When she couldn't stop the shaking she held the cup out to Elyscia, "you do this. I cannot find the strength after healing his leg."

As Yvette sat down in a rickety old wooden armchair, she sighed deeply and rubbed her eyes. Elyscia moved to Rylan's side and gently opened his mouth as she tipped the vial over his mouth and poured its contents until it was entirely void of the antidote. Rylan swallowed the concoction and remained still for a moment before he lurched forward and began to cough wildly; his eyes scanned the room and locked on Elyscia as she steadied herself from startling backwards, "Elyscia? Why are you here and not with the old man?"

Elyscia gave a staunch condescending look before crossing her arms and replying, "I had to save you, again. I swear that without my family's help you'd already be buried and forgotten."

"You're probably right," Rylan responded as he eased back down into the bed and grimaced at the repulsive taste of the antidote, "Why did you give me that foul drink?"

Yvette chuckled, "You're brother was the one to make it. He said he had a book from the Fang so I let the boy feel the sense of accomplishment for saving you. However, you should rest now. I'll take everyone over to the inn for the night and return in the morning to check on how you are feeling."

Rylan nodded as he looked at the ceiling, "Thank you for letting him do that, he's still rather green when it comes to our lifestyle. Where is the rest of the group?"

Orsen's gruff voice answered as he arose and gathers his things, "We separated from Lord Tiberius and your brothers to ensure we were treated as soon as possible. They should be within the walls now, if not close by."

Rylan nodded as his mind began to drift. Brilla moved to Orsen's side and exited with Yvette as Elyscia stood in the doorway, "Why did you have to come back now of all times?"

"Because this was the closest route to King's Hold and back before the harvest." Rylan responded as his eyes closed and he fell into a deep slumber.

❊   ❊   ❊

Night loomed against the setting sun, the storm turned from its torrential downpour into a broken drizzle as Sayren spotted the illuminating light of the lantern's glow from the latch within Havenhome's walls. After searching the remains of the assassins they'd encountered, only coins and jewels laid amongst them with random parchment detailing future targets were discovered. Although Sayren believed Tiberius would be enraged as he was unable to discover his conspirator that had sent the Fang, the noble remained calm and silently prayed words over his men before readying his horse and setting off. As the three riders approached, two men with readied bows emerged from behind the top of the wooden wall and a third's voice proclaimed, "Halt! You have no business here!" from the opened latch.

"I am Lord Tiberius of House Bernak!" Tiberius responded as he spurred his horse forward, "I have come to rejoin Lady Isabelle and her guard. You will open these gates for me immediately!"

A momentary silence filled the air before the guardsman behind returned, "Come down from your horse and stand in the light to prove whom you say! There's a curfew in effect because of highwaymen that have sought to harm our home. If you are noble, we will open the gates for you immediately."

Tiberius and Sayren looked at one another before Sayren gave him a silent nod. Toren sat back with a throwing dagger ready, while Sayren removed a rod from his side pouch. Tiberius slowly dismounted and began to make his way forward, "How long have you been plagued by bandits?"

With a scoff, the guardsman replied, "For years, it must have been at least five harvests since they first started raiding the border villages."

Tiberius stopped just at the edge of the light and opened his cloak to reveal his crest. The guard pushed the lantern closer to the latch's opening as the flames illuminated the two headed wolf. A quick gasp from the other end of the wall, followed by several quick footsteps through the thick mud, the loud rusted hinges of the western gate began to open. Sayren brought Tiberius his horse as the noble closed his cloak once more and stepped back onto his mount, "Thank you, now if you'll direct me to the closest inn we'll be on our way."

"Of course," replied the guardsmen as he outstretched his hand, "if your lordship would be so kind to help me recall the inn."

Tiberius scoffed and looked over to Sayren, "Do you recall where they said they were going?"

"Unfortunately not, otherwise I would gladly remind this fool that he addresses the House of Bernak." Sayren responded as he glared harshly at the man as the firelight revealed his face.

With a quick nod, the guardsman retracted his hand and stepped away, "Apologies my lord. I recall that the inn you're looking for is named 'The Raven's Roost'. It'll be down the road on your right. Do be careful though sir, the owner is quite mad."

Tiberius snapped his reins and preceded down the road with Toren as Sayren turned to face the man, "You'd do well to remember your place. In dark times like these every move we make could be our last."

Distant thunder rolled over the town as Sayren made his way back to the other two, carefully watching the guards close and lock the gate before sending two patrolling guards off into the shadows and out of view. A sense of unease washed over Sayren as he returned to Tiberius's side and motioned for them to remain silent. A single dimly lit lantern hung under the inn's upper floors. Gently swaying in the wind, the rusted chain's that held the sign for the inn creaked with each motion. As the three dismounted from their horses and headed for the door, Sayren saw the light disappear and the inn fall dark. Sayren tightly secured his horse to a covered post before grabbing his things and moving for the door.

Many of the tables and chairs within the Raven's Roost appeared to be held together with several additional boards and leather straps to secure them into a working fashion. Although the darken cedar bar had the least patchwork of the bar's features, only a handful of bottles sat dust covered atop a small shelf. Tiberius made his way forward, carefully moving several chairs out of his way to the bar, "Hello? Is anyone here? I'm looking for-"

Tiberius stepped away from the bar as an aged barkeep slowly arose from under the bar, armed with a readied crossbow trained on Tiberius's chest, and a grizzled face staring back at the noble, "You're looking for trouble is my guess, you bandit scum! I don't take kindly to your kind being here! Now get lost before you lose your life!"

"Good sir," Sayren said as he reactively strung his bow, "we are not bandits. The man you are pointing your weapon at is Lord Tiberius, Heir of House Bernak. You'd do well to lower your crossbow immediately. We only wish to purchase rooms for the evening and find our other companions that may already be here."

"No." The old man replied as he steadied the heavy crossbow on the bar, "No one else has come through here tonight. Even if you are who you say, you'll only bring us trouble by staying here. Now off with you before I lose my patience!"

Toren slowly made his way around Tiberius and when the old man was tightening his grip on his crossbow, Toren threw a dagger through the air and slicing the crossbow string before the blade sank into the back wall. Tiberius quickly grabbed the unusable crossbow and pried it from the barkeeps grasp before grabbing him by the collar and pulling him close, "Listen well. I have already lost three men today and I was forced to separate from two women under my charge. Now you can either tell me if Lady Isabelle, Rylan, and the others are here, or we will have a private conversation between you and my iron."

"Did you say Rylan, as in the leader of the Six Crows? He hasn't been here in years. The last time I saw him he was escorting some noble to King's Hold. Are you here to do the same thing?" The old man replied as he attempted to free himself from Tiberius's grasp with no avail.

"You must be Byra then," Sayren said as he lowered his bow and approached Tiberius, placing a hand on his shoulder to release his grip. Byra's old frame gave way as he fell to the floor as he attempted to regain his balance. "My name is Sayren. I was with my brother Rylan on that journey; I never had a chance to introduce myself."

"Father," A young man's voice called out from the second floor, "Is everything alright down there?"

Byra adjusted his tattered tunic before responding, "Get down here and get these men's horses to the stables Yvon! It's late and we'll be having guests tonight!"

Yvon slid down the railing, hopping off just before the last step, quickly bowed, and disappeared through the door. "Quite the son you have there, is he trained?" Tiberius inquired as he set the crossbow down on the bar and pulled a stool over.

Byra laughed as he fumbled underneath the counter, reaching for his keys through several bolts and daggers before emerging, "His mother taught him how to use her abilities since she's from Vaine originally. The boy picked up on her teachings quicker than I fell in love with her, but he still has a way to go before learning how to truly be a capable fighter by Alder's standards."

"I'm sure he'll be a strong man one day and live up to your expectations." Tiberius praised as he looked out the dust covered windows into the night.

Byra handed Tiberius a key and placed another two on the bar top for Toren and Sayren, "These keys will work on the rooms upstairs so when your friends arrive, I'll give them keys as well, I have eight rooms so I do hope that will be enough for the night."

Sayren sat beside Tiberius and retrieved his key as Toren grabbed the last key before prying his dagger from the wall and heading upstairs without a word, his tome in hand. Tiberius gave a silent nod to both men before standing and heading upstairs as well. "I trust you'll wait for the others before turning in for the night Sayren?"

"Of course Lord Tiberius, we'll discuss our next move tomorrow morning once the group is ready to travel."

"Very well, let us hope for a calm and clear morning to travel." Tiberius replied before grabbing his satchel by the base of the stairs and disappearing from view.

Byra pulled a tankard from under the bar and placed it in front of Sayren, "Tell me, how do you and your brothers deal with the daunting task of your father's shadow looming just beyond your grasp?

Sayren gave Byra a puzzled look as he held the tankard while Byra poured a dark stout, "I don't quite understand if I'm being completely honest with you. My brothers and I are all different from one another and nothing like our father. He was a lowly soldier who died fighting in the uprising. Why would I compare myself to him?"

Byra recorked the flask and chuckled for a moment before continuing, "I knew your father. He was quite a brave man who fought for not only the freedom of the eight kingdoms, but that of his people and his family. Your father, the king, was nothing close to a mere soldier and neither are any of his heirs."

Sayren slammed the tankard down, "I've already told one man that I am not an heir today. What lunacy gave the idea that I have a single drop of royalty running through my veins?"

Byra looked Sayren dead in the eye, "One man is a farce, but two is more than mere coincidence. Tell me your last name."

"I don't have one. Commoners aren't afforded a surname unless they are chosen to become a hero. Even then they are adopted into an already established house and given that family's last name."

"And how does a lowly commoner know such things as the goings on of the patronage of heroes?"

Sayren inhaled sharply before slowly exhaling, "Listen, Byra, I don't know much about my father, or even Rylan. We were apart for many years before he reunited us together. As much as I would love to live a life of royalty, I could never achieve something like that. My family has no ties to royalty." Sayren paused for a moment as Byra's tunic shifted and revealed the royal crest of House Bassadora emblazoned on his chest, "However, I feel as though you have closer ties than I ever would have...Royal Guardian."

Byra began to open his mouth to speak when Lady Isabelle, Aldis, and the others entered through the front door. "I see you've already met the other half of the group, Yvette. What travelers accompanied you have already retired for the evening upstairs. I've already prepared the kettle for your tea. Is Rylan with you?"

Yvette walked over to Byra and gently kissed his cheek as she placed her frail hands over his, "He's fine, he was poisoned by the Fang again. His young brother, Aldis, saved his life though. He's a very astute young sage. I take it you've already collected the payment for our guests?"

Byra voice instantly disappeared as a lump formed in his throat as Yvette began to tighten her feeble, yet strong hands around Byra's, "I haven't had the chance to ask just yet, but they are with Rylan and will surely uphold their honor and pay. What say we go take care of your tea dear before the kettle gets cold?"

Yvette gave Byra a cold, stern look and released his hand before turning and disappearing into the back, "Have a good night's rest everyone. I will see you all in the morning for breakfast."

Sayren and Byra looked at one another, "You married?" Byra asked as he wiped away the sweat forming on his brow.

"I am, actually, eight years after this Harvest Festival to be exact." Sayren replied as a smirk began to form across his tired face.

"Be smart and let your wife lead, otherwise you'll find yourself sleeping away from her warmth on many a cold night." Byra scoffed as he placed the remaining room keys on the bar and proceeded to the back.

Aldis and Sayren met eyes as the others grabbed their keys, "We need to talk brother." Aldis halted Sayren as he paused for Orsen and Brilla to disappear up the steps. "The guards of this town are acting very odd, don't you think?"

Sayren finished his drink and started making his way to the stairs, "That is because those men are with the bandits. I'm not positive, but I believe that the town may have fallen under their control. If that is the case, we'll need to be certain about our next move should they make one of their own. Will Rylan be able to travel and fight in the morning?"

Aldis nodded in agreement, "I've been watching the shadows as we made our way back to the inn, and it seems that there are eyes everywhere. If they are connected to the bandits, we'll be attacked either late tonight or early in the morning. Rylan's not in the greatest of conditions, but if he can stand, he'll ride and fight after some rest."

"Agreed," Sayren stopped at the top step and placed his bow on his lap as he sat watching the doorway, "I'll take the first watch for the evening and I'll wake Toren next, and then it will be you. If we are attacked make sure you get the nobles out of here as quickly as possible and make for Rylan. He'll know how to escape the town and find us. We'll lead them to the Sen Portal and stall for as long as we can with talks of treasure and shiny things they will no doubt be enamored by. Can you do this for me Aldis?"

Aldis reviewed the plan silently in his head for a moment, "Yes, I believe so. Should I take your things to your room?"

"No, but thank you little brother, now get some rest." Sayren replied as he placed an arrow on his bow and silently notched it in place.

From just outside of the inn's windows, lit lanterns passed to and from either side of view, the light illuminating the metal armor of the guards moving outside. Yvon silently made his way in from the back and moved up the stairs and sat next to Sayren, "What's going on? Why are there so many guards surrounding us?"

Sayren remained motionless, but softly whispered, "tonight we will find out just how many guards it takes to put down an archer. Are you ready to fight if need be?"

Yvon cracked a childish smile, "I'm only sixteen, but yeah. I've been itching to take on the guards since they took my sister."

Several shouts erupted from outside as the first guardsman burst through the doorway and found an arrow impaled through his chest as he fell lifeless at the foot of the staircase. "So it begins." Sayren mocked as he restrung his bow and awaited his next target.

CHAPTER 6

With early festivities of the Harvest Festival underway in Dalkas, the Ogre's Nest was filled with patrons. Both commoner and noble alike filled the square as music and laughter danced through the air. Mead tankards collided in celebration of a hard day's work done and another successful year coming to an end before winter's arrival. Many patrons within the Ogre's Nest sat commending one another for a successful quarry and any fallen comrades that were no longer with them. Amelia danced across the floor between mercenary and noble alike, her arms filled with tankards and plates of lavish food. Several other women were out mingling with the men, however, Amelia's focus was undeterred as she steadily moved through the tables delivering food and taking new orders without a moment's hesitation. A relentless cheer for song started as a single shout before growing into a loud roar as patrons called out for Amelia to sing.

"Play the Song of Harvest!" One shouted as he thrust his mug into the air.

"Nay, sing a song of old heroes!" A noble in protest from the other end of the bar returned.

Amelia blushed as she returned to the bar and looked to the stout fellow standing on the other side, "Tonight's bunch seems rather enthused about getting onto my bad side; what would you have me do, Fontaine?"

Fontaine gave a hearty laugh before bellowing, "To song and merry-making! Let our drinks be as incredible as our fair maiden Amelia's voice and we'll all leave happy!"

A roar of cheers and applause erupted as the men began to clear a space in the middle of the room for Amelia and fell into a low hum as they awaited her to begin. Amelia ran her fingers through her hair before shouting, "So what shall it be? Shall I sing a song of bounty or a song of deeds first?"

"How about you sing a song of a single, powerful man that garnered the respect of both noble and commoner alike?" Mauro replied as he stepped into view from the cluster of men near the threshold of the inn's main door. Amelia, frightened at the inquisitors' sudden appearance, dropped a tankard of mead in surprise. "I didn't mean to cause you to drop another man's beverage," Mauro's voice called out to the room as he scanned for his target, "but I must intrude for a few moments to inquire any information of a man. He is the leader of the Six Crows, a man by the name of Rylan. I was told he frequents this tavern and I need to speak with him. Who will speak of him here?"

A staunch silence fell over the patrons, both noble and commoner alike. Although many had never traveled with, nor fought against Rylan, the respect was absolute. With an inquisitor present inside any location outside of the Royal District meant that the person of interest would more than likely never be heard from again. Amelia began to pick up the mug, but Mauro placed his foot over the tankard and gently lifted her face with his cold, leather covered fingers.

Mauro commanded the presence in the room with another cloaked inquisitor in addition to three noble guardsmen each armed with a club and an angered expression. He scanned the room with only glances and angered stares returned to him before he made his next attempt at persuading the crowd, "I see that this is in face the correct place and that many of you would show support to this man even though he is wanted for questioning on the king's business. I will offer you a compromise to any men who come forward with information that I want; tell me where he lives or where he is currently located, and I will buy twice the tab of the patron as well as keep him with me as I present to King Sepius Vasilli 'a man of the king'. Now will any of you assist me?"

Not a soul responded, and Mauro's temper began to rise, until a solemn hand raised itself over the crowds from the darkest corner of the room. Mauro motioned for the hooded figure to come forward as a sea of angered faces and whispered insults washed over the room as if it were a raging sea. Making it through the clustered bar made it an arduous task as the figure had a severe limp as he made his way to the inquisitors.

Mauro pointed to the man, "I see this is the only one who would stand for his king over a man not even kin. What is your name?"

As the figure grabbed his hood and pulled it back, the face of Kraste painfully stood upright and gave a slight bow before the nobles, "I am Kraste, Lord Inquisitor. I have what information you seek, but I would not ask of you any money."

"Ah," Mauro laughed jokingly as he placed a hand on Kraste's shoulder, "an 'honorable' man of the king at that. What would you ask of me in return for your aid?"

Kraste pulled back his cloak to reveal his injured leg, "I need to have my leg mended sir. I crossed blades with Rylan of the Six Crows not a day past in an honorable duel and he saw fit to strike my leg in an attempt to kill me without respect. I was able to fend for my life, but the dog ran off with his brothers on their way to a border village named Havenhome."

Mauro gazed down at Kraste's leg with disgust before nodding in agreement, "I do agree your leg will need to be mended. I will see to it that you are taken care so that you may lead us to Havenhome. However, do you also know where he lives?"

The tavern began to grow uneasy as whispers continue to spurn insults; however, the Fang also seemed to be angered at Kraste's upheaval of information about his failure. Nervously Kraste glanced back at the senior members of the Fang sitting at the table he had come from and with a silent nod of approval, Kraste returned his attention to Mauro and bowed, "The Six Crows all reside in the same house just outside of the militia district. Although most of the brothers are gone, two still remain at the residence." Kraste paused for a moment before looking at Amelia with a malicious grin before continuing, "That barkeep there, Amelia, and Rylan were lovers at a time and both are still very close. She would be able to tell you more about the mission Rylan has taken."

Mauro snapped his fingers and the guards quickly secured Amelia by the arms and began to bring her outside. Almost in unison, the entirety of the bar patrons stood and readied themselves for combat, but when Mauro remained calm at the act, many of the men stood uneasy.

"Leave it to a Fang to cause such misery! He's nothing more than a poisoned dagger!" One of the braver men near to Kraste proclaimed as he stepped forward to strike the assassin down with his sword. In a single movement, the other inquisitor leaped in front of the sword's path, grabbed the man's wrist, and contorting the mercenary in such a painful way he found his sword clanging against the stone tile and his arm pinned behind his head as the inquisitor looked to Mauro. "Very well Daliah, do it and let's be off. I would prefer to be done with this business by sunrise so I can rest before heading out of the capital."

Daliah grabbed the back of the mercenary's neck before sending black like tendrils from her hand into the man's body. With the appearance of veins, many of the onlookers turned away or gagged at the sight of the black veins swept over the man's face with several loud pops and cracks as the man screamed and pleaded for her to stop. A sudden twist of her wrist and the man's neck snapped and the room fell utterly silent with looks of horror and disgust on the faces of both common and noble occupants. Daliah released her grip and let the body fall lifeless onto the stone tiles as the tendrils returned from her victim and into a burned scar emblazoned on her palm; the blood slowly trickling off the dark vines as then disappeared. With a wave of his hand, Mauro and the others proceeded to exit with Kraste limping close behind, leaving the Ogre's Nest. A wave of discouraging misery washed over the patrons inside as the tavern's sorrows drowned against the festivities and cheers emanating from the square.

❀   ❀   ❀

Within Naria's private chamber, many of her splintered pieces of armor lay about the floor as well as several fine dresses Alkith had made for her with each passing harvest. She lay motionless in her bed, still incapacitated from her fight with Lora and the others, but surprisingly alive. Alkith had managed to return her to her bed using his speed faster than the healers could arrive and prepare to use their abilities to stop the damage to her body. With their combine powers, the torn ligaments in her legs and fractured forearms were mended quickly and without any long term damage.

With the feeling of a heavy pressure against her stomach, Naria opened her eyes to the dimly lit candles illuminating her room from the dark night sky and found a young boy barely old enough to wield a sword lying across her. "Luca," Naria whispered as she gently brushed his golden hair away from his face, "what are you doing here? You should be sleeping in your room."

A subtle creak in in the hinges of the door alerted Naria of Alkith's entrance and slowly eased Luca off from her chest and tucked him under her arm. "I didn't want keep the boy from his own mother," Alkith said as he sat on the edge of Naria's bed, "I see you've recovered. Care to tell me what happened?"

Naria started to sit upright when she suddenly recoiled from the immense pain in her head from where she had collided with the floor, "I was remembering father when a man burst into our hall and tried to lie to me. I saw through his lies and killed him, but not before using my power. After I had dispatched the man, the guards turned on me and I can't remember. Did you take care of them?"

Alkith looked through the window at the stars, staring into the vast darkness, "No, fortunately one of my men who saved me earlier, also protected you. He's had the unfortunate luck of being in the wrong place at the right time, but I cannot fault him for the results. He even rescued me earlier today when we came across a larger willow bear. In your case though, Gauld found you just before those turncoats could do anything and dispatched them. He ran into some trouble with Gianni after he entered the hall to bring you to me. Thankfully, I was able to intervene before I lost both my second and my sister. Will you be able to move about tomorrow? I suspect Alder will arrive before the setting sun."

Naria flexed her muscles to test her strength, but other than a few spots of soreness, all seemed well, "I'll be fine should you need me, but I promised Luca that I would take him to the Kay district to fetch some honey loaves that he's talked about ever since you brought him one back. Would you mind taking him back to his room when you leave? I'm still very tired and wish to go back to sleep."

Alkith nodded and brought Luca into his arms as he turned to leave. As he slowly opened the bedroom door, the rusted hinges gave a loud creak as Alkith looked into the hallway to find Ellice, the female heir of Ulferth, resting on the opposite wall with her pale skin and silver blonde hair reflecting the fire light. "Lady Ellice." Alkith bowed as he proceeded away from Naria's door with Luca beginning to stir in his arms.

Ellice bowed her head, "Lord Alkith." She returned as she made her way into Naria's bed chamber and sat down in a chair just off to the side of the bed. "I see you've been busy since I left. Have you made any headway into finding what I asked about?"

Naria sighed as she rolled over and sat up, "Unfortunately no, I found the few remaining mythical beasts have all but scattered to the wind. Only the ancient ones have said that when they return it will be up to the heirs of all eight kingdoms to overcome them and win the coming wars."

Ellice gave Naria a puzzled look as she leaned in closer, "What did they mean by wars? Shouldn't there be only the war to reclaim the thrones of our bloodlines?"

Naria shrugged and brushed her hair behind her ears, "I'm not entirely sure. Whatever the future holds for Thesia and ourselves is unclear. We will simply have to be ready for whatever comes to stand against us, foreign or neighboring."

A silence fell between the two as a strong breeze brushed against the window, both women readied with concealed weapons. After a few passing moments both heirs relaxed and Naria motioned to Ellice, "How did you fare with the recruiting in the north?"

"Better than I had originally expected," Ellice grinned as she proudly produced a folded parchment from under her shirt, "I was able to gain the pledge of four tribes bringing our total of loyalist to nearly fifteen. With over a hundred tribes in the north, however, I fear we will need more than what we will be able to draw into our fold before your brother's plan brings Alder into the fold and we set off to recover our claims. I may require your assistance if my brother and I cannot force Ulferth to bow to us, would you find that possible?"

Naria exhaled after hearing Ellice's request from the numerous times before. She placed both hands over Ellice's open palm, "I can't promise you that. You know my brother has this wild ambition of giving my hand away to a noble of our foreign allies as means to allying our goals."

"You've told me a thousand times, and I'll hear it a thousand more, but you and I both know that if they do decide to perform such a thing, Luca will certainly have to be taken into hiding or he'll be killed for being a legitimized bastard with rights to two kingdoms." Ellice's tone changed to a more serious feeling with a cold truth that plunged deep into Naria's heart.

"I will never allow Luca to be harmed," Naria said as she tightened her grip on Ellice's hand, "If it comes to marriage to that foreign leader, I'm sure his father would take him under his wing. He may be rough around the edges, but his son shows potential to master both royal arts."

Ellice's eyes widened, "Both houses? He has your curse and the ability to-"

"Yes, I've even seen him start to use some of the archaic relics of both houses with ease." Naria responded calmly as she patted Ellice's hands before lying back down in her bed. "Unfortunately I am very tired, Lady Ellice, and I don't wish to keep you from your rest either after such a journey. We can talk more on this at a later time."

Ellice arose from the chair and bowed, "Certainly, you'll need your strength should Alder arrive tomorrow. I can only imagine the surprise on the Six Wing's face when you show him his son."

      ✤   ✤   ✤

As the night seemed to drag on, Rylan found himself restlessly struggling with his wound. With each attempt to find a comforting position, a stinging pain drove itself up his leg and forced him to gently reposition himself on his back, staring up at the ceiling. Drops of rain cascaded endlessly onto the roof as time seemed to move at a snail's pace. Rylan could not relax knowing Kraste was still alive and would have notified the elder members of the Fang. If he hadn't been killed for his failure, there would surely be another, much larger, detachment heading towards them to finish their directive. Rylan's mind seemed to race, however, a wave of warmth washed over him from the antidote and sent him almost instantly into a daze. His eyelids grew heavy and his body seemed to go numb as he drifted to weightless slumber.

Rylan found himself resting in darkness within his dream, sounds of a calm wind brushing through trees rushed around him. He felt no pain, but a surreal sense of calm, yet he cautiously attempted to stand. Rylan's body felt as light as a feather as he arose and began to rub his eyes, a bright sun hung above him as he stood in one of the noble courtyards of King's Hold. His surroundings were as he remembered as a child, vibrant green grass and trees with the royal flags flying, unburned, atop the stalwart bastions of King's Rest. Although things seemed so familiar around him, there was a devoid of any signs of residents. Rylan began to move from road to building searching for anyone who may still be around, but with each threshold crossed, he was met with abandoned rooms collecting dust.

A loud noise from outside forced Rylan to rush back through the doorway to see the citadel itself crumbling to the ground and sounds of a raging battle grow louder the closer to the inner walls. Rylan moved without hesitation; in a full sprint, bounding forward with each step carelessly running headlong into the approaching fray. As the symphony of clashing weapons another filled the air, arrows began to land closer to Rylan until one struck him in the knee and sent him crashing down to the ground, snapping the shaft and forcing a cry out of Rylan as he clutched his wound. Rylan could hear the shouts of not only fighters commanding their forces to advance, but the sounds of innocent bystanders crying out attempting to flee the combat. Although the pain seemed intolerable, Rylan forced himself up and continued forward, staggering in pain with each step as crimson red flowed down his leg and onto the cobblestone streets beneath his steps. As he drew close to an open segment of the Alder district where many of the tournaments were held, he reached for his sword, but grasped at air as he looked down to see he was weaponless. A spear lay just in view as it lay partially concealed by a collection of large fermenting barrels. Rylan gingerly bent over to grab the bloodied spear, and found a young, impaled woman grasping the shaft of the spear as she choked on her own blood. He leaped back as the woman reached out to him before exhaling and falling limp against the blood soaked ground. Rylan looked on as the battlefield raged with many of the royal standards stood throughout the battlefield, however, many of the opposition Rylan had never seen before and the men seemed vastly different. Roars from mighty beasts tore through the sky as shadows zoomed overhead between the many clouds.

Several of the men clashing nearest to Rylan noticed him and stopped fighting as Rylan began to walk forward. An invisible wedge seemed to separate the fighters as Rylan approached. As he continued across the field, many of the soldiers seemed to be vastly different, men in lavishly designed clothes fighting with thin swords as well as men in full suits of armor wielding odd weapons with fixed blades at the end. Some of the soldiers around him appeared to be wielding powerful magic; others appeared to have no magic ability at all. Chants began on both sides, many of them in foreign languages to Rylan as they filled the air and the people around him began to step back forming a large circle between him and another masked individual who stood with a very ornate set of silver armor, a pair of crossed antlers resembling a crown emblazoned across the chestplate. Dark black locks of hair swayed in the winds with a white and gold colored mask adorning the figure's face without a sign of battle anywhere visible on Rylan's opposition.

Rylan felt his body get heavier as he found his sword and metal once again in his possession, "Who are you?" He shouted, drawing his sword and pointing it at the figure.

The masked individual turned to meet Rylan's gaze, "I am your doom," a deep voice bellowed from the man as he raised his hand and dark shadows began to appear around him, "You will not stand against my expansion, you or your cursed abilities. Your lands will burn and your armies will fall against my might!"

Rylan felt his power surge within him as five more wings of metal formed behind him, "I will not let you hurt my family or my home! You may bring your strongest men, but it will never be enough to stand against me or the men of Thesia!"

With a maniacal snicker, the man clenched his outstretched hands and turned the shapeless shadows into large wolf-like beasts with drooling mouths filled with jagged teeth and glaring red eyes, "I will not need to stand against you. You will invite me into your castles without having to draw a blade. My power is not like yours; I do not draw my magic from within, but I draw strength from the god that empowers my will and allows me to destroy all those that would stand against my empire. I will bring you and your lowly Thesia into a new dawn and a brilliant era of new found powers that you could not begin to dream! I will rise up your people to heights you will never dream; this will only happen once I rid the world of your honor and stop the heroes that would follow in your footsteps from becoming reality!"

Rylan brought his metal around him and turned the metal-like feathers to target his opponent, "That will never happen! I will never allow you to bear such tyranny to Thesia only to drench the land in your dark ways!"

"Nor will I, my honor will be resolute against you and any that stands with you." A female's voice called out as she emerged from the defending forces with two swords engulfed in vibrant blue flames. Her aura and appearance seemed familiar to Rylan, but her identity was a mystery.

"No man or woman of Thesia can stop my might! I will be a god once I erase your kind from existence!" The masked man roared as he pointed to the defenders.

A man of pure metal stepped forward, his hands empty but a glow from within the cracks of his armor glowing with a bright yellow, "I'm not from Thesia, nor am I from your world! Your line will never stand against the men and women who will stand against you and your tyrants! I pledge my life to stopping you and your kind every time you seek to gain a hold on the people! You will fall!"

A loud roar erupted behind the defenders as they rallied their spirits and forced their attackers to step back in fear. With a loud bang, the opposing forces charged and clashed, concealing the masked man from Rylan as he attempted to confront and vanquish his foe before he could escape. Rylan shoved, kicked, and slashed his way through the field of battle as it continued to rage around him until he reached the other side and saw the man turning a corner down an alleyway and out of view. Rylan sprinted forward as he chased after the man, yet once he turned, a bright light blinded Rylan and forced him to cover his eyes. Rylan slowly removed his hand from over his eyes and found a corridor filled with cases of arms and armor of all designs. Rylan turned to see where he had come from but found he was standing at the end of the hallway with only walls around him. Cautiously moving forward, Rylan gazed upon the sealed glass containers that held magnificent weapons of intricate patterns and carvings. Rylan turned his attention to the other end of the hall, a set of double doors slightly cracked open and the sounds of a heated discussion raging from within. As he approached the large barred doorway, a loud horn began to play as the crack widened and Rylan passed through.

A large chamber revealed itself with many beings of indescribable characteristics sitting around a large circular pool in the floor and starring quietly at Rylan. One figure arose, its appearance seemed like a man, but his body did not seemed natural to Rylan's eyes, "Hero of Order, you have finally stepped forth to begin our war. What has made you journey to our realm, wielder of metal and might?"

Rylan attempted to answer, but found he could not make a sound. He grasped at his throat as he felt the crushing presence of the being drawing nearer to him. Rylan gasped for air as the figure placed his hand on Rylan's shoulder. Rylan began to choke as he felt the pressure instantly leave his body and his voice returned, "I don't know where I am... or how I... arrived at this place. Where am I... and who... who are you?"

A quiet whisper echoed through the room as the other individuals sat gazing at Rylan. "Fear not, my champion," the figure holding Rylan calmingly spoke, "You are in a place that only a chosen few can reach. We are the creators of all that you've seen and much more that you have not. Many beings like yourself call us 'gods' or 'deities' and you may as well if you so choose. We would choose to name ourselves as 'Creators', although there were many more before those you see. We are what remains and we have molded the worlds as we best could."

Rylan gazed confused at the beings within the room, "I do not know what to think or say. This seems so strange to me. Why did you call me champion?"

A few chuckles followed by another round of whispers filled the room as Rylan turned back to the creator next to him for answers, "You are my champion. It will be easier for you to understand if I explain this in the ways you've learned in your small years. I am Athus, Creator of Honor, Truth, and Tactics in your world. I shape minds of beings across the stars to instill a sense of pride, but impartial code of conduct for battle. Although my dream is for that sense to become a standard, Suthred, the Creator sitting across from my seat is my opposite, is a dishonorable 'thing' creates deceit, greed, and calamity with the pride he plants in the minds and hearts of beings. He has forced my hand and forced a new war to begin in your homeland that will shape everything that will come after you. I have selected you to be my first champion, just as he has selected the man hidden behind that mask that you spoke with earlier. Although you will fight one another for the remainder of your lives, I fear the struggle between our differences will continue further throughout the stars until we have the very struggle for life itself."

"I do not wish to be a part of something that I have no choice in. I do my utmost to live honorably, but to ask such a task of me is far beyond what I wish for my life. I live to protect my my family. I must refuse you and your title, Athus. I do apologize for any inconvenience." Rylan bowed as he finished and attempted to return through the doorway.

Whispers stopped as the room fell silent and Athus removed his hand from Rylan's shoulder, returning the immense pressure on Rylan and forcing him to kneel. Athus walked in front of Rylan, and with a raise of his hand, Rylan found himself lifting off of the ground, "You must think you have some sort of power here, you insignificant mercenary. You may be the Six Winged Death, but I can take your wings just as easy as I gifted them to you. I have chosen you; I do not require your permission in how I move your path. You will be my champion or you will watch your world descend to darkness and hatred. Now, return to your world and see what awaits your people should you falter in your destiny."

Athus threw Rylan effortlessly through the air, sending him

crashing through the doors, and slamming against the blood soaked tiles of the finished battle around the citadel's courtyard within King's Hold. Rylan felt the pain of landing as if it were real and as he sat upright, many of the fighters he had seen laid dead in piles with men dressed in black cloaks tossing lit torched onto the piles. Rylan reached for a broken spear as he stood upright, the metal spearhead scraped against the ground and caused several cloaked figures towards Rylan as they drew weapons and rushed towards him. Rylan steadied himself and counter attacked with his broken weapon, slicing, piercing, and sending his enemies in all directions as they pressed towards him with ever increasing numbers. Sounds of monstrosities around the citadel forced Rylan's attackers to halt their advance and beat a hasty retreat as their cloaks masked their movements as if shadows upon the ground. Rylan attempted to draw forth his metal, but with each attempt he could not feel the presence of his metal. Scanning the courtyard, Rylan found the doorway to the Great Hall open as pillars of fires shot skyward and mighty beasts crashed into the walls, sending splintered shards of rocks flying across the courtyard. Rylan sprinted for the doorway to escape the oncoming barrage and managed to dodge what stones soared past him, until a larger rock caught him across the back of his head and sent him tumbling along the ground. With a steady stream of blood flowing down his neck and a strong pain holding him in a state of dazed confusion, Rylan clumsily made his way back upright with his broken spear and made his way through the doorway.

Sounds of grunting and wood scraping against the stone floor tiles forced Rylan to ready himself and turn his gaze towards the noises. Standing at the opposite end of the Great Hall was a creature built like a hairless bear with the snout of a boar, its tusks crimson and draped with the prizes of its victim's gored flesh. Rylan attempted to slowly back outside, however, the beast turned its attention towards him and gave a loud grunt, scraping its claws on the tile. Rylan felt his heart race as fear momentarily gripped him and forced him to stagger outside and return to the courtyard with his pursuer close behind him, drawing closer with every thunderous impact. Rylan turned to face his newest threat to find it almost upon him in a head long charge.

Without a moment to react, the creature drove its horns into Rylan's right leg as he attempted to dodge and found himself flung backwards with a deep gash in his leg sending excruciating pain throughout his entire body as he writhed on the ground pressing his free hand over the wound to slow the bleeding. As Rylan staggered backwards, the beast began to parade around its wounded prey as it gauged its next attack. Rylan could feel his wounds increasing in severity as his eyesight continued to blur and his leg began to numb, a wave of cool air seemed to brush over him, "If this is what you want to happen, then at least let me die with my honor, using my metal!" A crack of lightning overhead forced the beast to momentarily turn away from Rylan as he felt his power returning, a swarm of metal shards plummeting towards him. Rylan dropped his spear and outstretched his hand as the monster began to charge his right side. With the beast nearly on top of him with its tusks aimed for Rylan's chest, the shards of metal rained down as metal stakes, slamming through the beast and pinning it to the stone tile, its tusks a breath away from piercing Rylan. With a pained exhale, Rylan slumped against the broken chunks of rock as he began to feel his body go numb; his eyelids grew heavy as he could feel himself drifting away; however, the sounds of Athus's voice rang clear, "You have accepted your fate as my champion. You will not know your enemy, but you will see Suthred's games at work as he attempts to destroy your Thesia. You must stop him and change the hearts of your kinsmen to side with honor for all, it is the only way you will stand together and survive what draws near to those dark shores."

Rylan felt those words sink in as the image of his masked rival began to burn into his mind as he drifted. A sudden feeling of plummeting forced Rylan awake and upright in the bed, his body sweating and his leg felt somewhat stiff around the wound. Rylan looked around the room as the first signs of daylight began to pierce the holes in the back walls. As he arose from the bed and made his way over to his other garments, Rylan reached into a hidden pocket inside his leather brigandine, producing a vibrant silver ring with etched feathers encompassing the outside and the seal of the Orden Forge within. Rylan felt his magic surge as he held the ring within his grasp and found himself at ease since their journey had started.

Rylan carefully returned the ring and pulled his shirt over his head as he prepared, all the while thinking how Lord Tiberius and Lady Isabella were searching for the very thing he had never lost; one half of the absolute right to rule, the Ring of Alder. A sudden loud crash forced Rylan to draw his blade and jerk the door open to the apothecary's main room. Inside, Aldis and Tiberius stood bracing the door, each winded and incrusted with a solid layer of mud adorning their garments, "Rylan!" Tiberius called out as he bounced back from the men slamming against the opposite side of the door, "We need help, now!"

❀   ❀   ❀

As the morning sun cresting above Dalkas's royal palace, the main courtyard teemed with movement. Many of the groundskeepers were out tending to the gardens around the main sitting area as well as trimming the hedges that surrounded the courtyard to protect from prying nobles and esteemed guests. Apart from armed bowmen patrolling atop weather-warn stones, the entrance to the courtyard held the only visible seal of House Bassadora, a magnificent white crow crafted into the ground and several black banners of Golden Griffins, the sigil of House Vasilli, draped about to conceal any other symbols of the past. Standing in the middle of the courtyard with his protégé, Lord Gaius LeBlanc stood with his three metal wings bared at King Sepius's Grandson, Briar.

Gaius readied his attack and motioned to Briar, "Prepare your shield as I've shown you, I would hate to tell your grandfather you couldn't stand up to royal expectations."

Briar brought forth his inferior supply of metal and forged it into a large shield in front of him. "I'm not scared, Lord Gaius, you won't defeat me!"

Gaius chuckled before sending his metal shards bombarding down onto Briar's shield, the enormous weight of each strike forcing Briar further and further back as he attempted to withstand the barrage. As his first wave finished, Gaius recalled his metal, and Briar changed his metal from a shield to two war hammers and rushed forward. Gaius had little time to react, stepping backward, and formed his shield to block Briars' furious onslaught of blows. Gaius, although the far superior skilled fighter, gave Briar ground as he inched backwards to strengthen Briar's resolve.

"What seems to be the matter father?" Mauro called out as he entered the courtyard with Daliah, the patrol of Noble militia, and that of their five captives. "It would appear the young prince has begun his ascension past you in spectacular fashion!"

Briar smiled as he heard those words and tripped over himself, falling flat on his face as Gaius gave a long sigh and shook his head, "You need to stay focused Briar. If you let yourself get distracted in the middle of a battle, you'll never survive." Gaius turned his attention to Mauro and scowled, "What are you doing here boy? Can you not see this is the Royal Estate? What madness has driven you to bring common rabble into this place?"

Mauro shook his head as Briar returned upright and began to brush the dirt off his clothes, "For only a young man at the age of ten to be holding his own against a hero is still quite an incredible feat to accomplish. If you must know though father-"

"Address me properly boy." Gaius commanded as he pointed his shield towards the inquisitor.

"Ahem, very well, I hold official business with King Sepius in regards to the rebels and the traitors residing within our capital's walls. If you would point me in the right direction, we will be out of your way."

"Very well, Briar let us take a short break to drink some water. Then we shall work on your footing."

As Gaius and Briar began their walk back to the royal estate, Mauro noticed Faust, Heir Apparent to King Sepius, step out into the courtyard from behind one of the hedges and beckoned them forward. Mauro and Daliah both bowed in unison and motioned the guards to bring the prisoners with them. Faust's appearance was entitled, shirtless with a robe draped over his shoulders, his hair a glowing brown as the rays of sun danced over him, bathing him in its radiance. Although Daliah's gaze was fixed on Faust, Mauro stepped forward, bowing once more, and motioned back to his prisoners,

"Good morning to you Lord Prince Faust. I bring your father a gift. Do you know where his Kingship is perhaps?"

Faust's soothing voice returned, "My Father? I am not his keeper; I wouldn't know where that man has been. I do, however, spy a beautiful creature behind you. Your name is Daliah if I remember correctly, yes? It has been a harvest since I've seen you. What made you pursue the Inquisitor's purpose?"

Daliah blushed as she stepped forward and bowed, "You're too kind your grace. I do recall our dance at the Royal Gala; you had just defeated one of the heads of households in a game of Castles and Kings. It was an honor, Lord Prince."

Faust walked over to Daliah and brushed his hand through her hair, her face turning a bright rosy red before Mauro gave a subtle sigh to interrupt, "Prince Faust, the prisoners we have are-"

"Lord Inquisitor, what difference does it matter what kind of prisoner they are. Take them to the dungeon to be tortured and silenced. Nothing has changed." Faust's attention was firmly focused on Daliah as he spoke, his eyes locked with hers. "Shall we leave the work to your cohort here and go discuss how your opinion of the Royal Inquisitors thus far?"

Mauro's rage flared, however, he took a deep breath to regain his control and motioned to the guards, "Take the women down to the holding cells, and leave the two men here. I'm certain the king will wish to speak to them."

Faust glared at Mauro, "You would insinuate you know what my father thinks? Do you wish to be buried now for your insinuation, or would you rather apologize to me before I lose my temper?"

Mauro gave a slight bow before turning away from Mauro and kneeling with all but Faust following suit, "My King, I have brought you the beginning of your absolution. I apologize for such a long delay on behalf of all the inquisitors."

Faust turned to see his father, Sepius Vasilli, standing with his aides behind him. His aged figure draped in regal robes as he slowly made his way to his son before slapping him across the face, "Idiot boy!" Scolded Sepius as he turned away from Faust to Mauro, "Lord Mauro, I see you have brought me guests, but they are shackled and chained. What ferocity may they possess that would require such restraint? One of them is even a child."

Mauro waved to the guards to remove the cloth sacks from atop the heads of the prisoners. With a quick nod the guards removed the bags and revealed Abigail, Amelia, and Ophelia bound and gagged. Both Wilhelm and Ebon appeared in much worse condition with several minor lacerations and bruises covered their faces. "My King, these people have been accomplices in a terrible plot. It was discovered that a lone masked man, who undoubtedly sides with rebels and other heirs, kidnapped and tortured a noble by the name of Larus Carthill. Although it was unclear why he chose Lord Carthill, I was able to discover that the noble had also participated in concealing the late Queen Maree and her sons from capture. Although Lord Larus did not survive the process, I was able to discover his daughter had married, to my best knowledge, the oldest heir before abruptly running away and disavowing their claim to House Carthill. I present to you Ebon, Wilhelm, and Abigail Carthill, children of the traitor, and coconspirators of aiding a man known as Rylan of the Six Crows. Rylan and his brothers are no doubt the heirs we've been searching for my king. I present them to you for to pass judgement upon them as the one true, rightful king of this kingdom."

Sepius stepped forward and looked at the prisoners, "I don't believe I have ever seen you all since you were young children barely walking about the streets as I returned triumphant from our glorious revolution. Before I pass judgement on any of you all, I must ask; why did you betray me? Have I not ensured Alder's safety and rightful domination of this land? Have we not prospered as a people, together? Why would you turn against me for such insignificant sons of a cowardly dictator that let the lands fall to ruin while he sat atop his throne and celebrated a false unity with the other kingdoms?"

For a moment the courtyard was silent, a solid wave of tension formed over all inside the courtyard as Sepius waited for an answer. A slight breeze passed through the hedges as no one answered. Sepius motioned to the guards, "Since they do not wish to answer, take the women away. Faust will see to their confinement until I have decided what to do with them. Inquisitor Mauro, I wish for you to stay here and unbind these two men. I wish to make them a proposition."

As the guards and inquisitors rose, Faust draped his arm over Daliah and proceeded out of the courtyard with the guards pulling Amelia, Abigail, and Ophelia behind them in their heavy chains. Wilhelm and Ebon both remained on their knees as the guards cautiously untied their gags before unlocking the shackles and stepping back. Both men slowly arose as Mauro took his place beside Sepius while the guards readied their blades. "I must commend your father on raising such stalwart sons," Sepius spoke calmly as he pointed to both men, "I don't believe there are many men that would stand against king and country for family. Most men nowadays will commit such dishonor for a small purse of coins. I wish I could simply release you both back to your father's estate and allow you to serve me as the rightful king, however, I could not allow such defiance go unpunished. No matter what I do, fourteen houses must remain in place for me to be anointed King of Alder. I will spare your family, your sister, and the child, but I must hold one of you accountable for such actions. If I allow you to fight until one remains alive, would you do that and save your family?"

Wilhelm stepped forward, "Never. I cannot allow such a charade to mask that you would never allow anyone who stands against you live, no matter how insignificant the offense. I will not speak for my sister, but knowing that your words are nothing more than honeyed poison, I would rather die with my honor than kill my brother and condemn my family."

Sepius nodded and began to raise his hand until Ebon stepped in front of Wilhelm, knocking him in the side, "If we fight, you'll guarantee the safety of our sister and niece? If you give me your word as King and as an honorable man, I will fight."

"What are you doing you idiot!" Wilhelm screamed as he clutched his bruised side, "He will kill them regardless, whether by hanging from the walls or dragging them to the headman's block, they will certainly die!"

Sepius nodded to Mauro as the inquisitor drew a dagger and

tossed it onto the dewed grass, "You have my word." Sepius grinned as he spoke.

Ebon swung his fist wildly at Wilhelm as he attempted to move for the dagger. Wilhelm blocked the blow with his forearm and quickly uppercut Ebon in the stomach, forcing his brother to his knees gasping for air. Wilhelm stood over Ebon's body for a moment before looking to the guards, both behind him and standing atop the walls with readied arrows, before turning to the dagger. Wilhelm gingerly bent down to grab the dagger as Ebon began to stand and out stretch his hand to his brother, "Wil, do it for our family. I accept that one of our lives will be taken, but we'll spare our brothers the hardship of returning to see us all hanging from the towers as the crows feast on our bodies."

Wilhelm looked down at the dagger and began to tremble, it was his father's. He tightly gripped the handle before turning towards Mauro, "I am sorry brother, but I will not let them lull you into a false peace. We were dead the moment they found us. Forgive me." Ebon leaped forward as Wilhelm focused his ability and released his free hand, his skin began to red as the guards behind him began to writhe in pain and Ebon fell to the ground paralyzed. Mauro moved in front of the king as Wilhelm continued forward, "Please stand back my king, he wields forbidden magic! Archers, bring him down!"

Wilhelm leaped forward to plunged Larus's dagger into Mauro as a hail of arrows rained down and struck him several times over, forcing him to the ground gasping for breath and breaking his control of the magic. As the archers began to restring their bows to fire another volley, Ebon quickly leaped for the dagger and began driving it repeatedly into Wilhelm, his eyes welling with each wound he inflicted until his arms were exhausted and a pool of crimson blood began to move along between the stone tiles until they reached the glass.

"Inquisitor," Sepius placed his hand on Mauro's shoulder, "you're in my way."

Mauro quickly stepped to the side, carefully avoiding the blood. Sepius stared down at Ebon as he pulled the dagger out of his brothers back and tossed it aside on the grass, "It is done; now I humbly ask you uphold your word, my king."

Sepius brushed his grey beard as he looked at Wilhelm's blood outlining the stones, "I will do just as I have promise, Lord Ebon Carthill. I fear though that your brother might have spoken the truth. I want you to keep that dagger and go to your sister, ask her if she would stand with me as a subservient lady or if she would stand against her king and side with her husband. Should she agree to kneel before me and serve willingly, she will be spared, but if she refuses, you will prove your undying loyalty by taking her head. This will prove to me that you are worthy of your title and your house. Do this and you will be dressed by my tailor and stand among the heads of house as an advisor to me and my family. What say you?"

Ebon buried his fist in the blood of his brother as he foresaw what he would be forced to do. His realization of the cruel lie Sepius had played had tainted his heart, to kill his own brother he gagged at the thought of killing his sister as well. He swallowed what little pride he had as he stood, his hands and knees covered in blood, and bowed to Sepius, "Your judgement is resolute; I will do as you ask, but I ask only that my niece is spared the pain of hearing what may happen should Abigail deny you. Please allow me to wash my hands before I ask her, I do not wish her to know that her brother was killed by the other."

Sepius nodded in agreement and motioned for the guards to aide Ebon as he took the dagger and made their way towards the dungeon. "Tell me Mauro, where is this Rylan you spoke of now?"

Mauro with drew a parchment with Kraste's dreadfully written statement, "He makes his way towards King's Hold to assist Lady Isabelle, the new hero, and Lord Tiberius Bernak in finding her gift to you my king. A member of Serpent's Fang wrote this statement stating he saw Rylan guiding the nobles, and was even able to wound him in the duel. Rylan's current condition is unknown however. With your permission, I would request to take thirty men and capture him. I am certain that both nobles do not know that the heir rides with them. His brother will also be accompanying them. I do not suspect they will be aware of our intentions until it is far too late."

Sepius nodded in agreement as he smirked while looking over Wilhelm's corpse. "Take fifty men; if this Rylan is the heir, then he will also be the Six Winged Death. I do not wish to throw men needlessly to the butcher. Take the men and ride tomorrow, tonight we should celebrate such a day has finally arrived. Also do me the favor of fetching some servants to dispose of this traitor's body, but take his head, I have a fetching idea that will be the perfect present should you manage to take the heir alive."

Mauro bowed, "Yes my king, right away." He gave one last look at the rising sun before heading towards the estate and motioning to a few of the servants. Sepius stood basking in the sunlight as he felt the warmth was over his wrinkled skin, a spark in his mind forced him to open his arms and began to laugh before turning to his aides and proceeding to breakfast.

CHAPTER 7

Quickly grabbing his axe and running to help brace the door, Rylan looked through the cracks of the doorway and saw two guardsmen attempting to breakthrough, "What happened?"

Aldis bounced off the door as he attempted to reply, "These are... they're the same bandits that Sayren fought. We were suspicious that they may move on us out of retaliation; however Sayren killed a number of them before any made it inside and forced us to leap out of our rooms. Only myself and Lord Tiberius evaded capture that I'm aware of, but we've been unable to get close enough to find the others with these two pursuing us."

Rylan's anger began to boil, "If that idiot would've only listened and not gotten involved with matters that do not pertain to us, we'd be moving without having to deal with this mess. What happened to Byra and his family?"

"They were on the lower level when we turned in for the night," Tiberius answered, "last we saw of them before this whole mess kicked off. Are you in any condition to fight?"

Rylan tightened his fists and attempted to recall his metal, "Move away from the door! I'll handle the guards!"

All three leaped backwards as the two guards burst through the door with weapons drawn, "Great idea that was, now there here with us!" Tiberius shouted at Rylan.

A faint whistle whirled through the air as Rylan's metal pierced through the men from behind and reformed into a singular wing behind his back. Tiberius scoffed and headed to the doorway as he peered outside, scouring for any other guards that may be nearby.

Rylan quickly returned to his equipment and finished preparing for whatever stood against them. As he returned to the front door Tiberius leaded against the edge of the doorway with his shield and sword ready, while Aldis searched the men's bodies for anything useful. "Come little brother, these men are not worth our time. We need to rescue the others before anything worse besets them. Lord Tiberius, do you see any other enemies about?"

"No", Tiberius kept his gaze focused out into the morning light, many of the buildings still silent, however the shouts of men near the inn were still audible, "We need to make our way over to your brothers and Lady Isabelle. There sounds to be a large amount of brigands gathered though."

Rylan drew his sword and brazenly walked outside, carefully stepping over the bodies of the dead. Rylan motioned them forward as he pressed up against the closest building, carefully watching the back door of the inn. As Tiberius and Aldis made their way over to Rylan's side, the door of the inn swung open and three men carrying Yvette exited. Yvette was bruised, but did not struggle as the men threw her to the ground and drew their blades. Rylan rushed forward without hesitation, his metal shards dispersing from its winged resemblance as they formed spear like rods. One of the men made his way to Yvette and raised his sword to plunge into her chest when Rylan lurched forward, his metal soaring through the men and slamming them into the ground chocking on blood spewing from their mortal injuries. Rylan carefully looked over Yvette as she lay quiet, "you need to get up and conceal yourself within your hut. You'll be safe there until we return."

Yvette nodded slowly, returned upright with Rylan's assistance, and proceeded back to the apothecary with Tiberius and Aldis both drawing close once again to Rylan. "What are you doing?" Tiberius grabbed Rylan's shoulder with an abrupt shake as he questioned him.

"I'm saving the people who saved me Lord Tiberius. I mean no disrespect, but you'll need to trust me if we're to get our companions back and escape this town alive." Rylan answered as he shook his arm free and proceeded towards the back door, his metal dissipating back into its shards as he passed by the dying men.

Aldis watching horrified as Rylan's determination showed the kind of man he had heard stories about while in the academy of a mercenary that could killed relentlessly and without remorse, all while protecting any noble willing to pay for such a protector. As Rylan stepped through the doorway and out of sight from his little brother, Aldis quietly followed Tiberius with his staff in hand, carefully watching his surroundings before passing through the doorway and back into the inn.

Rylan silently made his way across the floor, his metal hovering just below the ceiling waiting to strike. The hallway and rooms were in a state of disarray as he made his way to the main area, with broken boards and shreds of clothing scattered about. Rylan could hear unfamiliar voices echoing from the outside near the main road, but Tiberius's attempts to move silently behind him caused a subtle clang of the shield colliding with obstacles as he closed the distance to the dining area doorway.

"Oi, what's Lothos want us to do with the bodies?" An unfamiliar voice shouted from within the hall as he called out to another. Rylan quickly moved across the doorway to gain eyesight on the individuals conversing. Both appeared as guardsmen; however the guard crest was replaced by a burning axe. Their modified appearance was that of the actual bandits that controlled the town instead of the façade they had in place to mimic a regular militia. With the first man dragging arrow riddled bodies into a pile, the second appeared to be pulling down Toren's bags and Sayren's shattered bow, "He probably can't here you while he's gawking over that healer. After she tried to heal that blasted bowman's hand he hasn't taken his eyes off of her."

"She probably reminds him of the boss," the first thug said as he flung the bodies onto the pile, "I still can't believe we lost thirty men from two mercenaries, a priestess and that noble bitch. Not to mention that old bastard and his wife nearly snuck up behind Lothos while he was beating on that bowman, any idea where that other noble went with the kid?"

After reaching the end of the stairs, the second man placed the items he was carrying onto a table near the main door and scratched his head, pondering before giving his answer. "I'm not too sure if I'm honest. If it were a simple noble I'd bet he's run off to cower in some dark corner with that sage until he messes himself. That noble isn't simple though, he is the one they call 'Wall of a Thousand Winds'. I've heard that even though he's the middle child for the Bernak family, Lord Tiberius is one of the best soldiers the kingdom has ever produced. My guess is if he hasn't already found a way to escape the walls, he'll be mounting a counter attack. Lothos knows that though and has men searching for them. We'll catch him and that kid soon enough. I think I'll check that old man's room now, surely he has to have some coins stashed away."

Rylan stepped out into the room, weapons readied, and slid a chair with his axe to draw the two bandit's attention, "Excuse me, I don't want to hold you both up from whatever it is you think you're doing, however I must ask where your 'Lothos' has taken the people that were staying here. If you do me that favor I'll spare your lives and be on my way. What say you?"

Both men laughed simultaneously as they pointed towards Rylan, "You must be joking, you couldn't hope to harm us, let alone fight Lothos, just give us your stuff and we'll let you leave here with your life." One said as he drew his sword.

Rylan did not hesitate as he stepped forward, "Lord Tiberius, what I am about to do will have to be settle between us before we move on with our rescue. If you wish to save Lady Isabelle before they endure any further hardships, it will require that we do not hold back any further. Rylan began to channel his focus as he drew his metal forth, "Aldis, I swear to you that I will explain everything once this is over and we are all together, but for now please just bear with me."

As the inn itself seemed to shake, many of the floorboards began to ooze liquid metal from underneath. The bandits looked on in horror as the metal seemed to move around their feet until it began to draw itself around Rylan and take form as five enormous wings of metal with the six flying into place from the back hallway. With fear in their eyes both brigands dashed madly for the door to escape, however Rylan twitched his axe hand and shot barbed metal rods forth, tearing through both men's legs before jerking backwards and sending both men to the floor. "Now I will ask you once more," Rylan's steady voice turned cold, "where did your leader take my people after you attacked them?"

Both bandits begged and pleaded through their agonizing screams and pleas for release. Undeterred Rylan sent another spike forward and drove it crashing downward into the first bandit's chest, instantly silencing him as the other man's dread increased as he continued to scream until he began retching uncontrollably. Rylan made his way over to the man and stood over him, "Tell me or I'll make your death more excruciating and prolonged than you can fathom."

"Please-please spare me! By my father you're him! You're the Six Winged Death! I'll tell you everything!" The man writhed in pain as he tried to calm himself and inadvertently attempted to adjust his leg. "Argh, he took them for gold! I- I mean hold, he took them to King's Hold; they left not too long ago! Please spare me; I have a son to look after!"

Rylan's gaze met the man's, his blank, emotionless eyes gave the man Rylan's answer as several shards showered the man's chest as he shuttered for a moment before settling motionless. Rylan turned back to his companions as the metal retracted from both men and began to form a magnificent suit of armor with two wings remaining. Tiberius made his way out to the room, his body shaking slightly from the sight of the six wings, but he maintained his composure as best as possible. Aldis stood in the doorway mortified, his eyes fixed on Rylan and mouth agape as he continued to processed the events.

"Lord Tiberius, I expect you have some disbelief to what you see before you. I meant what I said however; if you wish to save our group, we will have to unshackle our strongest abilities to crush our enemies. Will you fight with me to save Lady Isabelle and the others?"

Tiberius swallowed the lump in his throat as he attempted to maintain his disposition, "Are we to say that our enemies are the same? You stand before me as Heir to the Throne of Alder, yet my house was one of the first to turn against you and your bloodline. Were this a different location and circumstance, would you not spear me to the ground where I stand?"

Rylan sheathed his sword, "What happened was not because of you, nor did you swing the strike that killed my father. If I were to consider you my enemy, I would be forced to consider all of Alder, from King Sepius to each ragged pauper my enemy. I was taught not to hate a man for the deeds of prior generations, but to give every man a chance to decide his own fate, regardless of what becomes of the opinion of his family. I did not seek out the throne nor do I desire it. I wish to keep my brothers safe from a world that hates them for the perceptions of one disillusioned fool. I need your answer though Lord Tiberius; will you stand beside me to save our families, or will we part ways here and decide our fates while Lothos marches further and further away?"

Tiberius sighed before sheathing his sword and lowering his shield, "I would only ask that you do not stand in the way of Lady Isabelle when we return. If you promise that this will be our only meeting then I will stand by your side, not as a noble, but as an equal to see our families returned safely."

Rylan nodded and extended his hand to Tiberius, "If that is all you ask then consider this our last engagement, although your father and I have had dealings in the past as well as many other nobles who know of my existence. I do well to keep my family close and my allies closer. How else do you think I have been able to thrive as a mercenary for so long with only myself and my brothers?"

"I see." Tiberius nodded as he shook Rylan's open hand and headed for the table with the parties belongings, "We'll need to be provisioned should we follow the bandits on the road to King's Hold."

Aldis quietly made his way over to Rylan as he began to stare at the metal armor, meticulously making mental notes of its structure and design, "Actually we won't need to take that long. Although we will not be sure whether Sayren has stuck to the plan, in the event any of us were capture, we each have crystals that will allow our journey through a Sen Portal just outside of the town to the Royal Estate within Alder's District inside the walls of King's Hold. If we can acquire our horses we should be able to get there quickly enough to close the gap."

Tiberius and Rylan nodded in agreement as they grabbed what supplies were still usable and made their way to the back door. Aldis quickly looked for any other guards patrolling, but the area around them seemed entirely empty. With Aldis in front, the three returned to Yvette's hut, hid the supplies and made their way to the stables. Rylan marched through the rickety stable doors, waiting to find any bandits that may have been anticipating their arrival after the earlier commotion, but there were only a handful of villager corpses scattered about with Toren's horse missing. "Odd," Rylan whispered to himself as he scanned the room accounting for all the other horses. After motioning to Tiberius and Aldis all was clear, Rylan mounted his horse and transferred most of the metal into armor for his steed, leaving a single wing tucked behind him. As Tiberius tossed his saddle onto his horse's back he asked, "Why waste your metal on the horse? The beast won't do you much good if you're dead."

"Better to have the suspicion off of myself, it makes it far easier to defeat a multitude of foes before they realize what's going on if they don't know where the danger lies." Rylan replied as he snapped the reins and made his way to the door. Aldis pulled his horse next to him as he prepared to open the door, "Once these open, we'll need to make our way to the eastern gate before we are noticed. Once there, I suspect they'll have reinforced the walls to prevent Lord Tiberius from escaping. From my notes, the eastern side will be far better built due to it facing the uncontrolled area of King's Hold."

Rylan nodded as Tiberius too his place behind him, the sounds of clanging metal growing louder on the outside, "I suppose they know we're here now. I suppose you'll have a chance to see what six wings worth of death looks like Lord Tiberius." Rylan gave a malicious smirk and motioning for Aldis to blast open the doors.

From outside the barn three rows of men stood ready, armed with a large shield and either a spear or sword. A bright light began to shine from within the barn before a thunderous boom shook though the men and the doors fragmented outwards. The jagged splinters flew towards the guardsmen, piercing many of the unprotected spaces between the shields. As the first row fell and the others recovered from the disorientation, the sight of a storm of metal shards sent many routing, screaming to spare them as Rylan sent his ability forth to leave none left standing as they rode past. Sounds of pleading men being gored by metal echoed throughout the entirety of the village as Rylan, Tiberius, and Aldis pushed their steeds to a full gallop as they rushed the eastern gate of Havenhome.

With twin archer towers and an enclosed gatehouse holding the winch, the eastern gate held superiority in defensive capabilities in comparison against the western gate. With only two archers atop the towers and four more on the ground, it seemed their capabilities had become stretched thin. As three of the guards quickly attempted to form a line between Tiberius and the gate, he swung his sword, sending a massive arch of razor air that sliced through the paltry shields and severed the men in two. Rylan took aim at the archers readying their bows and sent out a storm of shards that pierced through their leather armor and shot back into the open air. As the three grew within a few paces from crossing over the threshold and back onto the road, the final guardsman began a mad dash for the gatehouse to release the wench and seal the riders inside. Aldis reacted before Rylan or Tiberius could make an attempt to halt the runner, pointing his staff towards the gatehouse and focusing, the door slammed closed just before the guard stepped through and sent the man flying backwards as he collided with the door, falling unconscious against the cold, morning dirt. All three burst into laughter at the sight as they escaped Havenhome in pursuit of Lothos and their companions.

❀   ❀   ❀

"Hey archer, where is this 'secret place' you kept squawking about when I threaten to kill your little friend Yvon?" Lothos cruel voice cracked as he laughed from the middle of the group with Elyscia draped across his saddle, unconscious.

Sayren walked in front of the group clutching his right arm, his hand crushed by Lothos after they had dragged everyone down the stairs and began to question their intentions. After Orsen was taken from the group, Brilla revealed their plan to venture to King's Hold in an attempt to procure valuable ancient trinkets to secure favor with King Sepius. Sayren glanced behind him to see Byra, Yvon, and Isabelle moving with their hands bound and armed men on both sides as they marched, "The passage is just up this way, the forest will have undoubtedly overtaken most of the markings used by royal members in the past, but I still have my tricks to find it."

Lothos laughed as he uncorked his waterskin and began to drink, "Let's hope you do. I'd hate to have to hurt your other hand. I wonder what's happened to your other companions; I'd wager they've been cornered trying to get out of the stables in a feeble attempt to run home with their tails tucked firmly between their legs."

"You'd better hope so," Isabelle barked as she gritted her teeth, "if that's not the case, you'll have no chance to survive your next encounter with them."

Lothos spurred his horse as me moved beside her and hoisted Isabelle onto her toes by her hair, "I highly doubt that, you fair-scented bitch. If you want to see your pretty house again, you'd better learn to keep your mouth shut like your little priestess behind us; otherwise you'll end up like the other nobles who couldn't shut up."

Isabelle grimaced as she nodded and Lothos released her. Sayren sniffed the air as the smell of freshly made bread floated through the air. "We're here. If you're men clear the vines away on our left then we should see stone pillars. The portal should be just beyond."

Lothos motion for the men standing behind him to begin cutting down the vegetation, and continued next to Sayren, resting his foot on Sayren's shoulder in attempt to provoke a response. "You know," Lothos started as he adjusted his foot, "with twenty men, you'd expect that even if your friends survived, they would decide against fighting against such odds.

As bits of vines and leaves fell to the dirt, the outline of weathered stone bricks began to come into shape. An old rusted gate crashed to the ground as the men cut its supporting vines, an almost clear path with low hanging branches revealed itself as it winded back towards the portal. Lothos dismounted his horse and laid Elyscia back atop the saddle before motioning for the group to proceed into the pathway, "Any tricks archer and I'll gut your healer first."

"No tricks Lothos, just an abandoned portal hidden by an overgrown gateway." Sayren said as he attempted to move his hand only to have an intense stinging pain shoot from his fingertips to his neck. He tried to focus on the metal rods still sitting on his knees, but the agony kept them motionless. Although he knew the portal was just beyond the trees, the smell of food put him on edge. Only he and his brothers should have known about the portal, meaning whoever was already there would be a force to be reckoned with.

Lothos's men began to exit the path into a vast open surrounding with waist high grass that surrounded an old derelict shack that appeared to once be a barn and a centralized circular building with many broken lanterns and flag posts. The bandits spread out as they began to smell the fresh bread and readied their weapons. Sounds of wooden boards creaking inside the building forced everyone's attention towards the thick dark wood doors as they slowly creaked open. Lothos grabbed a large cleaver slung over his back and motion for his men to move forward, "Whoever's in there, come out now or be slaughtered!"

"My, I haven't heard such uncertain ferocity in years," A familiar voice echoed from within the dark walls, "I don't believe you'd speak so boldly if you knew who you're barking at."

Lothos tightened his grip and ordered one of his men forward, "We'll see just who you are after my men drag you into the daylight!"

From within the shadowed interior, the voice began to chuckle as Lothos's men stepped towards the doorway to find Alkith standing, his mask donned, with his hand outstretched ready to strike. Alkith brought his ability to bear as he released a large blast as Lothos's men attempted to flee.

"You should know better that to anger a spirit of a fallen soldier, you raider scum. You will leave this place immediately and never return!" Alkith shouted as he stepped deeper into the shadows.

Lothos felt a strong chill run up his spine as his fleeting confidence left him with only fear. He attempted to continue to speak, but found himself speechless with a lump in his throat. While the majority of the group looked on at the building, Sayren stepped forward and called Alkith's bluff. "I've seen you before, you masked coward. You're neither a spirit nor a soldier. You lead the group that attacked Lothos's other men along the western road. Why don't you step under the sun and reveal yourself, unless you are afraid that you'll be discovered as a fraud."

Alkith laughed as he stepped forward into the doorway to the portal building, however he pointed at Lothos, "You there! I take it you are the leader of these men?"

Lothos nodded shakily as he stood frozen by fear and uncertainty.

"Very well, you must have come here with a purpose. I desire to return to King's Hold where I was slain. You will do this or suffer a far worse fate than your departed swordsmen. What will you choose?"

Sayren looked to Lothos as he locked eyes, "You cannot honestly be putting any truth into this façade of honeyed words, can you?"

Lothos regained control of himself as he felt a rage building within him, "You must be completely insane archer! If you think I'd be foolish enough to believe you over a fallen spirit that killed my men then you must have been hit much harder in the head than I thought." Lothos turned his attention to Alkith and bowed, "Oh spirit, I am deeply sorry for any offense given to you. We are on our way to King's Hold. If you wish to return than we will oblige, however I must ask that you show favor to us in return."

Alkith grinned under his masked as he looked at Sayren, "Very well, if you take me to where I rest then I shall gladly reward you. Although I must tell you that I am not the only spirit who roams King's Hold. How do you plan on taking us there warrior?"

Lothos walked over to Sayren, placed his hand against his back, and shoved him forward, "This man says he can take us there through the portal inside the building, but I'm not sure if he actually can."

Alkith flashed forward, instantly moving before Sayren as the others looked on in horror, "I see. I feel a presence from this one. He will be able to get us through the portal without difficulty. I will stay by him until we arrive at my destination. Shall we make our way?"

"Y-yes, of course, alright boys let's move for King's Hold!" Lothos shouted as he pulled Elyscia off of Toren's horse and made his way to the doorway. With muttered cheers mixed with concerned whispers, the group moved into the building. Old rafters creaked against the slightest breeze that flowed through the cracks between the worn stone bricks. Although the room was almost completely devoid of any light, the portal began to illuminate as Sayren stepped onto the portal's steps. A vibrant blue glow enveloped the room. Alkith looked over Sayren's body as the Sen Crystal adorned around his neck also glowed.

"What's going on archer?" Lothos called out as he stepped onto the main level of the portal.

"It's nothing to worry about." Sayren answered as he removed the crystal and moved towards the portal's center. He began to imagine his destination, the outer courtyard of the Royal Estate within the Alder District. A sudden shift in the air made the bandits inch in closer to one another as the symbols turned from their prior blue to a vibrant red. As the red glow began to glow brighter, Sayren open his hand, the crystal floated in air for a moment before shooting several symbols within the portal's boundaries. Sayren quickly closed his grip over the crystal as the air began to swirl and the red light began to illuminate to the point of blinding. A bright light shot into the sky as the group felt themselves being lifted upwards before landing firmly on the portal within the estate's grounds.

"Damn!" Lothos shouted as he pushed his way through the dispersing men as he looking upon the decaying estate, its grass over grown and concealing most of the manor where the royal family would've stayed. "Move yourselves! We've money to make!"

As the bandits began to pushed outwards towards the gateway, Alkith grabbed Sayren's armed and pulled him back just out of earshot, "You need to keep your allies close. Once we arrive at the governor's estate my men will be there to engage and eradicate this oaf and his cohorts. If I can separate Lothos from that woman I will try, but you'll need to have your brother assist in getting her away from him."

Sayren gave Alkith a surprised look as he scoured the area around him, "All of my brothers made it away from these men before they could be captured. None of them should be here yet. Why are you helping me?"

"I'm not helping you on purpose. I'm getting rid of a thorn in my side. Fact an Heir of Alder was dumb enough to get himself captured is mere coincidence. I simply need you to ensure my men don't cut you down to size before you are reunited with the other heirs."

"I told you before," Sayren grabbed Alkith's cloak, "I'm not the damned heir. I am a hunter and a mercenary. If you insinuate that one more time I'll rip off that damned mask and beat you bloody. Are we at an understanding?"

Alkith patted Sayren's hand away and grinned, "You wouldn't like what you find under my mask Sayren. I'm sure it would bring you nightmares."

Sayren huffed, "If any of the people I'm with are harmed, you won't have to sleep to have a nightmare, I'll personally show you fear that you couldn't imagine."

Alkith laughed as he brushed past Sayren making his way for the gate, "Not with your injuries you won't!"

With Lothos and his men combing the overgrown grounds, many of the men began to pick through the skeletal remains of soldiers who perished during the revolution. Although most of the weapons were severely damaged or eroded, many of the guardsmen for King's Hold were decorated in ornate, jeweled armor. Sayren walked over to Byra as he looked on in dismay as many of the rusted armor pieces had the same symbol as Byra's crest.

"I take it this was quite the battlefield?" Sayren asked as he paced himself with Byra.

"Aye, this was one of the worst battles during The Uprising. Although most of the royal families were at King's Rest, many of the royal servants and heroes stood with the Queen's Guard. When the fighting broke out, most of these soldiers were caught off guard and spread out, forced to fight by themselves against overwhelming odds."

"If you don't mind me asking, where were you when it all started off?" Sayren asked as they drew closer to the gate with Isabelle and Brilla walking behind them. Brilla was still very much shaken as Isabelle held her under her arm. Byra waved Yvon over as the men around him dispersed to pry through the dead bodies pinned against the walls.

"If I told you were I was located, you'd only need to look to your left at the manor. I was given the day to relax and see my newborn daughter by Queen Maree. As I left the manor the gateway flew open and the traitors rushed through the gate hoping to catch everyone off-guard. Most of those poor souls died instantly, however the rest of us tore through and held our ground until the majority of us died with the endless storm of arrows that cascaded down. We were holding the manor until the Six Winged Death made his way to us and we were able to finish off the remaining enemies within the district's walls." Byra lowered his head as he gave his respects to his fallen brothers and sisters. "It's not right that they've been left like this to rot and be scavenged for their renown. If I wasn't so old I'd give them a fight worth remembering."

Sayren patted Byra's shoulder as he pointed towards Alkith. He casually strolled between rummaging brigands making his way over to Lothos who stood with Elyscia slumped up against his leg. "Be ready," Sayren said to the others, "He's gonna cause a distraction that should force most of them to run off after him. We'll need to be ready for any of the men that stay behind."

Lothos turned his attention to Alkith with a startled expression, "What riches do you have near your resting place spirit?"

Alkith moved his hand over Elyscia, "I have the gift that gives men strength beyond reason. If you recall during the conflict within the district, Alder's Royal Guardian fell near King's Sepius's estate. Several others strong warriors fell there as well when the Six Wings lead his troops in the counter attack. What are you doing with this woman?"

Lothos choked as he attempted to swallow, "Well…she's a prize I have claimed."

"I will take her."

"Wait, what?" Lothos asked surprise. Alkith quickly launched a foot into Lothos's midsection without warning, grabbed Elyscia by the arm as she began to fall, and disappeared as he teleported away outside the compound.

Lothos leaped to his feet as his face turned red with anger, "After that slimy specter! He's off to his body at the governor's place!"

Many of Lothos's troops dropped whatever they were holding and rushed out the doorway with Lothos leading the charge, however three men remained as they eyed Isabelle and Brilla. With their weapons drawn the three moved towards the group with Sayren and Yvon moving between them ready to defend. As the first two raised their weapons into the air, the third ran one man through with his spear and threw a dagger into the other. With a puff of smoke, the figure disappeared, revealing Toren with his tome in hand.

As the bodies dropped to the ground Sayren walked over to Toren and embraced him, "Damn it Toren," smiling as he tightened his arms, "if you do that again, even a broken hand won't save you."

Both brothers laughed as they backed away from one another while Brilla rushed to Sayren, grabbing his hand and began to mend as well as she could. Although he tried to thank her, Sayren's jaw clenched from the immense pain as his bones began to reset. Yvon rushed over to the gate and pushed it closed, setting a weathered shield in the latches. As Brilla finished her attempt, Byra and Isabelle made their way over to the others, "I beg your pardon Sayren, but we need to rescue my daughter, will you be able to fight?"

"I will do whatever I can, regardless of my hand." Sayren said as he attempted to clench his fist, his fingers tingling as he reopened his hand. He had regained the majority of his movement; however he was unable to quickly move his fingers.

"Please sir," Brilla said as she placed her hands around Sayren's, "You're hand will take time to heal. If you press it, your hand may end up with permanent damage."

Sayren nodded as he reached for a sword lying in the tall grass, grasping it with his uninjured hand and start towards the gate, "I cannot promise anything priestess; I will do whatever it takes to save that innocent girl. I have a score to settle with that masked bastard as well if I get the chance."

Toren quickly followed behind as Byra proceeded over to the manor with Isabelle and Brilla, "Ladies please stay inside the house; we have no way of knowing who else may be coming through that portal and I wish to keep you both safe."

Isabelle gave the old man a look as she peered through the old doorway into the manor, "I don't mean to be a bother, but I'm not the type to sit back while others fight."

Byra grinned, "Oh, I know my dear. I am not asking you to stay for your safety, but for Lady Brilla. I have heard stories of your deeds, even this far distance away from your home. If anyone should have the misfortune of attempting to capture you, just do what you did to that merchant fellow."

Isabelle blushed as she lowered her head before nodding in agreement and taking Brilla inside, closing the doors behind them. Before returning to the others, Byra bowed his head once more for his fallen comrades before slowly dropping to a knee and pulling up the path stones. Brushing away the dried soil, the remains of cloth wrapped weapons revealed themselves. Byra pulled two of the weapons out of the dirt and removed the wrappings, one a long polearm with a standard size sword blade on the end, while the other appeared as a normal sheathed sword. After pushing the stones back into place over the other wrapped weapons, Byra returned upright and made his way to the gate, throwing the sword to Yvon as he drew close, "This is no longer practice boy. When you draw that sword, you will not be fighting with blunt wooden sticks. You will claim a life with every swing of that blade. If you aren't ready to do that, go stay with the women, but if you are, pulled back the gate and let's be off."

Yvon wrapped his hand around the leather grip of the sword and removed the sheath. Although it appeared to look like any other sword, the entirety of its shape was made from a singular piece of metal. Its sole edge made it a difficult sword for combat, however as Sayren looked at Yvon as he held the blade, he appeared to be wielding a strand of fabric flowing in a breeze. Yvon sheathed the blade and pushed the shield out of the gate's latches, "I won't stand by while my family is in danger. I will fight with you father."

Toren and Yvon pushed open the estate's gate as the portal began to glow once again, this time with Rylan, Tiberius, and Aldis standing with weapons ready as the light dimmed. Rylan looked out into the estate grounds as he saw Sayren and the others staring from the gate. Rylan rushed forward with Tiberius and Aldis scrambling to keep pace. Sayren stepped forward as Rylan closed the gap, "It's alright brother. We're all safe, except for Elyscia who was taken by the same masked man that attacked me in the woods."

Rylan slowed to a walk as he pulled his metal back into its armor shape and looked down the roadway towards the clamoring group of bandits with Lothos in the front barking in audible commands. "I am glad to see you are safe, where is Lady Isabelle and the priestess?"

"In the manor Rylan," Byra said as he stepped forward and patted his hand against Rylan's arm, "They are both safe and unharmed. I don't suppose you would know about my Yvette?"

Rylan nodded, "She was a little worse for wear, but she is safe inside her apothecary store."

Tiberius arrived at the gate with Aldis a few steps behind, clearly unprepared for the run and breathing rapidly to catch his breath. Lady Isabelle made her way over to him and embraced him as he turned to see her. "I am so relieved you are safe my lady. Are you hurt?"

Isabelle tightened her arms around Tiberius, "I am fine, just relieved to see you are unharmed."

"I will not force you to go with us Lord Tiberius, but I would be indebted to have you with us when we engage those thieves." Rylan said as he faced the nobles.

Lady Isabelle turned to see Rylan standing with his armor, the same way she had been told was the appearance of the Six Winged Death, and shrieked as she hid behind Tiberius, "What in the eight are you?" her voice filled with terror and shock.

Tiberius moved forward to Rylan and nodded, "I gave you my word we would see our family's returned safely. By my count our accord is not finished. I am with you."

Rylan bowed before turning to the fleeting figures racing towards King's Rest, "When we reach them, leave none standing. Anyone who would seek to hurt us has accepted the fate they have chosen. If that fool in the mask is around, I will handle him personally!"

CHAPTER 8

A lkith quickly flashed from place to place, staying just out of reach from Lothos and his band. He carefully beckoned them forward, ensuring their complete focus as he drew closer to the governor's manor. As he arrived, he carefully opened the wooded gate just enough to squeeze himself and Elyscia through.

After making his way through, he quickly ran up the stairs with what strength he had left and sat on the steps, setting Elyscia down beside him with her head resting on his shoulder. As Lothos and his guardsmen flung open the doors and prepared a strong line of spears and shields, Alkith raised his hand into the air, "Ah. I see you've made it Lothos. Here I thought you were slow in every sense of the word, but I see even the common stupid can hold surprises."

Lothos clenched his teeth as he allowed his anger to boil over, "The only fool here is you! You fake spirit! If you wish to die a quick death then hand over the girl now and tell me where the treasure is! You're vastly outnumbered!"

Alkith threw his head back laughing, "Oh am I?" he said as he dropped his hand. With a loud thud, the doors of the manor abruptly flew open and Alkith's trained soldiers poured out around him and formed a wall of towering shields and shimmering spears. "As I see it," Alkith mocked, "you're the one outsmarted and outnumbered. What say we make a compromise; you tell me where you have my supplies, as well as where your leader is cowering, and I'll leave you to rot in my dungeons. Otherwise my men will kill yours and you'll be the one who let them die."

Lothos grunted and motioned his hand towards a pair standing next to one another behind him, "Keat! Caros! Deal with these fools. Everyone else is to tear whatever remains to shreds!"

As the two stepped forward, Alkith threw his hand forward, commanding his troops forward. As both forces began to draw closer to one another, Caros began to generate streaks of electricity from his arms. Lothos readied his sword above his head and charged with his forces rushing behind him. Spears shattered against shields as sparks danced into the air as blades collided with one another, screams of wounded men echoed against the walls as sprays of red mist spouted into the air. Caros dodged a spear aimed for his head and instantly grabbed the wooden shaft and discharged his magic, a shriek of agony erupting for a moment before the sound of several gargled noises and the smell of burning flesh forced a small opening in Alkith's shield wall. Keat instantly leaped over her brother and forced bursts of air into the middle of Alkith's soldiers sending them staggering backwards and splitting their battle line. With his forces split, Alkith drew his blade and readied himself if he was forced to fight, "Damn it," he thought worriedly, "Where are you, you slow bastard? I didn't imagine it would take me having to fight lowborn criminals to force you out of hiding."

"Lothos!" Rylan's voice boomed over the walls as he and the others made their way in through the courtyards threshold. "I'm coming for your head, and I-" Rylan's voice stopped immediately as he saw Alkith standing with his sword drawn and the mask upon his face. His mind erupted with the blurred image of his enemy, Suthred's champion. Without a moment of hesitation Rylan raced forward and began cutting down anyone standing his path. Sayren, Tiberius, and Yvon attempted to keep pace; however the men not already engaged against Alkith's line impeded them and forced them to halt their advance to fight their way towards Lothos. Byra and Toren made their way forward as well, carefully standing shoulder to shoulder to protect one another.

As Lothos buried his sword in a fallen spearman, he turned to see Rylan rushing straight for him, without enough time to retrieve his sword; he grabbed the hatchets at his side and swung for Rylan's throat. Rylan did not attempt to block the strike, but use his metal as a platform to step over the blow and reach the empty space between him and Alkith.

"Bastard!" Lothos screamed as he attempted to strike Rylan from behind, however Rylan sidestepped the strike and sent a swift knee into the bandit captain's exposed chest, knocking the wind out of him and sending him to the ground breathless.

"I figured you'd show up sooner than you did Six Wings. What was the hold up?" Alkith smirked as he eased Elyscia onto the doorframe and began to step back into the shadows of the manors darkness.

"You're not going anywhere. If you wish to finish our business now, plague, fight me!" Rylan roar as he swarmed the doorway with metal shards shattering pottery sinking into wood resonated in Rylan's ears.

"If that was your best Rylan, you'll surely have to hope your brothers can save you." Alkith's voice beckoned from the shadows as a beam shot forth forcing Rylan to leap out of its path, nearly tripping over Elyscia.

Rylan paused for a moment before dashing through the doorway and returning his metal around him and charging straight through the manor until he burst into the central atrium where Alkith sat atop a waterless fountain watching Rylan closely. Rylan shot forth several metal rods that crashed into the fountain and forced Alkith to flash behind Rylan and send a well-aimed fist into Rylan's exposed ribs. Rylan quickly swung his axe backwards to create space, however Alkith stepped back and instantly pressed forward, thrust his sword at Rylan's throat. With only moments to block Rylan parried the strike with his sword and quickly countered with a slash of his own while cascading a swarm of shards at Alkith. Alkith dodged to the side and disappeared once again as the shards struck the wall and missed their intended target.

"I never thought it would be you that Suthred chose, you fleeing coward!" Rylan mocked as he removed the metal from around him and cast them in a wide circle around him as he gripped his weapon's handles and waited.

"What in the eight are you talking about? I am not fighting for anyone named Suthred you idiot! Clearly your time in hiding has addled your mind and the truth your refuse to accept! Now face me like the honorable boy you were when we first crossed paths!" Alkith's anger ever so slightly emerged in his tone as he spoke.

Rylan sent a handful of metal at a post near Alkith, "I have not addled, nor have I changed from how I was all those nightmares ago! I will protect my brothers and my family! You and your deceit will not harm them if I have a say!"

Alkith emerged from behind a pillar near Rylan, "Then be silent bastard!" his hand brought forth an immense beam aimed at Rylan's head.

Rylan quickly gather his metal into a shield a few steps in front of him as the magic collided and began to melt the metal. As the molten metal burned and began to fall to the floor, Alkith continued to press his attack, amplifying his blast to a smaller, more focused attack. He unfortunately failed to notice Rylan's fragments of metal flying across the atrium as they struck the stone pillar and lacerated his unprotected arm, halting the beam and forcing him to recoil for protection.

Rylan grinned at his success as Alkith grunted as he pulled a fragment from his forearm, "It's time we concluded our fight. Fall to your knees and you have my word your death will be quick."

Alkith stepped away from his cover and stood before Rylan as his metal shifted into its six wings, "I don't believe you're in the correct mindset. I didn't wish to make our battle dishonorable, but your state leads me only to concern. Halvor, Ellice, I unfortunately must ask you to step in. Stop his wings and he'll be all but defeated."

Rylan began to scan the atrium's doorways for any others standing in view, however there was no sound, no movement. A sudden chill of icy air forced Rylan to leap towards the fountain and look up to the roof where both Heirs of Ulferth stood ready as the ground beneath them began to freeze. Ice began to form down the pillars as Halvor continued his ability, forcing Alkith to join them atop the roof as all three looked down at Rylan.

"Surrender Rylan, there's no point to continuing this frivolous attempt to stand against us." Ellice stood with her arms crossed, watching Rylan's movement as he scanned the floor as the ice continued to draw nearer.

"You must be forgetting I still have my six wings" He retorted as he send his metal soaring towards them, a grin emerging from his face.

Ellice uncrossed her hands undaunted, "pity." As Rylan's metal drew close, she waved her hand and caused the humid air to freeze around the fragments and sent them plummeting down to the ground where Halvor's ice covered with another layer and held them firmly in place.

Rylan's rage began to build as he realized he had played into their trap effortlessly. See his defeat before him Rylan stuck his sword into the crack sprouting plants from under the fountain. "I yield. You make kill me now so that Suthred may claim his victory."

All three heirs looked at one another puzzled at Rylan's words, and with no idea what he meant Alkith leaped down to the ground as the ice began to recede. Alkith removed his masked as he walked over to Rylan and placed a hand on his shoulder, "What are you talking about? Who's this Suthred you're talking about Rylan? I know we've been apart for many harvests now, but I think it's finally time for you to return to your place next to all of us."

Rylan shuttered for a moment as his eyes flashed and he fell to his knees, forcing Alkith to drop his mask and grabbing Rylan's arms to secure him as he fell. Although he was motionless for a moment, Rylan gasped back to consciousness and looked up at Alkith before striking his head against Alkith's nose, "What the hell are you doing here and where are my brothers?"

Alkith slammed his fist against the ground as he felt his broken nose begin to stream blood, "You idiot! I save you and this is how you thank me? What the hell has gotten into you?"

"What do you mean you 'saved me'? I came to save Elyscia and kill that animal Lothos, but then everything is blurry. All I remember is that... that masked bastard! Where is he?"

"You're one to talk", Halvor mocked as he landed on the atrium's floor, "the only one who wears an actual mask around he is Alkith."

Alkith sighed as he retrieved his mask only to see a large crack forming from the left eye to its edge, "Damn. Halvor is right... I'm the one you saw in a mask, but you haven't answered my question, who's Suthred?"

Rylan's head ached as he attempted to remember anything past the point where his saw Alkith, "I don't know how to explain it to you at the moment. Where are my brothers and Lothos now?"

Ellice sat down atop the roof shingles, "Sounds as if they're still going at it, but the sounds have died down quite a lot so I'm not sure who's all left standing. Perhaps before we move to see what's going on, you should answer a few questions we have. It seems fair since you yielded to us."

Rylan exhaled and with a shift of his hand, the metal shards trapped inside the thick blocks of ice burst free and reformed behind him, "Don't remember doing that, nor can I afford to lose my family. If you want answers you'll have to help me with the bandits who have been attacking your supply lines."

Alkith set his mask aside and pulled Rylan's sword from the dirt, "Let's get this over and done with. We've much to discuss after Lothos has been dealt with."

❖   ❖   ❖

Sayren attempted to follow Rylan as he closed in, but the clashing forces closed his opening just as suddenly as Rylan had forced it open, leaving Sayren in close quarters with Lothos and his men. Quickly driving his sword through the closet bandit, Sayren attempted to move his injured hand and control his metal arrows, however an intense burning in his hand forced him to grimace and clutch his hand next to his chest as his arrows fell to the stone path beneath the raging battle. Two bandits turned to Sayren as he attempted to retrieve his sword and found himself trapped between them. With a nod, both enemies raced towards Sayren, but found themselves engaged by Tiberius and Yvon as they met sword with sword and held the two off long enough for Sayren to command his arrows to his unscathed hand to form a lightweight blade and reengaged. With Tiberius and Yvon now close by, the three began to make short work of the thieves as their front line continued to press forward.

Caros turned his attention to Sayren and his allies as he retracted a bloodied spear from one of Alkith's men while hurling a sword through another's chest. Keat followed suit as she used her winds to smash a soldier against the estate's wall and knocking the man unconscious. Sayren and Yvon stood on Tiberius's flanks striking at any opportunity as the thieves hopelessly attempted to strike Tiberius. A sudden bolt of lightning struck Tiberius as Caros closed the distance and landed a strong kick into Yvon's chest before either could react. Sayren attempted to catch Caros before he could defend himself, but quickly found himself propelled backwards as Keat unleashed her winds. Both bandits stood laughing as they walked further away from the fighting an approached Sayren and the others as they backed up and readied themselves, "I wondered how strong the noble would be, but it appears that he has no strength left in his winds. Maybe they should have called him 'Wall of a Thousand Breezes'.

"I do not like the fact some no-name vagabond thinks they have a nerve to address me in such a way," Tiberius growled as he readied his shield and rushed Keat.

"Where do you think you're going?" Caros grinned as he thrust his spear forward forcing Tiberius to block and instantaneously fly backwards as Caros discharged another powerful shock.

"Damn it all! Byra, Yvon, attack with me and we'll stop them now before they have another chance to attempt an insult!" Sayren ordered as he rushed forward at Caros, but as he readied another strike with his spear, Sayren turned towards Keat and attacked with his sword. Byra and Yvon quickly moved in as Caros attempted to change targets and found himself on a crumbling defensive stance with each strong blow after another from the father and son. Caros leaped backwards opposite from Keat and unleashed a massive of arc of lightning at Byra and Yvon. Without hesitation Yvon stepped forward, outstretched his hand, and absorbed the lightning directly into his hand. Caros grinned as he saw Yvon fall to a knee, his hand firmly clenched.

"Didn't your old man teach you not to interrupt adults when they're in the middle of something brat? Maybe that will learn you." Caros mocked as he readied the spear in front of him.

"I was taught a bounty of things," Yvon replied as he arose with the cloth over his arm burned away and a faint outline of darkened lines dancing atop his forearm, "he taught me how not to let lesser opponents unsettle my nerves."

Caros gritted his teeth and leaped forward, "Little bitch! I'll run you though in front of that old man!"

Yvon didn't respond, but sidestepped the spear and launched a strong, well-aimed kick into Caros's side. Caros toppled to the ground and was quickly forced to block Byra's overhead strike that nearly separated his head from his shoulders. Caros grunted at the immense pressure of Byra's strike, but quickly tossed it off to the side and swept Byra's legs out from under him, sending the old guardian crashing to the ground with a loud thud as he made contact with the stone tiles and lay motionless as Caros arose.

With his opponent between him and his father, Yvon leaped forward and attacked with an almost endless stream of fluid strikes and kicks that held Caros captive as Yvon effortlessly landed attack after attack unguarded. Caros, pained and furious, roared while unleashing several lightning bolts that cascaded down at Yvon, but the young fighter simply outstretched his hand once more and allowed the attack to connect with his hand. This time Yvon remained upright as Caros halted his attack; much to his dismay Yvon's arm was now completely covering in intricate patterns of a beast wrapping around and arcs emanating from it.

Yvon exhaled and sheathed his sword, "You rely on your skills far too heavily. If you surrender now, I can promise your life will be spared, however if you should chose not to; your life will be forfeit and damned."

Caros looked Yvon up and down, carefully contemplating whether Yvon had bluffed or was set in his serious demeanor. Looking down for a moment, he noticed Byra attempting to push himself upright; however upon seeing the old man, Caros stabbed his spearhead through Byra's right shoulder. "Tell me little boy," Caros mockingly shouted over the raging battle, "Will you still attempt to attack me with your old man impaled on my spear? If you kill your friends now then I just might let him live, otherwise I'll be force to char him into burnt ashes."

Yvon swept his hand to the side and stood undaunted. Caros aggressively discharged his lightning through the spear and into Byra's body; however the old man didn't make a sound. With his mirage suddenly disappearing, Byra stepped from behind Yvon, uninjured and readied for combat.

Byra patted Yvon on the shoulder before turning towards the remaining bandits clashing against Alkith's broken wall, "I'll leave him to you. Don't give him a chance to escape his fate."

Yvon nodded before dashing forward, Caros retrieved his spear from the ground and sent a flurry of strikes as he recoiled backwards in fear. Yvon dodged each attack with a speed that went beyond the bandit's comprehension, forcing his error to leave his defense absent, allowing Yvon to launch a strong left hook into Caros's stomach and dropping to his knees. Yvon stopped after a few steps and turned to once again face his opponent. Caros clutched his shirt as he gasped for air, his eyes filled with tears from the excruciating pain. Driving his spear into the ground and bracing against it as he stood, Caros flared his nostrils and unleashed a massive discharge of lightning, however Yvon remained undaunted, once again catching the bolt with his hand, instantly dissipating the attack as more of the design blackened into view on Yvon's arm.

Caros felt a strong presence begin to emanate from his opponent as his hair began to stand on end. Yvon began to slowly walk towards Caros, this time his eyes focused and his sword pressed back against his arm. Fearful that Yvon was about to attack Caros took aim with his spear and launched it forward at Yvon's chest. With Caros's spear soaring through the air, Yvon merely side stepped as he continued forward at a gentle pace, "You have committed your life to one foolish attack that was so poorly aimed, I didn't even have to block. Tell me, just how much confidence did you place into your last attempt?"

Caros fumbled his words as he tried to keep his demeanor, "You... you little brat... I'll... I'll break you with my lightning!"

Yvon continued forward as Caros blurted his threat, keeping his sword readied. Yvon lifted his free hand and closed it into a tight fist, "Your lightning? Do you mean your ability that I've been storing inside my body? Funny thing about our abilities, no matter how different, if you train hard enough there is a similar energy between them all. I learned the skill of my mother's bloodline that gives the ability to absorb another person's abilities and return it back without the ability to nullify it."

Caros roared as he leaped madly towards Yvon, his eyesight red with pure rage as he carelessly stepped into Yvon's striking range and found the blade running across his chest. Caros toppled to the ground screaming in pain. Yvon remained calm as he continued to mock Caros, "You're feeling your own powers work against you. It's easy to absorb energy and repulse it; however the key is to change the very fabric of the ability itself so your opponent cannot withstand their own weapon. Combine that with my sword and you'll see that there is no chance for you to win."

"Kid," Caros said as he uneasily arose to his feet, "You talk too much for a fighter; you're almost as bad as my sister and her incessant need to talk to stray animals. It's pointless when we're on the field of combat. Now come at me with all you have and let us meet our fates."

Yvon silently nodded his head and readied his sword as Caros stood, his breath heavy from his chest wound that continued to trickle a steady stream of crimson from his chest. As the sounds of the raging battle seemed to grow louder, both men rushed forward, bolts of smaller electric discharges danced behind Caros as he pulled his arms back before slamming his arms together and discharging an explosion of arching lightning, forcing Yvon to roll under while still being hit by Caros's attack, thrusting his sword upwards into his chest, and grabbing Caros's face with his free hand and discharging all of the stored magic at once. A loud scream broke the sounds of battle as all of Caros's muscles tightened to and suddenly went limp. Yvon turned to see what damage had been done by Caros's last attack, the lightning had struck down many of the combatants on both sides, however as his eyes reached the end of the strikes destructive path, Byra lay twitching on the ground. His guardian crest stained crimson from singed hole above his heart as he slowly fell to his back clutching his polesword. Yvon turned to see Sayren and Tiberius struggling to stop Keat as she glared at him from behind her winds. Without hesitation Yvon returned his gaze to Byra and the man standing over him with his sword poised above the old man's chest, Lothos was covered in blood and visibly winded, however with the majority of Alkith's troops cut down he had begun to turn his attention to his captured prey.

*   *   *

Sayren and Tiberius struggled to hold Keat back as she continued to pushed harder with her winds until the colossal gust became too much and sent both men stumbling backwards, "You bastards! I'll have vengeance for my brother!"

Tiberius looked to Caros' body as it lay still twitching from the current before turning to Sayren, "Putting her down won't be easy, although she's lacking in her skills, air is only amplified by anger. Much like a storm, she'll get much more ferocious unless we can subdue her quickly. I will do my best to counter her winds, however I would ask you to attack from her blindside and help close the distance so we may finish this foray."

Sayren nodded and dashed off to Keat's right, drawing her immediate attention, but before she could lash out at him Tiberius charged directly into her with his shield and sent her backwards until she returned her abilities and propelled herself forward. Tiberius attempted to shield himself from the oncoming blast, digging his shield into the ground as he braced behind it, however nothing seemed to happen. Tiberius checked his right to see Keat standing with a malicious smile painted on her crazed face as she cackled and shot forth a strong gust directly into Tiberius' side, denting his chest plate and hurling him through the air backwards as he bounced off the hard dirt, landing with a loud thud as he collided with a rumbled pile of stone that once resembled a statue of King Ralford.

Keat attempted to laugh, however she was forced to immediately contend with Sayren as he attacked with a flurry of strikes. Although she was fighting an injured man, Sayren's skill was still overpowering her knowledge of hand-to-hand combat. In an attempt to place some distance between them, Keat unleashed a massive burst of wind sending dirt and pebbles cascading into Sayren. Although he blocked the vast majority of the debris, many of the denser objects pelted his injured arm and unprotected stomach. Before Sayren could react, the wind suddenly stop and Keat launched her foot into his stomach and sent him to his knees as he began gasping for air, "Not so strong are you now archer?" Keat mocked as she continued to land one kick after another into Sayren's stomach. Sayren could only gasp for air as his opponent continued to attack him mercilessly until he saw Tiberius rushing towards him out of the corner of his sight.

"Sayren!" Tiberius roared as he charged head long into the fray, slashing an unsuspecting bandit that stood over one of Alkith's fleeing men and continuing forward towards Keat as she halted her attack and began to turn to face him. As she readied her free hand to unleash her next gust, a metal arrow pierced her palm and forced her to clutch it in agony as she turned back to Sayren as he sent his other arrows into her knees. Tiberius quickly took his chance to strike and plunged his blade through Keat's back as she wailed in agony, "You coward! I thought you nobles never attacked from behind!"

Tiberius twisted his sword as several audible cracks could be heard as his blade splintered her ribs, "For those who would seek to hurt any I care for, no code of honor will save you from your inevitable end!"

Keat attempted to free herself as she began to use her winds to propel herself forward; however Tiberius quickly retracted his sword, spun to gather the strongest gust he could muster, and slammed his shield into Keat's chest. She soared through the air without ever glancing the ground until she collided with the perimeter stone wall, the sound of bones shattering against rock momentarily suspended the battle as bandit and soldier alike turned to see Keat's crumpled body plummet to the ground, a mural of blood splashed against the wall. Many of the bandits stopped their attacks against the few remaining soldiers and turned their attention to Tiberius and Sayren. Tiberius quickly drove his sword into the ground and pulled Sayren to his feet, "Looks like we'll be fighting a little while longer, how many can you handle?"

Sayren looked at Tiberius, his eyes staring the noble directly into his eyes, "You must be out of your mind! I just got kicked repeatedly until you decided to actually do something and you expect me to fight more people. You're the Wall of a Thousand Winds, you fight them and I'll come help you when I'm good and ready!"

Tiberius sighed deeply as he retrieved his sword and began walking forward towards the approaching enemies, "If you need to take time to recover, princess, I'll be over here fighting to save our companions."

* * *

The sounds of clashing metal echoed through the battlefield as Lothos cut down the last member of Alkith's group before turning to see the bolt of lightning careening past him and striking Byra. He crimson stained face grinned smirked with pleasure as he saw the old barkeep fall to the ground. Clutching his sword in both hands, Lothos proceeded over to Byra and stood over him, "Any last words old man before I kill you and then your companions?"

Byra lay confused as he fumbled his weapon and began to cling to Lothos' leg, "If you wish to live, run now before you don't have legs to stand on."

Lothos laugh as he plunged his sword down into Byra's chest, "I'll survive this day you old fool. You won't though, and neither will that pretty daughter of yours!"

Byra looked back as Toren picked up Elyscia and began to back away from the battle, his eyes focused on Elyscia as she stirred. Lothos drew his gaze towards Byra's daughter and gritted his teeth as he saw Toren sneaking away with his prize. Lothos retracted his sword from Byra's chest as the old man gasped and proceeded to make his way towards Toren. A sudden roar from behind him forced Lothos to turn and block Yvon's Sword as it crashed down upon him, "Oh did I just silence your father little brat? Shall I tell you his final words?"

Yvon's rage had completely over taken his mind as he attacked recklessly. Lothos blocked each attack with ease until he saw his opening, parrying Yvon's attack and sending his fist directly against his face. Yvon stumbled, dazed by the power of the strike and sluggishly parried Lothos' advance as he began to strike with both hands, driving Yvon to a knee as the weight of the attacks were too much. Lothos laughed as Yvon drove his sword into the ground as he began to weigh upon his blade to keep himself upright. As his vision began to blur, Yvon could see Lothos drawing close readying his sword to run him through, however his eyes grew heavy as his sight turned to black and he fell to the ground. Lothos laughed heartily as he placed his boot upon Yvon's chest, "This is all you had? You little brat, you weren't worth my attention."

A sudden, loud thud from the manor forced Lothos to turn and see the door flying through the air. Reacting quickly, Lothos sliced upwards with his sword, slamming his blade into the door and sending both flying past and into a group of his men standing near Tiberius. Enraged, Lothos grabbed two finely engraved hatchets from their holsters on his side and turned to the doorway where Rylan, Alkith, Halvor, and Ellice stood with weapons drawn and ready.

"What's with you bugs? It's as if every time one of you disappears, you go and find more vermin to stand by your side!" Lothos barked as he motioned to the five men near him to engage.

"I'm insulted that you don't know when a royal steps forward, you bow and accept your fate." Ellice sad as she stepped forward, her fingers freezing over into claws of ice, "I'll take care of these petty fools who follow him; you three can handle that oaf who would insult our blood."

Lothos grunted as he felt the sting of Ellice's words echo in his head. "I'll be sure to remind you of just how royal you are when me and my men are done with you, you common whore!"

Rylan and Alkith both looked at Lothos, "You shouldn't have said that!"

Before Lothos could contemplate the meaning behind their words, Halvor leaped into the air and brought the crushing weight of his axe down at Lothos. Barely dodging the ground breaking strike, Lothos nimbly rolled out of the way and lunged at Halvor, only to find Alkith blocking his hatchets with a single sword, "Perhaps you should learn who we are since you're about to die. I am Alkith Kay, Heir to Kay!" Alkith finished his words with a strong knee into Lothos' stomach, doubling over and forcing him backwards. Halvor quickly followed up with his next attack, slicing horizontally at Lothos' middle. Lothos blocked the attack, catching Halvor's axe and trapping them in his hatchets. Lothos grinned as he attempted to press his advantage, but found himself on the receiving end of Halvor's head as he struck Lothos directly on the bridge of his nose, "I am Halvor, the rightful Ulferth in the north!"

Lothos released his weapons as he covered his face, blood streaming from his nose as he recoiled in pain. He opened his eyes, to see the blurry outline of Rylan standing before him, his six wings in full display for all to see. "I am Rylan, the Six Winged Death. My brothers and I make up the Heirs to Alder's Throne. You have sought to harm members of both royal houses and their subjects. Punishment for such an action is death, several times over. With the heirs of both Kay and Ulferth present, your death will be carried out immediately. Let this serve as a lesson to all who seek to harm true royals, you will never succeed."

As Rylan readied his metal as Lothos backed himself against the stone wall and concealed a small dagger inside his sleeve. Rylan walked forward, his metal forming two separate swords primed to sever Lothos' head from his shoulders. As Rylan reached Lothos, the bandit took his chance and lunged forward at Rylan, thrusting his dagger into Rylan's unprotected stomach. Lothos grinned, "Looks like The Six Winged Death will be killed by the smallest piece of metal. What will you do now Rylan? Will you beg for me to kill you quickly?"

Rylan lowered his head down onto Lothos' shoulder as he slowly exhaled. A silence flooded the courtyard as Rylan stood resting against Lothos, "Actually," Rylan whispered into Lothos' ear as he stepped back to reveal His other wings had encased Lothos' hand, "You'll beg me to end this quickly."

With a cold stare that could only be matched by Halvor's ice, Rylan began to work, stabbing both blades through Lothos' knees, before crushing the bandit captain's hand along with the blade. Lothos wailed in agony as he felt the metal compress and his bones began to shatter. Drawing two new blades from his remaining metal, Rylan plunged them into Lothos' arms and drove both into the stone mortar. With his body contorted, Lothos begged, "Please stop this!"

Rylan's blank stare gave his answer. Rylan gathered what shards were left and sent them into the air only to bring them cascading down onto Lothos, defenseless to the onslaught of raining metal barbs that tore through him and drove themselves into the crimson soaked dirt. After a few cries of undiscernible pleas, Lothos fell silent and Rylan returned his metal behind him as he reset his six wings. Rylan turned to see Alkith standing with an all too familiar grin on his face, the same smile he wore whenever he had tricked someone into doing his bidding. Ellice stood next to Halvor, her finger tips coated in deluded blood from her icy talons. All three heirs walked over to Rylan and nodded, "Well then," Alkith said as he surveyed his complete loss of his detachment, "Now that the thorn in my side has been dealt with, we come to our next matter at hand; what shall become of your noble sponsors?"

Rylan placed a hand over his sheathed blade, "They will see the fulfillment of the contract we have with them and they shall return to Dalkas, unharmed. As will my brothers and I, unless you wish to finish what your ambush attempted."

Alkith ran his fingers through his sapphire hair, "You seem to forget that you surrendered to us. You don't have a say on what we decide."

"I fear you will have more to contend with than just myself if you should decide another fate for them." Rylan's tone was firm, but maintained a calm demeanor as he conveyed his statement.

Halvor stepped forward and placed his hand on Rylan's shoulder, "Before anything is decided, you should see to your companions."

As Rylan turned to his allies, his heart sank as he saw Yvon and Elyscia kneeling over Byra with Tiberius and his brothers standing quietly behind them. Rylan sank his metal into the ground and raced over to Yvon's side, Byra's pale cold hand reaching out for his. Rylan gingerly placed Byra's hand in his, "You were supposed to outlive me old man, now whose going to give me grief for all the trouble I try to get into?"

Byra grinned, lightly tightening his grip on Rylan's hand, "You protected our family, I couldn't have asked for a stronger leader. I am sorry I could not see you take your father's place. It would have truly been a sight to behold."

"You and I both know that I would never be king." Rylan replied grimly.

"Your father would always ask me, 'what makes a good king?', and every time I would say 'his actions, not his blood'. Just because you have Alder's royal blood running through you doesn't make you a king, your sense of duty and justice makes you more worthy that the snake sitting on the throne." Byra's voice grew soft as he finished and began to cough.

Rylan turned to Yvon, "You're father is a good man, stay with him and I will see he is taken care of."

Yvon's face streamed with tears, "It's my fault. I dodged the lightning that hit him, if I could've-"

Rylan pulled Yvon's face into his chest, "The battlefield is not a place of life, or second chances. If you take up arms, you cannot chose when you will live or die, but you can choose to fight and protect those you care about. Your father has fought for many years, don't let his last moments be of his son crying as he faces an honorable end to his journey. Tell him you are proud to be his son. Tell him you are proud to call him your father and your teacher."

Yvon composed himself and took Byra's hand as Rylan released him, gave Byra one last nod, and moved over to Sayren. As Elyscia and Yvon continued to talk with their father, Rylan, Sayren, and Toren stepped to the side as Rylan began to explain the heir's sudden appearance.

"I don't know how I'm to properly explain this to you," He started as he adjusted his armor, "to put it simply, the three people behind us are royal heirs to the kingdoms of Kay and Ulferth. That masked individual you both saw on our way to Havenhome is Alkith, the oldest son of Kay's Royal Bloodline, while the other two are heirs of Ulferth, named Halvor and Ellice."

Sayren looked Alkith up and down before returning to Rylan, "That man tried to kill us and you're telling us that he is a Royal Heir? What are those three doing here, and why are they helping us?"

Rylan sighed, "It is hard to explain, however we are heirs to Alder's throne."

"How was that hard to explain?" Toren responded.

"It's not as simple as you'd expect. When the uprising happened, you were both young and stuck with Queen Maree as Byra and I repelled those that sought to kill us all. King Ralford, our father, fell to Lord Gaius LeBlanc before we could reach him with his remaining guard. Once the city was retaken I sat with the other heirs and discussed how we should handle the affairs, however with no known supporters and few loyal soldiers left, it was decided that all heirs would go into hiding. It was a different time and I was still very angry. I made a pact that once an heir felt they had enough power, they would return to King's Hold and begin to amass and army to take back our homes. When we escaped, Sayren became very sick and we were forced to turn to allies within Dalkas, hiding among nobles, and remain in the shadows. Although Sayren recovered, we were forced to split up and find our own means of power. It wasn't until I found Bansel of the Silver Dragoons, was I able to return to find Byra and my metal. Since then I have fought to keep our family out of Sepius' sight. With the other heirs already here though, I was asked to join them, but each time I refused, simply because we had a life and no need for royal blood. I kept this from you because we have never needed power outside of ourselves to survive. Whatever happens, I only ask that we return with Tiberius and Isabelle. They will not sell us out and we'll be able to continue our simple lives."

Rylan's words held firm in Sayren's heart, his peace of mind that he had known for all his life only made sense to maintain, however Toren's mind drown him to thoughts of potential power, "You mean we've been royals this entire time and you've kept it from us because you didn't want to take what's rightfully ours?"

Rylan looked Toren directly in his eyes, "Would you have our family fight the entirety of Alder's armies? Or perhaps fight Lord Gaius LeBlanc, and his noble guardsman that have trained to kill us since they enlisted? Maybe you feel that we would be better fighting the Metal Serpent and his son?"

Toren chocked on the lump forming in his throat as Rylan's tone unsettled his nerves. With the daunting task of any one of those options he began to realize the sizable task any one of those would be to accomplish. Toren attempted to responded, however he was surprised when Alkith suddenly appeared beside him, "Sorry to interrupt this little bonding moment, however we are going to need to talk to the heir of Alder."

Rylan gave Alkith an angered look, "I've already told you I won't bring my family into this."

"Oh no," Alkith waved off Rylan's comment as he swung his arm around Sayren, "Although you may be the eldest son of Ralford, you are not the legitimate heir. No bastard son can hold that title if he is not accepted by a noble court. As records show up to the uprising, you were never taken before any court or council, first legitimate son of Ralford and true heir to Alder's throne is Sayren."

Rylan leaped forward, tackling Alkith to the ground as he reared his fist, only to have it caught by Sayren, "What does he mean?"

Rylan attempted to wrench his arm free, but Sayren's demeanor had changed, "This is no time to discuss this! We need to leave hear before we are caught up in all of their dealings. Believe me when I tell you this is not the life you want for our family."

"I don't think that's your decision to make any longer, brother." As his cold words echoed into Rylan's ear, Sayren grabbed his brother's leather gambeson, throwing him backwards, and extending a hand to Alkith.

Alkith smirked as he latched onto Sayren's hand to help him stand. After dusting himself off, Alkith turned to Tiberius with Sayren close behind, "And who might you be?"

Tiberius bowed, "I am Lord Tiberius Bernak, Heir to the Bernak House, known as the 'Wall of A Thousand Winds'. It is a pleasure to make your acquaintance, Prince Alkith of Kay."

Caught almost completely off guard, Alkith gave Tiberius an odd look before chuckling, "Ah," he said with a cheery tone, "I see you were paying attention when we dealt with that last bandit. I don't believe I've given you enough credit Lord Tiberius; you are a true noble, I can only imagine what you observe within the confines of court."

Tiberius gave a simple wave of his hand, "I am unfortunately no politician sir, I am merely observant on the field of battle. I must ask that you pardon Lady Isabelle, Lady Brilla, and I; we are merely seeking to gain Lady Isabelle's approval of King Sepius to become a Hero of Alder."

Alkith raised his hand quickly to stop Tiberius, "You'll have to excuse my rudeness, however I do believe I heard you say King Sepius, am I correct?"

"You did," Tiberius nodded, "Although his claim may not be legitimate with King Ralford's sons still alive, he is still the one that sits upon the throne in Dalkas. I must serve my family, as they serve

House Vasilli. I do not wish to place Lady Isabelle into the middle of royals as they fight for their proper place on the throne."

Alkith nodded in agreement, "I would not condone such action either. Heroes of any kingdom must be seen as defenders of common folk, not elite forces for a king. If you don't mind me asking though; what is it that she was tasked with finding?"

Tiberius glanced over towards Rylan as he pressed off the ground and began patting himself off. "We were tasked with finding Alder's Ring."

Sayren and Alkith both turned to Rylan, "Where is it?" Sayren said as he marched up to his brother. "I know we have it, you've kept a ring on you as long as I can remember."

Rylan moved away from his brother and stopped next to Tiberius, "I'll give you the ring, but you must promise me you'll never speak of any of this to anyone. Although it looks like a simple ring, it bares the power of all rulers of Alder. Whatever may happen, Sepius must not wear it. If he does his power will outmatch even my own."

"...Stop," Byra's weak voice called out as Yvon and Elyscia carried him over to Rylan, "You are the rightful heir you fool. Your father acknowledged you before the uprising; the sage was never able to transcribe it into the records... but I kept... the parchment. You'll... have to find it if you truly wish to protect your family. It's... it's..." Byra's voice fell to a whisper as his body went limp and his head slumped against his chest.

"What did the old man say?" Alkith's inquiry fell on deaf ears as Rylan embraced both of Byra's children before reaching for the small bag containing the ring and tossing it to Tiberius, "Take it Tiberius, I want no more of any of this. I will deliver you and the ladies back to Dalkas tomorrow. Sayren," Rylan's defeated tone carried throughout the courtyard as he bowed, "You are the heir to Alder. I will see the nobles back to their homes and collect your family, all I ask is that you keep our family protected and together, regardless of how you wish to proceed."

Alkith chimed in with an overjoyed tone as he wrapped his arms around Sayren and Toren, "What say we return to King's Rest for a meal and some much deserved relaxation?"

Toren's eyes shimmer at the notion of food and rest, his head bobbing excitedly; however Sayren held a blank stare as Rylan and the others proceeded to exit the courtyard carrying his forgotten childhood guardian out to be laid to rest. His mind raced as he contemplated his actions; was his quick reaction against his brother senseless, or was it proper for the Heir of Alder?

CHAPTER 9

As Sayren and Toren entered King's Rest, the outside desolation of Alder's district seemed to immediately disappear and the stunning beauty of the lavish courtyard in the setting sunlight. With Ellice and Halvor walking at a quickened pace, Alkith remained by both brothers as they stood in awe. Trees trimmed properly with lanterns hung from the branches, precise stone walkways without tarnish or blemish that withstood the patrols marching over. A calming presence washed over Sayren as he recalled blurred images of nobles parading about laughing and joking. His memory, although very obscure, was slowly returning as he gazed upon the weathered banner of Alder swayed in the calm breeze. For the first time he could recall the sight Ralford as he stood pointing at the different standards of each kingdom while Maree stood holding Aldis in her arms and a very young Toren clinging to her dress.

"So tell me what you think of all this?" Alkith asked as he moved through Sayren's memory and returned him to reality.

Alkith ran his fingers through his hair, "I can recall this place now, the way it was before the uprising with my family. I don't understand though, how were you able to retake such an enormous place? A handful of men pushing out the entirety of the uprising forces all those harvests ago?"

"It was not an easy task," Alkith started as he placed his hand on Alkith's shoulder, "We barely had a hundred men for each kingdom, many of which were injured or so impacted by the horrors of their king's falling, they could do nothing more than wet themselves and cower in fear. It was through sheer luck that Rylan was able to wield your father's metal with his own. The guardians decided to stand on the offensive to protect the main heir's, and a unified decision to sally forth to meet our foes together that gave us the victory. With barely any knowledge of commanding, each of us was thrown headfirst into combat to survive and save those that we cared for. I couldn't tell you what your brother or the other heirs had to fight through, however with every corner in Kay's district, I continued to press forward, cutting down men two to three times my age. I was young and scared, but I knew that if I didn't, my men would not stand behind me and we would surely die that day. I could not let that fate befall my sister or my mother. For all the atrocities I committed that day, I knew that it was for a cause greater than just my name. Each of the heirs had to prove that even though each king had fallen, the next in line were far more than capable of meeting the challenges that we faced and overcoming them. After the walls were secured and I returned, your family had left along with Epharth's Heir, Elwarth, and Parthus' eldest, Alessia. There was a letter addressed to us though sitting on the main table of the King's Court table. 'When the time comes, we will stand together again and retake our blood rights.' That was the oath each of us took before we left this place, an oath to grow stronger than we were on that day and gather the strength we needed to once again take our family's place on the throne."

Sayren listened to Alkith's story as he recalled lying in his bed, sweating through his sheets and his body feeling as if it were on fire; sounds of screaming men and clashing metal echoing from the far reaches of King's Hold into his window. He could hear the wails of his mother from outside the door as the hand maidens scurried around the room like rats in the open, each tending to Toren as he kicked and screamed to see his father while Aldis cried out from his interrupted nap. Each moment that passed felt like an eternity as Sayren lay sick, until the door burst open with a young, blood-soaked Rylan standing in the doorway with Byra standing close behind comforting Queen Maree.

"It took eight harvests for Naria and I to recruit a sizable force to recover a town, however we were severely over matched in the way of supplies and we lost our guardian. After we returned here to find only Halvor and Ellice, I set out to gain new allies across the sea," Alkith's voice fell soft as he remembered his travels, "It took me what seemed like an eternity to find another suitable ally that was willing to assist us. Once I arrived at a continent far larger than ours, it was ruled by a single empire; however the lands were separated to ruling houses that answered to one specific ruler. I was able to convince them through some very longwinded discussions that they should aid us in our reclamation and in return they would have the rights to set up a post in Kay, as well as send both goods and men through without problem."

Sayren looked at Alkith curiously as he finished, "You gave them entrance into Thesia? Do you realize how long it has been since foreign troops have ever landed here?"

"I do, however I realized that without Kay's or Alder's main forces, we'll be lambs to the slaughter. We needed support if we enter open conflict with them. Even if we only use them to defend King's Hold and our families; our forces will never amass a large enough quantity to win against either kingdom." Alkith's voice grew bold as he waved off Sayren's notion of danger.

Sayren continued to press his point, "If we allow them here, who can know what they will bring with them. On top of supplies needed, there is also the fact you're the only one that knows anything about them. I could not base my assurance that they will land and not have other intentions by your word alone."

Sayren's voice began to escalate, drawing the attention of some of the troops around the courtyard, forcing Alkith to pull Sayren close to him and whisper, "No one but the heirs know of this plan. I would prefer to keep concealed to avoid any wandering ears of the other kingdoms catching wind and reporting it back to their masters. I will personally give you the same guarantee that I did for the other heirs; our allies, the Idrailian Empire, have promised to send us enough men to retake Kay. Once we do that, we'll have enough combined strength to challenge Alder and finish the war."

Although not convinced, Sayren agreed with Alkith that affairs of such importance should stay between the heirs. As they continued towards the inner doorway, the large doors slowly open and revealed Naria walking with Luca clutching her hand tightly.

Halvor, Ellice, and Naria all bowed to one another as they crossed paths; however Naria halted as she looked past the other heirs and saw her brother with the two men standing next to him. Alkith bowed to Naria, motioning for Sayren and Toren to follow suit. Naria returned the bow and proceeded over to Alkith, "Are these men of ours? I don't recall seeing them before."

Alkith chuckled as he embraced his sister and kissed her check, "No my dear sister, these are the sons of Alder. I don't suppose you'd remember Sayren or Toren since you all were still very young at the time."

"I recall exactly who they are," Naria smiled as she looked at both brothers before passing Luca off to Alkith and hugging both firmly, "I can't believe it has been so long since we've seen one another. Tell me, what has Rylan been doing these past years?"

"He's been doing just fine; he had neglected to tell us about this part of our lives though. We've parted way for a while until he completes his travels with a pair of nobles and returns with our youngest brother Aldis and my family." Sayren replied as he returned the smile before gesturing towards Luca, "Who might this strapping young fellow be?"

Before Naria could explain, Alkith interjected, "He's mine actually. A bit of an odd turn of events for me, however he's becoming quite the skilled fighter even at such a young age."

Sayren nodded in agreement, "Sounds like Rylan; he was a fighter ever since he was young and never wasted a single moment to have fun. I preferred to lay about instead of practice though."

They all began to laugh except for Toren, who stood just outside of the conversation fiddling with the tome inside his satchel, carefully watching the glares of soldiers as they passed by. "I apologize for interrupting," Toren bowed as he moved closer, "would it be possible to continue this inside so we may eat, I'm famished."

Sayren laughed as he placed his arm around Toren and nodded in agreement, "That would be quite wonderful. I need to see how my hand is doing; do you have a healer in King's Hold by chance?"

"Certainly," Naria replied as she retrieved Luca from Alkith and gave him a momentary glare of disapproval before continuing, "We'll see to it you return to Alder rooms and my personal herbalist will see to your hand. What happened to it?"

Sayren smirked, "A very unfriendly fellow that didn't particularly like my arrows silencing his men. He decided that the most effective way to impede my marksmanship would be to crush my hand. I was taken care of by a healer earlier, however it was a rushed attempt."

"Then it's settled," Alkith said as he turned towards King's Rest's main doorway, "let's get you both moved in. Dinner should be ready soon so you'll be able to sit down and meet with the others. We'll have much to discuss tonight now that all of the heirs have returned."

Sayren patted Toren's shoulder before moving alongside Alkith as they continued to discuss what had taken place since the days following the uprising, Toren still following behind the others with his hand on the tome, his nerves unsettled by the number of soldiers about, watching his every move.

❖   ❖   ❖

With Byra's body lying against the royal estates outer walls, Yvon stood with Rylan and Tiberius while Isabelle, Brilla, Aldis all attempted to comfort Elyscia as she wailed uncontrollably over her father's cold body. While the sun continued to plummet closer to the horizon, Rylan paced back and forth while Tiberius stood with his arms crossed, "what will you do now Rylan? With your brother taking the throne, you know you won't be able to remain in Dalkas."

"I know," Rylan replied as he continued to walk, "this puts everything at risk. He's chosen to take power and pride over the safety of his family. This is exactly why I didn't want to join with the other heirs."

Yvon, holding his father's polesword, lifted his head, "It's beyond what you can do at this point. If Sayren has decided to take his place as the heir to Alder's throne, you should support him as his brother. However you should finish the task at hand. Once Lord Tiberius and Lady Isabelle have returned to Dalkas, I would say to collect your things and return to your brother's side."

"That will be difficult," Rylan replied as his head sank, "I lied to my brothers to keep them safe. If I were to return I'm sure I will never be held in the same regard, but staying in Dalkas only ensures that Sepius will be one step closure to eliminating all of my father's heirs."

Tiberius glanced over to Isabelle as she held Elyscia close, tears flowing for one of her protectors. "I cannot say that it will be easy,"

168

Tiberius began as he turned Alder's ring over and over in his hand, "if we return any King Sepius retrieves what you've held in your possession for so long he will wish to know how it came to pass and will certainly desire to speak to the man who found it. If you have any enemies within the noble court, they will surely turn against you and call to light the absence of your brothers and any other family-"

"Damn!" Rylan cursed as he clenched his fist, "We need to leave now! If that bastard Kraste has returned he could send men after Sayren's wife and daughter. I do apologize to both of you, but I cannot risk delaying our return any further. Aldis! Come over here!"

Rylan's sudden shouts startled everyone; Aldis began to race towards his brother before tripping over the tall grass. As he arose and brushed himself off, Aldis quickly moved to Rylan's side, "what's wrong brother?"

"I need you to listen carefully," Rylan started as he placed his hands on his younger brother's shoulders, "Sayren and Toren are at King's Rest. I need you to go to them and tell them you are Aldis Bassadora, youngest son of Ralford. Your brothers will explain why when you arrive, however I need you to pass on a message. Tell them that I've gone to finish my contract with House Bernak and retrieve our remaining family. I fear that the Fang may make a move against them before we return."

Aldis looked to Yvon and Tiberius before slightly bowing and stepping away from Rylan, "Very well, I wish you a swift journey. Lord Tiberius I do hope you have many good years ahead of you, and Yvon I am sorry for your loss. Your father was a very good man for what little I was able to know him."

"Thank you, young sage. Peace be with you and your brothers." Tiberius bowed slightly as he moved over to Isabelle.

Yvon stepped forward and embraced Aldis before following Tiberius, Rylan nodded to Aldis before watching his brother adjust his bag and take his staff in hand as he proceeded out of the gateway.

With Aldis now away from the group, Rylan turned his attention to his noble companions, ensuring to maintain enough space between him and Elyscia as she slowly released her grip on Isabelle and clutched Yvon as she continued to stream tears down her face. Tiberius lifted

Isabelle to her feet and handed her the ring, folding her fingers over the warm metal. She looked him in the eye then back to Rylan, her eyes although pained filled with rage as she rushed forward screaming, "How could you? You, the Six Winged Death, you let him die and now attempt to stand before us! If you hadn't disappeared, Alder would be different and this wouldn't have happened! I hate you!"

Rylan quickly readied himself as Isabelle drew but a few steps away and pushed her hands forward, cascading bright violet flames outwards in such a vast area Rylan could not dodge. With little time to react, Rylan pulled his metal from the ground into an angled wall, forcing the flames to fall to either side. Although Rylan was not directing burned by the blaze, the immense heat emanating from Isabelle's rage felt as if Rylan had stepped into the middle of a raging forest fire. Although Rylan did not wish to hurt her, he had no other option but to draw his sword and readied himself to strike. "Stop this now!" Tiberius roared as he pushed a crushing wind at Isabelle with only his open palm, although Isabelle's flames were burning at such a high degree, Tiberius' winds dissipated them and forced Isabelle to guard herself from the unceasing winds. With Rylan seizing his opportunity, he quickly dashed around his scorched metal and planted his feet into the ground with his sword pointed directly at Isabelle's unprotected side. Tiberius halted his attack and rushed forward, but stopped when Rylan outstretched his hand, motioning for him to stop. "Lady Isabelle," Rylan's voice conveyed calmly as he held the edge of his blade a hair's width from her ribs, "I cannot change what has happened. My father did not intend for an uprising, nor do I ever plan to pursue a tainted throne. I have lived my life to hold what family I have left together. Lord Tiberius has agreed that upon your return and presentation of the ring, we will part ways and you will not see me again. I have done many things in my life that have given me much strife; however I cannot simply stand by while my remaining family is in danger. We will return to Dalkas, and once we enter the city you, Lord Tiberius, and Lady Brilla will precede to your destination while I go to mine. I gave you that ring because I saw in you the chance to be more than just a noble hero, but a champion of the people and their voice against a corrupted false king. If you cannot be that, then return to me the ring and return to being a simple commoner with the power to protect those around you. I will not force you to do either, such would not my place. You have a great tutor in Lord Tiberius and he will teach you how to wield your greatest power; your voice."

Isabelle glared at Rylan as she stepped away and moved towards the portal, "Very well." Her angered tone echoed as she stomped away, fist clenched around the ring, "Let us be off and conclude this business."

Tiberius motioned to Brilla as she stood shaking at the events that had just unfolded before her eyes, "The Six Winged Death lives." She murmured moving to Tiberius's side and proceeded to the portal without a further sound.

Yvon called out, "Rylan!" as he waved him down.

Rylan proceeded over, sheathed his sword, and once again burying his metal wings into the ground, "Will you stay here to bury your father?"

"Aye," Yvon replied as he eased Elyscia off of his chest, "Please see that she makes it back home and helps our mother until I can return to bring them here."

Rylan shook his head, "I will see her home. Once you have finished go to King's Rest and get one of my brothers to return you. We are indebted to your father and will honor his name for his sacrifices throughout his many years."

Even with the prior night's events, Elyscia clasped her arms tightly around Rylan's chest and buried her head. Rylan gently placed his arm around her and proceeded to the portal, pulling his Sen Crystal from his pouch. As he stepped onto the portal, Rylan looked over to King's Rest in the distance and pondered what had made Sayren react in such a way. After a momentary pause of recalling the look upon Sayren's face, he pushed the discontent out of his mind and focused on returning to Dalkas, not to mention the process of explaining everything to Abigail. As he tightened his grasp on the crystal, his mind recalled Byra's last words on his legitimate claim to the throne. As the winds kicked up around him he felt Elyscia whimper, "Dad..." before the flash of light erupted around them and they were off.

❀   ❀   ❀

A calm breeze gently rustled the leaves around the abandoned forest portal; birds chirped their afternoon melodies to wild deer that grazed on the remaining berries still populating the area. With the portal awakening and the sudden emergence of the cascading light, most of the wildlife dispersed immediately, turning the symphony of sounds into a muted, lush landscape. As Rylan emerged with the nobles behind him, he carefully scanned the surroundings, wary of the lull that blanketed his ears. With Elyscia pinned to his side, Rylan was unable to draw either of his weapons; however he cautiously motioned the group to follow as he exited the doorway and continued across the overgrown space between them and the exit. Tiberius stayed close behind the others as he watched the rear in case of another bandit force awaiting their return, however there was nothing to be seen or heard.

"Tiberius," Rylan waved his hand forward as he approached the gate, "Take Lady Isabelle and Brilla first. I want to say something to Elyscia before we return to the village and make our return to the capital."

"We will await you at the edge of the woods, do be quick though." Tiberius replied as he moved to the front and began pushing branches aside from Isabelle and Brilla as they made their way to the road.

Elyscia pried her tear stained eyes away from Rylan's chest before sulking.

"Please Elyscia," Rylan said as he placed his hand under her chin and lifted her eyes to meet his, "I need you to be focused for whatever may happen next."

Elyscia wiped her eyes as she attempted to compose herself. Her hands quivered as she reached up for Rylan's hand; however Rylan stepped away as she did, "Why would you move away from me?"

Rylan bowed his head, "I made a promise to your father that I would not bring any of you into this madness. Even when I saw you the last time, I knew you were the most beautiful woman I had ever had the chance to grow with, but I could not bring myself to betray your father after all he had done and given up just for my brothers and I."

Suddenly enraged Elyscia lashed out at Rylan, "After all this time! You left me and my family the day after my birthday, I stayed up all night with my sister because of how madly in love with you we both were and you left before either of us could see you! We thought that you hated us! Even after Laelia was taken from our home, I wrote you letter after letter for you to return and save her! You never came back! I hated you for abandoning us; I hated you for abandoning me! Did you even care?"

Rylan was stunned by her accusations for a moment before collecting himself and maintaining his calm tone, "I never received those letters Elyscia, had I known that she had disappeared I would've dropped everything and returned. I can only imagine what happened to you through all that. I can't go back to fix everything, however I didn't feel that I, nor Byra, would've allowed me to return only to fall entirely for you. I could not protect you back then, and now I have little choice in whatever becomes of our lives. When I leave, you need to bring your mother here and remain hidden until your brother returns. Once he brings you back to King's Hold you should decide what you want to do with your life. If you wish to stay, it will not be easy and you will live in danger until all of this has concluded, but if you wish to start new somewhere else, then I beg you not to hesitate."

"And what about you, will you runaway too?" Elyscia asked as she calmed herself after a deep breathe, "Or will you stay and fight with your brothers?"

Rylan gave a heavy sigh as he looked about, "I'm not entirely sure myself. I cannot leave my brothers to survive, however once it is discovered that all of Thesia's heirs have reunited to retake their thrones, I will not be safe to wander the roads of my home."

"Then let's run away and never look back. If we leave together once you return, we'll never have to deal with the politics of this world and we can be truly happy together." Elyscia's eyes sparkled as she began to dream her words into reality.

Rylan leaned in and kissed Elyscia's cheek gently as he wrapped his arms around her and whispered, "If only that were possible, I would go with you in a heartbeat. That future can never be, we each must choose our paths, and I fear they will not intertwine. For that I am most regretful; however I can only hope that it will save you heartbreak that faced my family. Please be safe in whatever you choose. If you see Sayren, please give him this and tell him to claim his right."

As Rylan backed away, he laid the axe at Elyscia's feet as her eyes began to tear up again. She maintained her composure long enough for Rylan to bow, turn towards the road, and disappear into the forest. Her heart sank to an unimaginable depth as she felt alone once again, her illusionary future shattered. Elyscia fell to her knees as she clutched herself and silently screamed as Rylan emerged onto the road with Tiberius and the others.

"Will she be alright by herself?" Tiberius asked as he pointed back towards the abandoned portal, "She's already lost her father and we're leaving her to return on her own."

Rylan's dismayed appearance gave Tiberius his answer, "We have no other choice. Should any remaining bandits remain at the town, they'll surely attack us on sight. I would not endanger her. Bandits would never risk losing a chance to get a heavily laden purse. Once we return, if we make it through the town, we'll head to the stables and grab the remaining horses to make our journey back."

Isabelle, realizing Rylan's axe was now missing from his back, proceeded over to his side, "I must know before we continue any further together; Why do you not retake the throne that is rightfully your family's?"

"I only want peace for all of Alder." Rylan responded as he looked to the golden rays of setting sunlight as they pierced through the trees.

"You mean you would let your people starve, children traded, and women raped, all for a peace? How can you say such farce knowing that the people you should protect are disregarded by the man on the throne? Would you simply stand in the shadows as we are tortured for pleasure of fat nobles who see nothing wrong with what they're doing?" Isabelle's enraged tone began to grow louder with each breath as she stood directly in Rylan's path, forcing him to answer.

"I must." Rylan answered calmly as he remained unmoved, "If I or my brothers attempt to retake the throne, the lands would be torn into chaos, with brother fighting brother, families murdered or displaced simply because of where they reside. I would not see such needless bloodshed for a more pointless reason as a title. I gave you that ring to do what I cannot. Each time you have stood up for yourself and others you protected, you show courage needed in a true Hero. Anyone can hold a title for the power it gives, but few can match what the title means. Lord Tiberius is a soldier, but holds the title of Noble. He could be like the men and women you mention that would do terrible things to those beneath him, but he upholds the honor and duty instilled in him from his upbringing. He makes a difference that I could not make without putting honorable men and women like him at risk of falling prey simply because of his nature. I will not be the cause of such bloodshed in my home; that is why I choose peace. That is why I choose to stand aside for a terrible king, not because he has power, but because he is powerless without the people that surround him. Now do you understand why I cannot interfere with my birthright? It pains me every time I see a family torn apart by the terrors that hold Alder within its grasp; however, I do not have the power to change our path without turning our home into a battlefield of death and loss. I hope you can understand why things must be why they are."

Isabelle stood silent for a moment, she minded astonished by Rylan's explanation. "I understand..." She responded after a few moments of silence before backing away, "I apologize for acting like such a child. I'm unable to fathom how you must feel in your position, but I will not let our people suffer at the hands of such monsters once I become Hero. You have my word."

Rylan began to walk forward without the slightest acceptable, his mind raced with atrocities committed in the name of the crown and struggled to keep his mind on the task at hand. Tiberius silently followed as he watched Isabelle sigh before making way towards Havenhome. Brilla silently trailed behind the others, carefully watching Rylan with such intensity, that even Rylan himself could feel the glare burrowing a hole through his leather. Although the afternoon roads were clear, a feeling of eyes watching them from just behind the cover of the trees filled the group with unease. Rylan noticed sets of wheel indentions stood out along the edges of the road; however the patterns of hooves vastly outnumbered any cart he had seen pulled before. Rylan began to ponder, "There must be more patrols going through this area or several other groups have tried to make their way to King's Hold."

With the outline of the walls focusing into view, amber rays of sunlight concealed the wooden parapets. As Rylan and the others approached the gates, a voice called out, "Halt! Why do Nobles of Alder approach without a steed or house sigil?"

Tiberius stepped forward to confront the voice, "I am Lord Tiberius Bernak, we have returned from our journey and seek entry. What business is it of a common wall guard to question a Noble?"

A familiar chuckle erupted from the man atop the walls as Rylan slowly gripped his sword's hilt, "Who said I am common rabble, Tiberius? I am one of many hands of King Sepius. My name is Inquisitor Mauro LeBlanc and I've come to find the man you recruited to guide you to King's Hold. Where is Rylan of The Six Crows?"

Keeping his calm demeanor, Rylan released his sword and stepped forward, "I am here Lord Mauro, what would make you seek me out so far from Dalkas?"

As Rylan finished speaking the gate swung open and noble militia men poured forth, surrounding him with weapons drawn and readied. "What's the meaning of this inquisitor?" Tiberius shouted angrily.

Mauro slowly emerged from behind the wall and made his way to the group, "My Lord Tiberius, you have quite the disconcerting tone, are you with the mercenary?"

Tiberius clenched his fist, "No." His voice angered at the notion, "I am not fond of men working for me to be detained without reason. So tell me, Inquisitor Mauro, why have your men pointed their weapons at my guide?"

Mauro gave his malevolent grin before pointing at Rylan, "The man you paid to guide you has been rumored to be an Heir of Ralford the Tyrant. He has also been named as an accomplice to rebel factions both within the walls of Dalkas and those of the other heirs scurrying about the shadows. He is mine to drag before King Sepius himself for questioning. Does that sate your curiosity, Lord Tiberius?"

"It does," Tiberius answered without glancing to Rylan.

"I wish to know my accuser, Inquisitor Mauro." Rylan replied as he undid his sword belt and allowed his sword to fall against the rough ground in a sign of his surrender.

Mauro sneered at Rylan, "You've some nerve interrupting nobles as they are speaking to one another. I will grant you your answer though. Several of these townspeople have claimed to see you in possession of six metal wings, as well as Lord Larus Carthill within Dalkas. I've heard enough tales of your butchery to satisfy my curiosity and find you as an heir. That does leave me with some troubling realizations however. Where are your brothers?"

Rylan had to think quickly as he had not accounted on such an event occurring so soon, let alone Lord Larus betraying his own blood. "They're lost to King's Hold, Inquisitor. We were attacked by the bandits that run this town, and during their assault, my brothers fell protecting those still here."

"Is that true Lord Tiberius? I trust the word of a noble over that of a traitor any day." Mauro moved over to Tiberius as he motioned for one of his men to retrieve Rylan's weapon and restrain him.

Tiberius nodded, "Yes, we were attacked by wild bandits who sought to kidnap us and use the chance to steal any valuables we possessed. He and his brothers fought bravely to protect us, and although I was not able to witness their deaths, Rylan was distraught over their passing for the time we remained there."

"Hmm," Mauro pondered as he moved past Tiberius to Isabelle, "Lady Isabelle, is what they say true? Did they die protecting you?"

Isabelle clenched the ring in her hand, "Yes," she muttered as she stepped past him and move to Tiberius' side, "Rylan's brothers were lost attempting to protect us, when they fell it was left to Lord Tiberius and Rylan to defeat them."

Mauro's curiosity peaked, "You did not aid them?"

"I did," she quickly replied, "I could not fight initially do to my power's wide uncertainty. I would've risked burning everyone had I not restrained my flames until it became absolutely necessary."

Mauro ran his fingers through his hair before returning to Rylan's gaze as he circled around his men. "If you're brothers are lost, then where are your metal wings? Why do you not fight us? You would certainly be able to silence many of us before ever being injured."

Rylan could feel Mauro's attempt to clearly bait his reaction, however Rylan endured, "I do not wish to harm anyone, nor do I desire the throne. If you take me to King Sepius, I will abdicate what right I have to the throne and he will rule with absolution and free of interference."

Mauro's grin soured before Rylan's eyes as the inquisitor's plans had been sullied, "You don't seem too reluctant to give up something that has been yours since birth. Why would you not even attempt to claim your right? Did you not wish to honor your father?"

Rylan restrained himself, the plunging daggers of Mauro's words attempting another provocation was met with a deep breath and long sigh before restating what he had told Isabelle, "I love Alder and its people, I have grown with them for many harvests. If I were to attempt such an action against King Sepius, it would surely tear our homes and many innocent families asunder. I would not have simple folk of this kingdom forced into a squabble between two men. That is why I wish to abdicate my place for his majesty so he may be absolute in his rule."

"Very well, I will not delay this any further." Mauro replied as he moved directly facing Rylan and shackled his wrists in heavy manacles before moving to Tiberius, "I trust that you and Lady Isabelle will be present for the interrogation. I believe that his majesty will want you there to confirm his declaration."

Tiberius bowed slightly, "Of course. We shall depart immediately for Dalkas and prepare ourselves. I would ask that something be done with the bandits infesting this village and the Serpent's Fang that attempted to kill us during our travels here. Three of my men were killed, while the fourth has gone missing."

Mauro scowled at Tiberius as he turned to the gate and waved his hand, Orsen emerged with several bandits around him, their leader standing behind the group with her arms crossed. She appeared around the same age as Tiberius and Rylan; however her body was covered in scars and burns. With cold blue eyes she emerged to the front of the pack and stood next to Mauro. "You see," he said as he put his arm around the woman only to have it brushed off, "King Sepius has employed several groups to occupy border towns in order to restrict the movement of rebels in and out of Alder. These people captured your soldier as he was fleeing from the village in an attempt to return with word of your deaths. I wondered why your story did not collaborate what I was told upon arriving, however I don't think many nobles would opening discuss their failings in front of commoners. I do not find that unworthy of your status, however I would ask that you deal with your underling before he becomes a problem."

Mauro discreetly handed Tiberius a dagger and motioned for

Orsen to be brought forward and knelt down in front of his lord. Orsen fell to his knees and bowed his head, "Forgive me Lord Tiberius, I was not able to protect you or Lady Isabelle. I accept whatever fate you deem necessary."

Tiberius knelt down and whispered as he handed Orsen the dagger, "You have served me well for many years and I would not do this if there was any other way."

As Tiberius backed away Orsen nodded and aimed the dagger at his chest. With a swift motion, Orsen plunged the dagger into his heart and twisted as he grimaced silently before falling to the ground, a pool of crimson slowly forming around his body as the blood began to trace the outline of the stones along the path. Rylan lowered his head as the bandits retrieved his body and dragged his body to the trees before tossing him into the woods as if he were common garbage. His mind raced as he thought of his fate should Sepius decide a fate for him after releasing his claim to the throne. A fate much similar to that of Orsen would be the least of his worries.

As Rylan stood watching Tiberius and Mauro conversing with one another, his mind raced until it arrived upon a memory during his childhood. A short time after his mother had returned them to Dalkas to hide amongst the nobles, they had begun to secretly venture out into the open to gather food. On one cloudless day in early into the spring, Rylan hand gone with his mother to the Horseman's Square for a celebration of the new season. As he moved with her throughout the crowded square, passing by vendors of all sorts of foods and trinkets, he saw a beautifully crafted suit of armor made by Orden Forge. Rylan broke free of his mother's grasp and raced through the crowds to gaze upon the ornate armor. As Maree attempted to make her way to Rylan concealed by a large cloak, several guards brushed by her and knocked her to the ground. Her hood fell back as she landed onto the ground and sat gazing up at the cruel grin of Sepius as he stood with his young son as they moved about observing their subjects.

"Seize her!" Sepius roared as he pointed towards Maree. Several armed guards rushed Maree, grabbing hold of her and pinning her on her knees, kneeling before the king. "My, my," Sepius mocked as he slowly took a knee and held her chin up to maintain eye contact, "I would call you a fool to ever dare set foot in this place again, however I must thank you for saving he the coin it would've taken to drag you out of any hole you may have hid yourself in."

As Rylan stood gazing upon the armor, several people began to push him about as the remaining guards opened a large space. Rylan turned to see his mother held by the guards and attempted to push his way forward. As he neared the guard closest to him, a hand grabbed the back of his collar and yanked him backwards, holding him in place with another hand pressed itself against his mouth to conceal his screams.

Sepius called out to Faust, "Son! What shall we do to this traitor?"

Although Faust was still the same age as Rylan, his twisted mind had already begun to form as he replied, "Bring the horses, father! We shall deal with her with horsemen in the Horseman's Square!"

Sepius began to laugh hysterically at the notion and beckoned his men to bring horses for the task. Many voices amongst the crowd erupted in murmurs of the disgusting idea of such a thing, but not a soul moved forward from them to stop such an attempt. Rylan tried with all his strength to break free of his capture until a man's voice whispered to him, "Stop it before you needlessly die for nothing. Your mother's fate is sealed, however you may still live and claim vengeance on the men that would do such an atrocious thing to a woman and a queen."

Rylan gazed up at the face of a young man who seemed barely older than himself, yet he realized the truth in his words. Rylan reluctantly ended his frivolous attempts to break free and began to remember any and all of the many faces that stood within the circle. Faust and Rylan met eyes for a moment before the sounds of hooves drew the young prince's attention away and back to his father. Sepius called out for his men to fasten ropes around Maree's limbs and await his command to begin her execution. As Maree's tears began to fall, Sepius called out to his people, "I do this not because I enjoy or find pleasure in such atrocities! As King I am bound by the laws set before me by the first kings to eradicate any and all who would carry the blood of a royal line! Believe me, my people, if there were any other way, I would gladly take it! Queen Maree may be yet saved though, if her sons yet live and come forth, I will spare her life in exchange for theirs! I promise it will be quick and painless!"

With the ocean of whispers increasing, one man stepped forward and fell to his knees pleading, "My king! I would ask you spare her life so that she may continue her charity to the people of Alder. I would humbly ask you make her a hero!"

For a moment the crowd stood in silence as Sepius looked upon the beggar, his face devoid of expression, yet his eyes darted from one place to another as he formulated his response. Sepius turned to his son and winked before the ground beneath the man erupted with several impaling metal spikes as they tore through the helpless man. Eruptions of chaotic screams filled the square as Sepius' metal retracted into the ground and the impaled man crumpled to the ground. "A traitor," Sepius called out as he outstretched his hands to the crowd to calm them, "one of many that have sought our ruin. Those among us that would seek all we have changed together will always attempt to change the fates that Ralford himself sought to challenge. They do not care for you; even this queen lied to you as she gave you charity but openly beat her own children simply because she could. That is why she is alone and sentenced to death!"

Rylan attempted to call out against such dishonorable lies; however the crowd had turned in favor of their new king and began to spout curses and anger from their mouths. With a victorious grin and one final look to Maree, Sepius snapped his fingers, ordering the horsemen to spur their steeds forward. Her screams split through the air as the ropes tighten around her and began to stretch her muscles, stifling the crowd. After a few moments Sepius stepped forward with his metal forming into a dagger, dragged its sharp blade across her throat, and silenced her screams as crimson blood spilled onto the stones like flowing waterfalls. Sepius turned once again to the crowd, proudly displaying the blood soaked dagger, and proclaimed, "Thus another tyrant dies!"

Cheers and applause began to grow louder and louder until Sepius called out for his horsemen to sever the ropes and collect Maree's lifeless body. Rylan's anger erupted as he struggled to break free from his captors grasp until the young man threw him against the ground and pressed his leg upon Rylan's chest as he leaned forward, "What's done is done kid. No matter how many you get you'll never be able to bring her back. If you wish to survive, work for me. If you want to become strong, train with my men. If you seek revenge, learn all that you can. Tomorrow is not a guarantee for you, but I can give you a fighting chance when your time comes."

Rylan's ears could barely hear as the crowds continued their celebrations, but his captor's words rang true. Although he did not wish to simply leave his family to their fates, Rylan knew he would have to grow strong in order to protect them. Taking the man's outstretched hand, Rylan agreed to follow him and learn. It was the first time since the uprising that he had desired to grow stronger.

"Rylan," Mauro's voice began to drag him out of his memory and back into reality as he looked about to see Tiberius, Isabelle, and Brilla disappeared and left only the bandits and Mauro's guards around him. "I suppose you were deep in thought about something?"

Rylan shook away his remaining daze as he looked at Mauro, "I'm ready to return to Dalkas, shall we depart?"

Mauro laughed as he waved to the bandit leader. His men moved aside as the woman approached Rylan, wrapped her arms around him, and aggressively kissed him. Surprised, Rylan leaped backwards as he stared at the woman bewildered. Upon closer inspection of her appearance, it was Laelia beyond the shadow of a doubt. Rylan's mind could not fathom what to say, however his anger erupted as he roared, "How could you! It's your fault they're dead!"

"Seize him." Mauro commanded as his men wrestled Rylan to the ground. "You'll need to control yourself Rylan, otherwise I'll be forced to have my men blind and muzzle you."

Rylan struggled to see Laelia, "You killed your own father! I can only wonder how disgusted he would be to find you leading such a disgraceful life!"

Mauro sighed and motioned to one of his men to fulfill his promise. As the men continued to struggle to restrain Rylan, Laelia moved around to stand over his head, "I have no father." She replied with a cold, heartless tone. "I was left to die by my family, by you, and I was lost until I found my strength to fight back. Now I lead while you fall. Come whatever may, I will not be wounded by your words. I hope you die painfully, traitor."

Rylan struggled as the guardsmen tied the cloth over his mouth and threw a sack over his head. Although he could not see Rylan could hear Mauro, "I didn't want to return so quickly, unfortunately with his confession, we'll have to return immediately so that King Sepius will have his unquestionable right to rule... do knock him out though. I don't want to explain to his majesty how he was able to recall his metal."

Rylan quickly attempted to break free, but as an armored hand connected on the side of his head Rylan could only muster a single, poorly made symbol in the dirt. As Mauro's guard lifted Rylan's limp body from the ground, a faintly drawn crow revealed itself.

CHAPTER 10

A s Aldis enter the dining hall with his brothers, many of the seats around the table were empty. Heirs of Barner, Parthus, Vaine, and Epharth were indisposed or not within the walls. Alkith and Naria sat at one end of the table dressed in finely woven clothing befitting their customs of marvelous golden designs woven into their bright blue attires to signify royal status. Halvor and Ellice sat on the opposing end dressed in furs and their bloodied weapons still around their waists. Although the tailors on hand were very exquisite in their detail and designs, the three brothers stood peering over one another as each brother held different coloration and appearance. While Aldis had simply modified his sage robes, Toren had asked for an immaculate designed tunic emblazoned with his family crest and a strong red fabric to encircle it. Sayren asked for a simplistic design, similar to one of his father's wardrobe, and although it to several attempts to find anything of the late king's attire in the citadel, one of the weavers recalled seeing King Ralford ask him to construct an outfit for his fortieth birthday, only a year before the uprising took place. It took five thread-weavers nearly three hours to finish, and after several failed attempts, their abilities finally flowed seamlessly through the white tunic, carefully etching ancient designs into the folds and a simple, yet majesty gold and silver crow soaring across the chest.

As the heirs took to their seats, Sayren noticed Alkith mesmerized by the design and gave him a silent nod as they met each other's gaze. Alkith's chuckled, "I remember that design, your father wore it to

184

show up the rest of the nobles when we sat down for the Harvest Feast. You do him a great honor."

"Thank you," Sayren responded as he smoothed down his tunic to remove any wrinkles, "I must say you do us quite the honor by helping us with such a revelation; however I believe we will have to return soon to collect my family and our brother."

Alkith nodded as he waved to one of the masked servants to begin serving the food, "I agree entirely, however you should eat and prepare yourselves before returning. If you left now, you'll end up only starving yourselves. I believe we would all prefer to accompany you to meet your family and welcome them into our glorious reclamation of our birthright."

Halvor lifted his goblet, "Let us drink to the final heir's arrival! Now we may final set to break this dreadful stain that sits in our place upon our father's thrones!" Everyone lifted their drinks and sipped, with the exception of Halvor who finished his drink in one motion before slamming the glass down and loudly demanding, "Another!"

Toren couldn't help himself as he cracked a grin across his face and began to chuckle until Aldis nudged him with an elbow to his ribs to stop. Sayren nodded to both of his brothers as he sat across from them to restrain themselves from any outbursts that may be taken offensively. "Tell me Naria," Sayren spoke as he watched the servants begin to scurry about the room collecting wine and placing dishes filled with lavish cuisine across the dining table, "where is Luca?"

Several of the waiters hesitated momentarily before continuing their duties, surprised by the question. Naria's face froze as her eyes widened before nervously answering, "I'm not sure who that is Sayren, is that one of the soldiers?"

"No it's that kid you were with when we first arrived." Toren blurted out as he blindly stared unaware at a large boar that sat roasted on a silver plate in front of him with numerous plates of bread and soups he had never laid eyes on before.

Ellice effortlessly moved her knife through a tender piece of pork on her plate as she responded to their comments without drawing her attention from her plate, "For sons of King Ralford, I would've thought they all would be a bit more courteous at dinner."

"You'll have to forgive us," Sayren returned, "we have not had the opportunity to reeducate ourselves on the ways of royalty."

"That's been quite obvious since you walked in. If you were taught anything you would've refrained from entering with something so similar to an appearance of a fallen king. Such an action is disgraceful." Ellice's tone was cold and harsh as she focused on the meal before her. Toren gave Aldis an infuriated look before gazing across to Sayren. Although clearly caught off guard, Sayren was taxing himself to maintain his composed demeanor.

With most of the food placed in their designated locations and servants maintaining a silent presence along the walls, the sounds of clamoring metal and racing footsteps grew louder and louder until the doors to the dining room burst open with Yvon knocking several guardsmen to the floor with his sheathed sword. "What the hell are you doing sitting around?" Yvon questioned as he moved over to Sayren only to have Halvor arise from his seat and turn to face him.

Halvor's fists began to tighten as he began to call forth his ice, "I feel for your loss boy, but barging into a royal chamber is punishable by death without an invite."

"I did," Yvon said as he brushed past Halvor without a second glance and maintained eye contact with Sayren, "Rylan said that you would return me to Havenhome to collect my family and bring them to safety, yet I come to find you sitting about in fancy clothing eating your dinner."

Sayren arose from the table, attempting to conceal his relief to excuse himself and motioned for his brothers, "You're right and I apologize. It was not my intention to be so engrossed in all the frivolities of royal etiquette. Come brothers, we have a job to finish."

Toren grinned from ear to ear as he heard his brother's insult coated words leave his mouth and happily arose with Aldis following suit, a slightly dismayed look upon his face. As the four made their way to the door, Alkith abruptly arose from his seat and startled many of the servants, "Although I admire your dedication, the word of a bastard is not the same as the rightful king. I must insist you stay here Sayren, at least you will be safe should something go wrong."

"With all due respect," Sayren responded as he turned and gave a slight nod, "I am the oldest brother here and I will not allow my brothers to needlessly walk into harm without being by their side. Should you truly wish to ensure my safety, you may accompany us as well. Surely no one would dare to wound eight heirs that walk side by side."

Gianni has sat silently in his chair, watching and waiting, however as Sayren finished his sentence, he arose and pointed at the curtained windows, "You do not see because you have not been here; anytime more than two of heirs have the cursed misfortune of drawing unwanted attention and bringing unnecessary bloodshed in their wake. We are cursed to walk alone until we all unite and regain our thrones!"

Sayren merely turned to leave as Gianni barked at him, "Clearly," he exclaimed before disappearing down the hall, "you are simply too scared to fight now that you have that option."

Gianni roared in anger, bringing roots from the doors and loudly slamming the large oak doors closed and forcing a gust of wind to cascade through the room throwing food and drink away from them and crashing down at the feet of the servants. "Pick that trash up now and get out!"

Alkith grinned as Gianni's temper clearly got the better of him and incited a reaction he had not seen in at least ten harvests. Brushing off some bread crumbs that had manage to stay upon his coat, Alkith headed for the single side door where the servants had come from, "Gianni, Halvor, I suggest we gather what men are willing to fight and die. I will be riding to their aid, not because that ass Sayren decided to trick us into a reaction, but because should my plans be moving as intended we'll need all that we can to fight off the entirety of Alder's army."

"Finally, a straight forward battle for once instead of all this shadowy business!" Halvor echoed as he beat his chest and smiled to his sister.

Ellice nodded, "We'll go, but our men will not follow us to such a folly. If they come with us, it will only be if Ulferth wishes to meet us in open conflict."

"If they're men then they'll march with us regardless of who or where we fight!" Halvor barked as his angered tone coated his beard with dribbles of saliva.

Naria arose and moved over to her brother as Gianni stood

brooding as he contemplated his actions and Halvor argued with Ellice over use of their soldiers, "What will you do should an army actually arrive, brother?"

Naira looked worryingly into his eyes, "Well, my dearest sister," Alkith's devious grin emerged as he removed a Sen Crystal from his coats inner pocket, "should everything go according to plan; then you may just see 'him' return to us for good. If not then we may never see him again and we'll need to keep those brothers from attempting anything reckless."

Although reassured that Alkith had everything under control, Naria maintained her unease as her brother moved through the kitchen ordering many of the young children to fetch Gauld, his men, and a few things Naria could not make out as he moved further away. With the sudden noise of the hall doors reopening, Naria observed Gianni motioning to one of his archers to fetch more men and meet him at the gate, while Halvor appeared with his shoulders lowered in defeat as Ellice lead the way with her chin held high in victory. As the others disappeared to go prepare for war, Naria sighed and silently made her way out of the dining hall and over to a large library filled with books and Luca sitting in front of a large stack of tomes reading away.

"Ah, Lady Naria, it is good to see you. Young master Luca has been studying Thesia's History quite extensively. He's even been asking questions about the men you met today from Alder." A robed sage conveyed as he cautiously made his way down a ladder placed behind a row of bookshelves near Naria's left.

"Very good to know, Sage Maneth, it has always been a pleasure having you around the records to maintain our history and teach Luca. I must unfortunately ask something of you." Naria replied with a worrisome voice.

"Of course my lady, one moment and I will be there to assist you. I simply need to put this last tome on your last encounter into its place." Maneth's voice momentarily lulled as he ran his fingers across the books until he found a certain red leather bound book and placed the pages on Naria's encounter within the hall inside the back of the book and gently slid his finger along the spine, stitching the newest pages into the book before returning it to its place and emerging before Naria, "How may I be of assistance?"

Naria's mind recalled seeing Alkith's mischievous grin before placing her hand on the sage's shoulder, "I must ask you to look after Luca until our return. We should not be gone for very long, however I can only suspect that in the coming days, we may finally begin our next phase into our recovery of our thrones."

Maneth's brow grew heavy as he scowled for a moment before sighing and nodding, "Of course your majesty, I would prefer to accompany you and the others should history decide to progress, however I would ask that you allow me to send a few young pages to follow with you and record whatever may happen."

"Certainly," Naria agreed as she moved over to Luca only to find him fast asleep with his finger placed over a section of the book labeled only with 'Six Winged Death'. She smiled and gently kissed his head before moving back to the door. Naria and Maneth bowed to one another before Naria closed the door and left to dawn her armor.

❖   ❖   ❖

As the Sen Portal near Havenhome activated and the four men exited, Yvon instantly began to scan for Elyscia, his sword tied to his waist while his father's polesword tightly gripped in his hands. Although the forest was quite, Yvon noticed a set of footprints leading off in the direction of a mostly collapsed shed. He outstretched his hand in the shed's direction as Sayren emerged with a Darkwood bow that was located with Byra's stash of weapons. Both readied their weapons and moved to the collapsed shack as Toren and Aldis looked on waiting for a signal.

Sounds of wooden planks scraping against one another until Sayren and Yvon were at the broken doorway, "Elyscia? If you're in there its Yvon, I'm with Rylan's brothers. We're here to get mother and leave this place forever."

For a moment, silence filled the surrounding area as everyone held their breath. Finally Elyscia emerged with Rylan's axe tightly clutched in her hands. As she and Yvon made eye contact, she released the axe and ran into Yvon's arms. Before the axe head sunk into the ground,

Sayren quickly grabbed the handle, and sent a pulse shooting through handle and into Sayren. Rylan's axe slowly began to melt and take the form of an ornate sword inscribed with ancient symbols that Sayren could not discern as he pulled the weapon upright.

As Elyscia held Yvon, she turned her head to Sayren, "Your brother asked me to give that to you."

"Thank you," Sayren replied as he marveled at the craftsmanship of the blade's design before searching for a sheath, "Rylan didn't happen to leave a sheath behind did he?"

"No." Elyscia replied as she buried her face into Yvon's chest and started to cry once again.

Yvon looked to Sayren, "I'm sure we'll be able to locate a spare somewhere in the town."

"I'm not certain that would be a good idea to stick around once we've acquired you mother." Sayren replied with a worrisome tone. Yvon's notion of staying within the town undoubtedly suggested that his desire to utterly annihilate whatever forces remained within the walls. Although Sayren wished to change his mind, Yvon's focused appearance was resolute, even as Elyscia mourned upon his shoulder.

As Toren and Aldis made their way from the portal room and towards the road, sounds of marching soldiers approaching forced them to quietly wave down Sayren and the others to hide themselves. Sounds of snapping branches and crunching decaying leaves under leather boots grew louder as Aldis concealed himself within the bushes as Toren produced his tome, opened to one of his pages and vanished like dust carried away by the wind. A patrol of Mauro's men made their way into the courtyard as Yvon, Elyscia, and Sayren hid within the collapsed shack and silently watched. As the soldiers boldly enter the overgrown courtyard splitting themselves evenly as they began their search, three towards the shack and three towards the portal room. One of the men heading towards the portal chamber stopped as he heard the rustling of branches emanating from where Aldis had shrouded himself. Armed with his spear, the soldier thrust his spearhead into the bushes several times before retracting it. Devoid of any signs that he had struck what was once there the soldier peered through the bushes for a moment before shrugging and quickly returning to his group.

Sayren, relieved that Aldis was uninjured turned his attention to the three soldiers approaching him and quickly strung his bow. As they drew closer to the shack and further away from the others, Sayren released his first arrow, striking the female soldier in her neck and sent her to the ground clutching her throat as he restrung his bow and took aim at the next target. As the soldiers screamed out for the others, Sayren quickly released his second arrow into the man's chest, puncturing his heart and silencing his alarm immediately. Before the third solder could react, Yvon emerged with Sayren and ran the other woman through with his polesword driving into her stomach before pushing the pole's blade out of the soldier's side, a cascade of blood flowing from the large wound as she tightly held her side screeching in agony.

With the first group downed, the remaining soldiers quickly took a defensive stance with their backs to one another as Sayren readied his bow and Yvon slowly edged forward. Aldis emerged from the forest and tossed a sphere directly over the three soldiers as they turned to see what Aldis had thrown above them. When the sphere was directly above the group, Aldis exploded the orb, causing a bright light to blind the men directly underneath and force them to cover their eyes. Unable to see around them, the soldiers began to swing their weapons madly, almost striking one another as they began to move away from one another.

Toren seized the opportunity as he emerged from the portal doorway and launched himself onto one of the soldiers, driving his dagger repeatedly into the blinded man's chest. Hearing the sounds of their comrade's shrieks and gurgles, the remaining man and woman turned their attention towards Toren's direction. Before either one could close the distance, Toren quickly rolled towards the woman and plunged his dagger into the woman's stomach before shifting behind her and sending his small knife into the base of her neck and twisting. Before Toren could make his way to the last man, the guard regained his vision and stared at his fallen company scattered among the tall grass. As his eyes met Toren's strong glare, he readied his sword and pointed, "I know you! You're the bastard that injured the militia! I'm going to run you through and bleeding you dry!"

"If that's what you believe will happen then come try, you know I'll be right here." Toren calmly replied as he retracted his weapons and allowed the woman to collapse to the ground.

Toren watched as the last soldier roared and charged head long towards him, unaware of his surroundings. Toren grinned as he kicked the dead woman's spear upright and watched as his opponent impaled himself through the stomach and immediately dropped his sword to grab the spear. Toren watched as the man attempted to remove the spear, his hands bloody and unable to grip the crimson spear as he grunted and growled with every attempt to free himself.

"What are you doing out here?" Sayren questioned the soldier as he made his way over to him.

"We've... already got your brother. Once his majesty kills the rest of his family, he'll hang his corpse from atop the wall so all will know he is the true king of Alder and you'll be left with nothing. Now do what you must."

Sayren looked to Toren and gave him a brief nod. "With pleasure." Toren said as he grabbed the man's arm opposite Sayren and drove his knife into the man's armpit. The man wretched in agony as Toren twisted the blade.

Sayren knelt down beside the man and wrenched his head backwards, "What do you mean 'the rest of his family'? Answer my questions and I'll make it quick for you."

"I don't know! All I heard what that they had captured his wife and kid. We were dispatched with Inquisitor Mauro to retrieve you lot to be questioned for their connection with late King Ralford. Now please... Just end this."

Sayren watched as the man continued to struggle with his injuries, but could not maintain his composure at the thought of Abigail and Ophelia lying dead at Rylan's feet. Taking one of his metal arrows, Sayren drove the point into the man's skull and began to make his way towards the road. Toren retracted his dagger and instantly motioned for the other to quickly follow as he caught up with Sayren.

Elyscia quietly handed Sayren's sword to Yvon as he drew closer to the brothers, "What did he say?"

Sayren took the sword from Yvon and recalled his arrow from the man's lifeless body, "He said they have my family and they know who he is. We'll deal with these bandits then move to Dalkas and free Rylan."

❊   ❊   ❊

As Yvon and Sayren lead the group to the edge of the town, both large wooden doors were released and swung open. Although no guardsmen stood atop the walls, several bandit guards stood ready at the doors threshold with weapons bared at their approach. With the sun nearly set behind the brigands, it was unclear if there were any additional reinforcements lurking behind the walls.

With the group still making their advance, one of the men moved forward with his spear, "Halt if you wish to draw another breath!" Shaky and nervous, the guard attempted to raise his shield as if to expect an attack.

Sayren continued forward with an arrow notched in his bow, "I have no time for your games, move or be silenced!"

Without another word the guardsman shuffled back into his spot on the line and readied themselves for combat. Sayren quickly rushed forward, pulled back on the arrow and released. His ability to see forward a few moments gave him his target; as the bandits reacted to Sayren's arrow, the man on the right edge of the line lowered his head under the shield as the arrow sank into his unguarded knee. As the injured man fell to the ground, Sayren released his metal arrows and sent them careening into the remaining shields, driving them back with tremendous force. Yvon, Toren, and Aldis raced forward and unleashed their own attacks upon the guards, quickly dispatching them and entering the town. Elyscia quickly came behind them and started looking for their mother, "I can't see her!"

"Stay with us!" Yvon barked as he wrestled a shield free and stood near Elyscia, "If you run off, I won't be able to protect you!"

Sayren scanned the surroundings as he noticed more and more bandits moving from behind buildings and beginning to surround them. As he readied another arrow, several of the villagers also seemed to stare from within their houses as almost fifty men and women surrounded the group with spears and axes, warily guarding themselves as they secured their perimeter around the gate. Aldis quickly began to form several orbs around him while Toren grabbed a spear and laid his hand on his tome.

"Any of you advance and I'll personally gut you myself!" Laelia's voice barked as she approached with her elite guard trailing her steps with focused eyes on the brothers as they made their way from the manor house to her subordinates.

Sayren stepped forward, his arrow trained on Laelia as she entered the half circle, "What are you to these outlaws, their leader or just another lieutenant?"

Laelie scoffed as she motioned off to her right side, "I'm the one who leads this terrible band of lawless pillagers. I take it you're one of Ralford's other sons? You're one of Rylan's brothers?"

Sayren carefully watched as two bandits emerged from a metal barred hut with the two children he had freed during his first encounter with the bandits, "You bitch. If you hurt them I'll break you down to what little soul you may have still have. Release those children and we'll settle this!"

Laelia began to cackle as the two children reached her and she placed her hands over their small chained wrists, "Do as I trained you and you'll receive extra food this evening."

Both children looked at one another and over to Sayren before the older sister nodded to her brother and began to release their abilities. A bright orange glowing stream flooded from the young boy while a vibrant gold released from the girl. Laelia's arms began to absorb the magic and begin to show the intricate tattoos across her arms and her neck. Before Laelia could tell the children to stop and face Sayren, Yvon had rushed forward and launched a well-placed kick directly into his sister's side.

Yvon returned his foot to the ground and clenched an open fist towards Laelia, "For our father, I will be the one to take from you everything you hold dear!"

Injured, yet enraged, Laelia turned towards her younger brother, "You little brat! Our father left me to die! I hope he died slow, filled with the agony that he left me to suffer with! I was going to allow you and Elyscia to walk away from this unharmed, however now I think I'll simply turn you in like the others!" Laelia waved her hand out towards her subordinates, "If any of you interfere, I'll deal with later! If the heirs attempt to intervene, you may hurt them but do not kill them unless you wish to pay me their ransom!"

Yvon looked back to Sayren who stood with his brothers, weapons ready for combat, and with a single nod from Elyscia, Yvon focused his sights on Laelia and sprinted forward. The two quickly locked eyes and unleashed a furry of strikes against one another. Although she was empowered, Laelia's magic did not seem to give her an edge against Yvon's determination as she attempted to press the advantage with every opening, yet always seemed to be just shy of connecting a strong blow that would give her the upper hand.

As the two separated, many bandits began to chant and cheer for their leader. Yvon's brow was beginning to sweat in the cool autumn wind as he began to refocus his breathing and regain his stamina. Laelia was not about to give him the opportunity as she quickly closed the space between them and began to unleash her glowing fists. Yvon attempted his best to block the burst of strikes, yet for every blow he was able to deflect, another two seemed to find their mark. Without any physical abilities of his own, Yvon could do nothing but brace against the cascading attacks that began to wear on his limbs until Laelia shot her foot directly into his chest, sending him tumbling backwards before tripping over his own feet and falling to the dirt face first. A roar of applause and cheers erupted as Yvon struggled to return to his feet. As he looked around, many of the cowering townsfolk that had once remained blissfully unaware, had now crept outside their shadows and behind their windows to observe the fight. Although the crowd had begun to grow, Yvon could see his sister's lack of attention as the towns folk began to creep in amongst the bandits as they cheered for both sided.

"Don't you see little brother," Laelia slowly moved forward with her tattoos still fully illuminated, "father taught you how to absorb and unleash magic. He never showed you how to harness the magic into objects to wield them with unmatched power! If only you had kept yourself in check I would've taught you how to become strong and unrivaled in power! Father left me to die at the hands of the bandits I now command because their leader was daft enough to attack me with his abilities only to have them turn on him! I clawed and dragged myself from a lowly slave to leader; all while our father sat content, inside his inn, never once forcing his way to find me or even what fate had befallen me!"

Yvon heaved his aching body upright and removed his shirt; several scars dotted about his skin, "Our father, your father! He was forced to remain inside that inn as if it were his prison due to the beating we received at the hands of those you command! When he grew disheartened, I began to search for you and found only more scars and bruises awaited me! I searched for two years, and never once did I hear your name or your fate! I never would've figured you would die at the hands of such low scum; however it never once crossed my mind that you would betray your own blood and seek to kill the ones who never stopped caring for you! No matter what you can do with your tainted strength, I will not let you destroy my father's honor!"

"Foolish little brat." Laelia murmured as she drew the magic out from her body and into the forms of a sword and shield. She feinted right and then seemed to instantly be directly in front of Yvon as she swung her weapon.

Yvon quickly rolled away from his sister and grabbed his father's polesword from the ground as the siblings readied themselves for another dance. Both combatants launched themselves forwards and clashed; Yvon's attempts to attack were quickly countered and forced him back on the defensive as Laelia's stifled his by strength alone. After several strikes against Yvon's weapon, he could feel its strong wood staff section beginning to crack against the weight of his sisters daunting attacks, fearing his father's weapon breaking Yvon avoided Laelia's downward strike, tossed the weapon towards Toren and unsheathed his sword.

"What's wrong little brother? Is your pointy stick already breaking? I promise you that your sword will fair no better against my might!" Laelia mocked as she strutted around her brother, confidence spilling from her like a raging waterfall.

Yvon could not withstand much more of a battery from his older sister's attacks, yet he felt a sense of dread as all his attempts to attack had been blocked or countered effortlessly. Without any other seemingly feasible options, Yvon thought to himself about what Laelia had said earlier, "to harness magic into objects and wield them." His mind couldn't begin to fathom how to do such a thing, but with little option left he knew he would have to attempt such a feat without any practice.

Both Yvon and Laelia began to move opposite one another as they circled one another within the crowd, each waiting for an opportunity. As Yvon continued around, his foot caught against an uncovered stone and forced him off balance as his sister rushed forward to seize her victory. Without a chance to attempt drawing magic with the sword, Yvon swung wildly at his sister, missing by a wide margin before she once again brought the sword high above her head and slashed with all her might. Yvon's muscle memory after endless hours of training forced his arms to return his sword back into a block position as he closed his eyes and attempted to counter. As the two blades collided, Laelia's orange blade shattered into dazzling glints of magic as it began to attach itself to the blade's edge. A violent burst discharged from the blade's distruction that Laelia was sent careening backward into the air before she landed with an unforgiving thud against the hard dirt at the edge of the circle. She shared the same expression as those that looked onwards towards Yvon as he arose to his feet, his eyes transfixed upon the sword as faint orange shards moved about the sword and began to give an etched outline of an incomplete design.

"What did you do?" Laelia screamed at her brother as she dusted herself off and changed her shield composed of golden shield to another sword, this time a large two handed sword with magic seeming to fall off of the blade as if fog had settled around it.

Yvon moved his focus back to his opponent as he readjusted his grip and widened his feet; "I suppose I've found your weakness, dear sister. If you wish to pursue this folly of yours, then by all means let's continue without more stalling."

Laelia bared her teeth as she tighten her grip on her weapon and charge forward. This time, readied for the strong attack, Yvon braced himself to counter and as the two swords met, the golden mist falling from the blade move forward and sent Yvon stumbling backward, not from the strike, but from the pressure of the mist as it fell upon his skin. Laelia gave him a smirk as Yvon's arms felt heavier than ever before. Not allowing her brother to adjust to the hindrance, she dashed forward and pressed her attack, however this time Yvon used his own momentum to spin, swing the blade to counter and absorb the two handed sword with the mist before anymore could weigh him down. With the new energy absorbing into the metal blade and removing the mist from his arms, Yvon could feel his sword's own power as a completed design of symbols and began to illuminate the blade with a brilliant white aura around its sharpened edge.

"Someone give me a weapon, now!" Laelia barked at her men as they stood in awe at Yvon's feat. From the crowd, a sword fell into the dirt. Yvon allowed her to retrieve the blade and remained back as Laelia's frustration began to boil, "Why are you waiting? If you're so great to absorb my weapons, then let see how you fair when I cleave you in half!"

Yvon slowly made his way forward, his mind calm and focused as his sister's hand shakily held the blade. "Die bastard!" she screamed as she rushed forward, wildly swinging her blade as she closed the space between them. Yvon exhaled and quickly parried the strike, sending Laelia's sword flying across the open area and quickly outstretched his hand to push her away. As his unblocked palm connected with his sister's body, an enormous pulse of energy dissipated from both of Yvon's hands, sending both Laelia and his own sword backwards.

Cheers from the surrounding villagers exploded as Laelia's body fell against the rough ground beneath her, her eyes blank and limbs motionless. Yvon stood baffled at the sight before turning to see his sword lying upon the ground, its aura gone, but a single line within the design now sat etched upon the untouched part of his blade. Yvon quickly ran to Laelia and lifted her head, strongly shaking her arm as he attempted to force a reaction, "Sister, say something! Do something, anything! Please don't let me have done what I fear most!"

As sounds of rustling leaves echoed throughout Havenhome, Laelia's body remained silent and her eyes blank. Yvon's eyes began to well with tears as his heart sank, even if it was meant to be. His heart could not bear the thought of losing two members of his family within the same day. Gently resting her body on the ground and crossing her arms, Yvon stood to retrieve his sword as Elyscia walked over to console him. Many of the bandits, although shocked by the events, held fire in their eyes as they began to ponder what should be done with the group and who would next lead. As the men began to close in on Sayren and his brothers, sounds of marching drums grew louder and louder until the sight of organized soldiers bearing the standards of House Kay, Evest, and Ulferth revealed themselves by the glowing light of torches gleaming in the setting sunlight.

"Sayren!" Alkith's voice called out as he and the other heirs rode forward into view, weapons drawn and ready, "Have you already gotten yourself into more trouble?"

Sayren scowled at Alkith as he turned to meet them, "I would dare say that I avoid trouble, it simply enjoys my company more so than others."

Alkith chuckled as he dismounted and stood before bandit and villager alike, "I see there is some confusion amongst these people. Do you not see royalty standing before you? Or have you simply forgotten how to kneel!"

In a frightened unison, men and women fell to their knees, Alkith's tone shaking their souls. Many of the bandits immediately dropped their weapons as Alkith produced his mask and held it beside his face.

"It would seem these men face your decision Sayren. As rightful king, you may choose to give them their lives, should the swear fealty, or face death as traitors and assassins against a member of a royal family." Alkith lowered his mask and gently slid it back into his pouch. "I dare say many of them possess strength to stand against you, let alone actually harm you in any way."

Aldis pulled on Sayren's tunic as he gazed around at the populace, "How could they accept servitude when we do not have a way to protect them or even house them currently?"

Sayren nodded to Aldis before stepping towards the gathered crowd, "For those of you who do not know who I am, my name is Sayren Bassadora, son of King Ralford, and rightful King of Alder. I wish to afford you the privilege of joining me in regaining my throne.

If you choose to do so, you will be rewarded with space within Alder's District inside King's Hold. Should you choose not to join me and my brothers, I would ask that you move into a separate group to the middle of town. You must make the choice now, for I cannot risk delaying further."

As men and women whispered amongst themselves, several of the bandits placed their weapons at Sayren's feat, bowed and moved to join him. Others spat on the dirt and moved to the other group wishing not to partake. As the crowd began to separate, it was clear that many of the older villagers bowed to not only Sayren, but the other heirs as well, proudly revealing their badges of servitude to the prior kings. With the last few people moved to their chosen groups, Alkith silently ordered his men to encircle the people who stood against Sayren.

"What are your men doing?" Sayren posed to Alkith as he pointed towards the circle.

Alkith gave Sayren a stern look before sheathing his sword and crossing his arms, "If any of these people that stand against you make it to Dalkas, or any noble that does not support you, they will surely notify Sepius and we'll have the entirety of Alder's forces at our gates within a week's time."

"What will you do then," Sayren responded as he noticed the soldiers drawing their weapons and closing in on the people, "Do you mean to kill them all? There are women and children amongst them!"

Alkith gave his silent command as his soldiers began to cut down the crowd without mercy, screams of both men and women alike erupting with crimson sprays as Sayren grabbed Alkith's collar and shook him violently, "Stop them, now!"

Alkith sighed as he waved his hand and the sound of a horn rang out. As the screams stopped and the soldiers backed away, Sayren turned to see only a handful of people remained, many of them bandits clutching innocent people in front of them as shields. Enraged, Sayren commanded his metal forth with near breakneck pace as the rods tore through the remain bandits, freeing the people as they rushed out of the soldiers encirclement and fell before Sayren's feet begging to be spared.

"And now those that once stood against you will now be indebted to you for their lives are yours to do wish as you please." Alkith's impertinent tone rang true in Sayren's ears, even if he did not agree. "Now you have your first set of troops for which you can begin to rebuild Alder's district within King's Hold. You can thank me later for such sensible actions."

Sayren's cold stare pierced into Alkith's very soul as he recalled his metal and once again turned to face him, "You would call that 'sensible'? Do you not see that you condemned innocent people to death simply because you thought they might turn against us? Has it not crossed your mind that we are still near the border between King's Hold and Alder? These people are from all eight kingdoms and do not hold allegiance to any king, but you're clearly too daft to see it!"

Alkith abruptly grabbed Sayren by the collar and slammed his back remorselessly against the ground before placing a knee over his stomach. "You must be the dumbest of your brothers," Alkith's cold eyes remained fixed with Sayren's as his face drew closer, "You forget that the only kings currently are the feeble collaborators that killed our fathers and attempted to kill us! We do not follow the rules of order as long as we are without a proper title. If you wish to do so, then you will doom yourself and your entire bloodline to fall before you ever obtain your throne! We must claw and scratch our way back to some semblance of our parents before we can ever hope to retake our rightful place! Should I have to kill innocent people in order to provide the necessary response to keep our secret safe and ensure that those below me stay in line, they I will do so without a second thought. You may be a Bassadora, but you have much to learn about being of royal decent. If you are done with your temper tantrum you should gather what supplies are available here and prepare these people to leave once your bothersome brother returns. I'm certain he will not wish to remain here any longer than he has to."

Alkith removed himself from atop Sayren and extended an open hand. Although still infuriated by Alkith's actions, Sayren begrudgingly took his gesture and arose to his feet before turning to his brothers and his newly acquired subjects. "Good people of Havenhome," Sayren's voice cracking as he spoke, "what has transpired here was never my intention, however it is a necessity to ensure our secret is held in place. I would ask that we bury any innocent men or women properly and with respect. Bandits that cowered in the face of death will be hung from the trees outside the western gate as a sign to any future brigands from entering this place. My brother Rylan will return soon with my family, and upon their arrival we shall make our way to King's Hold to where you may begin your lives anew and under the protection of House Bassadora. If you wish to enlist as soldiers you may do so, however I ask that you wait until we return and you settle into your new lives."

One elderly man stepped forward, once again bowing before he spoke, "I must ask your forgiveness sire, but I am not sure your brother will ever return."

"What do you mean? What is your name?" Sayren said as he made his way over to the elderly man.

"Horvik," he said before coughing. After the small fit had passed, Horvik continued, "Upon your brother's return, he was seized by a Noble Inquisitor named Mauro and several Noble Guardsmen. They left almost immediately after they bound his hands together with the nobles you pass through here with yesterday. I believe they were returning to the capital for him to be questioned by King Sepius himself."

Sayren turned his horrified gaze to his brothers as they returned a similarly frightened look. "If that's true then we will have to return and save him immediately."

"No," Alkith's voice interrupted as he made his way between the brothers, "your brother wished to return and retrieve your family. If you were to leave in pursuit, we couldn't protect you and you would face impossible odds trying to return. You would leave the very people you now hold yourselves responsible. Believe in your brother and his ability as The Six Winged Death."

"I don't care to hear your voice Alkith," Sayren as he returned without facing him, "Should I need your words, I'll ask for them."

Naria made her way forward as she place her hand over Sayren's shoulder and turned him to face her, "You know he's right. Even if you don't want to believe it, my brother is not wrong. If you leave now you put everything at risk. Your remaining family may be still in Dalkas, however if Rylan is the tactician I remember him to be, he'll have hundreds of escape routes if anything like this came to pass. Trust your brother to do what he must to protect his family, you must stay here and look after your people if you ever wish to prepare for what may follow Rylan upon his return."

"She's right," Aldis nodded as he stood next to Naria and gazed into his brother's distant eyes, "Rylan has always thought of every possible event and will surely have expected this to happen if he prepared everyone the way he always does."

Sayren looked over to Toren, who stood with his arms crossed, his eyes fixed on the dead mass of people as a subtle revealing grin appeared, "What about you Toren, what do you say we should do?"

Sayren's words pulled his mind out of the clouds and forced Toren to assess his surroundings, "I…uh…I think we should stay." An unsteady tone emerged from his mouth as he gazed upon the hundreds of soldiers that began to pour into the city and begin to secure the village, "There's nothing for us to return to inside Dalkas if Rylan retrieves the rest of your family. If we left, there are numerous chances we might miss them entirely and be confronted by whatever semblance of an army comes to eradicate our bloodline. We should stay and prepare, but it's your decision, not mine."

Sayren sighed deeply as his own mind concurred with Naria and his brothers. Although he still wished to leave and see his wife and daughter personally, the risk alone would be far too great. Sayren turned to Alkith and the townspeople, "My brothers and I will remain here, however that means we must prepare for whatever may come. Anyone who is able to work I ask that you assist these soldiers in preparing any defenses we may require in the event of an attack."

"My, my," Yvette's old voice echoed as she emerged from behind one of the buildings, "To think I have lost a husband and a daughter in one day places a heavy burden upon my heart. However, for as saddened as I may be, I'm proud as a mother to see Ralford's sons taking up the mantle and fighting for their blood right. Should any of you or your soldiers need medicine or poisons, please let me know. Yvon, Elyscia, come with me and we will take care of your sister. I wish to hear how your father passed."

Elyscia rushed over to her mother and wrapped her arms around her, only to slightly ease up as Yvette released a murmured whimper.

Yvon retrieve his weapons and Laelia's body before moving to his mother's side and bowing slightly.

As the three disappeared back around the corner, Halvor, Gianni, Alkith, and Sayren stood together gauging Havenhome's defensible aspects. "Gianni, I don't suppose you could create a sizable moat for us to use along the western wall could you?" Alkith asked as he surveyed the feeble western wall.

Gianni gave Alkith a scowled look, "you know I cannot do that with my magic, such a destructive thing would go against everything I was ever taught. I can awaken the trees and plants a distance away from the walls; however I would not be able to cover our retreat back through the portal when the time came."

"You want to retreat?" Halvor huffed as he lit his smoking pipe and exhaled a large plume of smoke, "If I knew we were only here to lose, I would've left to go north already."

Sayren pointed along the tops of the palisades to the places where he wished archers to be stationed and waved off a young man carrying a hunting bow, "That's not what he means, with our numbers, if anything more than a thousand strong troops arrive behind Rylan, we will not be able to withstand an assault, regardless of who we may be. It is sensible to hold a strong enough force here to guarantee we can weaken any advance while removing the majority of our troops to strengthen our position within King's Hold. It will not be a loss or a retreat; it will be a strong defensive tactic that allows us to save our men to fight another day."

"Well said," Ellice chimed in as she emerged from behind Halvor and rested herself against his arm, "I didn't think any of your line knew how to speak so eloquently when it came to being beaten, but I can imagine you eventually learn how since you became a married man."

Sayren smirked as Ellice's words reminded of Abigail's warm smile, "I never lost with my beloved. I simply chose to pick which times I would win and when I would abdicate an unwinnable pursuit."

All five laughed as the lighthearted moment gave a momentary escape to the serious matter at hand. "Very well," Sayren motioned with his hand to the western gate, "we should all go and decide what should be done. Once we've made our decision we should reconvene inside the lord's manor." With a unified nod the heirs separated and began to bark out orders to their soldiers as they each prepared for war, torches beginning to illuminate the town as the last few rays of setting sunlight disappeared.

CHAPTER 11

After being knocked unconscious and shackled, Rylan awoke to beams of morning sunlight shining through iron bars within his cell. A severe pain forced him awaken as his throbbing head began to increase. Rylan slowly relocated underneath the window welcoming the sunrise, alone with echoing sounds of approaching guards. Making a quick mental count of what he still had on hand, Rylan found himself stripped of metal, with the exception of his manacles. He felt almost naked without his armor, his Orden Forge armor was a precious gift that he had always held with high pristine. As the footsteps halted outside his cell, sounds of a key rotating a tarnished lock echoed around him until the door open. Five noble guardsmen entered with Mauro as the door slammed against the stone walls, the inquisitor's shoulder adorned with Rylan's armor.

"I see you've taken a fancy to my armor." Rylan grimaced as guards roughly lifted him upright.

Mauro grinned and bowed, presenting the shoulder piece as if it were the height of fashionable attire, "I think it suits me rather well. I doubt you would go so far to make usable metal for yourself that you'd destroy anything made by Orden."

Rylan scowled, "You know I very well could."

"Then I would surely lose an arm, while you would lose your life before you've even made it to see what remains of your family." Mauro scoffed as he motions of the guards to follow his as he turned to leave.

Rylan felt a pointed pressure against his back as he was sure there was a blade readied against him should he attempt anything. Unable to pursue anything further with Mauro as he exited the room with well-armed escorts surrounding him, Rylan focused on his plan with Sepius, should he have the chance to speak.

As they made their way from the inquisitor's prison, morning sunlight began to cascade over the high outer walls of the noble district. Ahead of the group, Tiberius and Isabelle both stood with armored attire and a flagbearer behind them. Mauro and Tiberius exchanged morning nods of salutation as both parties drew close to one another.

Mauro halted the group before stepping towards Isabelle, "Good morning Lady Isabelle, I am truly grateful you've decided to join us on this occasion."

Isabelle curtsied vigilantly as she eyed Rylan's glare only a few feet away, "Of course Inquisitor Mauro, should I become a Hero, I will be at the whim of his majesty. This is simply another way of expressing my devotion to such a title, and my liege."

A muffled chuckle sounded underneath Mauro's sleeve as he began to laugh only to begin coughing, "Although I was happy to make our return so quickly, I can't say I have enjoyed the lack of rest."

"Agreed," Tiberius answered as he motioned for his servant to join the group, "I cannot say I feel well rested either. With the harvest fast approaching, I fear that we will only see less and less sleep when this matter concludes."

Mauro gave a surprised look as Tiberius finished speaking, "What would drive you to believe such a thing? Surely with no further heirs there would be no one to contest the throne, or have I missed something?"

"I don't believe there is anything missing from what I've learned." Tiberius responded as the group began making their way towards the citadel once again. "However I would suspect that the other kingdom's heirs might seek vengeance and bolster the rebellious acts of their agitators within our borders."

Mauro silently nodded in agreement as he contemplated Tiberius' words, "You mean to say that should anything befall Rylan and the common rabble catch wind of it, we could see an increase in aggression against our kingdom and its properties?"

Tiberius motioned to Isabelle to stay close by him as she appeared to be slowing down, staring at Rylan's bruised and blooding head and neck. "That is quite possible, however I simply meant to imply that if word were ever to filter down into the lower districts that the Six Winged Death has been captured, King Sepius' right to rule would fall to quite relentless scrutiny. Such an action so close to harvest and winter would certainly spell economic hardships for Dalkas and several large cities."

Mauro exhaled heavily as his mind contemplated what he had heard, "That mere possibility would increase all of our duties several times over. Your family would be called to secure food transport and security. I can only imagine that we would be used to deal with any fool dumb enough to attempt to steal from our winter stores. Let us hope that does not come to fruition. It would save me much ache."

"I can only imagine what his majesty would do to you should you become unnecessary." Rylan chimed in as he held his head low, "I figure that if anyone in your situation is no longer required, King Sepius would surely take your head."

Tiberius, Isabelle, and several of the escorting guards turned their gaze to Rylan as he finished his audacious comments. Mauro continued walking as he replied, "Surely you must see that I am useful in more ways than a simple inquisitor. Although I base the majority of my time there, I am an invaluable asset towards the underworld dealings and spy networks."

"For someone so underhanded, you sound pretty boisterous with your shadows." Rylan responded with an openly displayed smirk fastened upon his face.

Mauro raised his hand for the group to halt as they arrived at the main gate for the citadel's walls, "Although I may have announced I am multi-faceted, I can only imagine just how anxious you must be getting if this is all that you've been able to distract yourself with."

"However poised you may be with your talents, I'm sure you'll one day met the end of your usefulness to the king and he will have you silenced like all the others who stood before him." Rylan responded before Mauro could advance to meet the gate's guards. "Do you not fear that day and the end you certainly face?"

Mauro sighed and motioned for one of his guardsmen to meet the others, "I fear death just as much as any soldier would, but I do not fear the pain of dying. I know that when my time comes to an end and I am betrayed or on my deathbed, I will not fear the end. I will fear whatever may come after it though, the very thought of anything after death frightens me."

Rylan nodded as he watched the guards exchanging words, "I can agree with your words. Our lives are filled with pain, whether physical or of the heart, but we all fear what may come after. Some have said that we are reunited with family, while there are some who would say that great men and women are taken to a place of eternal combat to where they fight and feast for all time with the first kings. If you fear death, have you made time for a woman, or child?"

Mauro cracked a smile as he released a chuckle, "I've never had the time for such compassion or trivial love. His majesty has always held me close to his side as to not allow the chance of such power to pass on to the next generation. With all the questions, what about yourself? I can imagine living in such fear must have kept you from having more than just one daughter. Did you hope to conceal yourselves long enough to rebuild your family?"

"My...daughter?" Rylan's face gave a puzzled look as Mauro's grin became a grand smirk adorning his face. "If you're worried about her potential you'd find little cause for alarm. She's shown barely any talent for metal. Even if she had grown to be where my mastery was for her age, I could never allow such a weak child claim a throne I did not want to begin with."

"So you'd show young Ophelia no love as she grows to be your only heir?" Mauro's voice sounded as if he believed Rylan's bluff in his answer; however he seemed all the more intrigued. "Even if you were to claim the throne you'd give her no privilege to the throne?"

Although his outward appearance remained unchanged, Rylan momentarily celebrated his accomplished ruse before returning to the question, "An act of putting someone so weak onto the throne would only serve as a sign of weakness to the other kingdoms and would surely spell disaster for Alder."

"Lord Inquisitor," the guardsman interrupted as he returned, "they will be lowering the gate immediately and a runner has been dispatched to notify his royal majesty."

Mauro cleared his throat before turning to the man, "Very well, see to it that you and the other guardsmen maintain your highest level of alertness as we enter. Should anything happen I will entrust you to lock down this city and deal with whatever stands in your way."

As the soldier saluted, Mauro made his way forward with Rylan, Tiberius and Isabelle through the massive threshold and into the outer courtyard. Rylan watched as several units of soldiers, comprised of at least thirty men each, moved into defensive formations on either side of him. Tiberius anxiously shoved Rylan forward as they neared the inner gate, his eyes carefully following the archer's arrows trained upon them from atop the inner parapets. Many of the inner walls had been draped with ornate Vasilli banners over where Rylan's bloodline once hung.

Rylan marveled at the sight of Dalkas' citadel, it had been over twenty harvests since he had last been inside the walls, but he could still recall how it looked before. Rows upon rows of tables set out for the men to relax while on watch, women in bright dresses scurrying about kissing their husbands goodbye for the day while each went about their duties. Many of the tables had broken or rotted from years of misuse, and only royal colors now moved about the walls as Rylan passed through the next gate and into the inner courtyard.

A cool morning breeze met the group as they entered the courtyard where the white crow lay underfoot; rows of royal guardsmen encased the courtyard while archers stood ready amongst the inner walls. As Mauro and Tiberius made their way down the steps towards a group approaching from within the estate, Rylan could make out the aged appearance of Sepius as he made his way towards the pavilion with Prince Faust and Lord Gaius following close behind. Several servants followed closely behind the trio with young Briar as they reached the pavilion and began taking their places.

"Good morning to you Your Majesty, Lord Gaius, Prince Faust, and young Master Briar." Mauro began as he and Tiberius took a knee, "I am proud to come bearing the sole heir to Alder's throne, Rylan Bassadora of the Six Crows."

Sepius motioned for both men to rise as he gazed upon Rylan and locked eyes with him. "I am happy to see your efforts finally come to bear such a bounty, inquisitor," he spoke as he motioned for one of his servants to move forward and present Mauro with a finely crafted, single edged blade, "may this be a sight for any and all to behold in how your dedication to the crown and Alder have been honored."

Mauro graciously retrieved the sword and bowed, "Thank you my great king. I could not ask for any gift other than to serve the rightful king. You do me great honor."

"Nonsense," Sepius grinned as he waived off the notion, "any man willing to go after the Six Winged Death must surely be awarded. As I am to also be aware that Lord Tiberius travelled with him, unknowingly."

Tiberius bowed, "Yes your majesty. I had contacted the Six Crows to assist myself and Lady Isabelle in recovering her gift to you for the harvest. We were not made aware of whom this man was until we were confronted by Inquisitor Mauro and he was detained."

"Seems convenient," Faust muttered to his father before gesturing to Tiberius, "How do you explain to us all, specially your king, that you unknowingly enlisted the help of the last remnants of Bassadora? Did you not see that man use metal when you held combat against members of the Serpent's Fang?"

Tiberius maintained his bow, "I did see him use a small amount of metal Prince Faust. I confronted Rylan about his ability, however he stated that he could only use a small amount of metal and was far more talented in combat than in his ability to wield any metal."

Sepius motion for Tiberius to arise, "I have no reason not to believe you Lord Tiberius. You've shown great promise and devotion to Alder as you've grown from a small boy into a soldier of renown. I also heard some of you lost some of your men during the journey as well, how did this come to pass?"

Tiberius lowered his head in dismay as he recalled the sight of his men buried in the dirt after their clash with the Fang, "I was accompanied by brave men who died protecting Lady Isabelle and Priestess Brilla when we were attacked by the Serpent's Fang. Only one man survived, and he failed to protect his charges when we were beset by bandits in Havenhome. I have already sent word to their families of their passing and thanked them for their service to my family."

"That is very diplomatic of you Lord Tiberius; perhaps you are getting a taste for politics after all." Sepius responded with a grin upon his face, "However we shall dispatch with further questions of your journey and that of Lady Isabelle's gift until after I've dealt with the bastard. Bring him forward would you Mauro."

Lady Isabelle nudged Rylan forward as Mauro outstretched his hand and seized him by the arm, Rylan's eyes transfixed on Sepius as he drew closer until the king held up a hand to hold. "I see you've finally returned to what was once your home Rylan, how do you appreciate my governance of Alder?"

"I've seen far worse things in the twenty harvests it's taken me to see you once again, however I couldn't help but notice you still have the white crow held within place, have you chosen to adopt the sigil for yourself?" Rylan slighted as he glared at Sepius.

"The last time I recall you having such distain for me, you had just lost your father. Or maybe you were there when I stole your mother from you? Is this why you hold such hatred towards me, or is it because I sit where you feel you belong?" Sepius smirked menacingly as he began to arise, only to be met with a coughing fit. A servant quickly rushed to his side, a blackened cloth outstretched as Sepius quickly pulled the handkerchief over his mouth to conceal the crimson trail running from his lips. "As for that old crow, it would've required me to remove the tiles around it, and I do so loved those blood-stained stones, they remind me of all those that stood before you, all those that stood against me."

Rylan clenched his fist in fury as his long list of allies had dwindled over the years, undoubtedly meeting their ends on his family's crest behind him, "I hold no distain for you, King Sepius. For twenty harvests I have had the chance to overcome my dislike of you and accept the fact that I no longer wished for a title I never wanted. I was there when you killed my father, and my mother. I watched as my friends and family met their ends by your hands or your shadowed puppets, however I still do not wish vengeance upon you. I came here because I wish to abdicate my right to the throne and take what is left of my life and disappear."

As Rylan finished speaking, Faust motioned to a servant on the outer part of the hedged area, and the servant disappeared momentarily as Amelia emerged from the bushes, her body spotted with dark purple and blue bruises, a thick metal collar around her neck, and a goblet shaking in her bloodied hands. Amelia kneeled before Faust as she presented him the goblet, her head lowered and avoiding contact with Rylan and Faust.

"Rylan, pay attention when your King is trying to speak to you boy!" Sepius screamed as he smacked Rylan across the face with the back of his hand, his rings scrapping against Rylan's cold skin leaving streaks of bright red. Amelia looked to Rylan, but he quickly turned his attention back to Sepius with concentrated eyes peering deep into Sepius' soul. "You make quite the offer for a bastard and the last living heir of King Ralford's blood. As promising as your bargain may be, I am without the Sword or Ring of Alder. You, as well as I, know that without either, my right to rule is all but naught with you alive, abdicated or not. Besides that," Sepius grinned as he nodded to Faust, "why would I ever neglect such a beautiful opportunity to break a member of the House of Bassadora before ending my opposition entirely?"

Enraged, Rylan attempted to leap forward at Sepius as the old king took his seat, but found both Mauro and Tiberius withholding his arms and forcing him to his knees, "Coward!" he roared as he desperately attempted to pry himself free of his restraints, "I will never give you the sight you wish to behold!"

Faust suddenly grasped Amelia's knotted hair and handed his goblet to one of the servants, "Let's begin with the pretty little whore, would that be fitting father?" With a sudden shuffle of boots, three men came scurrying out with a large block of wood and a wicker basket. A fourth, hooded, muscular fellow emerged wielding a large, polished axe and made his way to the other three as they began to set up an impromptu executioner's block. Faust threw Amelia to the ground and with his closing grip, began to constrict her airway with the metal collar. Amelia began to gasp and chock for air as she tried to breathe, however the executioner's assistants quickly grabbed both arms and dragged her over to the block as she writhed and struggled in pain.

Rylan attempted to lurch forward but was quickly met by a direct hit with Mauro's new sword hilt into his chest. Rylan coughed as Faust stepped before him and took a knee, holding Rylan's head upright with his hair, "What did you say? Did you just insult me?"

"I'll never let you rest if you kill her." Rylan cursed Faust as he spat in his face.

Although clearly angered, Faust paused to wipe the saliva off of his cheek before he launched his fist into Rylan's unguarded face. "I don't think you understand how this is going to happen!" Faust struck again, "We will take everything from you right before your eyes! I will rip them all away while you watch, unable to stop all that you care about die!" Faust attacked Rylan with several more strikes before releasing Rylan's hair and returning to his seat. "I want them to look into each other's eyes. I want him to see her soul leave her body!"

Sepius placed a hand over his son's clenched fist to warn him of his temper as the assistants each locked her hands in place and held Amelia's head in place atop the block. Rylan and Amelia met eyes as she continued to gasp for breath, her face beginning to turn a slight purple.

As the Executioner readied his axe, he turned his head to King Sepius and waited for his command. "Hold a moment." Sepius looked to Isabelle and motioned for her to approach, "Would you do me the honor of hold Rylan's head up, I don't want him to turn away from such a sight."

Isabelle looked at Sepius wide eyed as he finished and looked over to Tiberius for help. Although repulsed at the thought, Tiberius silently nodded to Isabelle to do as she was instructed. Slowly descended down the steps as she made her way to the others, Isabelle swallowed the lump in her throat before taking hold of Rylan's hair and firmly tugging it upward to ensure Sepius took notice of her compliance.

Sepius gave a large grinned and turned back to the executioner, "Do it." In an instant the axe descended on its mark. Isabelle recoiled at the sight and released Rylan's head, however Rylan did not move or breathe; he could only watch as Amelia's matted hair descended into the basket and out of view. With a dismissing grunt, the king's headsman pried his bloodied blade from the wood and released a stream of crimson into the air. As the blood splashed onto Rylan's face, both Sepius and Faust erupted into a strong laughter, forcing many of the guards and servants to follow suit even after several inaudible retches. A bloody river formed between the stone tiles as Amelia's body was dragged away by the executioner's assistants.

With the body out of sight and the laughter subsiding, Sepius looked to Rylan as their eyes locked and Rylan appeared stone-faced as he watched Sepius sip from his wine, "My, my Rylan, I must say that suits you quite well, maybe we should bath you in your allies blood before we send you on your way to meet them. Who should I send to the block next?" Rylan remained still as he stayed emotionless as Sepius grinned, "Maybe one of your loving brothers? You must know I nearly died myself when I found they belonged to my dear old friend Larus. Did you know he was once proposed to become my successor? I was appalled at the very notion of his blood ever resting in what I had brought to flourish inside King's Hold, all while I was to be moved to the southern border to oversee our relations with Vaine. I could not allow such a dreadful thing to transpire, so I joined the cause of overthrowing King Sepius and the others. It took very little effort as I was already in a position to get the other armies into Alder's district within King's Hold. You know what happened next, however when I found out that you had possibly joined his line with royal blood, I knew I had to exact my vengeance then instead of allowing such a thing to continue. I'll have you know that your brother Wilhelm Carthill is dead; his bones picked clean by the swine I will serve at the Harvest Festival to the people of Dalkas. I sent one of them to be consumed with what they had become. Your other brother, Ebon, though was able to see the error of his ways and dispatch with the festering disease that had infected his name. After he dispatched his brother I had him dispatch his sister. Such a stubborn one; Abigail was certainly faithful to you. I offered to spare her life if she named you and your brothers as the heirs. Alas, she too had to be removed, Lord Ebon, do come and join us."

From the doorway where Sepius and his subjects had emerged from, a figure dressed in brilliant white and gold emerged, his face clean shave, and hair pulled back, braided with strips of golden cloth woven into place. Ebon made his way to Gaius' side, farthest away from Sepius, but bowed as he moved into his noticeably preordained position, "Good morning your majesty. How may I serve you this great day?"

Sepius paid no mind to Ebon as he spoke, but instead looked to

Rylan and the inquisitor, "Mauro, what did you tell me Rylan had said he wanted to be?"

Mauro, swallowed the lump in his throat as he thought about Rylan's words about his usefulness, "A man of... of the king, your highness."

"Ah yes," Sepius smirked as he pointed to Rylan, "A man of the king. I must say I applaud your choice of words; perhaps I'll use that in my speech when I tell them that the Six Winged Death lies death at my feet. As I recall though, you are not the only heir of your father, you have three brothers. I know of Sayren and Toren; however your last brother's name eludes my sight. What is it?"

Rylan remained still and quiet as he continued to glare at Sepius.

"No matter," the king said as he gestured to Tiberius, "Tell me, heir of House Bernak, what fate befell the other members of your party?"

Tiberius looked to Isabelle, Rylan, and then finally to Sepius as he sighed, "They fell in battle your majesty. When we were beset by bandits, the brothers were forced to fight while Lady Isabelle and Brilla were overseeing the other captive's safety. We were grossly outnumbered and forced to fight beyond the means of a normal soldier. All three of Rylan's brothers fell to the bandits as they fought."

"Would you concur this?" Faust asked Isabelle as he sat forward in his chair and rested his chin upon his clasped hands.

Isabelle bowed, "Yes, Prince Faust. Brilla and I protected another family that was captured with us. I did not witness the brother's fall, but I could see Rylan's rage as each brother died. It was truly a horrific sight to behold as he fought with such rage. I could only imagine what damage he could've commanded if he had all six wings."

Sepius examined Isabelle's body language as she spoke, carefully watching her hand she held over a small pouch. "Tell me," he started as Isabelle concluded speaking, "were you able to recover the artifact you wished to find for me?"

"I was your highness." She responded nervously.

"If it is alright with you, I would like to see the gift now. Should I judge it to be worthy; I will bestow upon you the title of Hero immediately." Sepius' smile widened as he could see Rylan's glare dull as he began to worry about Isabelle's response.

"I must apologize, King Sepius," Tiberius interjected, "if such a thing is to happen, it would surely need to be in the eyes of at least five noble houses. Such a thing could not be done otherwise without adoption into a house."

Sepius scowled at Tiberius as he turned his eyes to meet his, "You are unfortunately right Lord Tiberius. I cannot help but asked myself why would such a selfless woman like Lady Isabelle be worthy of such a simple title as 'Hero', would you say you have power my dear?"

Isabelle once again looked at Tiberius before speaking, "I would only wish to have power to help those without it sire. Such is the responsibility of the strong to protect those that cannot. I cannot say that I hold the same power as Lord Tiberius or yourself, but with what I have, I strive to make every part of it worthy of a titled position."

Faust smiled at her and nudged his father's hand, "I do believe you're right father. She would be quite fitting. I would certainly agree to such a proposal."

Sepius clapped his hands together, "It's settled then, upon the death of Rylan and the House of Bassadora, a union between Lady Isabelle and Prince Faust, my son, will be arranged. Let us celebrate by concluding with dispatching Rylan's daughter, then we'll celebrate with a fine meal to discuss the betrothal."

Another inquisitor entered the courtyard with a young girl, shackled and a sack concealing her head. As the inquisitor bowed to King Sepius, he removed the burlap sack and revealed a very distraught Ophelia. King Sepius returned his malicious scowl to Rylan and watch as he gritted his teeth and strained every muscle to break free, but Tiberius placed are assuring hand on his chest, "The King would never dare harm a child, regardless of blood. Such a thing is disgraceful and will not be tolerated by nobles."

"Perhaps we should kill the girl and then parade what is left of Rylan's soul across Dalkas before hanging him for all to see his bloodline fail. What do you say father?" Faust's lively tone clearly displayed his unsavory ideals with the laws and intentions to effectively finish toying with his captive.

Sepius gave Faust a displease look, "Only someone foolhardy would finish off their opponent when they hold nothing. If you wish to ever be compared to me boy, you must learn that everything can be taken away from an opponent. Even people they do not suspect to be on their side. Perhaps you could learn that from your dear sister. Brilla do come out here."

From behind where Ophelia had emerged with the inquisitor, Brilla presented herself in her true colors. A regal white dress, trimmed with gold designs, and an ornate necklace with golden wings. Her hair tied back and an emotionless expression on her face, Brilla walked out in her actual occupation, the rumored daughter of King Sepius. "Good morning father, I'm glad to see you up so early this morning." A smile similar to his painted across Brilla's face as she glanced over Rylan and the nobles, a singular horrified expression painted upon their faces.

"Ah, it is truly a gift to finally have you back home and away from the wild clutches of the fallen prince." Sepius smiled as he reached for her hand and gently kissed it before motioning to Tiberius and Isabelle, "Since you were there my dearest Brilla, would you do me the kindest of telling me the legitimacy of their stories?"

Brilla curtsied as her eyes widened and her smile became far more malicious that that of her father, "Of course. Such a wonderful tale these nobles have spun for you. Daring deeds of heroism indeed, however I can only say that their stories are much like their honor, lacking. What Lord Tiberius and Lady Isabelle have told you are all lies. Even more so than that, Rylan's brothers yet live and are with the other heirs within King's Hold. I fear that they may already be readying an attack against us." Brilla could see her father's mind formulating, while Faust's rage began to whiten his knuckles as she continued. "If your inquisitor had pressed Rylan for further information and interrogated him on the whereabouts of his brothers, or that of the Sen Portal he had arrived from, perhaps you would not be sitting here with only one brother, but all four instead."

"Four you say?" Sepius turned to Rylan as he tugged his beard, "I only three boys. Did you learn of his name?"

Brilla looked to Rylan as she gave a quick wink, "Aldis. He is quite the aspiring sage. He would have gone to the noble sage's college to study starting after the harvest. If he was not related he could've become quite the historian."

Sepius gave a silent nod to one of his aids who lifted a bright yellow flag, and with an almost instant reaction, the courtyard filled with soldiers, weapons readied in clenched hands as they surrounded Rylan and the nobles. Several moments passed silently as Sepius contemplated his next move. "I could have you all killed for such treason. I had hoped for far better standards of you two," Sepius pointed to Tiberius and Mauro as he then turned his gaze to Isabelle, "as for you; I could never allow such a poisoned woman as you within my retinue. With such a devotion to your guardian, I would never be able to turn you to stand with us."

Tiberius remained in place as he still restrained Rylan's arm, "My king, I would never presume to guess your motives or actions, however Rylan had showed no notion for wanting your rightful crown. He even turned down the other heirs when they asked him to join them. If such a man does not want the crown, perhaps he can convince his brothers to do the same and you would rule without opposition. I will not ask you to spare me for my actions; however I ask that you allow Lady Isabelle to-"

"Enough!" Faust roared as he allowed his anger to control his mind. "Bring me that bastard's daughter and I'll gut her myself! Then I'll have Daliah gouge out the rest of your eyes before throwing you to the dogs as they feast on your still breathing bodies!"

Sepius quickly arose and motioned for the inquisitor to come forward, "Splendid idea boy, kill the girl and then take out your hate on those that would seek to destroy our name!"

As the inquisitor began to tug Ophelia's chained restraints, Isabelle stepped forward and revealed the Ring of Alder, "Sire please spare her! I do not wish to see an innocent child harmed, even if it means I sacrifice myself to do so! I bring you the ring as my token of duty; however I would ask to trade her life for this instead!"

Sepius outstretched his hand, "Hold the girl there. Gaius, if any of them so much as move, snap her neck. Give me the ring girl, now!"

"Don't! If you give him that ring, there will be nothing stopping him from killing us all!" Rylan shouted as he remained still. Rylan tapped both Mauro and Tiberius on their sides to ease up his arms should Sepius move for the ring. Reluctantly Rylan felt both men almost completely release his arms while still concealing their motive.

Sepius turned to Rylan, "I've heard enough from you! You are a prisoner and a dead man, stay there and watch as I show you just how I will dissect your every hope until there is nothing but sorrow in my wake. Today you die, and tomorrow your house will fall! No hand me that damned ring bitch!"

Tiberius nudged Rylan, wordlessly giving him the prompt to move, however Rylan remained still. Conflicted in his own mind Rylan realized their only hope of survival was to do what he had set out never to pursue. A needless and bloody war to claim something he did not desire, nor need. He looked at the bloodied stones before him and Amelia's helpless face burned into his mind. Rylan looked to Isabelle, her hand shakily extending with the ring in her palm. For a moment, a white crow, the symbol of his bloodline appeared in Isabelle hand and upon Tiberius' shoulder as he tugged against Rylan's arm. Everything seemed to flash as Rylan's mind resolved the conflict within himself and he lurched forward into action.

Rylan leaped forward, ripping Mauro's sword from his grasp and extended his hand towards the ring as Sepius seized it from Isabelle's hand, "I am Rylan Bassadora, the Six Winged Death and Heir of Alder, answer my call!"

"No!" Sepius roared as he tightened his hold on the ring, attempting to slide it onto his own finger, but the ring simply liquefied in his hand and flew to Rylan, "Kill them all, now!"

Rylan watched as the surrounding troops released their arrows and started their attacks as the Ring of Alder reformed itself around his finger, the polished, gleaming metal dulled and seemingly calcified itself in place as a single word echoed in Rylan's head, "Command."

"Stop!" Rylan roared as he extended his hand, and for the first time in Sepius' reign, metal not belonging to a wielder halted in its place. Arrows held their position in midair, royal guards slammed against their immovable armor, and Faust's partially formed blade seized his arm.

Sepius gazed in horror as he scoured the courtyard as Rylan made his way too him, "You cannot do this, such a thing is beneath your blood! If you truly claim your title as heir you cannot kill a member of royalty!"

Rylan silently moved past him and over to the inquisitor holding Ophelia. As he drew closer, Rylan could tell the man was stuck in place by their ceremonial armor under his robes and glanced over to Ophelia, "Close your eyes and don't open them till I tell you. No matter what you feel or hear; keep them closed."

As Ophelia tightly closed her eyes, Rylan waved his free hand over the metal shackles and watched as they fell to the ground. Rylan then turned his attention back to the inquisitor and callously forced Mauro's sword blade through the man's throat.

Brilla freed herself from her gold necklace and attempted to flee as Sepius launched his concealed metal from the dirt at Rylan's unprotected back, only to find it ricochet off an invisible barrier around Rylan and soar directly at his daughter's unprotected back. Sounds of a sudden shriek echoed through the courtyard as Rylan turned to see Sepius falling to his knees and tears streaming from his face at the sight of his impaled daughter pinned against the rock tiles.

"Sepius Vasilli," Rylan began as he removed the sword and waived his free hand once more, turning the arrows and weapons upon the soldiers who wielded them, "you usurped my father's throne, the Throne of King Ralford. I wished to avoid such conflict and allow you to rule unopposed, but you continued your rampage as you took from me my mother, Queen Maree. You then saw to the murder of my family, Lord Wilhelm and Lady Amelia of House Carthill. I was willing to let your transgressions pass still, if only to see my family safe and your title remain in your hands. I cannot, I will not allow you to stand before me unopposed any longer. For the crimes against you there is but one punishment I can honorably sentence you too. You will die by the pure metal of the First King. Arthlyn Bassadora made the ring with his entire ability before sealing it away within Dalkas; he placed the white crow upon the courtyard before you."

With subtle vibrations at first the stones began to gently vibrate as the white crow began to crack and fly into the air before forming several dozen white, metal crows in the sky above the courtyard.

Rylan clenched his fist as he backed away as the swarm of crows began to soar towards Sepius and his entourage.

Gaius quickly surrounded himself in a capsule of metal, while Faust concealed himself and Briar in a similar fashion. Frantic screams of horrified servants echoed throughout the inner walls as the metallic crows swept through them without resistance. As the echoes seemed to die out, Sepius surveyed the carnage left at Arthlyn's Ring; red stained stone tiles lay cracked or shattered as his servants lay in pieces along the ground. With his soldiers, servants, and his precious daughter Brilla dead, Sepius fell to his knees, "This is not a power of Alder; this is the work of a monster!"

"You'd be correct Sepius," Rylan answered as he place his free hand atop Sepius' shoulder and pressed Mauro's sword blade against his throat, "the bloody portrait of your reign was made at the hands of the boy who you attempted to break, the hands of the Six Winged Death. I will give it you, had me at a complete disadvantage; however you lost when you believed that my six wings are all that I learned to master. What will you do knowing you're line is now left with only a coward and his son?"

Sepius closed his eyes and cackled, "I will be at peace stupid boy. My son may never be me, but my grandson holds the potential to rule all of Thesia when he takes my place. While you protect your heir, I will protect mine to my last breathe, for they are cursed to clash one day and my grandson will stand the victor. Now do what you set out to do before my guards get here and kill you, I grow weary of this burdened crown."

"I never wanted to kill you, you old fool. All I ever desired was a normal life that my brothers could live and know true happiness. You stole that from them, and now I have no choice but to finish a bloody war you began so long ago." Rylan's solemn tone was neither hateful nor sorrowful as he pulled the blade across Sepius' throat and pulled back his hair.

Sepius' tired, elderly figure did not so much as lift a finger as he felt his limbs grow cold and numb, his sight began to blur and his sense of sound began to dull, but the sound of mobilizing troops rushing the courtyard gave him one last smile before his mind went blank and his lifeless body collapsed on the ground.

Rylan turned to Isabelle, Tiberius, and Mauro as the approaching footsteps grew louder, "I have no intention of any needless killing, if you wish to join my brothers, you are welcome to follow me. Should you decide not to I will be forced to knock you unconscious to prevent their suspicion. I cannot guarantee your safety though if you stay. What will you choose?"

Tiberius bowed, "I am with Lady Isabelle. As her guardian I could not leave her side, should she choose to join you, I would renounce my position as heir apparent to House Bernak and its holdings."

Isabelle walked over to Ophelia and gently took her hand as she led her to Tiberius, "I will not stand idle as innocent people of Alder are thrust into a feud they do not understand. I will fight with the rightful heir to ensure all people of Alder are respected and receive fair rights. I stand with you."

"Well I suppose it would be difficult asking you to leave me my sword, seeing as how you just murdered a king with it," Mauro sighed as he looked at his crimson stained sword, "Even if I were to stay, I'm sure that my father would have me killed for not attempting to stop you, Faust would kill me for allowing you to even free yourself, and I would almost certainly be ousted and left to feed the hungry dogs that the royal family keeps for his unfavorable friends. So I will be accompanying you, if you'll allow me to."

Rylan cleaned the blade with a piece of Sepius' clothes before handing it to Mauro, "I do not despise you for being steadfast in your work, but it will take time for me to accept you are the reason many of my family are dead."

As Mauro took the blade he looked behind Rylan to see Ebon cowering on the ground, his hands concealing his bawling face as he knelt in his soiled pants, "What about him? He is still your family is he not? If we are to leave I'd be sure to collect him before we do so."

Rylan continued to face Mauro as he spoke to Ebon, his tone cruel and pointed, "You killed our brother and sister. What do you have to say for yourself? Speak now before I leave you to a cruel fate brother!"

Ebon's body lurched forward as he pressed his face and hands against the stone, "Please Rylan! I did not do so without reason! I did it to save Ophelia's life! Sepius said that if one brother died he would spare her and Abigail! I didn't know he would force me to kill my sister as well, but if I didn't he was going to kill both of them and force me to watch as they flayed Ophelia's skin to the bone!"

Rylan could not hold his anger against his brothers as he turned and picked him up off the ground, "I understand now why you did what you did, but I am not sure how we will be able to explain this to Sayren. I assure you though we will approach him together when we reunite with them."

"I could never ask you to do such a thing," Ebon responded as he tightly gripped Rylan's arms before he turned to the dead inquisitor's body and drew his sword and dagger, "I will remain here and see to it that you are bought enough time to escape. Thank you for making me feel I am not totally lost in my disgrace brother, I will complete my promise to you today. I will ensure that Ophelia stays far away from danger as possible. I apologize for not being able to do so before this."

Rylan bowed as Ebon adjusted his grip, "I could not ask you to do more than you will. I'll ensure Sayren knows that his brothers and wife did not die for nothing. I hope for our forefathers to be fair in their judgment of you Ebon, and thank you."

Ebon made his way to the main gate as the sounds of armed guards preparing themselves into formation to enter. Rylan and the other made their way to where Arthlyn's metal lay, revealing a descending spiral staircase in its place, "Quickly," Rylan motioned for Tiberius to go first, "We will use these tunnels to exit Dalkas. I will lead the way once I have dealt with Lord Gaius."

As Isabelle and Ophelia proceeded down the stairs, Mauro stopped at Rylan's side and turned, "You should know I was not the one to start this set of events. Lord Carthill was abducted by a masked man that passed along a message: 'The noble houses of Alder will fall to the rightful king's hand and a new day will dawn with your crimson life blood upon the streets. The low born will rise and drive the knife through your frail king's heart. The Crow's wings will spread and the Six Winged Death will take his throne.' Hopefully that will shed some light on to who started this chain of events."

Rylan's mind once again recalled the masked individual's face as he made his way to Gaius' metal. Rylan pressed his hand against the cold steel and stepped away as the metal melted to the ground. Gaius stepped forward to confront Rylan, his expression filled with seething hatred and rage as his eye glimpsed at the bloody carnage that lay around him. Gaius fearlessly approached Rylan, moving within a breath's distance from his face, "You know I will kill you if you don't end this now like the coward you are."

"I didn't expect you to still have a spine after being on your back for Sepius after so long." Rylan's calm tone still held his hatred for his father's murderer, "I didn't come here to start this, nor will I continue needlessly killing. I may detest your very existence, but I am leaving with what remains of my family. If you feel the need to avenge your pseudo king, you can try and find me, I'm sure you can find another dog like yourself who'll bark when you command."

Rylan stepped away and began making his way to the hole in the courtyard as Gaius furiously clenched his fist, "I will warn you now though Gaius LeBlanc; you killed my father, but I am not him. I will not take pity on you or anyone you bring with you if you decide to pursue me. Consider this your only warning."

Gaius looked back to Sepius's bloody corpse before responding to Rylan's words, "I will find you boy, and believe me when I say you will not survive the hell that I will have at my back. You will die and then I will kill anyone who dared to stand beside you! I will avenge my king!"

Rylan waved off the notion as he sent one of the crows directly at Faust's shield. A loud clang followed by Briar screaming as Rylan descended down the steps, his heart burdened by the notion of leaving Ebon, but his brother was right; murdering his own siblings could not be over looked. A loud boom echoed in the stairwell as the front gate burst open, sounds of Ebon roaring into battle rang in Rylan's ears as he closed his hand and recalled the white metal crows back to their seal over him. As the last bird melted into shape, Rylan took a deep breath and exhaled slowly as he sat on the bottom step in front of the others. Ophelia quickly ran to Rylan and wrapped her small arms around him as she began to weep uncontrollably. Rylan silently embraced her and held her tight in his arms for a moment before kissing her forehead and returned to his feet, "Lady Isabelle, I do apologize for asking you to do such a frivolous task; however would you mind lighting torches as we make our way? It was how we were taught to distinguish our location should there ever be a need to use these tunnels to escape Dalkas."

"Of course, I will assist however I can." Isabelle agreed as she took another torch from the wall around the stairwell and ignited a flame.

Mauro looked down the dark tunnel passage before turning to the group, "I don't mean to question you Rylan, you certainly have much more knowledge about these caverns than I do, but how will torches help navigate where we should go if we are trying to make our way out of the city?"

"Fair enough," Rylan responded as he moved his hand along the side of the rock wall and pulled metal from the small cracks, "I will use the metal underneath the city to find our way out. We should hurry though, once we get outside the walls, we'll be at my brother's hunting hut where he has horsed tied up. They'll most likely be hungry, but they should take us to Havenhome without any hindrance."

※　※　※

As soldiers flooded the courtyard and began to collect the multitude of dead, Gaius barked orders to soldiers passed by too close, "You! Take two men and notified the city guards, no one is allowed in or out without my approval!" Gaius' frustration growing more prevalent with each passing breath as he continued to shout out commands, "Bring a healer to me at once! I need the Royal Guard here now!"

Faust sat in his chair, hands pressed against his forehead as he sat stunned by the events, his mind burning with the images of his father lying dead before him as Briar ran to the dead king and began to shake Sepius' body, begging his grandfather to wake up. Faust quickly yanked Briar away and shouted at him to return to his room until a servant fetched him, however Faust was unsure if any servant would dare step inside the courtyard, let alone the estate, should word break out. A moment of clarity surged into Faust's mind as he leaped upright and shouted, "Everyone stop!"

A sudden hush fell upon the tiled stones as Faust made his way to the stone stairs and turned to face his men, "You are all staring at the might of our enemies; my father was foolish enough to waste meaningless time attempting to slowly dissect his adversary. Such a mistake has forced us to pay a heavy price. Such a cost that I will not allow it to go without a response! Lord Gaius, I will entrust you with five hundred of the noble guard to take with whatever mercenaries you can muster to pursue our king's murderer. All other soldiers are to report directly to me as we handle this situation. This matter must be dealt with quickly and tactfully as to avoid hysteria within our walls. Now be about your preassigned duties!"

Once again the bustling commotion of armored soldiers rushed about the courtyard as Gaius marched forward with clenched fists to stand beside him, "What are you doing?" He muttered, "We will need our best troops to end that bastard's life and eliminate all that would choose to stand beside him."

Faust looked at Gaius, his facial expression dull, but there was a distinct flash in his eyes, "As my father's son, the right to rule falls to me, and as the next in line, I cannot needlessly throw away what men we have here to sate your lust for vengeance. I would not leave Dalkas undefended; however I will happily assist in providing funds to gather mercenaries to assist you."

"Are you mad?" Gaius shouted as he drew several eyes, "If you send mercenaries to fight, you would do your father's name, your name, the greatest dishonor!"

Faust stepped into Gaius, the two chest to chest, their foreheads pressed together, "You forget your place, Lord Gaius! As Heir to Alder's Throne, I have command of the armies! You would do well to accept my help before I hand the honor of avenging my father to another!"

Gaius reluctantly backed away, "Very well. I will do as you've requested. I would keep in mind though the smallest detail you have forgotten. With the Bassadora bloodline emerging from the shadows once again, your right to rule is put into question; not only its legitimacy, but your favor with the heads of the noble houses. You will need their seals of approval to ever call yourself king in Alder. I will take my leave and gather what forces I can. We can discuss other matters upon our return with Rylan's head upon my spear."

Faust stood motionless as Gaius made his way for the main gate, his mind recalling his less than desirable reputation with the noble houses. His time had been spent showing them the many ways they were beneath him, and had garnered himself a rather appalling notion of him having to grovel with them in order to gain what he had earned. Faust quickly made his way back into the estate to find Daliah lingering inside his room, "I require your assistance."

"Of course sire." Daliah responded with a quick bow, "What is it you require?"

Faust paced back and forth in front of her for a moment before spinning to stand face to face, "You told me a member of the Serpent's fang had fought Rylan of the Six Crows not but a few days ago correct?"

"Yes." She nodded.

"Take my coin purse and fetch him as well as any other members you can gather. My father was ruthlessly cut down by that crow bastard, and now that fool Gaius will ride out to kill him. If he succeeds, the nobles will almost certainly place him as king and we will be left to grovel with the rest of the noble pigs and their poor excuse of power." Faust's eyes seemed to flare as his mind began to finalize remaining details to ensure his succession. "On the chance that Gaius is able to accomplish such a feat, I would require him to perish a true hero in battle. I need you to accompany his forces, however if you succeed and return with Rylan Bassadora's head, I will see to it personally that you wield the title of 'Head Inquisitor'."

"That would be most gracious, Prince Faust. I-" Daliah began before Faust smacked her across the face with the back of his hand.

"I will be King and you will address me as such!" He roared as she clutched her face.

"Of course, as you wish, my king." Daliah bowed and quickly made her exit for the door as Faust watched the servants quickly scurried around the grounds carrying messages and bandages to and fro.

Faust grinned as he fell upon his bed and began to chuckle, "Finally," he whispered, "I will finally be what I deserve. I will be the true King of Alder."

CHAPTER 12

As Havenhome's defenders were finalizing their posture, Sayren took an uneasy stroll along the calm central road towards the western gate, now manned by Gianni's archers. Many of the citizen's that weren't capable of fighting had already been escorted back to King's Hold by Toren, while the remaining people had dawned what armor the town had in supply and sat around campfires dotted about the village. Aldis, Yvon, and Gauld had taken up residence with the other captain's within Raven's Roost and were overseeing the deployment of food and drink as the day progressed. Sayren stared into the setting sun as his mind raced about his family's condition. A sudden ringing of the alarm bell shook Sayren back to reality as he raced forward towards the gate as they opened. Escorted by Alkith's forward scouts on all sides, a small grouping of three horses entered the town. Sayren's heart raced as he saw Ophelia racing towards him, quickly dropping to a knee in the soft mud as she leaped into his arms and began to cry. Sayren closed his eyes as he pressed his hand against Ophelia's sullied hair and kissed her on the cheek as Rylan and the others dismounted from their steeds and moved towards Sayren and the other approaching heirs.

"I see you made it back in one piece," Alkith grinned as he opened his arms, "such a sight to behold, but I cannot help but notice you seem to be a few people short. Where's that lovely priestess and your remaining family?"

Rylan glared at Alkith as he made his way over to Sayren and wrapped his arms around both him and Ophelia, "I was unable to save them brother." Rylan's voice cracked as he delivered the news, "Our brothers and sister died protecting your daughter and our future."

Sayren lifted Ophelia into his arms and backed away from Rylan, "We could have avoided this fate if you had told us of our birthright brother. Now I must see to my motherless daughter and prepare for whatever demons you have chasing your tail."

Rylan stepped forward and grabbed Sayren's collar, "You will not insult me for keeping our family together as best I could. Nothing can last forever, but I imagined we would be much older before such an event like this occurred." Rylan sighed as he reached into his small pouch, grabbing Arthlyn's Ring and placing it in Sayren's hand, "You will not fight what is coming. I came back to tell you that I will fight Gaius and his army alone when they arrive tomorrow."

Alkith laughed as he approached and placed his hand on Rylan's shoulder, "You are quite the jest-"

Rylan instantly swept Alkith's hand off, released Sayren, and gripped Alkith by the throat as he brought himself close to the heir's ear, "If you dare touch me again I will take that mask that has cost me my family and us it to sever your limbs before taking your head."

Rylan's whispered words froze Alkith in place as he silently nodded and stepped away when Rylan eased his hold, "Rylan is right," Alkith choked as he rubbed his neck, "We shall depart immediately. He would face down an army to ensure his bloodline survives, and I feel that is most fitting. If he does succeed, then he will surely be worthy of his title as 'The Six Winged Death' and have a suitable place at our table as we retake our rightful thrones."

As the other heirs gave Alkith a puzzled look, they agreed with his position and instantly began barking orders with the exception of Naria. She stood just off to the side as Rylan bowed to Tiberius, Isabelle, and Mauro, thanking each of them for assisting and motioning for them to follow Sayren.

"Rylan," Naria asked as she slowly made her way forward as he turned to meet her, "Is that actually you?"

Surprised, Rylan could not believe his eyes as he looked upon Naria for the first time in what seemed an eternity, "Naria? You looked so different…as if the last time the young lady I saw has now fashioned herself into a strong and able warrior befitting the title of queen."

"Oh shut up," Naria said as she blushed, "I've been forced to wield the responsibilities of a people that I don't rule, in a place that I do not claim. I suppose you had the easier life of living without the responsibilities of those not of your blood."

Rylan smile, "Hardly. I have been so calculated in protecting my family and their secret that I lost what little time I had to find happiness. I suppose you have already had several suitors approach and ask for your hand?"

Naria playfully smacked Rylan's chest as she scowled at him, "Of course not. I haven't found a man worthy of my prowess, but my brother has seen fit to attempt an alliance of marriage with allies he has seemingly discovered across the sea."

Rylan sighed, "Of course he has. Your brother never runs out of schemes and ideas. I'm sure you'll tell me that he's also found himself waist deep in secrets and stratagems for any possibly in his grand campaign to retake your place in Kay."

"If he hasn't already I'm sure he will now that you and your brothers have returned." Naria said as she stared into Rylan's eyes.

Rylan momentarily lost himself as he looked into Naria's gaze and began to slowly inch towards her, until a sudden clatter of plates echoed from within the Raven's Roost and Aldis burst from the doorway as he raced to Rylan. Rylan barely had a moment to prepare himself as Aldis slammed into him, wrapping his arms around him and squeezing tightly, "Brother! I'm so happy you're safe!"

Naria started to chuckle as Rylan attempted to free himself for Aldis with no avail, "I see that you two need to catch up. It was a pleasure to see you once again Rylan. I don't believe I will be leaving until the morning, in case we are beset before everyone can return through the portal."

Aldis instantly released his brother and bowed to Naria, "I must sincerely apologize, Lady Naria; I did not mean to intrude."

"It's quite alright," Naria replied as he returned the bow, "I can understand the longing to see a brother after their fate becomes uncertain. Do catch up with Rylan; tomorrow will be quite the uncertain day."

As Naria finished her statement Rylan bowed, "Good evening Lady Naria. I do hope you stay safe whatever our futures may hold before us." Naira bowed once more before turning and walking back towards the noble estate.

Aldis and Rylan proceed back to the Raven's Roost to where they met Toren and Yvon both drinking ale from overflowing tankards and sharing stories attempting to out glorify the other. Although Aldis began to talk about Yvon and Laelia's fight when they first returned to Havenhome, Rylan's mind stayed transfixed on Gaius and the forces he would have undoubtedly raised in order to destroy him.

"Rylan!" Yvon belched as he nudged his shoulder with an empty tankard and a flagon, "I understand you must be focused for tomorrow, but even I know that my father would have wanted you to be happy on our last night as free men. He hated seeing a serious face in his inn."

Rylan smiled as he took the ale and took a long drink, "You're father was a great man Yvon, you do him a great honor to have stood up for him in the ways you already have. I'm sure he will be proud of you in the coming days."

Yvon slumped down in his seat and slammed the flagon down, "I don't think I'm ready though. My father taught me everything he ever learned, but I still don't feel prepared to follow in his steps to protect you and your brothers."

"I don't think my brothers and I will need much protecting now," Rylan smiled as he patted Yvon against his back, "It's good that you're not confident about whatever comes next, if you were then I'd think that Byra truly didn't teach you his greatest lesson; be ready for whatever may come your way, however also enjoy the time when you are not ready. It's what makes life worth living. Tell me, did your mother and sister already leave for King's Hold?"

"Oh no, we couldn't leave my little brother," Elyscia chuckled as she entered the room with Yvette behind her, each carrying a large platter of food, "since you left, this place has been bustling with hungry soldiers as they prepared to abandon this place. We've barely had enough time to breathe, let alone sit and have food for ourselves."

Toren lurched forward as he attempted to stand and nearly fell completely over before catching himself on Aldis, "This day has been awful. I've been working all day, and with no time to nap or even relax. Aren't we supposed to be royalty? Rylan what gives?"

Rylan turned to see Toren swaying toward him, and caught Toren by the shoulder as he eased him into an open seat next to him, "If you think that being a member of royalty is only to lounge about all day then you are sorely mistaken brother. If Sayren stands as king, it will fall to you and Aldis to maintain parts of the kingdom that Sayren delegates down to you."

"So the things he doesn't want to do?" Toren replied as he rested his head on the table.

"Something similar to that yes," Rylan answered as he took another sip of his drink before reaching for the flagon and refilling his drink, "but this is the responsibility of a royal family member. Even mother had duties that father had delegated down to her."

Toren began to snore as Aldis swiftly took a seat next to Rylan at the mention of their parents, "You remember them? What did mother do? What was she like?"

Rylan smiled as he tousled his little brother's hair, "That is far too many questions with so little time left before you need to get Toren to bed so you two can help bring everyone to King's Hold tomorrow. I'll tell you about her duty to the people though; she was given the duty to oversee the wellbeing of all who resided in Alder's borders. Mother took a stance on the matter that angered many of the noble houses, but the people adored her for it. Every year after the Harvest Festival concluded and we returned home, she would collect hundreds of furs and had them fashion into clothes for the poor as well as ensuring families were well supplied with food for the winter. Hence why she had priestess and priests that would assist her, and they still do so even now. That is also many of the people disliked our father, because they believed he did not care for his people."

Aldis sulked as Rylan finished talking and grabbed Toren, draping his arm over his shoulder, "Thank you for telling me Rylan, I'm sure our parents will be happy knowing we are finally returning to reclaim our rightful place."

Rylan raised his glass and nodded as Aldis began to drag his brother towards the stairs leading to their rooms, while Yvette and Elyscia placed the food on the table. Rylan watched Yvon begin to look at the food for a moment before turning a pale greenish color and racing for the door, Yvette laughing with each step.

"He's certainly his father's son." Rylan joked as Yvon disappeared into the night to empty his stomach.

Yvette turned to Rylan smiling, "Certainly, and you as well. I still recall the nights you both attempted to out drink the other, only to have to care for both of you the next morning as you couldn't get out of your beds."

Elyscia began to laugh uncontrollably as she recalled the woozy, young Rylan as he sat with a bucket between his legs next to her father positioned the exact same way. "I must say," she began as she reached for her brother's tankard and took a sip, "even though you were not of his blood, father treated you as if you were his own son."

"I practically was," Rylan answered as he tore off a piece of meat from the cooked chicken laid before him, "being the king's bastard son, I was not welcomed in many of King's Rest's locations. Byra took me under his arm and taught me many things that I still hold dear to myself today. I owe him more than I could ever repay for everything that makes me the man I am today."

"I'm sure my old fool would have expected you to say nothing less. Yvon told me how it happened and how you helped him," Yvette said with her tired, old voice as she sipped from her small cup of tea, "I cannot thank you enough for everything you did, I'm not sure how to repay you this time."

Rylan smiled at Yvette and reclined in his chair, "I couldn't ask anything more of you that what you've already done for me and my family. If I was to ask for something though, it would simply be to ensure you and your children leave here tomorrow with everyone who has chosen to remain for the night. I wish to fight tomorrow alone."

"Alone?" Yvon's voice echoed as he returned from the outside, his color returning to normal as he staggered over and sat next to Elyscia, "How am I supposed to fight by your side if you do it alone?"

Elyscia chuckled as she looked at Yvon, "Come now little brother;

Rylan always fights alone. Even when he was fighting for a mercenary group he would deal with almost all of the threats alone. I'm almost certain that's how you wish to live your life."

"You may be right," Rylan responded as he sipped his mead once more, "I have never been one to fight with an army, let alone any number of allies with the exception of my brothers. It's far easier to focus on combat when you only have to worry about yourself on the field."

"No wonder you've stayed unmarried for this long," Yvette said as she looked at Rylan and Elyscia, "If you think the battlefield is only suited for you then you'll be alone both in and out of combat boy."

Rylan looked over to Elyscia as she blushed and turned her eyes away, "You're right. If I ever took the time to actually find peace in my life, I might have already had several children. Unfortunately my brothers and their safety took precedence and forced me to deny myself such pleasures."

Yvette sipped her tea as she relaxed her weary, old bones, "Hopefully you will succeed tomorrow then so you may actually find some peace. Otherwise I'll feel as if I wasted so much time over nothing."

Rylan nodded, "Certainly. I'm not the type to disappoint if it can be helped. I think I shall retire for the evening though. I'll need all the strength I can muster for tomorrow. Sleep well everyone."

As Rylan made his way up the stairs, he could hear Yvon pestering Elyscia to follow Rylan up the stairs since there was a chance he die tomorrow, however a strong strike from a thrown wooden spoon from Yvette quickly silenced him. Rylan slowly made his way down the hall to an open door into an empty room. Although the sheets were disheveled and the floor littered with dirt, Rylan felt relieved as he sat down onto the bed and removed his boots, his feet aching after sprinting through the tunnels to the hunting cabin. After pulling his shirt over his head and tossing it on top the small table next to the bed, Rylan lay back in the bed and almost instantly felt his mind drift away into deep slumber.

❊   ❊   ❊

"Is this all the mercenaries you could muster, a single group of men willing to take up arms to kill their king's murderer?" Gaius roared as he stood looking over the Silver Dragoons. Gaius nearly threw his soldier across the room as he turned to his newly contracted ally.

"I'm sorry Lord Gaius; many of them didn't want to take a job where they knew nothing in regards to the details of the target other than the job was in the name of their king." Gaius' frightened guardsman replied as he cowered in his shadow.

"Is that so?" Gaius rubbed his beard as he looked at Bansel and proceeded over to him, "Is that why you came, or are you waiting to hear more details as well?"

Bansel adjusted his sword belt as he stepped to meet Gaius, "On the contrary, I already know what's going on. Last time a man came begging for mercenaries; it was for the revolution. That very same mercenary army attempted to withstand you and King Sepius. Needless to say, it was a slaughter after you took the field." Bansel took a breath and looked back to his men, "This time clearly has to be something equally dangerous and will require many more men than you can muster if it's in regards to what I believe is your opposition."

Gaius scoffed at Bansel's words as he crossed his arms, "You must think you're quite astute, I take it you were part of that pitiful force House Ashburn put together in order to stop us?"

"Not a chance," Bansel replied, "I didn't arrive in Thesia but a few harvests before. I wouldn't have joined them even back then. Any mercenary with the smallest inkling of suspicion would have questioned the purpose of such a force, the same inkling that many of these mercenary companies are wary of such a request once again. Without carrying on further with this pointless discussion, why don't you tell me what you and the king fear so much that would require such an army to assemble without marshalling Alder's regular soldiers. Is it the heir's emerging from the shadows?"

Bansel saw Gaius' knuckles turn white as he said Sepius' title, "Regardless of the reason, we are offering to pay you and your men five thousand gold to accompany me and my guards as me go to a town called Havenhome to eradicate a threat. Such an amount should be more than enough."

Bansel chuckled, "Five thousand for twenty-five hundred men and women of the Silver Dragoons? We would normally charge that fee for one hundred troops to escort a noble. You'll have to sweeten your offer if you want me and my men. How about you give us sole rights to escort you and the royal family during their trips for two harvests, such an agreement would be enough to secure our assistance fight this 'threat' you seem so afraid."

Gaius waved his hand as if the notion was simply absurd to even entertain, "You can follow my men or I will see you and your men conscripted on the spot. Now will you choose to take my deal, or shall I have one of my men fetch a magister?"

Bansel furrowed his brow in displeasure at the threat, but sighed, "Five thousand will see the Silver Dragoons at your side for this concord. However, I will ask that you have the agreement drawn up to guarantee our payment."

Gaius nodded in agreement and motioned to a soldier standing nearby, "Fetch me paper and quill. Also ensure my men are ready to ride immediately. I won't delay any longer."

"I do hope you don't mind waiting a few moments longer for us to catch up." A noble from behind Bansel said as he approached Gaius will open arms.

Gaius gave a surprised at the man as he hugged him, but instantly returned the gesture as he smiled, "My good friend Sancil, I thought you had all but disappeared. What are you doing here?"

Bansel instantly recoiled as he recognized Sancil's name. Lord Sancil Verdane was a prominent figurehead within the noble houses until recently. After a dispute with another head of a noble house, Lord Illard Varze, House Verdane found many of its members mysteriously deceased. Bansel recalled that the last bit of information regarding Lord Sancil and his daughters had disappeared underground as to limit their likelihood of meeting a similar fate. Although not as strong martially as House Bernak or LeBlanc, Sancil's prowess during sieges were second to none, worrying Bansel further as to their unknown opposition at Havenhome. "I will see to it that my men are ready to go, shall your men be leading the group or would you like my men to secure your forward position?"

Gaius seemed almost oblivious to Bansel as he spoke, but broke off his banter with Sancil after a brief moment, "You're men will be at our rear and flanks, I expect to march all night and rest just outside of the town before battle."

With a quick nod, Bansel turned to leave and Gaius found himself alone with Sancil, "What are you doing outside of your protection? If Illard finds out I'm certain he'll be daring enough to send men out after you again."

Sancil smiled and patted Gaius on his shoulder, "there's no need to be so worried old friend. If that fiend wishes to send more men after me, let him. I have lived long enough to discover there was only a single man ever contracted to kill my wife and sons. None of my contacts could give a name, but he is said to wield dual swords. I hope that once our business is concluded, you will assist me in tracing this man down and bringing him to bare justice and force Illard's nefarious deeds to light."

Gaius shook Lord Verdane's hand in agreement as he moved towards the door, "Let us be off then, I believe we'll give our foe quite the fright when we arrive with over three thousand men. Such a sight will drive fear into their hearts before we pierce it with our blades."

Both nobles laughed as they exited the cramped mustering hall and mounted their horses. Gaius' horsemen quickly took their position behind him, Bansel waiting with his Silver Dragoons off to side. As his forces began to move, Gaius ordered a handful of riders to proceed ahead and clear the road to allow easy passage out of the capital, many merchants and common folk scurried out of the force's path before ever drawing near to them.

Upon their arrival at the eastern gate, Gaius halted his forces as Daliah and Kraste rode towards them, "What are you doing here inquisitor?"

Daliah approached on her armored horse, her normal attire replaced with a hooded leather brigandine and gauntlets, "Prince Faust wished that I assist in your assault against our enemy and hire a large detachment of the Serpent's Fang to ensure or success."

Gaius looked to Lord Verdane, whose eyes narrowed as he began to inspect Kraste's swords strapped around his waist, "I don't see why we would need assassins for such an honorable mission." Gaius returned to Daliah, "I will welcome as many able bodied men as can be mustered. Fall in behind Sir Bansel and his Dragoons. We will be riding until we are just outside of the town. I take it the man beside you is the one who wounded our target?"

"Ah," Kraste chimed in with an enthused expression adorning his cheeks, "we are going after Rylan. I knew there was always something odd about him, but to be the Six Winged Death, it almost seems impossible for such a lowlife."

"Watch your tongue snake," Bansel growled as he approached, "If I had known you wanted to take on Rylan and the Six Crows I would have insisted on bringing all of my men. Those men are highly skilled and even though there are only a handful in number they will provide a serious resistance, I would imagine you already have a plan in regards to them."

Gaius huffed as he noticed several of the townspeople reacting to Rylan's name and beginning to murmur to one another, "Such detail shall be left alone until we make camp. We do not have time to stand around while he undoubtedly returns to his allies. Now fall in line and let's be off!"

With a loud snap of his reins, Gaius spurred his steed forward with his men following suit close behind. As the forces began to move, Bansel quickly returned to his men and signaled for one of his men to meet him. "I have a delicate mission for you," Bansel began as the rider arrived next to him, "return to our headquarters and notify Paithe that the little bird may be taking flight. She'll direct you on what to do after, but I need this done quietly and without drawing any attention to yourself. Do you understand?"

A silent nod assured Bansel before the young woman broke off and disappeared down an alleyway before they drew near to the Serpent's Fang. A sense of unease washed over Bansel as he scanned the masked riders that seemed similar yet vastly different from one another unlike his uniformed and standardized appearance of his own soldiers. Many of the Fang members appeared as if they were smiling and pointing him out as he passed; only increasing his sense of foul deeds looming before him. After a quick spur to his horse, Bansel focused on his duties and how he would face Rylan when both sides met.

❀　❀　❀

With the setting sun nestled into its nightly slumber, Gaius and his troops continued to pace along the final distance until a pair of scouts rode into torchlight, "Lord Gaius we've found it!"

"Hold!" Gaius commanded as he and Sancil rode forward to meet the men, "What have you seen for their defenses?"

Both riders looked at one another before the slightly brave man delivered his report, "With a seemingly weak western gate there appears to be no one atop the walls. We scouted around the town on foot; however the only lights we saw appeared off in the distance with a caravan seemingly heading towards King's Hold. This town's eastern gate is far better secured with guard towers and what appeared to be a winch control system located out of direct view of the gateway. There only appeared to be a handful of people with in the town, and gave the appearance to be villagers. I could only guess that if those people stand against you my lord, they could not number more than fifty, if even that."

Gaius gave a pleased smile as he read the report and tossed both men a gold coin each, "Thank you for delivering such advantageous news. We will set up camp just outside of the woods and begin our assault tomorrow after sunrise. If they are villagers then we should have little resistance in routing them before any blood is even shed. Consider yourselves up for promotion when we return to the capital with our enemy's head upon a pike!"

A fatigued cheer quietly erupted from his men as they began to split off into the woods to set up camp and begin to sleep. As the road cleared, Bansel approached with Daliah and Kraste a few seconds behind as Gaius and Sancil dismounted from their houses. "Tell me Lord Gaius," Bansel began as he stepped down off his horse, "What will be our plan of attack for tomorrow since you have received what appeared to be evidence for our victory?"

Gaius loosened his cuirass as the others arrived, undoubtedly ready to hear the same information, "Tonight we will rest and set guards up in case any suspicious individuals draw close to our men. When we ready ourselves for battle in the morning, I suspect we will have little to stand in our way. Rylan has hidden himself and his allies within a guard-less village that will undoubtedly leave his aide when we arrive. I, Lord Verdane, our soldiers, and the Silver Dragoons will march upon the eastern gate and enter the town, while Inquisitor Daliah and her allies make their way around to the western gate and maintain a perimeter should Rylan attempt to escape. Regardless of who finds him, I will be the one to fight and kill him. Should any of you come upon my traitorous blood, I would ask you do not kill him; however, should he resist in any fashion, bleed him dry and you will have yourselves not only my gratitude, but a hefty pouch of coins."

Bansel nodded in agreement, "I would ask how you wish to enter and my men to do once Rylan and his allies are found?"

Daliah chuckled, "If your men survive finding him, then I suppose they should cry for Lord Gaius and his soldiers to come save them."

"Watch what you say Inquisitor," Bansel returned as he turned to face her, "I do not take kindly to anyone who insults my men, especially members of a noble family that still owes me money. Lord Sorren Terzi, your uncle, still has an unsettled debt with me for killing my men after they had safely delivered him to his destination."

Daliah's face turned a shade of red made even more visible by the torchlight, "Such things are not my concern, and you will watch how you speak to an Inquisitor of the King."

Both Gaius and Sancil began to laugh as Daliah stormed off with Kraste giving a displeased look at Bansel, only to quickly ride away when Bansel raised a closed fist in his direction, "My, my Sir Bansel." Lord Verdane said as he placed his hand over the mercenary's hand and lowered it down to his side, "You surely have a strong spine on you. When we arrive at the gate tomorrow I would like to see that power that earned you the reputation of a 'Dragon Slayer', that should be more than enough to bring Rylan out of hiding. It's a rarity to even see a dragon, let alone a man who seemingly defeated one and stole its power, and as much as I would like to see it in combat, once Rylan emerges, Lord Gaius and our troops will engage him and his allies. You won't need to concern yourselves unless we are not able to handle one man and three disgraced nobles."

"You seem very confident for such a unpredictable enemy," Bansel replied as he brushed his steed's mane before one of his men took the reins and led it away, "You are up against the Six Winged Death, Wall of a Thousand Winds, a hero of uninhibited flames, and possibly the other heirs. If you wish to truly succeed tomorrow, we should mount the entirety of our combined forces at the eastern gate to ensure no one is able to escape. I can only assume that you want to kill him to avenge King Sepius, otherwise an official proclamation would have been circulated." Bansel carefully watched Gaius tighten his grip on his reins before bowing to both nobles, "Whatever the case may be, my men and I will see to your safety tomorrow after I show you my way of opening a gate. Goodnight Lord Verdane, Lord LeBlanc."

Sancil bowed to Bansel as he turned and made his way into the night, "I assume by your reaction that what that man said is true. Did Rylan actually harm King Sepius?"

Gaius sighed deeply as he attempted to ease his troubled mind, "He did far more than that. Rylan was captured and brought before Sepius this morning; he murdered the King, his daughter, nearly three dozen royal guards, and escaped with his daughter and Arthlyn's Ring."

"Wait a moment," Sancil pause as he ran his fingers through his greyed hair, "he murdered our king, escaped from Dalkas unharmed, and you didn't call the entirety of Alder's forces to bear down upon him?"

Gaius brow furrowed as he contemplated his next words, "It's not that I didn't desire to. If I had the ability to, I would have ordered them readied and marching as soon as it happened; however I was blocked by Sepius' upstart fool of a son, Faust. He refused to allow me on the grounds of being Alder's next in line, but promised to pay for any mercenaries that I could muster, as if that would have honored his father's murder. I believe our inquisitor's purpose here with the Fang is far more than aid to our cause. If we succeed in silencing Rylan, I believe we will be met with opposition upon our exit. Faust would likely be removed from power and another placed as his father's successor."

Sancil grinned, "I suppose you mean yourself? You did kill Ralford back during the uprising, and defeating his strongest son would surely put you well ahead of the most unpopular man in Dalkas. I agree that we should prepare for the worst tomorrow, and keep it between ourselves until it becomes necessary to inform the Silver Dragoons."

Gaius nodded in agreement as both nobles made their way towards a small clearing where they tied their horses with the others soldier's before finally making their way for a small fire made personally for them. "I do not care for unwanted casualties tomorrow. If any of the villagers move in the wrong way, we will cut them down and raze Havenhome as a den for the rebellious heirs that would try to destroy our way."

"I agree, they have already chosen a side, even if unknowingly. We should raze the town regardless." Sancil's mind began to devise uses for any innocent villagers caught in the battle as he rested himself against a tree and tossed a few more branches onto the flames, "If any of the townsfolk survive, we can capture them and proclaim to be enemies of Alder aligned with the heirs and their rebellion."

Gaius chuckled as he pulled his cloak over his body, "You've changed from engineer to diplomat in the time since I last saw you, hopefully you will be able to use that wit of yours tomorrow as well when the time comes."

CHAPTER 13

"**A**ldis, wake up." Rylan whispered as he shook his youngest brother. "Wake up; you've got to leave now."

Aldis wiped away the dreariness from his eyes as he awoke to his dark room within the inn, the sounds of bustling footsteps echoing from just outside the door. "What's going on? It's not even light outside yet, why do we have to leave?"

Rylan tossed Aldis' staff and satchel onto his lap and moved to grab the cloak hung behind the door, "Gaius and his men are here. I've notified everyone still in the town, I need you and Toren to escort them through to King's Hold and wait for me to return. Don't use the portal after you leave, if I fail they will surely place a heavy guard around it and march towards you and the other heirs. Do you understand?"

Aldis groggily shook his head as he arose and took his cloak from Rylan's extended hand, carelessly draping it over him and his bag. "I do brother, are you sure you don't want us to stay and help you defeat them?"

Rylan smiled as he and Aldis exited the room into the lit bar area where the others stood, "I'm sure little brother. Is everyone here and ready to leave?"

A unified, drowsy, "yes", was returned by the remaining villagers as they leaned against whatever was closest. "What are we to do if they're here?" Mauro questioned as he rested his back against the bar.

"You'll be making your way to the Sen Portal just outside of town with Aldis. He will take you to King's Hold to where I ask that you all decide whether you will stay and stand with my brothers, or depart and live your lives elsewhere." Rylan's tone became quite serious as he moved through to where Mauro was standing and retrieved his

Orden armor, now cleaned and polished. "What made you decide to go to such lengths?"

Mauro smiled as he placed his hand on Rylan's shoulder before standing upright and swinging his bag over his back, "If you are to die, you should die looking as immaculate as possible. I can't do much for your other clothes, and you have six wings for weapons, so I fixed up the one thing I could. It is my way of saying 'thanks for not leaving me to die'."

Rylan grinned, but with held his laughter as he mirrored Mauro and placed his hand on his shoulder, "Regardless of whatever happens, I do hope you'll stay. My brother will need someone with your talents by his side in the days ahead; such gifts are as rare as a true noble to wield them."

Mauro made an abrupt dash for the door and began heading towards the western gate, with all but Tiberius, Naria, Yvon and Elyscia following suit. "I don't suppose you all want something from me before you leave?" Rylan joked as he made his way to Tiberius.

Tiberius extended an open hand, which Rylan gratefully grasp as the two shook hands, "I saw Mauro working on that armor last night and I wanted to do something as well, however I cannot give you my power in a bottle or jar." Tiberius smiled as he released from the hand shake and produced both hatchets Lothos once held, "These were from that bandit that attacked our family. As thanks for your deeds and my inability to settle our debt for a completed contract, I wished to give you these to use as you saw fit."

Rylan took the hatchets with a proud expression on his face before tucking them into his belt and embracing Tiberius, "Thank you for the gift, consider our debt settled. I would ask that when you arrive at the hold you not only look after Lady Isabelle, but my brothers as well. A commander such as you will be invaluable to him as words spread of our return and people seek to join our cause."

"You have my word," Tiberius nodded as he backed away and made his way to the door. "A word of advice though for when you return," Tiberius waved his hand in the air, "Isabelle isn't her real name; once someone is adopted into a noble house, the hero adopts a new name presented to them by the head of house. Isabelle was my father's doing, however I preferred her real name, Liara of Orst."

Rylan bowed, "I will keep that in mind." As Tiberius exited into the early morning darkness, both Yvon and Elyscia rushed over and hugged Rylan.

"Don't you dare die," Elyscia said as she discreetly slide a folded note into Rylan's pouch, "Byra wouldn't forgive you if you were to leave us before you saw your bloodline back on the throne."

Rylan pulled Elyscia closer as he whispered in her ear, "I won't, but please do consider what I said. You have your own life to live; it does not belong to a cause that I will not force you to be a part of."

As all three released one another, Yvon quickly presented his sheathed sword and extended it to Rylan, "I cannot offer anything in comparison to the others, however I would humbling ask that you wield the sword my father presented to me in battle."

Surprised Rylan looked over the single edged weapon and asked, "Is this the one they say you used against Laelia?"

Yvon let out a chocked cough before responding, "Yes. I wouldn't have wished it upon my sister, but she left me no choice. I do not know what will happen if you should use it, or even what will happen if you should draw it from the sheathe. My request will not change though."

Rylan graciously lifted the blade from Yvon's open palms and tied it around his waist, "I will wield it with pride and honor, not only for your father, but for yours as well. I'm sure not many will be able to say they possess a weapon once brandished by the Six Winged Death. Now head out there quickly and ensure Aldis doesn't lose his way in the dark. I'm trusting in both of you."

Rylan waited for both brother and sister to exit before approaching Naria, "I suppose you've stayed behind to see if I'll let you stay and fight with me?"

Naria only grinned, "You won't be able to keep up with me if you wanted too. I'd have defeated the whole army before you ever had a chance to use one of your new toys."

"As if you'd be able to stand against one of them," Rylan returned as he began to don his armor, "You're always too tired to fight unless it's passed noon and you've had lunch."

Naria scoffed, "I do not." As she brushed against Rylan and began to move towards the door, "I actually wanted to tell you something important before you come to King's Rest."

"Oh? What might that be?" Rylan inquired as he playfully followed her.

Naria blushed as she attempted to speak and began to laugh. "It's about us," her voice clearly nervous, "I wanted to tell you that you have-"

Before Naria could finish her sentence, Gauld burst through the doorway breathing heavily as he placed his hand upon his knees, attempting to catch his breath. "Thank goodness I found you...your brother sent me to find you Lady Naria. He wishes you'll return immediately and attend to an important matter...he did not say what exactly."

Naria gave a heavy sigh as she walked over to Rylan and kissed his cheek, "I suppose we will speak once you return. Much has changed since you left, but now is not the time to discuss such things; you have a battle to prepare for."

Perturbed by the interruption Rylan nearly spoke, but withheld his words and politely nodded as all three exited the door way and made their way to the others at the gate.

As some of the remaining men raised the tarnished portcullis, Yvon took lead of the group and began to make his way for the portal. A subtle whistle echoed through the trees as Rylan silently recalled his metal and bowed once last time to the others as they disappeared into the night. As the last few pieces of metal made their way into a small pile, Rylan made his way over to the wench system and lowered the gate once more before using his metal to close the large wooden doors and sealing him within the town. With the sun's morning amber light peeking just above the trees, a bitter gust of wind blew through Havenhome as Rylan dawned his cloak, made his metal into a chair that he rested upon, an axe driven into the damp morning dirt, and awaited Gaius's arrival.

❊   ❊   ❊

With the sound of a several shouting soldiers, Gaius immediately leaped upright and pulled his metal from his horse forming a dual ended spear. Dazed by his sudden and alarmed awakening, he blurrily scoured the tree line to see his men all looking to the dawning sky to see a brilliant blue pillar of light penetrating the dim morning sky. "Quickly, to arms!" Gaius roared as he donned his cloak and bolted to horse with Sancil madly scurrying to collect his items scattered around him. As Gaius made his way to the rode on his horse, Bansel and his men were waiting, ready and awaiting instruction.

"It's good to see you made yourself ready for combat so quickly Bansel," Gaius grunted as he splashed his face with water to assist him in adjusting to the morning.

"Our reputation is one of preparedness, Lord Gaius," Bansel replied as he motioned to his men as they stood silently behind him, "and it is a reputation I aim to keep."

As Lord Verdane and the noble guardsmen groggily marched out of the woods, the poor sight of many of the Serpent's Fang stood about still half-dressed and only partially conscious. Gaius rode over to Kraste as he emerged from the woods with his cloak flimsily fastened and his sword belt contorted in such a way he nearly tripped over a scabbard as he clumsily made his way forward, "What are you lot doing?" Gaius screamed as he reared his horse in front of Kraste, nearly causing the man to wet himself from shock. "Get your men ready and escort Inquisitor Daliah to the western gate! We will approach from the east and attack. Should you allow our target to elude us, I will personally see you heads nailed to the city's walls as a monument to your failure!"

Daliah watched from the shadows as Gaius turned his horse towards Havenhome and spurred his horse, the Silver Dragoons and his men following behind, "You truly were worth keeping alive Kraste."

Kraste bowed as he adjusted his clothing and the remainder of his men emerged ready for battle, "You give me too much praise Lady Inquisitor, I am simply doing as instructed by the Elder Council. I was told to assist you and to fulfill the contract you had imposed. Your men will be ready shortly and we may proceed how you'd prefer."

"Good, see to it your archers stay just outside the western gate while we proceed around to the eastern gate. Should the fighting cease we will enter and finish off whatever remnants survive." Daliah stepped into her saddle and began to make for the road as Kraste fastened his cloak around his neck.

With his archers grouped together and given their orders, Kraste turned to the remaining men before him, "We may outnumber our targets; however we must still be prudent. Do not engage alone and ensure you reapply your poison once we are in position. There is to be no survivors, and no witnesses. If you engage a noble or the Six Winged Death, fight for your life, because if you do not; they will cut you down without mercy. To the contract!"

"To the contract!" The Serpent's Fang assassin's muttered in unison before dawning their masks and hoods, quietly beginning their approach on Havenhome.

❀   ❀   ❀

Gaius and Sancil cautiously approached the western gate of Havenhome as the morning sun crested over the walls and illuminated the absence of any guard presence from the palisade. "Open in the name of King Sepius of Alder!" Gaius shouted towards the gate in hopes of a response by one of the innocent villagers. Several quiet seconds past as the brisk morning air continued, but only silence greeted them as Havenhome remained quiet. "Open this gate immediately or face the wrath of Alder's might! I will not give another chance if you do not cooperate immediately!" Gaius roared, his temper flaring at the possibility that the only thing that awaited them within the walls were abandoned buildings devoid of his prey.

Again there was nothing, and with little remaining patience, Gaius turned to Sancil, "Should we see what the Dragon Slayer can do?"

Lord Verdane grinned as he motioned for Bansel, "Come forward commander and let us see this strength of yours in action!"

Bansel promptly spurred his steed forward until he arrived just outside the gate and dismounted, handing the reins off to one of his men and approaching the gate. Removing the glove from his right hand, Bansel measured his strike carefully before taking a few steps backwards. As he began to channel his strength, a bright red color began to envelope his fist and form silver scales over top of the skin. Bansel tightened his clenched fist one last time before rushing forward and striking the wooden doors, the red coloration instantly exploding in bright cascade of crimsons and currant hues. Both sturdy wooden doors splintered into countless fragments as they disappeared into dust and opened the way to Havenhome.

With their passage open Bansel calmly proceeded over to his horse, returned his glove onto his uninjured hand and reached for his sword, "Shall we precede Lord Gaius?"

Gaius, Sancil, and all five hundred noble guardsmen stood in wonder at what transpired, and with a mighty roar, Gaius thrust his spear forward and spurred his horse as he raced into Havenhome with him men close behind. Bansel motioned for his men to follow, pausing as he noticed Kraste's archers moving through the trees, but continued as his men began to pour through the gates.

With a small dust still looming from the gate, Gaius and Sancil road forward into the seemingly empty Havenhome, cautiously proceeding through what defenses had been created by Sayren and the other heirs, "Where are you bastard?" Gaius bellowed as he dismounted his horse and pulled his metal into three wings suspended behind him.

As the sounds of thundering feet marched through the town, Gaius' guardsmen drew close to Raven's Roost inn, halting immediately at the sight of a hooded figure sitting in a metal throne, a solemn axe resting beside it. Sancil quickly readied himself, placing his kite shield firmly in front with his sword resting upon it top.

"I told you what would happen if you came chasing after me Gaius!" Rylan's voice exploded from under his hood as he uncrossed his legs and sat forward.

Gaius stepped forward with is spear lazily dragging along the dirt, "You're a fool to think your feeble threats would scare someone like me! I killed your father, what makes you think you'll fair any different than he will if you fight me? I don't see your ring, or the Sword of Alder. You have nothing to protect you, save what little metal you can muster!"

Rylan sat silently as Gaius attempted to coax him into an indefensible state of anger by referencing his father, however it fell on a determined and focus mind.

"Would you like to know how we killed your sad excuse for a

brother?" Gaius laughed as he pulled a bloodied sack from his back and tossed it between him and Rylan, "He died with my metal planted in his back before he even had a chance to swing at the guards! Ebon looked disgraceful as he fell upon his knees and watched as I readied my sword to cleave his head from his shoulders! Do you know what he said to me? 'Please don't hurt Ophelia.' He begged me as I plunged my metal through his throat! After I'm through butchering you, I'll be sure to pay her a visit!"

Again Rylan silently sat on his metal seat, the cool wind still passing through the trees outside of Havenhome. Although he could feel his blood boiling, Rylan had to force Gaius to move first, he had to wait to draw him out.

"What, nothing to say from the great Six Winged Death? I thought you were supposed to be a great warrior, yet you sit silent like a muted beggar upon what little strength you have." Gaius tightened his grip on his spear as his responses failed to move Rylan, "Would you like to know how your pitiful father died?"

Rylan snapped back his hood as he bared hit teeth at Gaius, "Don't be stupid, this has nothing to do with my father. If you wish to keep your men alive you'll face me and be done with this idle prattle!"

Gaius smiled at Rylan's reaction, "He was a coward, boy! When he knew he was going to die he pleaded for his life, begging me to spare him! He was weak, just like you, and just like all those that stand with you!"

"Enough!" Rylan roared as he slammed his fists against the metal chair, "If you wish to stand their insulting me like a gossiping milk maid all day then do it with Faust, your coward prince of a snake! Should you actually want to fight, then attack me fool, let me show you what power you were spared that day so many harvests ago when you ran like a frightened child from King's Hold!"

Gaius barked, "Attack!" as he swept his hand towards Rylan. With a unified battle cry, all five hundred guardsmen rushed forward at Rylan with swords, spears, and axes readied to silence Rylan with a single strike.

With the distance between Rylan and his opposition closing rapidly, Rylan retrieved his axe and arose from his seat, the metal chair splintering into shards and forming his infamous six wings. As the final fragment rose into place, the guardsmen halted their advance and stood gazing at the horrific problem ahead of them. With a subtle exhale, Rylan unleashed his torrent of metal upon the attacking men, sheiks and cries of panic and agony erupting as they tore through the simple metal armor and shields that attempted to stand in their path. Before the survivors could ready themselves, Rylan unleashed his axe and sword into them, each stroke seemingly cleaving through several men as he roared through the ranks cutting down what men survived his metal wave.

Seeing Rylan's attacks, Gaius quickly formed his metal into a shield and helm, and launched into the fray, shoving men out of the way as he attempted to confront Rylan. With his men in utter disarray, Gaius forced his way forward until the sight of Rylan's Orden Forge Armor reflected the morning sun's light in an amber hue. Gaius launched his spear between his men and appeared to land a solid strike against Rylan's chest. Laughing at the ease of his success, Gaius attempted to retract his spear only to find Rylan's metal had surrounded the spear point and was holding it in place. Gaius grunted as he attempted to retrieve his spear once again, pulling with all his might as his spear remained in place. Rylan turned his attention to Gaius as the surrounding men were still stunned from Rylan's first attacks and took a step backwards before recalling his metal and dropping the cloak from his shoulders.

Rylan and Gaius began to circle one another, stepping over fallen soldiers and glaring at one another with each bloodied step. A large space began to form around the men as Sancil and the remaining guardsmen encircled the two and began to cheer for Gaius. Rylan's metal began to form armor around him as Gaius changed his spear to a longsword and readied himself to strike. With a pained cough from one of the injured men, both Gaius and Rylan leaped towards one another and began to clash. Rylan swinging with his axe at Gaius' head, yet Gaius deflected the blow with his shield and quickly spun, slicing against Rylan's back, the metal scraping against one another and sending Rylan stumbling forward. Not allowing his opponent to recover, Gaius charged shield first into Rylan's back and sent him sprawling near the edge of the circle as he collided with the stone path.

A loud applause erupted from the men as Rylan rolled to his side and arose, his metal scratched and dirtied from both Gaius and the ground. Gaius shook his head in disapproval at Rylan as he readied himself once more and dashed forward. Rylan side stepped Gaius as his shield impacted one of the guardsmen and quickly struck Gaius in the back with his axe, the metal denting and sparks bursting into the air as Rylan spun and regained his footing. As the attacked guardsmen slammed against the ground with Gaius close behind, the men erupted in anger as they attempted to attack Rylan while Gaius recovered. As the men once again closed in Rylan unleashed his metal into shards and tore into the ranks of guardsmen surrounding him, crimson geysers erupting from the victims of his fury as they pierced through, send his victims to the ground, motionless or crying out in pain.

Lord Sancil and a handful of guardsmen around him withheld themselves from the attack as they watched another drove of men fell to the ground while the survivors slowly backed away, once again forming a large space with Rylan in the center. A large pile of deceased or severely injured men lay over a large crimson pool beginning to form over the blood soaked dirt. A weary cheer for Gaius erupted as he re-entered the circle, this time with a sword in each hand and his back furnished with a thicker plate.

"This will only end with you dying at my feet bastard!" Gaius shouted as he pointed one of his blades at Rylan.

Rylan shifted his weight as his metal sunk into the ground, his axe changing to a sword similar to Yvon's, "The only end with come at the cost of your men's lives if you continue to use them as your shield."

Gaius charged forward and began to strike Rylan with a flurry of attacks as his face grew red with anger. Rylan parried each blow with careful precision and slowly gave ground as he stepped over body and weapon that surrounded their feet. Gaius madly marched over the bodies of his fallen men with each step he made, pained screams of men not yet dead fell upon guiltless ears. With their commander seemingly gaining the upper hand once again, many of the men began to cheer for Gaius. With one heavy strike, Gaius force Rylan to a knee, sending a loud roar of encouragement from the men to their leader. With Rylan forced to press both swords against his, Gaius unleashed a forceful kick into Rylan's unprotected middle and sent him backwards through the pools of blood. A crimson stained Rylan rose to his feet, each breath seemingly pained as he grimaced with each exhale. Both men stood glaring into the other's each, deaf to every noise but the sounds of shifting metal and their own thoughts. Rylan dashed forward and quickly juked to the side, launching a swift kick against Gaius' leg before moving towards the center of the circle. Gaius felt the muscles in his leg contort as Rylan pushed off, a searing pain driving itself downwards to his toes as he grunted in anguish and staggered to the side clutching his leg. Rylan started pacing the open space in the middle of the circle as he watched Gaius stomp his foot into the ground several times before marching forward, his swords readied by his sides. Both men leaped at the other in unison as they attacked, sparks dancing through the air as each strike parried itself with another. Enraged that Rylan was challenging his skill far more than he thought possible, Gaius sneakily attacked with several fragments, only to find them instantly blocked, knocked aside from several of Rylan's as they erupted from between the stones. After several more parried strikes, Gaius locked swords with Rylan and promptly struck him with his helm, dazing him long enough to strike Rylan's metal sword from his hand and piecing his armored forearm.

Rylan howled in agony as he leaped backwards, removing Gaius' sword from his arm. Without a moments reprieve however, Rylan quickly found himself back on the defensive as Gaius continued to attack mercilessly. Out of options and continuously parrying blows moments before they struck Rylan forced his metal to the surface and quickly attempted to strike Gaius from all sides.

Gaius quickly formed the same encasing shield as before around himself as Rylan's fragments flew through the air and clanged off. From within the metal, Gaius began to hear shouts of his men crying out once again as he reverted his metal back to their previous forms and attempted to strike Rylan, but found he had moved out of range and diverted his attacks to the remaining men.

Rylan sneered at Gaius as he recalled his fragments into his six wings and stood ready to cross blades with only Yvon's sword held with both hands. Both men raced forward as Rylan unleashed his wings at Gaius and forced him to shift his swords into a shield as they collided, successfully blocking the fragments as they struck. Before Gaius could reshape his swords, Rylan sliced Gaius across the side, under his cuirass, and rolled out of striking range. Rylan could feel a strange sensation from the sword as it seemed to vibrate ever so slightly and as he looked at Gaius, he could see metal falling to the ground from the noble's back and shatter upon the ground as they fell.

"You dare poison me? Have you no honor?" Gaius barked as he turned to Rylan with both swords in hand.

Rylan arose and sheathed his blade and fashion his metal into a sword and axe before answering, "This blade was a gift that is said to steal a person's soul. I will not grant you such a fate though; you will perish by my hands."

Gaius scowled at Rylan as he made his way forward and readied an attack. With a sudden lunge forward, Gaius forced Rylan to parry his first blow only to find himself struck by Gaius' second blade as it slashed across his back, tearing through his brigandine and lacerating his skin. Although not deep enough to strike bone, Gaius' attack forced Rylan to scream and drive him to respond with a wild swing. Gaius mocked, "Unsettled so easily? I expected more from a Bassadora!" as he parried Rylan's sword and kicked him in the stomach sending him staggering. Gaius leaped forward, thrusting his sword at Rylan's chest, but found him prepared as Rylan stepped out of the blade's path and propelled his sword down directly onto Gaius' extended arm, severing the limb in a clean stroke. Gaius howled as he reset his feet, swinging his sword with tremendous force at Rylan's head. Ducking under the strike, Rylan drove his sword's blade directly upward into Gaius' shoulder and bending the metal into a rod riddled with thorn like protrusions that secured it in place. Gaius dropped his sword as he fell to his knees and began to breathe heavily, his vision blurring from unbearable anguish.

"As I recall Gaius, you did something similar to my father." Rylan uttered as he made his way to face Gaius, his metal swarming over his armor and cutting it away. Rylan twisted his fist as the jagged metal shards began to tear into Gaius' unarmored flesh, his lips bleeding as his teeth dug into them in an attempt to withhold his screams. "It's no use Gaius, you will beg for your end before I take your life."

One of the few remaining guardsmen attempted to rush Rylan from behind, but found himself impaled by more of Rylan's metal concealed under the road. As the spike pierced the man's head, his helmet flew backwards and landed at Sancil's feet, a looks of disgust and dread affixed to the faces of the guardsmen as their comrade fell limp and slowly slid down the spike.

"I will not yield to you bastard!" Gaius shouted as the metal continued to sink deeper into his skin.

Rylan's face grew twisted and malicious as he knelt down to whisper in his ear, "I don't want you to. I want you to suffer for everything my family has suffered. For my father, my mother, my brothers, my sister, my friends, and all the innocent lives you ripped from this world so coldly. My metal talons will dig into your flesh until you beg me to stop. Then I will crush your bones until you plead for death. You will die by my hands, and you will enter death a feeble monstrosity when I have finished with you. All who come across you in death will never know who you are but a beast with no name."

As Bansel and the Silver Dragoons made their way forward, Gaius turned his pained gaze, "Order your men to attack, fool! I'm not paying you to watch me die!"

Bansel waived his hand as his men formed a solid wall of shields separating everyone from the western gate, "I agree Lord LeBlanc," Gaius returned as he stepped forward, "you are not paying us. I had no intention of ever standing beside a man like you after you stood by while an innocent woman was murdered. You and your king only survived this long because I stopped the younger man standing before you from attacking all those years ago. Neither my men nor I will help you, regardless of coin."

Gaius shrieked as the metal began to scrape against his bones, his remaining arm attempting to move, only to lacerate his muscles further from the thorns imbedded in his arm, "I may die here, but you will never rule Alder as long as there is a single man to stand against you!"

Rylan chuckled as he turned his fist and watched as his metal began to crush Gaius, retching sounds erupting from the onlookers, "That is fine with me. I never wanted to be king, nor will I take the throne. My brother, a true son of King Ralford and Queen Maree, Sayren Bassadora will wear the crown and usher in an era that you could never have reached."

Gaius began to shake as a stream of crimson streaked from his lips, "I…curse you…you and your brothers…the heirs…heirs of Bassadora to know only anguish for all your days!"

A loud crack erupted from under Rylan's metal, and Gaius fell silent, his head slumped and still. Rylan let out a long breath before recalling his bloodstained metal and watching the disfigured corpse of Gaius LeBlanc collide with the pile of bodies that surrounded him. As Rylan turned to the remaining guardsmen and Lord Verdane, all but the noble threw down their weapons and fell to their knees. "I didn't believe him when he said you were the Six Winged Death!" Sancil shouted as he began to step forward.

Rylan smiled as he drew his hatchets, "I am the one and only. I take it you will not yield and be spared?"

"I could not allow you to live for killing my friend; it would be most unforgivable on my part." Sancil replied as he stopped a few steps away from Rylan, "I would ask your intentions after leaving here though, if that is suitable to you?"

Rylan nodded, "I will return to King's Hold with my brothers and protect them however I can."

Sancil lowered his shield and sword as he shook his head, "You know as well as I that you should return and lead them. You are the rightful heir."

"I'm not sure you're aware, Lord Verdane, but I am a bastard of King Ralford. I cannot claim the throne." Rylan returned in a direct tone, his patience still thin after dealing with Gaius.

"The last I recalled; your father and the twelve noble heads of houses all stood around and watched you become legitimized. This happened just before Sepius betrayed everyone and sent his rebellion forth to kill your father with the other usurpers." Sancil sheathed his sword, walking directly to Rylan, his face red with anger, "By my eyes and that of the others houses still standing with House Bassadora, you are the rightful heir! Do you not remember, or is it that you wish to forget how you're father failed?"

Rylan pressed his forehead against Sancil's, "Don't speak as if you knew him! If you were truly one of my father's supporters, where were you when I lead the charge to repulse the men and save what people I could? Don't deny that you ran with your tail firmly tucked! You gave away your honor for your life, yet you would dare stand there and attempt to mock me?"

Sancil remained silent for a moment, slowly backing away before taking a knee and lowering his head, "I accept that I fled in fear for my life and that of my family's. I acknowledge that you were left to lead a small force against an army alone. If you wish to hate me I will not stop you, but I would ask that you think about what would've happened had we not attempted to withhold Sepius' army from Dalkas long enough for you and your family to disappear. It was on Queen Maree's order to attack and stop them. We failed and lost what little honor we had for ourselves. I will not beg for my life or ask for anything, but know that I loved your father and you, as much as my own family. You will always be the true heir to Alder as long as I draw breath with those that would support you and your brothers."

"Get up," Rylan sheathed his hatchets and lifted Sancil to his feet, "I'm not going to harm you Lord Sancil Verdane, that ceremony is obscured in my mind with the events that happened soon after. Will you return to Alder once I leave?"

Sancil placed his open hand on Rylan's shoulder and pulled him close in and embrace, "I cannot. There are more men awaiting our withdrawal from this place. Should you allow me, I would ask a favor in slaughtering a man that has plagued and murdered my blood for years. His name is Kraste of the Serpent's Fang."

As the two men spilt, Rylan motioned for Bansel to draw close, "Lord Verdane tells me that there is another force waiting for us outside, is that true?"

Bansel nodded as he pointed to the remnants of the western gate, "there are nearly three thousand men from the Fang outside these walls, more than likely made up of recruits and fresh assassin's that have never seen battle. Although the majority of their forces are hidden within the forests outside the eastern gate, there is a group of archers behind us that will surely attempt to eliminate anyone who tries to leave."

"Lord Verdane, how would you wish to proceed? You are the skilled siege tactician; I cannot imagine a better commander for our defense." Rylan turned to Sancil as he gestured to both gates.

Sancil looked back at the western gate for a moment before turning to face the east, his eyes twitching back and forth with every possible stratagem he could fathom, "I believe our course of action will not give us many options, or room for blunder. If a small force proceeds to eliminate the western archers, the majority of the men could exit to the east and stall in time for the first force to engage on their unsuspecting flanks and rout them without much resistance. That would be my course of action; however these are not my men. What say you Sir Bansel?"

Bansel bowed and turned to his men, "I would not ask this of you all if it were for any other reason, but who will stand with me in defense of the rightful heir of Alder? If you do stand with me, I will promise you here and now; I will do everything to ensure your families are safely evacuated from Alder and make their way to King's Hold with the rest of the supporters of the true king. Should you feel otherwise, I ask that you simply stay in the town until our battle concludes; the other forces we arrived with will surely not leave anyone alive should they find you. You have your choices, brothers and sisters, what say you?"

A resonating sound of armor clanging against shield erupted for the Silver Dragoons as they rallied and began to move forward. Bansel looked at the other two, "I believe we have our plan. I trust you can handle the archers by yourself Rylan?"

"I won't even need all six wings." Rylan smiled as he nodded and began making his way to the western gate, "Bansel, see that Lord Verdane fulfills his revenge, or at least keep him alive long enough for me to assist. I have a score to settle with Kraste as well."

"Very well," Bansel answered as he gave Sancil a puzzled look, "Which one will Kraste be?"

Lord Verdane gave Bansel a slight grin, "He'll be the one who tries to kill me personally. He has two swords and was the man who rode beside Inquisitor Daliah from Dalkas."

"Ah, perfect. I didn't like his arrogance. My men will protect you as long as possible until you cross blades with him. If he does get the better of you I will see to it that my men intercede on your behalf. We pride ourselves on protection." Bansel said as he fell in behind the last row of soldiers as they made their way to the gate.

Sancil retrieved a small necklace from under his hauberk and handed it to Bansel, "I do hope you will allow your pride to tarnish this once. Should I fall I will join my family; however I would ask you deliver that to my daughter, Lady Cassia, at Draedin Keep. Bring this with the message that she survives House Verdane and she may do with it what she wishes."

Bansel bowed deeply and placed the necklace into his small pouch, "On my honor, I will see to it delivered, should you not see it done yourself."

❖   ❖   ❖

Outside Havenhome, Kraste had positioned his forces on both sides of the forest, with spearmen furthest away from the gate, his inexperienced members in the middle, and finally his most elite troops closest to the gate to prevent anyone from reentering the town. Daliah leaned against a tree behind opposite of Kraste near the middle, carefully waiting and watching for any movement. A rhythm of moving armor began to emanate as Bansel's men drew closer to the gate, Kraste gave the order to the Fang to conceal themselves with their green cloaks behind trees and bushes.

As the eastern gate slowly opened and revealed a walled mass of shields closing off any visible gap. From behind the shield wall, Bansel's voice echoed, "Lord Gaius is dead! Surrender Kraste of the Serpent's Fang and you may leave in peace!"

"Who would make such an audacious request after failing to protect the man that would pay them?" Kraste mocked from deep in the woods.

For several moment's there was no reply until Bansel roared, "Charge!" as he leaped from atop the palisade, his fist red and scaled once again. As Silver Dragoons began to file out of the gate, Bansel landed fist first into the ground, exploding the ground around him in a burst of dirt and vegetation, sending several of Kraste's assassin's flying through the air.

Kraste gave the order to charge with a silent motion of his hand and cloaked soldiers poured from the trees, clashing against both flanks of the Dragoons. For a moment there seemed to be mass confusion within the Silver Dragoon's ranks until Lord Verdane shouted, "Form your line and push them back to the forest! We'll force them to fight us on unsteady ground!"

With the sounds of battle and sprays of crimson mist spewing into the air; it was certain that even with inferior numbers, Bansel's soldiers held a strong advantage with Lord Verdane commanding them. As elite troops of the Serpent's Fang dashed out of the forest, many appeared to be rushing away from Bansel as he emerged from the forest, his hand fully mutated into that of a dragon's claw. What men attempted to stand against him were effortlessly cut down or sent flying over the opposing forces by Bansel's fist.

After staying outside of the conflict, Daliah drew her daggers from their sheaths, crept forward and began to engage what few Dragoons had pushed too far forward in an attempt to further gain ground. As Daliah saw what little elite troops were remaining and being decimated by Bansel, she quickly moved her way through the battle, picking up a fallen assassin's sword, and engaging Bansel.

As the two crossed swords, Bansel attempted to swipe at Daliah's middle, however Daliah dodged the strike and slashed him just above his scales with her dagger. Bansel stepped back as the two were split by opposing footmen. As the Silver Dragoon spearmen attempted the thrust his spear forward, Daliah parried the spearhead with her sword, rotated effortlessly around the woman's shield and drove her dagger between the Dragoon's chainmail hood and her hauberk. As she fell to the ground clutching her throat, Daliah watched as Bansel countered each swing of the axe as the assassin dangerously attacked. Before the Fang could counter, Bansel caught the man's hand with his claw and tightened his grip. With a loud scream over the raging battle, the assassin's hand disappeared into a mangled form as Bansel crushed both the hand and the axe's handle, sending its head sinking into the ground. As Bansel and Daliah once again locked eyes, Bansel drove his sword through the injured man's chest and rushed forward. As the two crossed blades once more, sparks flew from the colliding foes. Daliah quickly attempted to swing at Bansel's knees as the two separated, but Bansel blocked with his claw and snapped the blade as if it were a simple river reed. As Daliah watched in disbelief, Bansel launch a knee into her stomach and sent her backwards and off balance as he sent a second kick directly into her chest, slamming her against a tree. Daliah slumped down to the ground unconscious as Bansel made his way over to finisher off, but from the corner of his right eye, a hulking Willow Bear rearing itself roared before swiping with its hefty paw. Bansel had only a moment to raise his claw to protect himself against the heavy strike that sent him off his feet and flying through the woods, colliding with a group of mixed combatants as they collapsed to the ground. As Bansel slowly arose, his vision blurred and hazed, he realized his arm had changed completely into silver scales with a strand running up his neck and around his eye. Bansel dropped his sword as the other soldiers looked on in astonishment, clenched his still human fist and burst towards the bear in a full sprint, his claw readied to strike. With a low growl, the Willow Bear slashed another paw at Bansel; however he leaped over and dragged his scaled claw over its back, sending strands of matted fur now bathed in dark red into the ground. As Bansel landed on the ground, his claw poised to strike again, the beast howled and rushed into the forest, disappearing almost instantly as it stormed through the large bushes.

"Commander!" One of Bansel's men shouted from the roadway forced Bansel to recoil from his pursuit and quickly rush back to the raging conflict, his eyes attempting to find Daliah, but found only fallen allies and enemies with no sign of the Royal Inquisitor.

As Bansel erupted back into the roadway with his sword once again in hand, he began to measure the battlefield. Most of his forces had eliminated what remained of the Fang on his side and turned to focus on Kraste's remaining assassins. Although they appeared to hold the upper hand, Bansel could see many of his injured soldiers beginning to show signs of the Viper's Kiss and quickly rushed into the foray in hopes of ending the battle and saving what men could be saved.

Seeing Bansel returning to the road, Lord Verdane continued to scour the battle for Kraste, many of the Dragoons forcing a small circle around Sancil for protections. A sudden break in the perimeter around Sancil revealed Kraste and two other swordsmen as they broke through.

"Lord Sancil Verdane!" Kraste shouted as he cleaved through another Dragoon. "The price on your head is the largest of your whole family! I've waited for the chance to pry my blades from your chest!"

Sancil readied his shield as he prepared for Kraste, "I will kill you this day and end your terror. You will never harm another man, woman, or child for as long as I draw breathe."

Kraste released a maniacal sound as he growled and leaped forward swinging both blades with all his might against Sancil's shield. Sancil struggled to block both strikes and the continuous flurry that followed, but managed to keep Kraste directly in front of him without need of his sword. With each blocked strike, Kraste's frustrated expression afforded Sancil the opportunity needed as he abruptly slashed upwards and connected with Kraste's open chest.

Kraste laughed, "That isn't going to work old man!" pointing to his hardened leather armor, that although slightly split, revealed a thick chainmail hauberk hidden underneath. "I studied you and all your tactics for combat! You simply don't stand a chance!"

Before Sancil could respond, Kraste unleashed another attack with his sword and quickly followed up with a swift kick to Sancil's forward leg, sending the nobleman to ground as Kraste spun around to Sancil's back and slashed with both swords. With an anguished shriek, Sancil arched his back as he released his blade and propped himself upright with his shield.

Kraste positioned both blades along Sancil's throat as he mocked, "Any final words before I send you to your family? Shall I pay your daughter a visit in Draedin Keep after I take your head?"

Sancil fell backwards, propelling himself as he drove his shield into Kraste's stomach, forcing him to release his swords as he fell to his knees. Before Kraste could recover, Sancil tackled him to the ground shield first and drove a concealed dagger into the assassin's leg. Kraste howled as he struck Sancil with a strong right fist across the side of his head and sent the nobleman stunned to the ground. Both men struggled to arise, Sancil armed with only his shield and Kraste with the dagger he painfully removed from his leg. "You may be younger than me assassin," Sancil cringed as his wounds began to sting through the adrenaline, "but you'll have to learn a lot more before you can ever stand a chance against an honorable man."

"Tch...I will see you dead on this road when I return home, a wealthy hero!" Kraste stomped his injured leg down before rushing forward, his unarmed hand clenched in a tight fist that slammed against Sancil's shield while swinging the dagger. Sancil blocked Kraste's fist, and using the momentum, thrust his shield into Kraste's arm, forcing the dagger to swing wide as Sancil unleashed a strong uppercut into the assassin's stomach. Even with his additional armor, Kraste felt the full momentum of the strike and sent him stumbling backwards as he stifled the urge to vomit.

Sancil attempted to step forward and press his advantage, however with his racing heart, the poison began to take ahold as he staggered to his knees and felt as though his body was unresponsive. Lord Verdane looked up as Kraste began to laugh while he retrieved his swords, the battle continuing to rage a few feet away from where the two fought.

Kraste gave Sancil a smile as he pressed his foot against Sancil's shield pinning it way from his chest, "Any more empty threats? No? You must be experiencing my special poison. After my run it with Rylan last time, I was forced to add something a little more potent in order to ensure my success if I ever crossed blades with him once more."

Without a reply, Kraste readied one of his swords above Sancil's chest, carefully aiming it to plunge through the nobleman's heart and finish another bounty. As Kraste raised his sword to plunge downward, a man launched himself into Kraste's side and sent both men tumbling over the battle field and away from Sancil.

Kraste leaped to his feet, swords readied to strike, but as he looked upon his opponent, immediately recoiled, "Who would dare to...oh it's you, Bansel. Have you come to try and save your other nobleman? He's not going to make it I'm afraid."

Bansel pointed the tip of his sword at Kraste as his silver scales seemed to continue their spread across more of his neck, a partial jaw bone structure along the side of his face. "Kraste...I will kill you!" he roared as he leaped forward and slammed his blade downward and forcing Kraste to withstand the attack with both blades. Kraste pushed back Bansel's sword and quickly attempted to attack Bansel with a flurry of strikes, but as he did, Bansel merely raised his scaled arm and watched as Kraste's swords futilely clanged against the hardened scales. Weary from fighting Sancil, Kraste disengaged from Bansel and rushed towards the tree line in hopes of using his cloak's camouflage as an advantage.

With his route mostly free of any enemies, Kraste darted for the woods with Bansel racing to keep up, his eyes filled with pure malice as he attempted to swipe at the assassin with every few steps. As he pierced the tree line, Kraste was alarmed to see the sight of his reserve troops all but scattered to the winds by a single figured draped in crimson splashes about his leather armor, an Orden Forged arm piece adorning his right side. As Kraste turned to rush another direction, Bansel seized Kraste's cloak and threw him back towards the road, colliding with several smaller trees as he fell just onto the edge of the stone road.

As Bansel and Rylan turned to one another, Rylan gave Bansel a concerned expression; however Bansel simply flung the ripped cloak aside and began to make his way back to the battlefield. Rylan made a mad dash to catch up to his ally before he reemerged back onto the battlefield, but upon exiting the woods and seeing the carnage that lay before him, his eyes glued themselves to Sancil's motionless body. An overwhelming sense of anger washed over Rylan as he recalled Amelia's pleading face. He drew Yvon's sword, gripped it tightly with both hands before rushing behind Bansel.

Kraste continued to attack Bansel ineffectively as the scales seemed to be harder than any shield and forced him to continuously readjust his position to strike at the opposite side. With all of his preparations, Kraste could feel the growing fear in the back of his mind. With a sudden, miscalculated swipe of his claw, Bansel felt

Kraste use the opportunity to move to Bansel's back and attempt to strike. Before Kraste could deliver his blow, Rylan blocked the strike and shoved Kraste off balance with his shoulder, slashing upwards as Rylan freed his blade. Kraste once again found himself struck across the middle, however even with his additional metal, the strength of the blow alone staggered him allowing Bansel to rush forward and attack with his own blade, slashing the assassin across his shoulder and revealing more of the chainmail hauberk.

"Damn you!" Rylan shouted as he readied his sword and slowly began to encircle Kraste, "You have no honor and shame your brother's name!"

Kraste spit at Rylan's feet, "Don't mention my brother! All we wanted was to ride beside you and you saw fit to destroy my younger brother's dreams! I will erase you and your brothers from history for what you did to mine!"

Without another breath wasted, both men attacked one another, Kraste attempting to strike with every motion while Rylan parried and dodged each attack and maintained his footing. Before either combatant could gain the upper hand, Bansel charged into Kraste with his claw, gripping the assassin's armored ribs and digging his razor sharp claws through the metal. Kraste screamed out in pain as he managed to kick Rylan back and strike Bansel aside the face with the pommel of his weapon, forcing both attackers away from him as he clutched his side as his punctured flesh burned from contact with the outside air. Kraste began to feel his breath become increasingly strained as he realized his lung was pierced, his vision slightly blurring as he watched Rylan and Bansel move to opposing sides.

With a silent nod across to Bansel, Rylan leaped forward and swung his sword downwards, and as Kraste moved to block, Rylan grabbed Kraste's arm and pinned it in place. Bansel quickly moved in, thrusting his at Kraste's chest and forcing him to bring his sword to stop the attack; however Bansel gripped the blade with his claw and plunged his sword through Kraste's stomach with tremendous force, piercing through the chain and exiting through his back. As Bansel retracted his blade, both men released Kraste and watched as the wounded assassin stumbled forward, his blades falling to the ground. Kraste swayed with each step, his vision blurred and his breath shallow, until he turned to face Rylan and Bansel. Before Kraste could react, Rylan moved his metal into a curved wall, halting Kraste's retreat, while Bansel made his way forward, his eyes glinted with fire. Bansel stopped a few paces away from Kraste, "Now you will burn assassin!"

Before Kraste's eyes, a brief moment of clarity through the pain, Bansel opened his jaw, a bright ember forming just beyond his lips. Kraste attempted to scream as the ember ignited into a raging burst of brilliant fire that jetted forward, enveloping him in searing flames. What little fighting remained immediately halted as the fire splashed against Rylan's metal wall and leaped into the air, a single horrifying shriek piercing their ears as Kraste burnt away to ash.

As Bansel closed his jaw and turned with Rylan to see the remaining forces, the remnants of the Serpent's Fang scattered to the winds, throwing whatever weapons they held and making a mad dash into the woods. Rylan turned to Bansel, "It's over now, come back."

Bansel's eyes seemed to flare again for a moment before he blinked and rescinded the scales. "This has cost my men greatly Rylan, they will need to know it was not in vain."

"They will be rewarded and given a place to stay in King's Hold. If I could offer more I would, but that will have to be decided by my grieving brother." Rylan replied as both men looked to Sancil before quickly moving to his side.

"Did... did you kill him?" Sancil's voice chocked as a small stream of blood trickled from his cheek.

Bansel took Lord Verdane's hand, "Kraste and the Serpent's Fang have been decimated. I don't think they will be able to do much of anything for a long while. After this, Alder will be safe from any snakes."

Sancil attempted to shake Bansel's hand, but could no longer feel his limbs as wave of cold washed over him. He looked to Rylan, "Don't sit in the shadows for too long Rylan, you have a duty to your brothers, but you also carry one for your people as well. Do not let them go unnoticed like your father began to do."

Rylan struggled to speak as a lump formed in his through, "I will serve my brothers," Rylan choked, "and protect the people of Thesia however I can. You should save your strength Lord Verdane, we will get help shortly."

"There's no need," Sancil said as his vision began to darken, "I give what strength I had to the both of you. I'm sure you'll need it for the challenges you'll face ahead. For now look after what men are still capable, they've almost certainly been tainted like myself."

Rylan looked to Bansel, "see to your men and have them collect the injured. We'll make way for the Sen Portal immediately." Bansel gave a silent nod as he squeezed Sancil's hand one last time before standing to direct his men. "I'll see to it that you are buried with the other nobles at Alder's crypt if that is your wish, Lord Verdane."

"Send me to the pyre so that I may pass along the winds to my family." Sancil said as he slowly closed his eyes, "I wish you only good fortune…"

As Sancil's voice died away, tears began to stream down Rylan's face until the sounds of approaching soldiers forced him to his feet, hatchets at the ready. Bansel quickly rushed to Rylan's side as ranks of soldiers appeared on the road, bannermen of Kay leading the ranks.

"Rylan," Naria's voice sounded over the marching boots, "Are you okay?"

Rylan gave a sigh of relief as he motioned for the Silver Dragoons to retrieve Sancil's body, "I am fine, but we will need your men's help to ensure these men get antidotes! We fought against the Serpent's Fang!"

"Brother!" Aldis shouted as he darted in front of the ranks and over to his brother, carefully examining his armor, "You're arm is hurt, Lady Naria brought healers to heal you. I also prepared more antidotes for the Viper's Kiss. I'm sure it will not cover this many men though."

As Rylan rested his arm around Aldis, the sight of Yvon and Tiberius approaching with Naria between them brought a smile to Rylan's pained face. As the two forces met, Naria's soldiers began to recover and assist Bansel's Silver Dragoons. After a few minutes past, the combined group made their way away from Havenhome and returned to the portal, leaving behind Gaius, Kraste, and what remained. Rylan went so far as to release what few Noble Guardsmen still drew breath, claiming that, "If you live, you can tell the truth of Faust's deceit and the assassination of Lord Sancil Verdane by the

Serpent's Fang." All of the survivors agreed and made their way back to their horses, disappearing before Aldis reopened the portal and began to send troops through to King's Hold.

Rylan, Bansel, and Tiberius stood together as the last group prepared to go through, "This will be the easiest fight we will face during this war." Rylan spoke as he clutched his arm.

"Agreed," Bansel responded, "I can only hope we can handle our enemies at their best."

Tiberius grinned as he patted both men on the back, "We will never have to do so. I despise politics, but even I can assume that what you two accomplished here will forever divide Alder's Noble Houses. Faust will never be king as long as the thought of the true king draws breath. You may have started a war, but you have also begun its end. When the day comes that a Bassadora once again sits on the throne, I will sheath my blade with content. For now, let us be thankful that we have strong friends at our side and a place to call home. We will deal with whatever comes our way tomorrow."

Rylan gave one final look towards Havenhome, "Today marks the beginning of our bloody war." As Aldis returned the three stepped onto the portal, he gave an enthusiastic smile before opening the gateway a final time and sending them home.

EPILOGUE

Three weeks passed after the Battle at Havenhome; many whispers flooded Dalkas and the rest of Alder with the Six Winged Death's return, sending a split between many of the people within the Kingdom. With the resurgence of House Bassadora, open conflict between mass groups erupted in the open streets, forcing many of the nobles to begin increasing their guard and relocating to their keeps for security precautions.

Noble Houses Verdane and Carthill, now without suitable heirs, were quickly replaced by Lord Neir Orstag, a former guardsmen captain, and Lord Alric Asina, a relatively unknown figure that had begun to grow renown near the border of Alder and Vaine, with Faust's assistance. Although still filled with suitable heirs, Lord Phalo Bernak was executed for Tiberius' treason. Lein, Tiberius' older brother was made his replacement. Mauro's oldest sibling, Lord Vikker of Althra, assumed the head of House LeBlanc after Gaius was recovered and his body returned to Dalkas. Vikker returned immediately from his lands and assumed head of Alder's army.

As the Harvest Festival arrived in Dalkas, many of the citizens celebrated the day with parades, gifts, and feast. In Dalkas' citadel, however, the halls were filled with echoes of the jovial outside as Faust sat with Briar and Daliah, his new wife, at his side. His hall was nearly vacant, save for Neir, Alric, and the few servants that remained loyal after Sepius' public death. A heavy brow rested above Faust's face as thoughts of his rightful position as king stood just beyond his current grasp. For Faust to now become king amidst Rylan and his brother's return, he would have to hold favor with at least three-fourths majority of the noble houses. By replacing the fallen houses with rising loyalists, positioning a power-hungry Lein into his rightful position, and using Vikker's rage at his father's murder, Faust had already earned himself valuable allies; however he didn't feel it was sufficient to maintain his power.

In a bold and unheard of move, Faust made Daliah the Head of Royal Inquisitors, executing the old man that inhabited the seat for an outlandish reason of inability to capture and eliminate Rylan, thus infuriating many of the older inquisitors that felt it should be a male dominate position. During his changes to the Inquisitors, he absorbed the remnants of the Serpent's Fang to be used as a spying faction for his attempts to destroy Rylan and his brothers while maintaining order within the Royal Inquisitor's Ranks.

With his moves now calculated, Faust sent Briar under Lord Alric's care in order to conceal him from the public eye while he continued to train. Although his instruction continued, Briar's prowess with metal seemed to alter as strange markings began to appear across his arms. His abilities went beyond control and manipulation of his own metal, extending to surrounding metal in small amounts; however after interacting with other objects, he would have terrible visions while the dark markings continued up his skin. Briar's powers rapidly expanded, however due to his condition, he also became unruly, starting fights with other children and adults, leaving them bloody or worse if Alric or his men could not find him in time.

With Alder divided and struggling, the other kingdoms began to ready themselves for an inevitable war looming on the horizon. Increasing Royal Guards, conscripting any able-body, and readying mercenaries across Thesia, from Ulferth in the north, to Kay in the southeast, Thesia's fate was placed on the edge of a thin blade.

❖   ❖   ❖

Sayren sat along the main table filled with each eldest, legitimate heir. He sat with Alkith in the center, Halvor, Gianni, and Adda of Barner to his right. Alissia of Parthus and Nikolaias of Vaine sat to Alkith's left. The outer grounds of King's Rest were open to the masses as tables and dancers filled the open space, cheers for heirs erupting in the crowd as the festivities continued. A separate table had been set aside for the remaining heirs to sit and enjoy the party as gifts were presented to each royal family as toasts were made.

Sayren looked to Ophelia sitting between Liara and Tiberius, her smile growing with each trick the former Lady of Bernak showed her. After a few attempts, Ophelia snapped her fingers together; creating a spark atop the candle Liara was using and gave a very pleased look at her father. Sayren gave her a proud wink, it had been weeks since she had smiled at him, even when they had returned from Havenhome, Ophelia would cry every time she laid eyes upon him. Alkith had discretely asked Liara to begin to tutoring Ophelia, ensuring Rylan was not made aware. As Sayren moved his gaze from his daughter to his brothers, he noticed both Toren and Aldis had their faced planted into their books; however Rylan was noticeably absent from the festivities.

During the time after he returned, Rylan spent the majority of his time down in the catacombs, silently contemplating his future and that of his brothers. After Sayren appointed Tiberius to Alder's Marshal, Liara to Head Liaison, and Mauro to Sayren's Spymaster, Rylan was refused a position by Alkith's request for his aid in his plans of retaking Barner's capital to secure Thesia's largest port for their allies across the sea. Sayren offered Bansel a general's position with a large purse for his men; however he and the Silver Dragoons elected to serve as Rylan's bodyguards for the conflict's duration. Sayren accepted his notion and placed Bansel in charge of Rylan's safety.

After he returned and found Yvon holding a letter with his head bowed, Rylan questioned him as to the letters details. Yvon simply delivered the message and proceeded back to Byra's old house that now served as a temporary apothecary for the masses that fled Alder in support of Alder's Heir and the 'Six Winged Death'. With every day that passed, Rylan moved down into the catacombs to practice against Rolanth's, the second king of Alder, metal golem. With each swing of metal Rylan could feel his anger removing itself as it was replaced with a familiar feeling of reassurance in his own abilities, not as a mercenary, but as a free fighter.

❊   ❊   ❊

With the celebrations roaring off in the distance, Rylan sat on an empty roof watching the birds fly across the sky, dancing with the cold winds of fall as it filled the air. Rylan knew the letters intent, but couldn't bear to open it at the current point with injured men and women slowly making their way to the celebration. He finally hardened his resolve and opened Elyscia's letter. As he read each line, her words seemed to have taken hold;

"I never knew just how many secrets you held, or the monumental weight that you bore, however knowing what I know now; I can see why my father always liked you. I took your advice and have set out on my own travels, not because I could not stand the thought of you not returning, but the images that haunted my dreams the night before I left Havenhome. I watched as they carried you in, bloodied and cold, a sight that I could not bear to envision outside of my nightmares. I could tell you where I've decided to go, but I won't allow your mind to become unfocused from your future." As Rylan read the words from the page, he could see the dried droplets of tears she had let fall during her composing. As he reached the last few lines, he gave a smile and wiped away the fountain attempting to flow from his own eyes, "My father believed in you, as do your brothers, and all those you have helped along the way. I am happy to have known you and grown with you, however I have one last bit of advice: Should you ever wish to claim your rightful place on the throne, or establish your place at the table with the other heirs; my father hid the scroll containing your legitimization with your father. I wish you only the best of days and a bright future as you return these lands to their rightful owners and begin a new era of prosperity across Thesia."

As Rylan finished his letter and refolded it into a small square, he tucked it away into his satchel just as Bansel emerged from the stairway to the roof, sweaty and panting for air.

"Just what do you think you're doing? We're supposed to be celebrating with the others at King's Rest, yet you have me chasing you down all across the district!" Bansel gasped for air as he finished his rant.

Rylan nodded as he arose and moved over to Bansel, "Don't tell me you're tired after a short investigation; how will you ever be able to defeat anyone if you get so winded."

"We, not just me...I don't plan on fighting on my own, not as long as you still have arms to fight with." Bansel said as he lightly hit Rylan's chest with an open hand, "Now let's go before there's no food left. I'm starving."

Rylan grinned as he abruptly turned and rushed over the edge, "See you at the bottom!"

Bansel set off sprinting down the stairs, barely connecting with a single step as he flew down to the bottom and rushed out the doorway to see Rylan standing on his metal as it lowered him onto the clean stone street, "Don't scare me like that you idiot!"

Rylan grinned as he sank his metal back into the ground before giving Bansel a smirk and proceeding back towards King's Rest, "Come on now, if you still want to get there before it's too late we'll need to hurry."

"Stupid bastard..." Bansel muttered under his breath as he quickly rushed up to Rylan's side as the two headed back to the festival.

Thesia's Fate will further unfold in in the next book of the Alder Saga...

Printed in the United States
By Bookmasters